YOU ARE NOT I

Also by Millicent Dillon

FICTION

Baby Perpetua and Other Stories

The One in the Back Is Medea

The Dance of the Mothers

NONFICTION

A Little Original Sin:
The Life and Work of Jane Bowles

After Egypt:
Isadora Duncan and Mary Cassatt

Out in the World:
The Selected Letters of Jane Bowles (editor)

The Viking Portable
Paul and Jane Bowles (editor)

YOU ARE NOT I

A Portrait of Paul Bowles

MILLICENT DILLON

University of California Press
Berkeley   Los Angeles   London

University of California Press
Berkeley and Los Angeles, California

University of California Press, Ltd.
London, England

© 1998 by Millicent Dillon

Chapters 18 and 20 have been previously
published in slightly different form in *Raritan*
(winter 1998).

Library of Congress
Cataloging-in-Publication Data

Dillon, Millicent.
   You are not I : a portrait of Paul Bowles /
Millicent Dillon.
      p.   cm.
   ISBN 0-520-21104-9 (alk. paper)
      1. Bowles, Paul, 1910–   —Biography.   2.
Authors, American—20th century—
Biography.   3. Composers—United States—
Biography.   4. Americans—Morocco—
Biography.   I. Title.
PS3552.0874Z63   1998
813'.54—dc21
[B]   97-26220
                                              CIP

Manufactured in the United States of America
9   8   7   6   5   4   3   2   1

The paper used in this publication meets the
minimum requirements of American National
Standard for Information Sciences—
Permanence of Paper for Printed Library
Materials, ANSI Z39.48-1984.

CONTENTS

ACKNOWLEDGMENTS

I acknowledge with gratitude the generous support of the John Simon Guggenheim Foundation and the National Endowment for the Humanities.

I wish to thank Alice Adams, William Abrahams, Carol Ardman, Lawrence Stewart, Trent Duffy, Ned Rorem, Elizabeth Kenny, Betty Ann Austin, Roberto de Hollanda, Virginia Spencer Carr, and Director Thomas F. Staley and Cathy Henderson of the Harry Ransom Humanities Research Center of The University of Texas at Austin.

I also wish to thank Director Jim Clark, Rachel Berchten, Nola Burger, and Katherine Bell, as well as the others at the University of California Press who have helped bring this work to fruition.

In the past decade, since Paul Bowles has become an international legend, he has been the subject of many interviews and articles as well as several full-scale biographies. Yet, for all this reportage, he remains elusive. The complex being who is Paul Bowles deflects direct inquiry.

I came to know Paul Bowles through indirection. My first contact with him was in 1976, when he responded to a letter from me that told of my interest in writing about the life and work of his wife, Jane Bowles, who had died at age fifty-six in 1973. In answer he wrote that my project was of the greatest interest to him. Almost gratuitously, he added that Jane's life had nothing to do with her work, a remark perhaps more indicative of the feeling he wanted to convey about his own life and work.

In March 1977 I went to Tangier. On that first visit of six weeks, I spent four to five hours each day talking to Paul about Jane. Only later was I to learn that after her death others had refrained from speaking to him of Jane, in response to an unstated message from him. As a stranger, unaware of this prohibition, I came to know him in a very paradoxical way, one that was deeply intimate and at the same time impersonal. Jane was my subject, but he was my primary source of information. To see her, I had to see through him. In our conversations he had the remarkable capacity to be forcefully present in his own right and yet to be almost transparent to my gaze at the same time. On several occasions I brought him information about her life and her work that he had never known. I returned to Tangier in late 1977 and again in 1979 to consult with him further. After the biography of Jane (*A Little Original Sin*) was published in 1981, Paul and I continued to correspond.

In 1992 once again I returned to Tangier. This time I was in search of Paul, to write of his life and work. Now that I was looking at him, he was, of course, no longer transparent. Gazed at directly, for all that he had expressed eagerness about my doing this project, he became a master of opacity.

One generally thinks of the process of interviewing as tracing an arc of knowing. That is, you expect that you will accumulate information and presumably knowledge of the subject from beginning to end. In my work with Paul, however, the arc of knowing was made up of starts and stops, of reversals and sudden leaps and reversals again. In my new relationship to him, the more I questioned him, the less, it often seemed, I knew. As much as my inquiry was a going forward, it was also a retracing, a stumbling back over feelings and facts and memories. Everything was made more complex by what I thought I knew but didn't know and by what I didn't think I knew but may well have known.

In the portrait of Paul Bowles that follows, I have, in my own turn, resorted to indirection. Rather than relying on the traditional mode of revealing biographical information, I have interwoven factual material with conversations and speculations. I have been willing to surrender the solidity of chronological factual material in order to render the fluidity of his being and his presence as well as the atmosphere that he himself is constantly in the process of creating. I have been in search of a different kind of knowing—one that is consonant with secrecy, one that, now I come to think of it, is more akin to the knowing one has of a character in a work of fiction.

At the same time, what follows is a meditation on the nature of biography. Those elements that provide the structure and basis for traditional biography but that usually remain hidden from the reader are here opened up to view. In that sense, this portrait is a biography turned inside out. My own subjectivity is admitted: it becomes the way "into" my narrative, starting with my earliest trip to Tangier, where, in search of Jane, I began to "find" Paul.

I do, of course, recognize that any reader, myself included, cherishes the reassuring solidity of fact before jumping into uncharted and possibly muddy waters. So let me present here a brief account of the life of Paul Frederick Bowles.

He was born in Jamaica, Long Island, on December 30, 1910, of New England parentage. His father was a dentist; his mother, a homemaker. An only child, brought up in a severely disciplined household, isolated from other small children, he began composing music and writing stories at a very early age. By the time he was sixteen, his work had been published in the avant-garde European literary magazine *transition*.

In early 1929, after less than a year's study at the University of Virginia, Paul decided to leave the U.S. Without a word to his parents or to the university officials, he went to New York, borrowed money for his passage, and took a boat to France. Returning to the U.S. briefly, he began studying composition with Aaron Copland in 1930. The following year he returned to Europe, where he met Gertrude Stein and many important artists in the literary and musical world. It was on Stein's advice that he went to Morocco with Copland to work on his music. There he encountered a world that influenced him so profoundly he would return to it sixteen years later and make it his permanent home.

In 1937, once again in the U.S., already recognized as an important young composer, Paul met Jane Auer. Born in 1917 in New York City, Jane was also an only child. She was of German-Jewish heritage through her father, Hungarian-Jewish through her mother. The twenty-year-old Jane that Paul encountered was wild, witty, unpredictable, fey, and gaminelike. She had had affairs only with women; he had had affairs with women and men.

They were married in 1938 and set off on a honeymoon to Central America. At Paul's instigation, they soon left the cities behind and went farther and farther into primitive places that he loved but that she feared. From Central America they traveled to Paris, where Paul continued to work on his musical compositions and Jane began a novel based in part on their visit to Central America.

Later that year they returned to New York for Paul to compose music for a theatrical farce produced by Orson Welles. In New York the marriage changed, and from that point onward they lived separate sexual lives. The marriage was to endure, however, through journeys that would be taken together and separately and through casual and not so casual affairs with others. Shuttling from New York to Mexico, back to New York, to Staten Island, and to Mexico again, Paul worked assiduously on a wide variety of musical forms—chamber works, operas, incidental music for the theater, and songs—while Jane continued to work erratically on her novel.

One day in Mexico in the fall of 1941, Jane brought Paul the disordered typescript of her novel. He went over the manuscript with meticulous care, suggesting a number of changes and excisions. The novel, *Two Serious Ladies,* was published in 1943. It was not a success, though even at the time it had enthusiastic admirers, particularly among writers.

By 1945, profoundly affected by his experience of working on the novel with Jane, Paul found himself wanting once again to enter into the imaginative world of fiction, a world he thought he had long since abandoned. Still deeply immersed in his work as a composer, he produced several brilliant and terrifying short stories, set in the exotic locales he had visited. The stories were published, and in 1947, armed with a contract to write a novel, he set out for Morocco. In 1948 Jane joined him there.

Upon its publication in 1949, *The Sheltering Sky* became an international best-seller. Soon after, *The Delicate Prey,* Paul's first collection of short stories, was published to great critical acclaim. In the next few years, traveling alone from Ceylon to India to Morocco to Spain and back to Morocco, he completed his second novel, *Let It Come Down,* which was published in 1952.

In March of the following year, Paul arrived in New York, accompanied by the young Moroccan artist Ahmed Yacoubi, to write the music for Jane's play *In the Summer House.* (It was not a success, but, like her novel, it had a coterie of devoted followers.) For a period of time after his return to Morocco, Paul wrote short stories and travel essays as well as a series of musical compositions. In 1955 he published his third novel, *The Spider's House,* an examination of the religious, moral, and political conflict within Morocco through the eyes of an American expatriate and a young Moroccan boy.

In 1957, while Paul was traveling in East Asia with Ah-med Yacoubi, Jane, who had stayed in Tangier, suffered a stroke. Her capacity to read and write as well as her ability to function in daily life were impaired. As a result of Jane's illness, Paul was no longer able to travel so frequently. Living in the apartment directly above Jane's, he was often called upon to deal with problems arising from her disability. In the next few years, as Jane's condition seemed to stabilize, Paul completed another novel, *Up Above the World,* which details the physical and emotional disintegration of an American couple traveling in an unspecified country in Latin America. He published a series of translations of tales by Moroccan authors, including those by his protégé, Mohammed Mrabet, and recorded an album of native Moroccan music for the Library of Congress.

In the late 1960s, after Jane's physical and emotional condition worsened, Paul took her to Málaga, Spain, where she was confined to a sanatorium. Though she returned several times to Tangier, in 1969 she was permanently institutionalized in Málaga. During her final illness, Paul continued to work on travel articles and wrote his autobiography, *Without Stopping.* He also produced further translations of Mrabet's tales.

For some years after Jane's death in 1973, Paul's work went into abeyance. But by the late 1970s he was once again writing stories. During the early 1980s, his new work and his earlier work, which had previously gone out of print, were published in many languages throughout the world. The release in 1992 of Bernardo Bertolucci's film of *The Sheltering Sky,* in which Paul played a part, served to intensify the legendary aura of his reputation.

PART ONE

It was March 11, 1977. I was waiting in the inner courtyard of the Hotel Villa de France for Paul Bowles to arrive. The sun shone brilliantly on the tiled surfaces and on the white columns of the surrounding arcades. The air in Tangier carried an odor that was strange and yet familiar; I had noticed it the moment I landed that morning. It was an odor of the natural world, of plants and dirt, of moisture from the sea, compounded by car exhaust and spices and a faint hint of decay. At first I had thought it was like the smell of an older California. But this was no California, old or young, with its arches and tiles and triangular shadows, with its suggestion of an undertow that had nothing to do with the sea.

At the center of the courtyard was a large circular fountain, faced with blue and white and ochre tiles. No water ran into its basin, which was filled with pots of scraggly geraniums. On either side of the fountain, the arcade, set off by a series of white columns and high arches, sheltered a row of large potted plants. At the front of the courtyard, a stairway led up to the hotel parking lot, beyond which were high gates opening onto a narrow street. Now and then hotel guests, mainly Europeans, passed by me. Employees of the hotel in Moroccan dress carried baggage in and out.

Paul had made the reservation for me at the Villa de

France, writing that it was where Gertrude Stein and Alice Toklas had stayed when they vacationed here before World War I. The hotel must once have been luxurious. Now it was charming but dilapidated; the water on, then off, on, then off; the electric cords frayed, only one outlet working in the room. My room looked out upon a garden enclosed by stone walls. Beyond the wall was a street leading to a bus stop and an enclosed market. In the distance were several tall mosques and many low buildings leading down to the sea.

Promptly at four o'clock, Paul appeared at the top of the stairway. I recognized him from his photos, though in truth the photos had not done justice to the actuality of his physical beauty. His white hair, his blue-green eyes, his lined but still boyish face conveyed a presence that was light and quick, luminous, controlled, and elusive. His voice was musical, complex in its range and overtones.

We got into Paul's Ford Mustang, and Abdelouahaid Boulaich, Paul's driver and helper, drove us from the city center to the Inmeuble Itesa, the apartment house where Paul lived. Constructed of gray concrete, it was surrounded by empty fields, littered here and there with small mounds of rubble. In the tiny elevator we rode up to the fourth floor. Paul unlocked the door to his apartment and led the way through the small foyer, stacked on the left with suitcases. Pulling aside the thick woven curtain, he beckoned me into a dark living room. The end wall faced a windowed patio, but the light to the room was cut off by a mass of tall, leafy plants, ranged together like a miniature jungle.

Before coming, I had asked Paul if I could bring him anything from New York. He had answered that he would be grateful if I would bring him a newly published book by Jorge Luis Borges, *Imperial Messages,* and a small tur-kish towel. When I presented him with several towels, he thanked me with evident delight. I had been nervous about meeting him, and now I detected in myself a curious grat-ification, a sense of pleasure that I had been able to give him something he wanted and needed. As I handed him the Borges book, I mentioned a recent article in which the elderly Argentinian writer was quoted as saying that in his final years he, who had always been so devious in his writ-ing, wanted nothing more than to be simple. "I liked his deviousness," Paul said.

A young American, Dan Bente, a teacher at the Ameri-can School, came in, and we all—he and Abdelouahaid and Paul and myself—had tea, which Paul prepared. He had been smoking cigarettes steadily before this, but now he began to smoke kif (a form of cannabis), as did Dan. I declined the offer to smoke, as did Abdelouahaid, but soon the thick, sweet smell pervaded the air in the room. Paul was in continuous motion, going into another room, com-ing back in, and soon going out again. From a back room, I heard birds singing—finches perhaps.

Mohammed Mrabet entered, pulling aside the curtain. I had also seen photos of him from the 1960s, depicting him as a handsome young man. In the flesh he looked older and heavier than in the photos, his face running slightly to puffiness. But he was still very muscular, and there was a raw, sensual quality in the way he moved. Im-mediately he took over center stage. He spoke English halt-ingly and, when he could not find the right word, moved to Spanish and occasionally to Darija, a Moroccan dialect. Whether laughing or telling a story—frequently a story involving violence—the energy of his feelings poured forth, unmeasured.

"I have had a bad life," he announced ("bad" meaning *hard* or *terrible,* I did not know), "so I have many books in me. A bad life in jail," he added. "I do not read, I do not write." (His books were produced by his speaking into a tape recorder in Paul's presence, after which Paul transcribed the tapes and translated the stories.) "A bad life," he repeated. "Nazarenes, Westerners, they do not know what it is to have a bad life."

"Even in the West," I said, rising to the bait, "there is enough suffering to go around."

"In Western civilization, the suffering comes from neurosis," Paul said coolly. He sat on the low couch beside me, but the next moment he was in motion across the room. Soon he was on the floor, leaning on his elbow. He smoked constantly. The conversation continued, much of it in Spanish, which I did not understand. Above the fireplace I saw some scorch marks and a curious mask with bared teeth.

The talk finally turned to Jane, but it was a curiously prepared conversation, as if the words had been said many times before. A performance was being presented, with Mrabet as the one taleteller, making large, fierce gestures, scowling and exhorting, and Paul as the second taleteller, prompting, correcting, his face subtly mobile and imperturbable in turn.

Gossip was offered up: that Brion Gysin had hated Jane, that Gore Vidal had hated Jane. I brought up a story I'd been told in New York about Vidal's version of the death of the lyricist John LaTouche, who had been a very close friend of the Bowleses. This led to Paul telling a story about LaTouche's family, ending in a description of LaTouche's mother: "All she ever talked about was food."

"Like that recording you made of a dinner party," Dan

said to Paul, "in which everyone talked about the food and how marvelous it was, and Jane said, 'Well, it's not going to change my life.'"

"I used to take my tape recorder along and tape without anyone knowing," Paul responded. "Jane hated it, but at least I have some things of her I wouldn't have otherwise. She always hated to have her voice recorded or her picture taken." Was this a statement to me about her desire for privacy, which I, as the biographer, had come here to violate?

Incident piled upon incident, story upon story. There was a jousting or a jockeying going on that I was not astute enough to keep up with. Mostly I listened, though now and then I offered a comment. When I did, the easy sliding from incident to incident stopped. There was a pause, and then the energy—and ritual—of the conversation picked up again. That I was the listener and that they were conscious of my listening and reporting was inescapably present here. I sensed a gathering together, a resolve, a circling about Paul for the sake of protection. Yet he had wanted me to come, he wanted me to do this book on Jane— hadn't he written that to me?

Suddenly Mrabet turned to another subject, unconnected to Jane, telling how he had stolen Carol Ardman's shoes. (Carol Ardman was a young American writer who had become very friendly with Paul; she came to Tangier frequently for extended periods.) From what I could make out, Mrabet justified his theft as an act of revenge against Carol for her having, supposedly, stolen the shoes of a Moroccan at a picnic. "Why are you so sure she took them?" Paul asked Mrabet. Mrabet said something in Spanish in an undertone to Paul. Then he laughed and Paul laughed. It was as if one scenario, the mischievous youth being indulged by the proud parent, had suddenly given way to another—that of the jokester, the trickster ironically acknowledging his jokes, his tricks, to a confederate.

Later, driving me back to the hotel, Abdelouahaid said, "Mrabet talks a lot." To which I responded with a cautious "He is like an actor."

I spent the next morning in my room, going over copies of Jane's unpublished notebooks and manuscripts and letters from her archive at HRC (the Harry Ransom Humanities Research Center of The University of Texas at Austin). Now and then I looked out the window. I saw two women in country garb, with large straw hats and red and white woven cloths wrapped around their bodies, descend the hill toward the bus stop. Next came a man in a cloak and a hood, leading a goat by a rope. He pulled to the side of the road as a car raced by him, honking. I recalled the muezzin's cries that had wakened me early in the morning. I had entered a world of visual and aural density, where it was hard to know background from foreground.

I turned once again to the material I had brought with me. At four in the afternoon, Paul, who was a very late riser, would come to pick me up in the car. Then I would go back with him to the flat and stay for dinner. I wanted to be prepared with my questions, if the opportunity arose to ask them, although I was reluctant to start my inquiries in the presence of Mrabet and the others.

Before seeing Paul, I was to have lunch with the writers Virginia Sorensen Waugh and Alec Waugh. It was Virginia who was responsible for my being in Tangier. I had met her in May 1973 at the MacDowell Colony. One night at dinner, after reading my work, she told me she thought I would like Jane's novel, *Two Serious Ladies*. Virginia had lived in Tangier for a number of years and had known Paul and Jane socially during the early and mid-sixties, although after Jane had been confined to a convent hospital in Málaga in 1968, Virginia had not seen her. "Paul goes to visit her there every six weeks," she added. As it happened, Jane had died on May 4, 1973, a few days before our conversation, but word of her death did not reach the U.S. until some weeks later.

Virginia's intuition had been correct, though "like" was not the precise word for my response to Jane's novel. I had been astonished by its originality, by the brilliant and unexpected prose, and by something in the tone that suggested a constantly shifting border between the life of the writer who created the fiction and the fiction itself.

I had not begun to write until I was almost forty, which is to say that I had spent most of my life until then not thinking of myself as a writer. I had originally been trained in science—in physics—and then, as many young women did in the early fifties after getting married, I stayed at home to take care of my children. To the extent that I had examined my own life, it was not on a writer's terms, with a writer's means.

Writers who begin to write when they are young begin early to view their life experience as raw material for their work: the people they meet, the events that occur. There is a continual monitoring of experience for the purpose of giving form to experience in words. Then life informs the work and work informs the life naturally, unconsciously, or so it seemed to me.

But I had not had that natural progression. Suddenly, at the age of forty, I'd been impelled to narrative. I'd published a book of short stories and a novel, but I continued to feel that when I wrote I was on a precarious edge—fiction/life, life/fiction. In Jane Bowles's fiction I recognized another kind of edge, one that might provide a clue to my own dilemma. This I say now, after so many years. Then, perhaps, it had seemed to me that simply in obedience to a natural impulse I had written to Virginia, asking for Paul's address, saying I was interested in doing a book on Jane. Although Virginia was initially reluctant to contact him about my request, she eventually passed my note on to him, and so I had come to be in Tangier.

Virginia greeted me at the door and led me up the steps to her apartment, where my first impression was of light-filled rooms, furnished with red Moroccan rugs and brass tables. Every wall was lined with books. Sun streamed in through open doors to a balcony that looked down upon a walled-in garden blooming with exotic flowers.

It was clear from the outset that our lunch was to be a "social" lunch, our conversation a "social" conversation. I did not ask about Jane, and, at first, neither Virginia nor Alec spoke of her. Then, at one point, Alec said to me, "You are very like Jane, charming like she was." (Charming? I had not thought of myself as charming for many years.) "Before the stroke," he went on, "she was the kind of woman you would make a pass at, but not afterward. Her limbs seemed all awry."

"It was," said Virginia, "premature senility that she had. When she was in Málaga, Paul said to me, 'Don't go to see her there. She won't know you. She doesn't even know me.'"

In the midst of that social lunch, the conversation had shifted. In my new capacity as a teller of a life, it was necessary for me to be reminded how terrible and prolonged Jane's deterioration had been. Looking back, Alec and Virginia were no longer able to think of her at an earlier time without recalling what she had become in her illness.

When I got back to the Villa de France, I was given a note from Paul.

> Dear Millicent:
>   This never happens to me, or perhaps once a year it does, but I'm in bed, I suppose with a liver attack, or what seems like one. (Dizziness, nausea and chills.) I can't prepare dinner for you, and I apologize for not being able to. All this should not last long . . .
>   Why I had to get sick the very day of your arrival, I don't know. (It came on last night.) . . .
> Until soon,
Paul B.

Why indeed had he gotten sick the very day of my arrival? Because of my arrival? I recalled what had happened in New York one afternoon in the apartment of the duo-pianists Robert Fizdale and Arthur Gold, who had known Jane well in the forties. I had been waiting for them in their living room, but they were delayed. After a while I got up and went over to a window, which overlooked Central Park. Standing there, I heard them come in; I turned just as I heard Robert Fizdale gasp, "For a moment, I thought it was Jane."

And then there was an evening when I went to see Karl Bissinger, who had done a series of remarkable photos of Jane in the forties. After he talked for a while, he paused and, looking at me with his photographer's eye, said, "You know, you could be her more serious sister."

It had happened on a number of occasions during my interviews with those who had known Jane. I would see the sudden small shift in the eyes of the person talking. And then would come the statement: You know, you look like Jane. It had been unsettling to me. And the telling of this, I find, even so many years later, is still unsettling, as if I am overstepping a line, violating that most rudimentary law of biography—not to confuse oneself with one's subject. I myself did not think I looked like Jane, but I couldn't quite dismiss what others were saying to me.

Had Paul had a similar response to my appearance? No, in his imperturbability I had seen no indication of this. You are making too much of this, I warned myself, letting things get out of hand, as usual. Later Virginia was to tell me that one day she did ask Paul whether he thought I looked like Jane. "Not at all," he replied, but then amended his comment with "Well, maybe the same physical type."

The next day, Sunday, at Virginia and Alec's invitation, I attended the Anglican church service with them. Unused as I was to attending a religious service of any kind, I was struck by the intermixture of spiritual and worldly considerations. The priest invoked protection from God for the queen of England and the government of Morocco and the president of the U.S. He read as his text a passage from *A Handful of Dust,* by Evelyn Waugh (Alec's brother). Praising the body as the temple of the spirit, the priest spoke of all sexuality as natural. Those who are chosen for celibacy, he added, should not take any pride in being better than others.

After the service Alec told me with some glee of the latest Tangier scandal. An elderly British doctor had recently taken a Greek mistress. The doctor and his wife lived in a flat above his clinic, while he maintained his mistress discreetly in an apartment in another part of town. But then one day the doctor brought his mistress to the church service. Everybody had known about the affair before, but this action on the part of the doctor provoked considerable consternation. The doctor's wife played the organ during the service, so the congregation was now forced to be a silent witness to this drama. Actually, Alec said, he was sympathetic to the doctor. He found the doctor's wife terribly dull.

I knew Abdelouahaid did not come to Paul's flat on Sunday, and I thought of Paul, ill and alone. He didn't have a telephone, so I couldn't call him, but I could, at the very least, so decency dictated, walk out to his flat and leave a note at his door expressing my concern.

As I got off the tiny, creaking elevator, Paul's door opened, and he came out. He greeted me without surprise. He told me that he had been very uncomfortable yesterday, nauseated and his stomach bothering him, but today he felt much better. In fact, he was just going out for a walk. Would I like to join him?

When we got outside, he suddenly felt cold—a stiff breeze was blowing—and he went back in for his overcoat. We proceeded through unpaved streets and passed a group of young boys. "Bonjour, Madame," some of them said to me, grinning. One boy asked Paul for the time. Paul gave him the time in Darija and laughed. "They always ask about the thing they don't care about," he said. Then he added, "Janie always said that the one thing you can be certain of is that you will never know what they will do."

We passed a small, decaying house with shuttered windows. In the garden were two cows grazing. "We almost bought that house," Paul said. "We thought it was a pretty little house."

He led, I followed, downhill into a flat, barren area, where there were markers for lots, in preparation for a new subdivision. "They came in and took all the trees off the property, and now, after the rain, there is runoff into pools where mosquitoes can breed. And still there are no buildings. It is too bad about the trees. They hate trees; they like to walk in the open."

We stopped to look at one of the pools, whose surface was covered with a thick mat of white flowers. "Those look like wild strawberry," I said. Paul leaned over to pick one of the blossoms, but he slipped, and his right foot sank into the muddy pool. Drawing it out, he looked with disgust at his soaked suede shoe. "Do you want to go back?" I asked, recalling that he had not felt well and that he had been easily chilled. In the short space of time I had known him, there was already being elicited in me a need, an urge, a desire to protect him. "You might catch cold," I added, gratuitously.

"I won't catch cold, but it's uncomfortable."

As we walked back uphill, I told him briefly about being in Texas. I mentioned the many photographs of Jane at HRC. "I have no photos of Jane," he said (though later he found a number of them stashed away among other papers in the flat). The one thing he most regretted was the loss of the first novel she had written, in French. "I had it, but then she wanted it back. I gave it to her, and she lost it. She always lost everything."

(What can I say about this conversation? It was social; it was not social. It was again glancing. It was the first time I had been alone with him. I did not question him as an interviewer, penetratingly. After all, we were out on a walk. I could not say that there was unease in his speaking; what he was saying to me, he could have said to anyone. I noted the fleeting quality of feeling, the quick transitions that covered over disconnections. Everything was polite, proper, at some distance, at some remove. If he felt pressure from me, he did not show it.)

As we came to his building, he invited me in for tea. I said, "No, I—" and made some excuse about feeling that I should leave. "Don't say no on my account," he said.

"I'm only saying it because I know how I would feel if I had slipped in the mud." I didn't—and I don't really know on whose account I said it.

The next afternoon at four, Paul called for me at the hotel. With Abdelouahaid driving, we went first to the post office, then to the market, made a stop for wood, and drove out of town to a freshwater spring, where Abdelouahaid filled a number of bottles. From there we drove up through a forested area to an open space where we could see out over the Atlantic. The day was beautiful and warm. I said that I could see why one would want to stay here. "It costs ten thousand dollars a year to live here," Paul commented. "The rent is cheap; only the cars cost a lot, my car and Mrabet's."

When we arrived at the flat, Mrabet and Dan were present. There was the ritual of tea and kif-smoking and conversation. Paul spoke of how extraordinary Jane had been in person, so mercurial. "It was a performance," he said.

Now Mrabet took over, or, should I say, Paul let him take over. He was the focus of all eyes, he was the storyteller enacting his story, in halting English, in Spanish. He was sixteen, he began, when he met Jane in the house of

Madame McBey (Marguerite McBey, the American-born painter, who had lived in Tangier for many years). At once he jumped to the last years of Jane's illness, when for a brief period Paul brought her home from Málaga. "Jane wouldn't eat or take medicine from Paul, but she would take it from me," he announced.

He entered upon a long account of what happened when he went with Paul to see Jane in Granada in 1968. (Later I was to read Mrabet's story of this visit—as it was told to Paul and translated by Paul—"What Happened in Granada." Of course, what Mrabet meant by "story," what differentiation he made between what was life and what was invented, was not clear to me then and has never been clear to me.) Telling the story aloud, he was the macho man, the tough guy who, when offended by others, immediately takes retribution—throws this one around or that one around, male or female. He acted the story out with vehement gestures and loud words. It was a bravura performance. Warming to his part, he went on to tell of his hatred for Cherifa, Jane's Moroccan peasant lover. He expressed rage that Cherifa had referred to him as "the man from jail" when she herself was the dangerous one, a woman who had poisoned Jane and tried to poison Paul.

Confirming Mrabet's judgment of Cherifa, Paul noted, "She once came after me with her fingers like this"—he held out the index finger and third finger of his left hand in a V. Cherifa had, he said, aimed her fingers at his eyes.

Suddenly Mrabet's telling changed; his voice grew more expansive, softer. He told of Jane once saying to him that she wanted to die. Why, he asked her, did she want to die? "Janie told me, 'I no like this life.'" He told her the life she had was a beautiful life. He told her that all people were small, that only God was big. "I told Janie everything that comes from God is good, and we have to say thanks to God."

Then Paul spoke of Jane in the convent hospital at Málaga and of his going to see her and sitting by her bed. At the end, he said, it was as if she were flying over an abyss and seeing death. When the nuns would come in and talk to her about Jesus, "she'd look at me and smile and it was as if she were saying '*ossir*.'" (*Ossir* was a word often used in Jane's mother's family, implying the denial of what had just been said. It may have been of Hungarian origin.)

 Everything about Tangier seemed to suggest that it was a world where disjunctions could resolve themselves without active intervention. At home, I would have straightaway asked Paul for a private interview. Here, I waited. He will suggest it; it will be arranged, I told myself. But several days passed, and he made no move to alter the situation.

Once again I found myself in the light-filled rooms of the Waughs' flat, at a luncheon that included two guests, Paul and myself. Once again there was the ready surface sliding of social conversation until the moment when Virginia announced that John Hopkins, a young American writer living in Tangier, was preparing an article about Jane's grave in Málaga. As the grave was unmarked, a movement had been initiated by some expatriates in Tangier to take up a collection for a stone.

At the mention of the stone, Paul stiffened. He said he wanted no marker on her grave.

"But, Paul, a lot of people will want to come to her grave," Virginia protested gently.

"That's nonsense," he insisted coldly. "The marker would be a symbol that someone is there. But she was never there. Only the body is there. We have not progressed from savagery," he added. Then, in a sudden transition, he told an amusing and terrifying story of a man who drank a cocktail into which had been mixed the ashes of a corpse.

By the time we arrived at my hotel, I had decided not to wait any longer. As I got out of the car, I told Paul that I hoped I would have some time with him alone, as I had a lot of questions to ask him. Yes, he admitted, someone was always at the flat; it was hard to have a private conversation there. At my suggestion he agreed to come to the hotel for an interview the following day.

Promptly at four in the afternoon, Paul appeared at the Villa de France, and we adjourned to a small, glassed-in room overlooking the garden. After tea was served, I asked his permission to turn on the tape recorder. His first words were about Jane's illness and the part that he thought drinking had played in bringing on that illness. Then he reverted to the subject of her unmarked grave. He said that he was very angry at those people who had suggested a collection to buy a stone, implying that he was too cheap to buy one. "I don't want a cross on Jane's grave. As far as I'm concerned, she has no grave. I don't believe in cemeteries."

When I said something about mourning, he asked, "Who wants to mourn?"

"It's a way to get over it."

"You never get over it. I mean, it's always with you. I'm no longer connected with anything. I think I lived life vicariously and didn't know it. When I had no one to live through or for, I was disconnected from life. Oh, I'm connected all right—so what?—with eating and sleeping . . ."

After a pause, I spoke of the profound impact Jane's writing had had upon me, how it had suggested a deep connection to her own being.

"When it happened—that feeling—" he nodded, "it happened right away, and people thought they had always known her."

I asked him about Jane's childhood. He said she seldom spoke of it. I asked about Jane's father, who had died when she was twelve. He said she never spoke of him at all. "It was as though she never had a flesh-and-blood father," Paul added.

I mentioned "A Stick of Green Candy," Jane's story of a young girl's struggle with her father about her imaginative life. I suggested that there might have been some connection with her memory of her own father. "Jane would have objected if you said her fiction had to do with her life," he said summarily.

"At some level, all fiction is autobiographical," I insisted.

"Of course," he conceded, but it was an admission that seemed given only out of politeness.

By now the small room was crowded with guests, talking and laughing. All around us were the sounds of tea time at a hotel: plates and cups being set out, forks and spoons clattering, chairs scraping against a marble floor. A waiter appeared, asking whether we needed anything. When he went away, I brought up Jane's notebooks at HRC, how they were filled with uncompleted stories and uncompleted drafts of novels and plays. He said he knew nothing about them. She did not discuss them with him.

"Would you discuss your work with her?" I asked.

"Not really. Sometimes I let her see a manuscript, but we didn't discuss it. We felt there was nothing to discuss. Her work was her work. My work was my work. Unless she'd ask me something. And sometimes I'd ask her, 'Do you like the idea of it happening this way?' She never made suggestions for amelioration."

I reminded him of a letter in HRC that Jane had written to him in 1949, just after the publication of her story "Camp Cataract." She told him that she believed it would never have been properly finished without his help.

"I don't know. How can you tell? I never would have written anything, probably, if I hadn't gone over the manuscript of *Two Serious Ladies* carefully, making corrections in spelling and punctuation. It was the excitement of participating in that that got me interested in writing. There were so many interactions and interinfluences. Two people are together and are very close—which we were—we don't have to tell each other what we're doing because each one knows what the other is doing. What you want, what I wanted most of all, is to present the thing completed and have her read it and say, 'It's wonderful.' That's all I wanted. As Gertrude Stein said, 'No artist wants criticism; all he wants is praise.' That's all she wanted too."

"I should have given her more on 'Camp Cataract,'" he suddenly added. "When I first read it, I said to her, 'Yes, I like it, but it's so strange and mysterious. I don't understand it.' She was terribly depressed by that, and then she tried giving it to other people, and none of them understood it. Nobody understood it. I should have. But I was so busy writing *The Sheltering Sky* . . ."

In her daily life, he recalled, she was always using the expression "I am at the mercy of . . ." He never really knew what she meant by it. "She felt ideas as such were far less important than what one knew; and one didn't know with one's intellect, one knew with some other organ, according to her."

"And you? Do you make that separation in yourself?"

"I consider myself a nonintellectual. All my creative work was done without any intellect at all."

When I expressed doubt about this statement, he said, "I mean, writing music doesn't require what one would call the intellect, and writing my kind of fiction doesn't require it either."

Perhaps we were talking about different things, what he called intellect and what I called intellect. "When I speak of intellect," I said, "I include the shaping intellect, that which gives form to the work, and in that sense at least, intellect is strongly present in your work."

"Probably is. Probably is," he admitted. "It comes out by itself." Again I warned myself not to take this admission for agreement.

"Of course, what preoccupies the reader of your work is the narrative flow," I went on.

"That preoccupies me too, the narrative. I believe in narrative, don't you?"

At that moment it came to me that if I loved narrative, I also feared it. After a silence, I said, "Of course I believe in narrative. But Jane's narrative is not narrative in the ordinary sense."

"No, not sequential narrative. It's what happens to the people, inside them. The meaning of it isn't implicit in events but in the reactions of the people to whom they happen." After a pause, he added, "I don't see anything in common between her writing and mine."

"Oh," I said, "I think there is."

"I believe you; I just don't see it." He was being polite again.

"It must make you irritable, this stranger coming and telling you—"

"I'm not irritable. I'm not an irritable person."

After that day, Paul did not come again to the Villa de France to talk of Jane. He made it clear to me that he felt uncomfortable, giving an excuse about the noise at the hotel. I had not realized—others would tell me this later—that in the four years since Jane's death he had become reluctant to go out to public places. (Nor had it occurred to me that at the hotel he could not smoke kif, which—I was also to learn—was so helpful to him in alleviating anxiety.) He suggested that I interview him in his flat, saying that we could talk better there. When I mentioned that other people were usually around, making discussion difficult, he said he would make the time to see me alone.

And so began our daily conversations about Jane, extended conversations that went on for four or five hours at a time. Each day he waited for me to begin. As he waited, perhaps he was steeling himself, as for an ordeal, but he never gave any direct indication that this was so. He did make it clear, however, how much he admired her work, how he regretted that it had not been adequately recognized in her lifetime.

I soon learned that if I came to him with my theories about Jane's writing—for theorizing, working at an abstract level, was part of my history (part of myself that was often at odds with storytelling)—he would listen politely, but the conversation would go nowhere. At such times his answers had the quality of reiteration, of having been so-lidified. But if I could make myself stay with the specific, a phrase in her work or in a letter she had written to him, a phrase that was provocative and mysterious at the same time, something new appeared in his response: a new incident in her life, a new memory. Then there would be a new story, a revealing that was like a skein unwinding after the proper thread had been pulled.

When he responded to my questions, he was forthcoming but in a way that is difficult to describe. It has been said of Paul many times that he is very deceptive; he even said so himself in his autobiography. Yet, listening to him, I did not have a sense of deception—there was withholding, yes, but not in the sense of a deliberate refusal to tell. Rather, it seemed to me that his withholding was a process akin to his method of telling a story, where what is revealed is revealed only at the necessary moment.

I was being immersed in a world of stories: her stories, his stories about her, his stories about the two of them when they were together, about the games they would play together. And then there were all the other stories, the subsidiary stories surfacing around me, arising out of the world of his daily life.

One afternoon as Paul and I were just about to begin work, Mrabet came into the flat and sat down. He began a story about taking Jane to the market, in which he featured as a central character.

"I take Janie with me in car. Janie buy three bottle wine, one kilo meat, chocolate. Janie like chocolate. I look [at the bill]. Seventy-five hundred francs. I told him [an Italian shopkeeper], with seven thousand francs I could buy—" Mrabet listed in Spanish a number of items that he could buy with this sum. "Janie told me no. I told Janie this day, 'Shut up.' "

"Glad I wasn't there," Paul said.

"Janie became small."

"Like Alice in Wonderland," Paul interjected.

"Italiano hit me." And then, broadening the base of his accusation, "Cherifa hit me. Ayse [a Moroccan woman who had worked for Jane] hit me."

"Ay, ay, ay," said Paul.

"Everybody hit me. Never buy anything from Italiano."

"And Angèle?" Paul asked. Angèle was a Spanish woman who had also worked for Jane.

"Angèle hit me."

"One time," noted Paul, "Janie had six servants altogether. Not all at the same time. They rotated."

"*Culpa*," announced Mrabet loudly. "Your fault."

"According to him," Paul turned to me, "everything is my fault because I didn't command her, make her do this or that. Nobody could make her do anything," he insisted.

Mrabet said something about men needing to control women.

"All right, it's my fault. It's all over, so don't tell me it's my fault." Whereas earlier in Mrabet's story Paul had prompted him to further telling, now the tone of his voice was aggrieved.

"Besides, Mrabet," I interjected, "Paul wouldn't have wanted to tell her."

"He has a different idea—the man has to command," Paul explained.

"In this world," Mrabet said expansively, "every woman has to have a man over her." Then he added something

about Paul not having been serious enough and supple-
mented it with an aside to Paul in Spanish.

"He says the man has to keep the bit in the mouth,
otherwise the woman runs away. Never let her do what she
wants, or it's too late," Paul translated.

"It was too late when he met her," I said.

"It's never too late," Mrabet pronounced and got up and
left.

Of course, there was much about this by-play that I did
not understand, including how much of what he said Mrabet really believed, how much was for effect, and what in
fact was his purpose in telling the story about Jane to begin
with. As for Paul, he had entered into the "game," the
story, readily, but then it had suddenly turned more serious
for him, as if in the midst of it a nerve had been touched.

Thinking of Mrabet's way of telling, fused as it was with
an almost terrifying energy of loud gestures and expansive
cries, I said, "He's an actor."

"He's a mythoman. He doesn't understand the difference between fantasy and reality, especially with kif.
He allows it to affect him. He likes that, making an em-
broidery in his mind, which he then speaks of as if it
were true. He tells it as though it's true, and people have
to listen to him and say, 'Oh, really?' And when I speak
to him later about it, he says, 'Well, you know the difference, don't you, when I'm telling the truth and I'm not?
I know the difference, you know the difference, so what
are you complaining about? It sounds better.'" It sounded
eminently rational, yet I remained puzzled. Something
about story was going on between them: story was being
enacted for multiple purposes—as attack, as counterat-
tack . . . And I was the audience for this multifaceted

unfolding drama, without enough clues to know either the plot or the background or the rules that were being adhered to.

I turned again to Jane, to her stories, to several fragments in her uncompleted work in which she spoke of sin and salvation. After listening to the fragments, Paul said, "The salvation—what is it? When she was there, in front of one, it was terribly hard to understand what she was talking about, for she often talked that way too, to me. Yes, I think that was a fundamental part of her mind's work. I would always say, 'What do you mean, Janie? I know what you mean by this and by that, but I don't understand what you mean.'"

Yet, oddly, I had had a sense that I understood what she meant. That I did not know her, had never seen her, had never heard her speak, did not know the emphasis she gave to this or that, had never been forced to see the necessary contradictions between the life and the writing—all this not knowing had made it possible for me to think that I understood. Now I saw, as I listened to Paul, that my understanding was premature; it had been arrived at too easily.

That night I had a dream about Jane. It is curious that all the time I was obsessed with Jane as a subject, I do not remember dreaming of her except this one time. It was a dream divided into two sections. In one section, shut off like a dream within a dream, I saw Jane as a young girl with sparkling eyes, surrounded by others, hurrying by. In the other section of the dream, I was in California visiting a friend, and I was told that a new story of Jane's had been found that everyone was talking about. Suddenly, in that section of the dream, I knew that the other part of the dream was wrong, that Jane was dead.

From the time Paul was nineteen years old, he was a compulsive traveler, moving whenever he could from one exotic place to another without stopping. But after Jane's final illness, he never departed from Tangier and its environs. Now he lived each day in an unvarying routine in a confined world. He awoke after noon, having been up late the night before. At four, Abdelouahaid would drive him to the post office to pick up his mail. Then he would proceed to the market, where he did his daily shopping. Occasionally he would take a walk, on the mountain or near the ocean, before returning to his apartment for tea. After the visitors left—there were always visitors—he would have a late dinner and in the early hours of the morning go to bed, starting the cycle all over again.

And yet during those hours I would spend with him— usually from four in the afternoon to eight or nine at night—his world did not seem either routine or confined. If anything, I experienced the time spent with him as an intensification of ordinary life. Admittedly, I was caught up in the obsessive pursuit of the biographer: the search for her subject. But there was more to this intensification than feeding my own obsession. Something about Paul, about being with him, made one feel that with him you were at the center of a world—his world, maybe even *the* world. How this was created, I didn't know. But it was obviously felt not only by me but also by those who clustered about him. It was there, palpable in the air, as pervasive as the smell of kif drifting through the apartment, this intensification.

Paul and I were walking through the medina, the old Arab quarter. We passed by the house where the English diarist

Samuel Pepys had lived and came to the Place Amrah, where Paul pointed out the house he had once owned. He told me he had bought it in 1947, soon after his arrival in Tangier, for five hundred dollars. In 1956 he signed the house over to Jane so that she would be able to give it to Cherifa. In turn, Cherifa sold it sometime in the early seventies.

We went on through narrow, winding streets, passageways paved with uneven stones. Now and then there was an opening to a brightly lit square, where white walls presented blank facades with here and there a small window like a half-lidded eye. Then we entered shadowy alleyways, going up and up in the dimmed afternoon light.

Leaving the medina, we walked through the streets of town, past the Carthaginian graves from centuries before, to the Anglican church. In a corner of the churchyard, Paul pointed out the stall of the man who sold potions for love, for revenge, for fertility, for wealth, for success. I noticed how, as he slept in his little covered stall, his bare feet were turned inward, his toes touching.

When we returned to his flat, Paul began to speak of his unclear position as a resident in Tangier: for some months there had been a problem about his residence permit. (I was to learn later that the question of the residence permit was a recurring one, apparently for other European residents as well as for Paul, but that it was always resolved.) His complaint, if that is what it was, was less lament than a resigned statement of powerlessness.

What would happen, he wondered, going on without a transition, when he died? What would happen to his papers and his books? He had to think about these things; after all, he was now sixty-six. "I guess one must think about death," I said, in the way one speaks when one doesn't quite know what to say. "Do you have a will?" I asked him. No, he did not. I wondered aloud whether an American will would be valid in Tangier. He did not know. I offered to find out the answer to that question when I returned home, once again responding to what I saw as his need for help, though, to be sure, he never asked for it.

After tea, we returned to our usual mode of conversation. I went on with my questions about Jane, and we spent several hours going over passages in her notebooks. But when our work was done and I was preparing to leave, I found myself telling Paul of the fragment of the dream I had had about Jane. I certainly had not planned to tell him of the dream, but it seemed to evolve out of our conversation about Jane. I suppose the dream was a kind of offering on my part, a way of saying that, although he was the one always asked to disclose, I too was obligated to some form of disclosure.

Paul listened; he did not comment on the content of the dream. He only said he thought that dreams were more real than life.

At the very beginning of *The Sheltering Sky,* the as yet unnamed protagonist, coming out of sleep, opens his eyes in a tawdry room: ". . . there was the certitude of an infinite sadness at the core of his consciousness, but the sadness was reassuring, because it alone was familiar." For a while he lies absolutely still. Then he begins to wake up, to know the time—it is late afternoon; he hears his wife walking about in the adjacent room. He knows he has had a dream, which he cannot recall, but he knows he will recall it later. The body of the novel that follows is itself like a dream recalled. It has the dream quality of being shut off from life, even as it refers to life. It is as confining as a dream, even as it moves the reader forward.

Before coming to Tangier, I had, of course, read *The Sheltering Sky* (as well as Paul's other works), approaching it initially as subsidiary source material for my research on Jane. Soon, however, I was caught up in the forward thrust of the novel, which tells of the journey of an American couple, Port and Kit Moresby, in North Africa after the end of World War II. After embarking at a port city, they travel deep into the desert, driven by Port's need to escape civilization. In an isolated outpost, Port becomes desperately ill with typhoid. After his death, in an access of guilt and madness, Kit rushes out into the desert. Alone in the vast Sahara, Kit attaches herself to a group of nomads who are passing by. The first night, she is raped by two men, first by an older Arab and then by a younger one, Belquassim.

The rape by Belquassim is described as follows:

> He was there all around her, more powerful by far; she could make no movement not prompted by his will. At first she was stiff, gasping angrily, grimly trying to fight him, although the battle went on wholly inside her. Then she realized her helplessness and accepted it. Straightway she was conscious only of his lips and the breath coming from between them, sweet and fresh as a spring morning in childhood. . . . In his behavior there was a perfect balance between gentleness and violence that gave her particular delight.

At this point in my first reading of the novel, I had become very upset. I found it difficult to accept that Kit would take such delight in being raped. Even if—especially if—she'd just gone through the agonizing death of her husband and was half out of her mind with grief and guilt, was delight the emotion she would be likely to feel? It seemed to me that this episode was one of those instances in which an author's personal reverie has broken through into his fictional world. Some fantasy of violation—of being violated—as pleasure had influenced the course of the narrative. It was a jarring note, with the voice of the author, as man, intruding.

Of course, it was one thing to come to this conviction before meeting Paul. It was quite another to come to it after having met him, after having spent hours listening to him, actually hearing his voice. At night at the Villa de France, I had taken up the book again and was rereading it in its entirety. Once again, when I arrived at that section of the novel in which Kit is raped and takes such delight in her rape, I was dismayed. I was still faced with the uneasy feeling that this was the author's fantasy. And if it is his fantasy, I reproached myself, what difference does it make? I reminded myself that I was in Tangier to find out about Jane, not to be distracted by extraneous issues.

When we began to work the next day, there was, at first, talk of interviews and interviewing. That morning, Paul told me, he had been interviewed by two journalists from the U.S. (Although journalists occasionally came to see him at that time, it was a relatively rare occurrence, nothing like what would happen from the mid-eighties on, when interviewers came in a flood. But in 1977, it should be remembered, all of Paul's books were out of print in the U.S.)

Some interviews, he added, are meaningless. "After all, it is the interviewer that makes the interview, not the interviewee." I mentioned having just read Norman Mailer's interview with Jimmy Carter. Paul shrugged and said he didn't particularly care for Mailer. "I don't care that much for him as a personality," I admitted, "but I do think he is very intelligent."

"He doesn't need you to care for him," Paul said. "He cares for himself so much it's all right."

"He liked your story," I pointed out, referring to Mailer's words about "Pages from Cold Point." In *Advertisements for Myself,* Mailer had written that through this one work Paul had "opened the world of Hip. He let in the murder, the drugs, the incest, the death of the Square . . . , the call of the orgy, the end of civilization. . . ."

"He puts down everything else I've done at the expense of that one story," Paul went on. "If you remember, he says that it's all 'cool,' which was a word that meant something in those days, in the fifties. It's all very cool, but it's not raised to the heights of personality. It's a 'miasma' issuing from the author himself. Imagine, a miasma. What does he mean?"

I did not know what Mailer meant. But now that we had begun to speak about Paul's work, I felt that I had to say something about *The Sheltering Sky,* to at least acknowledge that I'd been rereading it. It seemed to me that to say nothing would be an act of deceit. And if I were not straightforward with him, how could I expect him to be so with me?

I began by saying that it was a different experience for me to read the book in Tangier. That was true. But now my courage began to fail me. I could not say outright, "I think that section where Kit goes alone into the desert is your fantasy, Paul." Instead, I said that I had had "a lot of trouble" with the last section of the book.

He showed no offense. "Kit going across the desert into

ridiculous adventures—well, that bothered many people," he said evenly.

"Did it?"

"Of course, naturally."

"If I read that last section as a mirage, as a fantasy, coming out of the earlier parts of the book, I have less trouble with it," I told him.

"I'm not very fond of it, naturally; it's such an old work. It's the one ninety percent of the people think is the best one. It's the first one. It's the oldest one. It's less interesting to me than more recent ones, but that's always the case; you always like your youngest child best."

You always like your youngest child best? "Well," I said, about to disagree, but then I let it go. His response had stymied me, in particular his saying that as *The Sheltering Sky* was such an old work it no longer held much interest for him. Yet just preceding this, he'd obviously been nettled by Mailer's remark from so long ago, about a story almost as old as the novel. I decided to drop the subject, to go on to something else.

(And, in fact, it would not be until fifteen years later, at the point when I began to look at Paul directly, that I would come back to this question about the rape sequence in *The Sheltering Sky*. Then I would have to confront it again, to ask myself if the episode was or was not a fantasy of Paul's—and, if it was, what it suggested about him, about his own inner life.)

Turning back to Jane, I said that I had some questions to ask him about her private life. "The Gerofis [Isabelle and Yvonne Gerofi, long-term friends of Jane] and others have spoken to me about Jane's love affairs, what they have called her 'amours.' "

"What amours? With Cherifa?"

"Not Cherifa so much. They were talking about other women." And here I sighed.

"I don't know about that. Here in Tangier? Only Cherifa that I knew about."

"They named three others."

"What? It's impossible. Is it accurate? Could it be?"

"I don't know the answer to that question," I said.

"The tongues of Tangier are always busy, carrying grapevine news which turns out generally to be wrong. But—I don't know—if I can hear about it, I'll try to make sense of it."

I told him of the three women who were supposed to be Jane's "amours." He acknowledged remembering them. He dismissed them. He seemed embarrassed by the entire discussion. His reluctance to talk about the other women in Jane's life was in sharp contrast to his readiness to talk about Cherifa. That she had been dangerous to Jane, that she may have poisoned Jane, how she took advantage of Jane financially—these were subjects he was always willing to expand on at length.

"The Gerofis also told me that at the end Jane was afraid of Cherifa," I told Paul. "Was there something aggressive or threatening about Cherifa from the beginning?"

"No." She became that way, he thought, as a result of the situation she was in, being "spoiled" by Jane, being given a free hand. "I confess that I didn't want to know about all those things, and I tried to stay outside of it. It all seemed—well, it depressed me. Since I couldn't effect any change in it, I preferred not to hear about it. As Jane said, 'I know that glazed look you get when I begin talking about Cherifa.' And I did, I'm afraid."

After this talk of Jane and other women, he began to speak of Jane and himself. "When she first met me, she announced to everyone, '*C'est mon ennemi* [He is my enemy].' I thought it very strange. She said she meant it, that she had never found anyone so inimical to her as I. It wasn't true." He recalled how immediately after meeting him she wanted to go with him to Mexico and how when they went on the bus they talked and talked. "So she liked to talk to her enemy, there's no doubt about it."

The next day it was Paul who told me about his dream. It was after I said to him, "I wanted to ask you if you could tell me a little about Helvetia." Helvetia Perkins, an American woman twenty years older than Jane, had been her lover in the 1940s.

"I dreamed of her last night, the first time in years. Doing all this with you is sort of opening up things that I've blocked off, shut out for years."

"You'll be glad when I leave."

"Not for your leaving, no. But that I don't have to go over this any more, of course. Oh, yes, naturally. But it must be good for me; I don't know why. I blocked it all out simply because it was so awful. The whole sixteen years were awful after the stroke. A long time for things to be awful."

After a long silence, I asked him if the Helvetia period had been awful too.

"No, I wasn't terribly involved in it."

He proceeded to give a chronological and factual account of Helvetia's presence in Jane's life. He spoke of going to Mexico with Jane in the spring of 1940 and of Jane meeting Helvetia there in the late summer; of his returning alone to the U.S. in September to work on the music for the Theater Guild production of *Twelfth Night;* of his finishing that score and then beginning to work on the production of *Liberty Jones;* of his wiring Jane and asking her to join him in New York; of their going to live at the Chelsea Hotel; of Helvetia arriving from Mexico and staying with Jane at the Chelsea for a few weeks. Then Helvetia left; then he toured with *Liberty Jones,* and Jane accompanied him; then he and Jane went to live in Brooklyn, on Middagh Street, in a house leased by the editor George Davis for a group of writers and composers including W. H. Auden, Benjamin Britten, Peter Pears, and Golo Mann. In the summer of 1941 he went back to Mexico, to Taxco, with Jane—no, he didn't remember Helvetia being there at the time, though she must have been. He was sick with jaundice much of that year. After Jane finished writing *Two Serious Ladies,* she and Helvetia returned to the U.S. in Helvetia's station wagon—that was in April 1942. He had arranged for Helvetia and Jane to stay at Holden Hall, a century-old house belonging to his family in Watkins Glen, New York. A few months later, he returned to the U.S. with Antonio Alvárez, a young Mexican painter, and they too went to stay at Holden Hall. In the mid-1940s he and Jane and Helvetia and Oliver Smith, the famous set designer (and a distant cousin of Paul's), shared a four-story house on West Tenth Street.

All of this that he told me seemed a compulsive listing rather than the following out of a narrative line. It was a marshaling of facts that was as much a defense against telling as a telling.

When we'd finished our work for the day, Paul said that he was cold and went to stand before the fire. He referred again to the dream he had had about Helvetia. In the dream, Helvetia was weeping. He put his arm around her to comfort her, though he felt a sense of repulsion.

On March 27 I traveled to Málaga, to the Clínica de los Angeles, the sanatorium where Jane had been confined at the time of her death. A nun in a white habit led me through a sunlit hall to the office of the director, Dr. Ortiz. Also present in the dark wood-paneled room were a nun who had cared for Jane and a patient, Lenore, who had been devoted to her. Dr. Ortiz spoke slowly and deliberately of Jane's illness, which he called "schizophrenia," of her hallucinations, and of her treatment with drugs. The two women spoke of Jane's conversion to Catholicism and of her final days, when she lay unhearing, unseeing, unmoving.

The following day I went to visit Jane's grave in the San Miguel Cemetery, on a hill at the outskirts of the city. A cemetery worker took me along a path that ran between walls of tombs down a slope to a large open space where the graves were in the ground. He moved quickly between the gravestones, checking the numbers. Finally he pointed out an unmarked grave that was covered with rubble, old flowers from other graves, shards of broken glass, pieces of plastic and paper. Nearby, women in black, relatives of the dead, were scrubbing gravestones with soap and water.

I returned to Tangier. I was once again back to my daily life of going to Paul's flat, of talking to him about Jane. I told him what the doctor had said, what the nun had said, what Jane's friend Lenore had said. "I have covered it all up and put a sheet over it," he said to me.

Before I went to Málaga, he had indicated to me that he thought my going there would not be "worthwhile." But on my return, my having gone had an unexpected effect upon him. Now things came back to him. He recalled that when Jane became blind, the nuns passed their hands over her face, and when she didn't respond, they simply said, "No recognition." He remembered that neither he nor she discussed her blindness. She only said to him, "You smell good."

He recalled the way the nuns treated her, at times like a child. "They acted as though she didn't understand anything. I was terribly embarrassed because of the remarks they made about her condition in front of her."

He described the nuns circling around her like twittering birds, saying to her, "*Su marido aqui* [Your husband is here]." Once when he came, it was Christmas, and the mother superior began explaining Christmas to him. She took it for granted that he was Jewish because Jane was, he explained. Later when he went to the clinic, the mother superior told him that they had brought a rabbi to see Jane but that Jane had refused to see him. Later still they sent for a priest, and she was received into the church. "Anybody who has anything to do with organized religion is a fool," Paul said.

"It's as though that half of my life is gone," he added. And then, after a pause: "The sense of the ridiculous goes if there is no one to share it."

I brought up with him the question of privacy, his own as well as Jane's. With some irritation, he spoke of articles about Jane and himself—about their sexual relations, about her illness—that had been published in an underground publication. He found them "defamatory," invented "out of whole cloth," and a true invasion of privacy. He said something about what Jane would have wanted—

"And you?" I asked. What was it that he wanted said and not said? I spoke of Jane's letters, with their implications of their separate sexual lives.

"Yeah, well, no, that's all right."

"You don't mind."

"No, no, no, no. I object when people make bald statements about our private life together which have nothing to do with the facts whatever. But once they put these things in print, one has somehow, I think, to—not refute them, obviously, but to tell the truth, that's all—not inventions and fantasies."

He added that he thought it was very important to speak about sex and finances. He mentioned that he'd heard of a book about Montgomery Clift in which the author said that Libby Holman's lawyer told her that Libby had left Paul four hundred and fifty thousand dollars. (Libby Holman, famous as the original "torch singer," was a close friend of the Bowleses.)

"Would it were so."

"Wouldn't it be marvelous? I'd be fixed." He laughed. "It's completely false. She didn't leave me a penny. Nor did anyone expect her to. But—gossip. Well, for one thing, everybody spoke of Libby; they said she was trying to break up our marriage."

I said I'd never heard that.

"Good. I hear these bits of gossip here in Tangier over the years." Then he suddenly began to reveal how Libby had proposed to him in 1948. "Libby was over here and said, 'Jane told me that if I wanted to get hold of you, I'd better do it fast.' I didn't have any intention of becoming Libby's husband, naturally. What for? We were down in the south, and Janie was up here in the hotel. She said, 'Jane is perfectly willing, but I don't think she would be somehow; I don't think she'd like it. Of course, it would be nice because she could live in the house with us and so on and we would never put her out—' " Here he laughed.

"You're kidding."

"She said, 'I think Janie wants to be Mrs. Bowles.' Well, there was no question of any of it in my mind at any point."

"And then did she take it with good grace when you said no?"

"I never said no."

I laughed. "You never said no?"

"I never said anything. Well, I never do. I don't know why you have to say something. You just have to go on living. People can guess for themselves whether it's yes or no."

There was an ebb and flow in our conversation that day. It kept shifting and moving about: thoughts and feelings surfacing, then falling away. Against the background of what had been brought back to him by my visit to Málaga, Paul began to speak of Jane's life before the stroke. Her life had been a good life, she had a "happy" life, she was "happy as a lark."

"She was not a miserable girl at all before the stroke. Her whole life is divided into those two sections, which haven't much to do with each other—except in your book, and you'll make them have to do with each other, right?" (Yes, I had told him this was my intention.) "In my head they don't have to do with each other. I know they have, obviously. It's the same person. But I can't make them fit somehow. Before the stroke it was like she'd been plugged into the main current, and after the stroke it was operating on old batteries. It wasn't right. The same machine but not operating in the same clear fashion."

I had brought Paul pages copied from a notebook of Jane's that he had never seen. It was an undated fragment, a scene of a husband and a wife sitting at an iron table outside a hotel in North Africa. From the context it had obviously been written in the late 1940s, after Jane came to Morocco. It was a record of a conversation different from any other that Jane had ever written, as if more directly, more nakedly transcribed from life in its delineation of a husband who wants to go "further in" the desert and of a wife who is afraid to go but feels she must.

I read Paul the beginning of the fragment, in which the woman says, "I don't want to feel like we've fallen out of our lives."

Obviously startled, he said that he used something very close to this in *The Sheltering Sky*. He got up and brought back a copy of the novel and pointed out the page where Port says to Kit, "I think we're both afraid of the same thing. And for the same reason. We've never managed, either one of us, to get all the way into life. We're hanging on to the outside for all we're worth, convinced we're going to fall off . . ."

And then, as if it were necessary to deny too close a similarity, he pointed out that the two conceptions were not the same. His, he said, was about "falling off of the world," not falling out of their lives. Then he changed the subject. He noted how the pages of *The Sheltering Sky* were deteriorating, ruined by the Tangier climate. And it was true that there was a mustiness in the air, moisture having seeped into books, into paper, into walls.

I returned to the fragment in Jane's notebook, to the woman telling her husband that when she has nothing to drink she is afraid of going into the desert: " 'She turned and faced him and he saw that she was beginning to look hunted.' "

I read Jane's words about the husband: " 'Like herself he did not want to express anything more than crankiness. It was too late. His eyes showed pain.' "

I continued reading, with the strange sense of being an intermediary, reading to him her words that he had never seen, words she had recorded about him and about herself. I came to the final paragraph of the fragment:

> They both secretly enjoyed that they were not going to feel tenderhearted after all. . . . Her heart was bitter too. But they could not both reflect the same sorrow. She thought this would seem indelicate. It would happen some day surely that this little argument (which was their marriage melody) [this phrase is written and crossed out and written and crossed out] would be silenced and they too would be lost in that world of grief so heavy that those who share it cannot look into each other's eyes.

When I had finished reading, there was a silence. Finally Paul said, "That's very good."

Something had shifted, some milestone had been passed, some border crossed, some relief given.

5   Walking out in the country, Paul and Abdelouahaid and I passed a group of Moroccans leading a bull decorated with garlands. Paul pointed out that they were leading the bull to slaughter. He went on to speak about ritualized violence and the meaning it had for a culture and the individuals in a culture—how ritual could channel violence, whereas in societies bereft of ritual, violence grew more undifferentiated and meaningless.

We were in the flat, and Paul was talking about Jane in New York in the thirties and early forties, how at parties she would sit on one man's lap and then another's—to test her power, Paul thought. He said that she combined the innocence of a small child in her gestures with an extreme sophistication in conversation.

"How long did that childish aspect last?" I asked.

"Not very long, if I remember correctly, because by the spring of 1940, when we left New York and went to Mexico, it had already changed. And our personal life was changing too. I think that might have had something to do with it." The doorbell rang, and Paul got up to answer it.

When he returned, I asked him if he wanted to talk about the change in their personal life. "Well, yeah," he said, but obviously he was reluctant to go on. "Perhaps we could go into it more thoroughly another time."

"Another time" came the next day. In the middle of speaking about Jane's modesty about her body, he brought up the sexual relationship between them. It had gone on for a year and a half after the marriage. Then it had ended. That was the change he had alluded to the day before.

Now he went one step further. He told me that he had gotten very angry at Jane and hit her twice—once in France, on their honeymoon in 1938, and once in New York, in the spring of 1940. After that, sex between them had ended. He had tried to renew their sexual relationship, but she did not want to. Later, he added, she came and spent the night with him a few times, but they didn't sleep together, though he tried to persuade her to.

That much he said and no more. We went on to talk of other things.

As I left that evening, I said to him, "I have to admit it's upsetting to me, what you said about hitting Jane."

He answered, "Yes, it's upsetting, and probably in part because you think it's upsetting to me."

Now it was my turn to get sick. The following morning I awoke with a fever and chills and aches that kept me in bed for three days. Lying in the hotel room, I had a series of intense dreams. One I awoke from, knowing only that it had been a dream of discovery. A woman had taken me to Morocco, and there I was discovering—what? I did not know. In another dream, I was swimming on my back, swimming backward, doing the backstroke. Following me, going faster and faster, a man was swimming forward. His going faster forced me to go faster.

After a few days, recovered, I returned to Paul's flat. We began our conversations again. There was no acknowledgment of what had been said. I continued to ask him about Jane, going over the letters and the notebooks and the published work.

At noontime one day I went to see Lily Wickman, the owner of the Parade Bar. A striking woman with a gruff voice and a sardonic manner, Lily, like many other Tangier expatriates, had an exotic history. As a young woman she had toured Europe in a motorcycle act called The Wall of Death.

She told me that Jane had often come to the Parade Bar in 1968, just before her confinement in the Clínica de los Angeles. While at the Parade, Jane would walk up and down incessantly, wring her hands, take her wig off and put it on again, drink and then order food and not eat it, and order food again. The ceaseless and repetitive activity drove everybody crazy, Lily remembered; the customers kept complaining. Still, Lily noted, it was odd; there was a quality of gaiety in Jane through all this.

When I saw Paul, I told him what Lily had said, and I mentioned the gaiety. No, she had not been "gay" then at home, he said, "not with me." During that period she had left her apartment downstairs and had gone to live in the Atlas Hotel. From there she would go to the Parade Bar every afternoon and evening. "Why did she go to the Atlas?" I asked. "Because she wanted to go," Paul answered, with a hint of asperity. "I don't know why. She was not in a state to explain why she wanted to go. She was not *compos mentis.*" And then he added, "That was when she emptied my bank account."

Now, in heightened detail, not as a listing but as a coherent and intense narrative, Paul described how Jane had started making out checks on their joint bank account, handing them out freely to anybody nearby—including, he noted, Cherifa as well as a shopkeeper who had consistently been overcharging Jane. Even after Jane emptied the account, she still went on writing check after check. When he discovered this, Paul had to rush around Tangier making payment on the bad checks.

After that, Jane's behavior oscillated further and further out of control until, on the recommendation of Dr. Yvonne Marillier-Roux, her physician, he had taken Jane to Málaga, even though she was adamantly opposed to going. "I kept at her and I kept at her," he sighed, "and Madame Roux kept at her, and Jane sort of shrugged her shoulders, and she said, 'It won't do any good,' and so on. She knew that already. And she was so out of her mind or pretended to be—I was never sure . . ."

He took her to Málaga, accompanied by a Moroccan intern who was prepared to give her an injection in case her behavior became uncontrollable. Yet she was quite docile on the trip. She said that she knew they were refugees fleeing from the war and that they could never go back, but at least now they were out and safe. "No," Paul suddenly corrected himself, "I don't think she was pretending."

By the time they arrived in Málaga, it was eight-thirty at night, and the clinic was silent and dark. "A nun appeared with a candle at a barred window, way up high. She called out, '*Está cerrado! No puede entrar nadie!* [We're closed! Nobody can enter!]' So we had to stay overnight in a hotel with Jane, who was determined by that time to get away." During the night Jane kept asking the intern for a drink. When he refused, she tried to jump out the window, but the intern stopped her. The next morning Paul left Jane in the clinic and returned to Tangier.

When Jane suffered her stroke in April 1957, Paul was away from Tangier, traveling in Southeast Asia with his intimate friend and protégé, the painter Ahmed Yacoubi. He did not learn of her illness until his boat docked in Las Palmas, in the Canary Islands, on the return voyage. There he received a telegram from the novelist Gordon Sager, who was living in Tangier.

When Paul finally saw Jane, six weeks after her stroke, he thought she seemed very much herself, although she had developed a quirky habit of misusing small words, substituting, for example, "he" for "she," "fat" for "thin," "high" for "low." As the days passed, however, it became clear that the stroke had not been a minor event but a cataclysmic shock to Jane's nervous system.

In the Tangier expatriate community, the rumors were prevalent that Jane's stroke had been caused by Cherifa.

Many subscribed to the view that Cherifa had performed magic on Jane or poisoned her. These rumors did not take into account Jane's own medical history: for some years she had had inordinately high blood pressure and had been taking a medication called Sparine to reduce it. At the same time, she had been drinking heavily, even though Sparine and alcohol were a deadly combination in someone genetically predisposed, as Jane was, to vascular illness.

In early July, Jane had several epileptiform seizures. So quickly did her condition worsen that by mid-July Paul felt it necessary to take her to England for medical treatment. She was examined first at the Radcliffe Infirmary at Oxford and then at St. Mary's Hospital in London, where the damage to her vision was diagnosed as irreparable. (She was able to see only half the field of vision with each eye.) But in addition to the actual loss of vision, Jane kept saying that she had lost her capacity for imagining, for visualizing images. The solution, one of the doctors said, was for her to return home and learn to cope "with her pots and pans."

Paul and Jane returned to Tangier by sea. On the ship Jane suffered another series of epileptiform seizures, which left her in a state of mental confusion and amnesia. Paul tried to get her into the hospital in Gibraltar, but she refused. Once they arrived in Tangier, Jane's condition deteriorated even further. She seemed unable to move of her own volition. From time to time she would whisper, "Complete isolation, complete isolation."

By early September, in a state of extreme anxiety, Jane said that she wanted to go back to England for further treatment—or, rather, she said that she wanted to go, and then she didn't want to go, and then she did want to go, her old indecisiveness now having achieved mammoth proportions without the ironic detachment that had once accompanied her vacillations. Anne Harbach, a friend of Jane's, volunteered to accompany her to England, and Paul gratefully paid her way.

In late September, Paul traveled to England with Ahmed Yacoubi, who was to have a show of his paintings in London. Once there, Paul visited Jane at St. Andrew's in Northhampton, the psychiatric hospital where she was being treated. The doctors had advised electric shock therapy for Jane, but she had refused it. She told Paul that she was fearful of further damage to her brain. Paul did not press her to accept the treatment. When he left her, she was in a very agitated state, convinced that she would never see him again.

On his return to London, Paul came down with "Asian flu." Though he was ill and running a high fever, while in bed he began and completed a story, "Tapiama." It is a story whose subject matter is ostensibly unrelated to what he was going through at the time.

In this story, a man identified only as a photographer is staying at a primitive hotel in the tropics. Desperate to escape from the fetid heat in his room, he goes out into the night and wanders along the shore toward a point of light in the distance. As he walks, he tells himself that freedom is governed by a law of diminishing returns. "If you went beyond a certain point of intensity in your consciousness of desiring it, you furnished yourself with a guarantee of not achieving it." In the last analysis, he tells himself, freedom is nothing but the state of being totally subject to the tyranny of chance.

When he reaches the light, it turns out to be a blaze in a small boat. The photographer gets into the boat and is rowed by a naked man across a body of water to Tapiama, a settlement composed of a collection of palm-leaf huts, a dock, and a cantina. In the cantina are a number of strange and threatening people, including a soldier and a girl with gold teeth. The girl attempts to seduce the photographer, but he kicks her forcefully in the breast, and she retreats. He drinks two glasses of a powerful concoction called cumbiana and becomes aware of a profound change within himself. The "act of living" has become so different from anything he has previously imagined that he feels "stranded." The only thing that is clear to him is that he must stay where he is and suffer. He realizes that to "try to escape would be fatal . . . 'Oh, God,' he asked himself. 'Am I going to be able to stand this?' "

Leaving the cantina, he goes down to the river, climbs into the boat, and pushes it off from shore. Lying in the boat, he becomes aware that he has fallen into "a senseless nightmare imposed from without, in the face of which he could only be totally passive." Five naked men, each one indistinguishable from the others, enter the boat and begin to row it, not toward the beach where the photographer wants to go but through a swamp and a canal. Feeling shame, he passively accepts going with them. Soon his shame troubles him less. The story ends with his asking about a sound he hears; he is told it is made by a talking bird in the jungle.

When Paul finished the story, his fever was gone, and he got out of bed. Almost immediately he had a relapse and spent a month in the hospital. Meanwhile, Jane had agreed to have electric shock treatments. After the therapy she seemed improved, and Paul, Jane, and Yacoubi returned together to Tangier in late November.

However, Tangier was no longer the refuge for them that it had been. The political situation had become complex, and the government had initiated a police action, aimed at the expatriate community, to investigate any personal links between Moroccans and foreigners. Ahmed Yacoubi, who had been arrested earlier and then released, was jailed again on his return. Seeing that some expatriates were being arrested and others deported, Paul decided to go to Portugal with Jane and wait there until the political situation in Tangier was resolved.

In Funchal, on the island of Madeira, Jane made an effort to write, but soon she did nothing but sit silently all day and stare into space. When she did speak, she would talk only about going back to Tangier. By the end of March, convinced that her condition was worsening, Paul tried to get her to go to New York. He told her that she could get better medical care there—and, besides, he had already written to several of her friends, and they had agreed to help her if she came to the U.S. Still Jane refused to leave. Then, one day during their bleak time together in Funchal, Paul told Jane that he was going to kill himself if the situation continued on as it was. Finally, she agreed to go to New York.

Some days earlier, before Paul had spoken in detail of Jane's stroke and its aftermath in their lives, I had questioned him about a letter Jane had written to him in 1947. It contained one sentence in which she said that Oliver Smith was always very nice to Paul but that Paul was not very nice to Oliver.

"I don't know what she meant" had been Paul's initial response. Then he added, "I don't know. Why wasn't I nice to him? Maybe I wasn't nice to anybody."

I laughed, and he said, "Could be. I think I've always

been very self-centered. I know that. It's hard to be any-thing else, for me."

I mentioned the demands of the imagination, the de-mands of one's own work.

"Well, that was my excuse, naturally, to myself for not paying enough attention to other people. It was always I can't, I can't. I don't know what one lives for, really, for oneself, for other people. Someone who writes, who creates something—if he doesn't live for himself, how can he do that work? I mean, if his principal consideration isn't his work, he probably won't do the work."

I thought of this statement, of his need to pay attention to himself and not to other people, when he spoke of his days with Jane at Funchal. If through his narrative of the events following Jane's stroke I was becoming a witness to her suffering, through that same narrative I was also be-coming a witness to how he had not been able to bear her suffering. The burden that had been placed upon him was too great for him.

Earlier he had said that he had lived "through" Jane. But after the stroke, he seemed to be saying, he could not or would not endure living this suffering through her.

The process of his revealing these things to me, some-times obliquely, sometimes directly, was not a therapeutic process—yet images, feelings, doubts, needs were being examined. It was not a confessional process—yet admis-sions were being made. As a result, there was for me a strange kind of grieving going on, grieving by proxy, as a surrogate, as I listened to him speak.

At the same time, part of me continued to try to make connections thematically, biographically. I recalled certain passages in Jane's work that showed an almost prophetic preoccupation with suffering, mystical in intensity. Even in ostensibly comic narratives or in narratives that spoke of a character's desperate longing for happiness and pleasure, the inescapable necessity of suffering was always present.

I remembered one fragment of an unfinished novel where Bozoe Flanner writes to Janet Murphy, "There isn't any use in my trying to pretend that I do not believe we were put on this earth to suffer. I do believe it—But not clearly enough . . . Don't you know me? I am Bozoe Flanner. I am exiled from the earth and I love the earth."

In Paul's fiction, on the other hand—I couldn't help seeing this either—it was not the acknowledgment of suffering but the avoidance of suffering that drove his characters. In *The Sheltering Sky*, Port, unable to bear the suffering that closeness with Kit entails, retreats into constant motion, into existential speculation. Dyar in *Let It Come Down*, Stenham in *The Spider's House*, the Slades in *Up Above the World*—all share the same compulsion to avoid suffering. Only the photographer in "Tapiama" begins to allow the knowledge of his suffering to come to consciousness. He tells himself that "he must stay there and suffer; to try to escape would be fatal . . ." Yet finally he too must escape, succumbing to total passivity as he is rowed away by the five indistinguishable men.

7 From the time I had first come to Tangier, there had been talk about Cherifa: how dangerous she was, how she did magic, how she poisoned Paul's parrot, how she was responsible for Jane's stroke. I had asked Paul where I could find her, but he had said he didn't know. Finally, Dan Bente suggested that I ask Mo-

hammed Temsamany, who had been Paul's driver in the fifties. Temsamany agreed to take me to meet her.

It turned out, however, that it wasn't a simple matter of just going to interview her. First there had to be "arrangements." Temsamany would come to the hotel and have a drink and then another drink, but for one reason or other, it seemed, this would not be the day for us to go. Once he said that we couldn't go to Cherifa's because he had a toothache. At other times the excuse wasn't clear or, rather, several excuses were intertwined. Finally the day came when he announced that, absolutely, the very next day we would go to Cherifa's. It was necessary, he advised me, to take something along for Cherifa as a gesture of politeness, by which he meant liquor. When I gave him some money to buy the liquor, he mentioned that he had told Cherifa that I was Jane's cousin, writing a book about Jane's life. I didn't see any reason for this deception, but there was little I could do about it after the fact.

The next day, when I went to meet Temsamany, I found him drinking in the hotel bar. With him he had a large package, the cognac and wine we were bringing as an offering. We got into a cab, and he told the driver to stop first at a "take-out chicken" place, which he said was owned by one of his relatives. When he came out of the "take-out chicken," he announced that he had to go to the bank. I waited in the cab outside and, after quite a long time, he emerged. He gave the driver some instructions, and we were driven to a section of Tangier called Emsallah and deposited in front of a pile of rubble.

I followed Temsamany through an alleyway and up a steep flight of stone steps. Cherifa came out on the landing to greet us. I had expected a large, terrifying personage. Instead, she was slight, graying, her hair pulled back, her skin finely wrinkled. She smiled a lot. She was wearing jeans and a white sweater over a green shirt with white flowers.

We went through a passageway with a lightwell into a room without a window. Around the periphery of the room was a raised section for seating, covered with a material of yellow and muddy brown flowers. The walls were painted a shade of green with a lot of yellow in it. High on the wall opposite the entry was a picture of Cherifa's late sister, to whom I had been told she was very devoted, with her husband.

Through Temsamany, Cherifa announced how much I looked like Jane. I said something innocuous to Temsamany, which he didn't bother to translate; and he and I, at Cherifa's behest, sat on the raised couch. Temsamany brought out the wine and the cognac and placed them on the low round table before us. Cherifa brought out some pictures, one of Jane and herself at the beach, the other a photo of herself alone when she was younger. Then Cherifa sat down on the raised section opposite me, her legs crossed before her in tailor fashion. It would have been hard to guess her age, though later I learned that she had been born in a small village near Tangier in 1928 or so.

A young man in his twenties came in, and Cherifa introduced him as her nephew. From what I could gather, listening to the infrequent asides in English that Temsamany was making to me, she was trying to persuade Temsamany to help her nephew get a job, but he was refusing. Temsamany then suggested that the nephew leave. He went out, but then he came right back in again.

A neighbor appeared and looked with interest at the liquor on the table. Temsamany gestured for him to leave, saying that we had come here to see Cherifa, not him. The man shrugged his shoulders and smiled at me. In halting French, he told me that he had once worked for Paul for a few days. The nephew announced that he too had known Jane. They all mentioned again how much I looked like Jane. Then the neighbor and the nephew left.

The chicken was brought out, unwrapped, and placed on the low table, but neither Cherifa nor Temsamany seemed interested in eating. The liquor was by now flowing freely, and Temsamany, who hadn't been exactly sober to start with, was getting more and more relaxed. The more he relaxed, the less he translated. His gestures, however, were becoming larger. There was a lot of hand-clapping and hitting his left palm with his right fist for emphasis. There was also a lot of getting up and kissing Cherifa on the lips. She grinned and laughed and seemed to be going along with everything he said, as she too kept drinking.

Yet I was aware of the fact that, even as she was drinking, she was sizing me up. Suddenly, innocently, she asked Temsamany to ask me a question. The question was "How is Jane's sister?" "But Jane didn't have a sister," I replied. "Well, then," she inquired, "how are the aunts?" "They are all dead—but one," I added. Again came more statements about how much I looked like Jane.

Now Cherifa was becoming more voluble. She said that she had had a dream some days ago that a man and a woman were coming to see her. Since Jane's death, she announced, she had not slept with a woman. Temsamany rolled his eyes. Cherifa held up the chicken and swore on the chicken that this was true. She added that she had lost interest in that kind of thing. She asked Temsamany to ask me if I was "that way." I said no. Was I married? "Divorced," I answered. "Good," she said, "I like that." And children? "I have two daughters." Where was I staying? "At the Villa de France." "Ah," she said, "Janie stayed there when she met me [in 1948]. She walked down the hill from there and found me in my hanootz [market stall]." Then Cherifa added—all of this, of course, being translated somehow by Temsamany—that she had met Paul first and that Paul had said to her, "My wife must meet you. She would like you."

She brought up Mrabet, saying that she hated him and that Jane had hated him too. She told how she had cared for Jane and how, when Jane was ill in the hospital in Tangier, she had slept every night at her bedside. Returning to the troubles of her own life, she spoke of her late sister, who had had eleven children. Her sister became ill, her legs swelled up, and then her husband "started going away from her." After her sister died, her husband married one, two, three times. "He never comes to see the children," Cherifa lamented.

She opened her white plastic purse, which had been behind her on the low couch, and took out photos of her sister at her wedding and of her sister's children, all handsome young people. Then she showed me a photo of herself and a pretty girl, both in djellabas (cloaks). Cherifa said she was (used to be? I couldn't gather anything about tenses in this conversation) in love with this girl. Temsamany remarked that he had taken that girl out once and that she was mad at him.

There was even more drinking, and even less translation. I looked at Cherifa, whose role in Jane's life had been so mysterious. She was laughing a lot, exchanging stories raucously with Temsamany. At one point she got up and ran lightly up the stairs outside to the kitchen above. I was puzzled by this woman who had been described as so evil, who seemed so good-humored.

Now Temsamany was eating the chicken. Cherifa gave him a towel to wipe his hands. "No," he said and threw it down. He pulled out some paper towels that he had brought with him in his jacket pocket. But then he picked up the towel and wiped his hands with it. Cherifa, looking at me, said, "*Kif-kif, kif-kif.*" I, thinking she was offering me kif, declined. "No, thanks, I don't smoke." (Paul was to tell me later that she was not offering me kif. Rather, the phrase "*kif-kif*" means "very like," and she was merely saying once again that I was like Jane. How Cherifa's insistence that I was so like Jane was tied up with the fact that Temsamany had said I was Jane's cousin—which, of course, Cherifa did not believe for a minute—I never would know.) An instant later, Cherifa was volunteering that Jane hated Paul smoking kif.

There was talk of how good it was that we (Temsamany and I) had come to visit. At that point, my stomach growled loudly. "What was that?" Temsamany asked. "Someone else talking," he added. Cherifa laughed and told me how Jane used to do that and say, "Excuse me, Cherifa, it wasn't me; it was someone else."

Soon it grew darker in the room, and there was only the dim light from an overhead fixture with a tan-colored shade. I noticed a smell like a mixture of urine and spices; it seemed to permeate the walls. By now Temsamany had completely given up translating and had become a little surly in his demeanor. I felt that I had gone as far as I could go with this. I got up and said it had been a pleasure for me to meet Cherifa, but unfortunately I had to go, as I had another appointment. There were many protestations of "Sit—wait—stay—," but finally Cherifa's nephew went to get a cab. Temsamany and I left, though first there was a long and voluble good-bye. Going through the alleyway

I saw a man on crutches, wearing a djellaba. His toes were pointed inward so strongly that I wondered how he could walk, yet he moved along speedily.

The next day, when I told Paul about my visit to Cherifa with Temsamany, he seemed to find it "awful" as well as amusing. He laughed when I told him about "*kif-kif*," telling me what the words meant. I also told him that after I had seen Cherifa, it was hard for me to hold onto a sense of her as evil, to believe that she could have poisoned Jane. He shrugged, clearly indicating he did not agree with my judgment of her innocence. "I would probably feel sorry for her if I saw her," he added, "but I don't want to see her."

That afternoon we went over the copy of a manuscript of Jane's that I had brought him from HRC. It was a part of her unfinished novel *Out in the World,* a section dealing with a young soldier named Andrew, who meets another young soldier in front of a bonfire. Andrew is a man obsessed with his own secrecy. At the camp, "all at once he had a brief but clear vision of himself as an eccentric, a person so absorbed in his own experience that he was barely conscious of anyone else." Others are somehow "a mass separate from himself and against him the same way that a wall is against a person if he wants to be on the other side of it."

As I read these fragments aloud to Paul, with their starts and stops and crossings out and new starts, the words conveyed the sense of an experience that happens and rehappens and rehappens again. Paul listened and responded with a "So strange." I knew him well enough by this time to know that it was painful for him, someone who always completed everything, to listen to yet one more example of what Jane had not completed. Yet even as I went on with the reading, there came to me a possibility, like a shadow upon the words, that in the character of Andrew, Jane was using something of what she saw in Paul, mixing it up with something of herself, something she knew of his secrecy and of her own.

I had turned off the tape recorder and was about to leave. Then suddenly—I do not know how he began—Paul was speaking of himself. I started the tape again. From the context I can only guess that he was elaborating on a phrase he had once used about himself. The phrase was "I don't exist."

"Or I am a machine, right? A machine produces material which will perhaps exist after the machine is broken. Its only justification, then, for ever having existed will lie in the material it's produced. So the machine doesn't really exist."

Doubtfully, I asked Paul if this was something he was saying for the moment but next month, say, he would disagree with it.

"No. I don't think so. No. I wrote it all out in *Without Stopping*, when it first became apparent to me that I was a recording instrument rather than a person."

I sighed, and Paul repeated, "I wrote it all out. It's all explained. I think." After a while, he added, "Well, it's rather a foolish thing to say because everyone feels that he exists, obviously, you know, being hungry, sleeping—all those things. I didn't really mean that. That goes without saying—that there's an entity, which is a real existent."

"A core of yourself—"

"Whatever keeps the machine running. I take that for granted."

"So you're saying something that I don't quite under-stand when you say that the 'I' doesn't exist. Unless you mean it's not accessible in terms of thought—"

"What's not accessible?"

"The 'I' that you're talking about when you say, 'I don't exist as a single entity.' "

" 'I doesn't exist.' You can say that," he laughed. "Doesn't that make it clearer?"

I said that this was beginning to sound like one of those unfathomable philosophical conversations.

"By Martin Buber." He laughed again. "I just said it without thinking."

"But you see, Paul—" I began and then stopped. "I know you don't like to talk about your work, but this does come up again and again in your work."

"What comes up?"

"What we've been talking about," I said, "this existing or not existing."

"I don't know what you mean, that it comes up again and again. Does it?"

"I think it does. What is being dealt with often is how does one find the source of feeling and action in a self, in an internal self, if it is the external that is the only solidity?" I reminded him of the opening passage of *Without Stopping*, which describes him as a child of four, seeing a mug, saying the word "mug" to himself, and at the same time hearing the clock chime four, knowing that he was four. Only then did he know that he was Paul, that "I" was "I."

"Because the clock is real, and the four notes are real," Paul explained.

Suddenly he began to speak of the knowledge of the inevitability of one's own death. "Because one's not eternal, one doesn't exist. Obviously, that's a lot of nonsense. Nothing is eternal, of course; therefore nothing exists. You can't say that. But that's the way it feels. Subjectively, that's the way it is. I've never been anything but subjective, I'm afraid. Subjectivity presented objectively," he laughed.

8 For the past several weeks, I had noticed a change in Paul: he seemed to have become more actively involved in the work on Jane's biography, trying to ferret out for me as much source material as he could. Every day when I arrived, he had something new to present—a letter of Jane's, a photo of her, even a draft of one more unfinished manuscript, things he had come upon the night before, rummaging through unsorted mounds of material in his flat. It was as if he had become caught up in my obsession with me, trying to find whatever would contribute to a coherent narrative of her life. Each day our talks were becoming more intense and more dense. Each interview had its own shape, its own dynamic, its own emerging theme. Each one was like a miniature drama revolving around Jane as the main character.

But now that my visit was coming to an end, yet a new element had been introduced into our talks: he had started to speak of himself, directly. Facing him, I had been seeing a not quite developed photographic image, but now that image was demanding some kind of resolution.

When I saw Paul next, I did not begin, as I usually did, with a question about Jane. Instead, I asked him what he wanted to talk about. In answer, he brought up "The Waterfall," a story he had written in the spring of 1926, when he was fifteen, for *The Oracle*, the literary magazine of

Jamaica High School in Queens, New York. I had brought a copy of the story with me and had given it to him weeks earlier. It had been fifty years since he had last seen "The Waterfall."

The story tells of a father whose son has jumped to his death from a high point above a waterfall. Soon after the boy's suicide, the father, angry at his son for his cowardice, walks into the forest and comes to the very spot from which his son leaped. As he looks over the edge of the rocky cliff to the pool three hundred and twenty feet below, he finds he is unable to resist the pull of the mysterious waters below. No longer blaming his son for killing himself, the father leaps into the abyss, into "utter oblivion and peace."

"I hated it," Paul said, remembering how it upset him to write the story. "It was a terrible sort of dirty thing to me—I mean, to write it. But when I read it over, I felt, I've done that—against my father." And here Paul banged on the table beside him.

"Well," he said after a moment, "I won't say that I thought of it that clearly at that time. I probably didn't, but I know that I connected the father and son with myself and my father. Of course I was aware of that. I changed his character insofar as I didn't really think that if I had committed suicide my father would be angry about it. I thought he wouldn't give a damn. Just to make a good story, I had to have the father angry at his son. And then as payment for his anger, he has to be caught in the same trap that his son was caught in and pulled toward his own destruction."

"But then it ends in peace for him."

"A peace? Right. Well, naturally," Paul laughed. "There's

no longer any trouble. I don't know. It was fiction, naturally. I was a kid, so it's very hard for me to remember exactly how I felt except that I know that it upset me when I was writing it. My heart beat much too fast. I thought I was committing some sort of crime by writing it because I'm sure I connected that with wishing that my father would die. You feel better after you have gotten it out of you, whatever it is, the poison, and solidified it, and then other people can read it and you want them to read it. They don't know what it means, and you want them to judge it purely on its fictional merits."

But how was it possible for him, as a young boy, to "get into" the character of his father?

"Well, I assume that if I got into him, or seemed to, it was simply because I pretended to be my father. I knew him, naturally, very, very well. All too well." But then he corrected himself. "Probably I didn't. But I mean I knew him from my childish point of view. And I considered that he was my enemy, that he wanted to be my enemy, that he wanted me to be unhappy. For there was no way of being happy if he was around.

"I remember when I was so small that I couldn't get up the steps of the elevated [railway]—you know, those long steps that led up to the platform from the street. I was only about three, and I couldn't make them. I mean, they seemed this high to me." Paul gestured with his hands, indicating an immense height above him. "I couldn't get up. So he hit me each step." And here Paul took on the voice of his father, a harsh voice of authority: " 'Come up! Keep walking! Keep walking! Stop dragging!' I couldn't reach the damn steps. So it was agony then to go on the elevated because I was going to be hit all the way up." He laughed and went on, his voice less charged. "Sharp slaps on the back of my legs"—he hit the table again—"walking behind me, hitting me.

"So it was no fun. Nothing was ever fun. Everything had to be put away before he came back [at night]. Anything that was left out was confiscated and destroyed. So I was very careful to hide everything away—this is at the age of four."

Before this, I had been struck by the remarkable musicality of Paul's voice, how when he said a word or a phrase, the tone moved so easily on it and through it, how even when he said something and laughed, there was a movement of tone, of pitch, on the laugh and on the word. But when he spoke of his father, his voice was different. There was no melody in the words, but rather a tightening, a flattening of pitch. One heard in his throat a constriction, as if the memory of the restraints placed upon him as a child still resided in the muscles and cells of his body so many years later, long after he had escaped—long after his father was dead.

"This just popped into my head," I said.

The whole question of Paul's anger, and especially his mention of hitting Jane, had lain fallow in my mind for some days. It was so much at odds with the Paul I encountered on a daily basis that I didn't know how to deal with it. But now that I was getting ready to leave, I had to bring it up.

I reminded Paul of an incident in *Without Stopping*. At the age of ten or so, Paul had a rock fight with Gordon Linville, a boy who lived next door. He hit Gordon on the head with a rock, and the boy bled profusely. The wound healed, but a scar was left on his forehead. Paul felt that the injury was unintentional, but Gordon and his older sister insisted that Paul had deliberately hurt him. "To assuage my feelings of guilt," Paul writes, "I kept trying to be friendly with him, but we always ended up fighting. There was an illogical and babyish quality about him that both infuriated and excited me, and I determined finally to arrange his fate and watch him undergo it."

Paul's scheme involved setting up a club called The Crystal Dog Club for boys in the neighborhood. After getting permission from his parents to hold the club's meetings on the third floor of their house, Paul circulated fliers announcing the founding meeting, at which there would be unlimited ice cream. When Gordon Linville showed up with the other boys at the first meeting, Paul maneuvered things so that Gordon was the first one to be initiated.

"He was already blubbering a little when the blindfold was applied," Paul notes. "That was perfect." Gordon was trussed up with a rope and dragged to the edge of the open stairwell. Now Paul arranged it so that Gordon was led to believe that he was about to be dangled out a third-story window. Paul's plan was for the boys to lower Gordon over the stairwell edge bit by bit and then, at the right psychological moment, to let him drop. But Gordon was heavier than expected, and when the boys let him over the edge with the rope, they could not hold onto him. Gordon plummeted to the bottom of the stairwell—two floors below—and began to scream. Paul's parents, Claude and Rena, came running, examined the boy, and, finding him unhurt, sent him home. The club was then disbanded by Claude's edict. From Paul's viewpoint, of course, it had already served its usefulness. "We decided that nobody else would have behaved in such an abject manner. Shortly after that the Linville boy went away to school."

"Oh, that's right," Paul responded vigorously. "Yeah, yeah, yeah, yeah, yeah. Yes. Yes. It wasn't really that I didn't like him. I wanted revenge against him; I don't know why. I thought he was helpless and an idiot and a dolt and should be ashamed of himself." Again Paul laughed. "I remember there's a conversation in *Without Stopping* between my mother and my father, and my mother says, 'Pragmatic,' about these [Linville] children, and my father says, 'Bovine.' "

"And was that what aggravated you about him?" I asked.

"It's hard to say what drove me mad about him. But I wasn't angry."

"You must have been angry at him in order to hang him over the stairwell like that."

"No. No. I disagree. I wasn't angry at him."

"Okay, so what was it if it wasn't anger?"

"I wanted to scare him, and I wanted to hear him blubber. Which is exactly what happened. He was like a small child, but he shouldn't have been. He was much too big to blubber."

"Hm," I said, waiting.

"There was a lot of sadness in him—when I thought about it. I think it wasn't hate for him. It was just wanting to see him suffer. Don't you think?"

"How do you distinguish those two?"

"Distinguish between what and what? Between hatred and sadism?"

He had used the word "sadism"; I don't think I could have or would have, but now that he had used it, I took it up. "Offhand, I would think sadism would have an element of—that you'd have to hate somebody to want to hurt them—"

"No. I don't think so. Not at all. I think you can be

fascinated by someone if you're a sadist and want to see that person suffer without hating him at all. Without liking him or hating him. Why? Because—" Here Paul sighed. "Why? Because you feel that the person must suffer, and you want to see it happen."

"Now, that's pretty complicated," I said. In fact, I feared the discussion was resolving itself into too stark simplicity.

"Well," Paul admitted, "perhaps I'm kifed. . ." We had been talking for some time, and Paul had been smoking kif, though he did not seem "kifed" to me in any way. "I was just trying to distinguish between how I would have felt had I hated this Gordon Linville," he went on.

"Had you hated him, you wouldn't have done what you did?"

"No," he said slowly, and then faster and rhythmically he added, "No, no, no. I would have done something private. Hatred doesn't require the establishment of a club and printing the stationery and having meetings and so on. No, no, no. A diabolical intent explains that, but not hatred. I didn't feel any vengeful feelings toward him at all. I just felt that I wanted to humiliate him in front of all the kids in the neighborhood. Which happened. They all helped me. They did it."

"What was it you said about somebody who was in some way bound to suffer—?"

"Who must suffer."

"By 'must,' you mean something in them?"

"Yes. I'm speaking in general terms. You said, how do you distinguish between aggression through sadism and aggression through hatred? And I was trying to pull them apart. That's a very easy way of saying the person must suffer. It doesn't really mean much. In my case, it meant that the boy was a slob. He wasn't dignified, the way he played. He complained, he snuffled and sobbed by himself and"—Paul imitated a sobbing complaint—"went over to the others and for a minute would look as though he was going to hit them but never did. It wasn't hatred for him; it was disgust for him, really. He was a sufferer. He always got everything. If someone got hit on the back of the head with a rock, it was Gordon Linville.

"I was sitting on the bus here in Morocco years ago between Casablanca and Marrakech," Paul went on, launching into story, "and a mother was there with two little girls. They seemed very nice, both of them all dressed up. But as we drove along, one of the little girls by the window suddenly vomited and was terribly sick, and the other one just sat primly, looking the other way. And the mother had to clean up and so on. Then the bus went on and it stopped, and the same little girl banged her head on the chromium railing ahead of her. A-a-ch! And then we were nearly to Marrakech, and a hornet came in the bus and stung her." Paul laughed and went on, "The mother turned to me, and she said, '*Cela, c'est tout les malheurs* [Everything bad happens to that one].' Which is exactly it. It was a joke between Janie and me for years. She would suddenly turn to me when we were out with other people, and she'd say, '*Cela, c'est tout les malheurs.*'"

There was a silence, and suddenly the light in the room began to dim. "Seems to me the light has gotten lower, don't you think?"

"It certainly did."

"It was a hundred and fifty watts and then a hundred— and now it's zero."

I got up and looked out the window. "There's not a light anywhere."

Paul went out of the room, saying, "I hope I have a flashlight."

"Well, at least you're not in the elevator," I called out, thinking of being stranded in the dark in that tiny, rickety cage.

"There's no light anywhere except in the sky," he said from the kitchen. A minute later the lights came on again. "That was quick," he said, as he came back in.

"Now, just let me ask you this—" Lights or no lights, what he had said about hatred was so different from my own sense of the word that I had to go on. "For instance, you would say you felt hatred for your father?"

"Yes, well, that's very different."

"But that did not mean wanting to see him suffer?"

"No. No. I just wanted him not there. I wanted to get rid of him. No, no. I hoped he would evanesce." At his sounding of the lyrical word, we both laughed. "I used to say that to my mother when I was a small child."

"And she didn't mind your saying that?"

"No. She would just say, 'Well, you don't understand.' I'd say, 'Why don't you just leave and go away?' She'd say, 'Where?' And I'd say, 'Well, somewhere else.' 'No, but where?' 'Well, to Grandma and Grandpa's house.' 'No, they can't have me.' And so on. She would get it down to there was nowhere for us to go."

"Do you think she found him very difficult too?" I asked.

"Very difficult. Indeed she did. Oh, yes. Terrible." He paused for a moment and then went on. "She said later that he only became pleasant when I left the house, when I went away. And she had to suffer him, oh, until I was seventeen."

"Something about a son," I ventured.

"Apparently. He didn't want me. He may have wanted somebody else. Not me. It was something strange; I don't know. My grandma said he was like a tomcat that comes and eats its kittens. He wanted to come back and eat me," Paul laughed.

"In later years were you ever able to talk to him in a way that was tolerable for you?"

"You mean, after I was married and so on? Oh, yeah. I'd go and visit."

"And it wasn't so bad?"

"No, no, everything was fine. In the first place, he wasn't responsible for me financially. In the second place, he wasn't responsible for me in any way at all." He paused. "The whole early years were completely forgotten, as it were. No one ever mentioned them at all. As though they'd never happened."

This could have been a stopping place, but I did not stop. "As I've gotten to know you in this curious way, you seem to me not to get angry, even in the ordinary way, the way most people do."

"You're speaking of me at the present date?"

"It doesn't seem as though anger is part of your—"

"No, I don't care enough to be angry. It's true."

"I ask this question because at one point you said to me you got angry at Jane twice," I reminded him.

"Ah. I struck her twice. I beat her twice."

"What could have made you angry at her?" I asked, finally.

"What could it have been?" he mused. He began talking about their honeymoon in France in 1938. "She'd come from Paris to Cannes," he began. "We were taking a siesta on the bed. I think she'd just come that morning. I don't know. Something I wanted. Something she didn't want. Or vice versa. Wanting to go out to a bar—probably had to do with that. Well, I was very angry with her for having stayed in Paris. Because she wanted to go out with all these people and drink and drink and drink, and I finally left her there in disgust and set out for the Côte d'Azur. I got in touch with her after a few days, and she came to Cannes. But I was still annoyed with her for having stayed behind in Paris. She kept talking about all these people and, as I remember, upbraiding me for being a killjoy, not being sociable, and so on. Well, I wanted just to be with her alone. I didn't want all these friends that she kept dragging around. I don't know what happened. I don't remember what I hit her with either, something that was there." He laughed abruptly. "A cane, maybe, or something."

"You must have been astonished at yourself for doing it."

"Well, I was very sad a minute later, naturally. Because she burst out crying, and she said, 'Well, I don't care; I love you just the same.' So then I felt horrible." Again came the brief sound, a nervous laugh or a disowning laugh. "It all ended very well. It was all right," he assured me.

"And then the other time was in New York [in 1940]. I was furious because when I came back to the Hotel Chelsea, I found the room full of people and smoke. And I wanted to go to bed; I was working on a show. We had only one room. There must have been eight or ten people in there, and they had no intention of leaving. They had bottles out, and they were all drunk. I went into the bathroom, and a woman wearing Jane's beautiful satin peignoir—it was a very fine object her mother had bought her and kept telling her it cost a fortune—was lying in the tub, wearing this thing."

"Passed out?"

"Yeah. So I couldn't even use the bathroom. It was rather like *Streetcar Named Desire*. I said, 'Get that woman out of the bathroom.' Jane said, 'These are my friends. They'll leave eventually.' And I said, 'When? I have to go to bed.' 'Ah, stop—' Arguing, you know. Well, then, after they left, I remember I—hit her. Also the same. She was already lying in bed." Again came that same sound, a laugh but not a laugh. "And I never did again. But those were—I never hurt her really."

"No," I said. "And then when she said, 'I love you all the same—'"

"Just the same," he corrected me.

"Just the same," I repeated, "that must have dissolved you completely."

"Of course." And here we both laughed briefly, a laugh of relief, perhaps, that we had gotten through this telling. "It was horrible," Paul added.

After a moment, I began to speak of how difficult it was to deal with anger, something I knew well in myself.

"Well, it's so self-corrosive," he commented. "Fear and anger are the worst emotions one can feel, I think. But they're really the same emotion, I mean, aren't they? Except anger generally comes right after fear."

I said something about anger stopping everything, taking over.

"Well, if you expect the worst, you can hardly be angry," he said.

"Say that again."

"One can only be angry if there is a discrepancy between what one feels should have happened and what did happen. Fear one can have all by itself, all by oneself. But one can't be angry all by oneself. There has to be an object, someone to be angry at. And really, you have to agree to be angry, with yourself. But you don't have to agree with yourself to be afraid. You have to say, this matters to me so much that I hereby decide to be angry about it, and in that flash of a second you are angry. You have to admit that it means enough to you for you to be angry about it, don't you think? It requires a certain assent, whereas fear doesn't at all. It's automatic. It generally is. It comes before you give it a chance—before you give yourself a chance to keep it away. You can't be angry with a bee for stinging you, for instance, can you? Unless you're an idiot," he laughed. "Your expectation is that it will and it does, if it does. There's no anger connected with it."

I thought of Paul's first volume of stories, *The Delicate Prey*. "There's an interesting thing that you do in many of your early stories that has to do with expectation," I said.

"Expectation on the part of the reader?"

"Yes. An expectation is aroused in the reader that something terrible is going to happen. And at the same time, you, the reader, believe that this should not happen."

"Should not happen?"

"Should not happen."

"M-m-m," he said, waiting.

"And then the course of the story is the inevitable occurrence of this terrible thing against your feeling that it should not happen. It is being *made* to happen."

"Being made to seem inevitable."

There was a knock on the door, and several visitors came in. Hearing Paul clear his throat, one of the men offered him a lozenge, then turned to me and offered me one. I said, "Thanks, I need one. I talk more than he does."

"Yes," Paul said.

I turned to him. "Really?" I had made the remark as a

joke, but was it true? After a moment, I answered myself, "I don't know."

"This mutual analysis," Paul said, and he laughed.

9 Jim Kalett arrived from New York to take photos for the book on Jane. In the afternoon Paul led us into the medina so that Jim could photograph the house in Place Amrah. As we walked through the narrow, winding streets, children pressed upon us, clamoring for money. One boy asked Paul if he was a Muslim. "No," he said. "Then why are you here?" the boy retorted. At the next turning, another boy about twelve, holding a little girl about two, asked Paul for money in English. Paul responded in Darija: "Why should I give you money?" The little girl began to cry, and the boy said in a reproachful tone, "She didn't cry until you spoke Arabic," and Paul laughed.

Later we went back to the flat, and Jim took photos of Paul, who seemed very much at ease before the camera, and of Mrabet and of Abdelouahaid. Suddenly I had the sense that everything was now open to public gaze. Conversation too had changed. It had become public conversation.

Before leaving for Málaga to photograph the clinic and Jane's grave, Jim Kalett decided to go for a day trip outside Tangier. He asked if I'd like to come along. I had not left Tangier since my arrival except to go to Málaga and to go on several short drives down the coast with Paul and Abdelouahaid. I felt reluctant to take any time away from my conversations with Paul. "You don't know when you'll come back to Morocco again," Jim insisted. So finally I agreed.

We drove on almost deserted roads through stark country between high ridges. Here and there in the cliffs were holes, caves, our driver told us, where cliff-dwelling monkeys lived. We followed a narrow road that turned and climbed to Xauen, a town set into the flank of a mountain. It was where Paul stayed when he wrote the last kif-driven section of *Let It Come Down.* Paul had once described Xauen as a "Poe landscape," but I found it to be surprisingly green, almost fertile, with a rushing stream running through its center. The sun shone brilliantly on the white houses with the terra-cotta roofs; only the covered passageways were in shadow. Many of the entry doors of the houses were blue. As I looked up at the mountain behind the town, I saw a small figure, a woman, making her way up the steep slope. The driver said she had been to the market. "She will climb for hours to get back to her own village."

When I arrived at Paul's the next afternoon, Mrabet and Dan Bente and Abdelouahaid were present, as they had been on my first visit six weeks before. I spoke about my trip to Xauen and mentioned having seen the woman climbing the mountain. Abdelouahaid told us that he had an aunt who lived in one of the hill towns and she had to climb for two and a half hours to get to her village when she returned from the market. "Those people are the uncorrupted ones," Paul said.

The conversation turned to Cherifa, to her use of magic, just as it had on my first day here. I will leave, and things will go on just as they have before, I thought. Even before

I leave, it's already going back to how it's been. But as Mrabet was going on and on about Cherifa and her evil powers, I found myself objecting to the mythic image of her that he was portraying. I said something about the effect on her of the world she lived in, of the place women had in Moroccan society.

According to one myth, Paul observed, women were once dominant in Morocco. They were Amazons, warriors who hunted en masse and caught men and subdued them. But then the Arabs came to Morocco, and their armies subdued the women. "Men here still have a horror and terror of women," he added.

Mrabet began a diatribe—was he being particularly provocative that day?—railing about Israel and proceeding to attack all Jews. "Mrabet," I said, "you are offending me by what you're saying; I am a Jew." "But you are an American," he replied. Then he noted that Jane was a Jew. Abruptly, he apologized to me for any pain he had given me.

It was a day in which conversation was impelled forward by some unclear imperative and then, just as suddenly, was brought to a stop. It was on that same day that Paul gave me a piece of silk he'd bought for Jane in Thailand in the late sixties, but which, because of her illness, she'd never been able to use. As I accepted his present, I felt a deep sadness at the thought that I would leave Tangier in two days, that I would not be able to see him and talk to him every day.

On the last day of my visit, I was invited by Paul to stay for dinner. Mrabet, who was a very good cook, made the dinner and then left. Paul and I ate and talked, but as the evening wore on, I began to notice a change in him. I had stayed for dinner with him several times before this, but I had never noticed any such shift. This time it was as if—and here I must go slowly—as if he were allowing the kif he was smoking (and which he always smoked from afternoon through evening) to let him let go. His voice changed slightly; it became less densely layered. He was more relaxed, slower, his gestures less precise, off guard.

Part of him was withdrawing, not through an active process but through submitting to the action of the kif. He had allowed the kif to take over, and it seemed to me, that for all that I was the one who was going, I was really the one being left behind.

10 In October 1977 I returned to Tangier for two weeks. Once again I spent four to five hours each day with Paul, checking facts, correcting errors, going over information I had unearthed from other informants about Jane, attempting to pin down an accurate chronology of her life.

I made another visit to Cherifa. Because I had seen her with Temsamany, I wondered if his presence might have skewed my vision of her. This time, when I went to see her, I brought along as translator a young Moroccan nurse called Naima, someone Cherifa didn't know. We took a taxi to Emsallah and wandered about for some time, trying to locate Cherifa's house. Naima asked the help of a woman passing by, and she led us to a house in an adjacent street. But the woman who opened the door said no one named Cherifa was there.

Naima then suggested that I show the woman who was helping us the picture of Cherifa I had with me. It had been taken by Jim Kalett, and I intended to give it to

Cherifa, along with some other photos he had shot of her nephews and nieces. "Ah, yes," the woman said, when she saw Cherifa's face, and she immediately led us to Cherifa's house. Naima and I climbed the steep stone stairs to the landing and knocked on the door.

When Cherifa answered, she showed no surprise. Yes, she remembered me; she thought I was going to come earlier. Then she said, as Naima translated, "I am glad it is women. I am old-fashioned. I believe women should be with women and men with men."

I noticed she had a handkerchief wrapped around her right wrist. She told us that she had broken it falling down the steps. She was old and lonely, she added, and could not work. Though the words, as presented by Naima, were pitiful words, Cherifa's demeanor did not seem pitiful at all. There was a sharpness in her, a darkness close to rage. It was clear that she had been drinking. I gave her the photos. She looked at the one of herself briefly and remarked that she did not like it, that she looked too old in it.

We were led into the room with couches along the wall, with the table in front of the couches, where the chicken had lain upon which Cherifa had sworn her undying allegiance to Jane. Three of Cherifa's nieces were sitting there. A question was asked of me: Do you have children? "Two daughters," I answered. No comment was made. Cherifa made some remarks to her nieces, who sat quietly. Naima did not translate.

We were offered an orange drink. Suddenly Cherifa said that Jane had written a book about her but that she, Cherifa, had never gotten any money from it. (What book did she mean?) If she was going to talk to me, she wanted money. Again came the lament: she was poor and old; she wanted to be taken care of for the rest of her life. No, she would speak of nothing, tell me nothing, unless I gave her money and a promise of much more.

Gone was the earlier Cherifa, the ribald one who had joked with Temsamany. In her place was an angry woman, making demands. To Naima, I said, "What is she talking about? How much does she say she wants?" "She won't say," Naima told me. "She wants you to say how much you'll give her."

Hopeless, I thought, hopeless, and I felt a surge of anger at being held up this way. "I have not got a lot of money," I told Naima to tell Cherifa. It was the truth. I had only a small advance on the book and a fellowship to last me for at least three years of work. As it was, it would not be enough to get by; I would have to borrow to make it through. But even if I had had money, I would not have given it to her.

"Tell her," I said to Naima, "that I have seen many people in New York and many people in Tangier about Jane, but I do not give them money. Tell her it is up to her. If she doesn't want to talk to me, that's all right; I won't put her in the book." I picked up my tape recorder and got ready to go. Suddenly Cherifa relented. It seemed she would rather be "in the book" than not in the book, whatever being in the book meant to her.

The conversation that followed was like a performance, made up of sudden bursts of speaking and miming. Ordinary sequence, at least the kind of sequence I was accustomed to in telling, was dismissed. Instead, there was another kind of telling, driven by announcements and protestations. Cherifa said she was like a man; she said she was whatever she wanted to be. She told of asking Jane for money, of telling Jane that she would leave her if she didn't give her money. Jane had said she had no money but she would ask Paul to give her his house in the medina, and then she would give it to Cherifa. Jane did give it to her, but it was only a little house, Cherifa complained. She could rent it out for only a small sum.

Erupting into pantomime, Cherifa skipped to the time after Jane's stroke. She became Jane being ill, having a seizure, biting her tongue. Then she was herself, Cherifa, taking care of Jane, going to the phone to call Madame [Doctor] Roux, calling Paul. She acted out her own ceaseless efforts to take care of Jane, never resting, not going to bed, lying down only when the other maid, Aicha, came.

I asked about the night of Jane's stroke. (I wondered if Cherifa would say something about having given Jane majoun, a cannabis jam, which Paul suspected she had done.) "It was Ramadan," Cherifa said. Jane had been drinking without eating, she ran up the stairs, she went into the bathroom and poured cold water on her face and her eyes, she had had alcohol and kif, she could not see clearly, her talking became broken, she could not speak at all. Cherifa called Christopher Wanklyn (a Canadian writer living in Tangier) for help. He called three doctors. They put ice on Jane's head.

And now that I had that answer, what did I know? It was like all the other questions that I asked her. When she answered them, what did I know?

As Naima and I got up to leave, Cherifa reverted to pathos. She had no family, no one. (What about the nephews and nieces?) She was old and lonely. Going down the steep outside staircase, she grasped my hand. Her grasp was sure and strong. I thought of what I had been told about Jane's handshake, how soft it was, almost without resistance. I thought of Cherifa's toughness, of the way she alternated between pathos and demand. I thought of her capacity for self-preservation. I thought of all I did not know and could never know about her and the world she lived in.

In the taxi going back to the hotel, Naima said, "It is a good thing you prepared me. All the way through, even at the end, what she wanted was money. And her language— I have never heard a woman talk that way—rough, low talk, like a man. The three nieces tried to get her to talk differently, but she said, 'Go to hell, I can talk any way I want.' I would have been afraid of her if I was alone," Naima added, "but I knew you were there to protect me."

I, protect her against Cherifa? I laughed to myself at the thought. To Naima I only smiled and nodded.

When I saw Paul the next day and told him about my visit, I ended by saying that, after what I had seen, it certainly seemed possible to me that Cherifa could have poisoned Jane. Paul shrugged and said, "Well, I don't know . . ."

After my first visit to Cherifa, when I had declared that I could not imagine her poisoning Jane, he had demurred, implying that I was out of my depth, that I didn't understand Cherifa. Now that I'd said I could indeed imagine the possibility, he equivocated.

Dan Bente's family arrived from America, and we all— Mrabet and Abdelouahaid and Paul and myself—went with them for a "real" Moroccan dinner at the Marhaba Palace. That evening Paul seemed very much at ease, witty, charming, courtly, making everyone feel that to be there was to be part of an important event. We sat in a corner of the restaurant on couches piled with pillows, against hanging curtains. The colors, the golds and the browns, shone in the candlelight. Even the dark wood gleamed, throwing back pinpoints of light, as the food and drink were served.

Looking at Paul, I thought I detected an openness I had not seen in him before. That afternoon I had spent several hours with him going over Jane's story "A Stick of Green Candy," her last completed work, written in Morocco in the early fifties. It is an intense and curiously fragile story about a young girl who, against the orders of her father, plays in a clay pit. There she imagines herself to be the head of a regiment of soldiers. A young boy invades the clay pit, and the girl falls in love with him. As a consequence of her love, she loses the capacity to believe in her own imagining.

Paul had seemed particularly moved by our conversation that afternoon, and now, looking at him at the Marhaba Palace, even as he spoke so easily to the others, I thought I detected the effect of the story still lingering in him. It was as if in going over Jane's story with me, he had been led to something about the revelation of secrets in himself. Seeing this in him had the paradoxical effect of making me feel that I was sharing a secret with him.

Of course, when I went to see him the next day, he was once again the Paul he always was, friendly but reserved, charming but withholding. It must have been the romantic atmosphere of the Marhaba Palace that had misled me. Or perhaps it was only the particular vulnerability of the biographer, the need to feel oneself a "secret sharer."

Abdelouahaid had invited Paul and me to drive out into the country with him to see the house he was building. The morning of the day we were to go, it rained. We had agreed that if it was raining we would not go, yet at three in the afternoon, with the sky still threatening, Paul and Abdelouahaid arrived at the hotel. Paul said he was coming along, but he didn't know why; he really didn't want to go. I had never seen him this way, so anxious and irritable. As we drove out of the city, the clouds continued to threaten, but it did not rain.

We followed the main road east, past fields and hills on either side, and then after an hour or so turned south, on a small road. From there we turned onto an even smaller road, hardly more than a dirt path. We drove partway up the slope and then stopped. The hillside above us, leading to Abdelouahaid's house, was sodden with mud. Abdelouahaid got out of the car and began to climb. I got out and began to follow him, with Paul behind me. As I walked a few paces, the mud attached itself to my shoes, and they grew heavy with the thick additional layer. Abdelouahaid, however, moved swiftly ahead, with an amazing lightness of tread. Suddenly Paul stopped; he said he was not going any further. He went back to the car and began to try to scrape the mud off his elegant suede shoes with a twig.

Far up on the hillside, Abdelouahaid called out to me to come on. I did not mind the mud, as I was wearing heavy walking shoes, but I hesitated. I returned to the car. I had seen how upset Paul was, and I had the sense that if I were to go off and leave him alone in the car, it would be an act of betrayal. He would feel it that way—or maybe I would feel it that way; perhaps both would be true. I knew that I was giving this small incident a great weight, yet in my situation with Paul small incidents often assumed a great weight for me. What he took seriously, I took seriously. I believed that whatever it was he felt, I had to give his convictions their "just due." (In his work, the thought, the anticipation, of betrayal is never absent.)

Paul got into the car, I got into the car, and we waited for Abdelouahaid to finish whatever it was he wanted to finish in his house. When he returned soon after, he told me that I should have gone with him. He was obviously disappointed with me. I mumbled some excuse about the mud. He drove down the hill backward, rapidly, with great ease.

Returning to Tangier, we took the road along the coast. There were clouds and mist over Mt. Moses. Far in the distance, across the Mediterranean, we could see the Rock of Gibraltar in sharp sunlight. The color of the rocks and of the dirt in the slanting sunlight was a combination of subtle ochres and complex reds. With the window open, we heard birds singing and the bleating of goats in the distance. There was a buzzing sound in the air. Paul, once again his usual charming, social self, said that it was a winnowing machine.

When I returned to Tangier once more, in June 1979, it was with an eight-hundred-page manuscript in my backpack. During the two weeks I was there, I spent hours each day with Paul to make sure I had not erred in my presentation of the facts. I trusted that he would not ask me to make any substantive changes in the manuscript out of a need to protect himself, and indeed he did not do so. His comments were factual and rhetorical. Was what I had said true? Was it clear? That was also a consideration for him. The factual corrections I accepted. The rhetorical suggestions were another matter. I considered that room for difference existed there.

In December 1980 I sent Paul a copy of the book in galleys so that he could catch any errors, as I had made a number of additions to the text since he had last seen it.

In January he sent me three pages of corrections, a number of spelling corrections of Moroccan names and places, and, again, rhetorical suggestions. At the end of his corrections, he wrote, "It's a beautiful biography and a terrible story . . . this time I saw myself as a consistently blithering idiot who stood by and watched the process of destruction, instead of taking hold and stopping it. And yet I knew there would have been no way . . ."

On July 7, 1981, shortly after receiving a copy of the finished book, Paul wrote to me: "I've read and reread the book so often that it's made me dream of Jane. The scene I remember most vividly is one where she and I were sitting with others around a table talking. Suddenly she became fractious and began to upbraid me. I was angry, so I rose and walked toward the door. I heard her call out: Good bye. And then I heard myself saying: There is no good bye from me to you. As I walked through the doorway I woke up. (The first dream I ever had of Jane where we weren't on good terms.)"

 To be a biographer—or perhaps I should speak only for myself—for *me* to be a biographer meant that I was in the grip of an obsession. That obsession had played itself out in my daily life, as I examined detail after detail of Jane's daily life, trying to see the forces that shaped her and the choices that she made and did not make in her life and in her work. At the same time, as I submitted to this obsession, I recognized that it was necessary to make a constant and conscious effort not to confuse her life with my life. It was an effort made even more necessary by the supposed physical resemblance between us and by certain bizarre coincidences in her life and mine. (For example, her mother's name was the same as my mother's; her grandfather's name was the same as my grandfather's. She lived in Woodmere, Long Island, at the same time I did. At thirteen, after her father's death, Jane and her mother moved to Manhattan, to the very building where my family lived when I was born. Jane broke her right leg in 1931; I broke mine the same year.)

After the biography was published, the obsession began to relent. Jane's image, her life, her work began to recede slowly in my consciousness. At times I had the sense that I was in a decompression chamber. I was going toward a state of equilibrium, in which forgetting and remembering worked out their own necessary truce.

In relation to Paul, however, an entirely different process was taking place. He had not been my subject; I did not have to struggle against any conscious identification with him. Whereas I had never met Jane, I had met Paul—in his flat, in Tangier, in life. As the months went by, I reached no equilibrium with respect to him. There remained with me his image as I had seen him on that first day I arrived in Tangier—the day I noticed those triangular shadows— and there was also his image in the days that had followed: transparent, opaque, and transparent again.

In the years following the publication of Jane's biography, Paul and I continued to correspond. He sent me several of his new short works. In turn, I sent him some of my new stories. In 1983, when I was editing a collection of Jane's letters, including some newly found correspondence, I asked for his help with names and dates, and he wrote me a long and detailed response. In 1985, when I was preparing a theater piece about Jane and her work, I sent him a copy of the play and solicited his comments. (Paul was not a character in the play, but rather a disembodied presence to whom her letters were addressed.)

In one letter to me, he asked if I would be his literary executor, a role that I accepted with some trepidation, given my inexperience in business negotiations. In many letters he spoke briefly of his life in Tangier, of the increasing number of interviewers coming to see him, of a course in creative writing he was teaching in the summer for the American School of Visual Arts. Now and then, a more intense, even personal, note would be inserted:

November 17, 1981

. . . Mrabet went to London three weeks ago, and is still there. I think he'll be back, although if someone were to offer him a job there, he'd accept it, I imagine, assuming he had official permission to remain. Naturally I miss him, but I can understand that he has no life in Tangier. In spite of that, I hope he comes back . . .

June 5, 1982

. . . When I used the word "work," I meant inventive work, which for me is the only satisfying variety. For you, too, I'd imagine. When you speak of "mind" and "memory," I assume that by "mind" you mean invention . . .

August 24, 1982

. . . You can see that I'm more worried about the books and manuscripts I have here than I am about the posthumous fate of my works, if indeed they have any fate other than to be rapidly forgotten.

I want to get through this will-making so I won't feel irresponsible. It seems selfish of one to die leaving everything in a state of chaos—rather like jumping out of the window into a busy street . . .

Why should "mind" work against invention? What one has besides "mind" is memories, which one doesn't want to use in fiction. Memory is everpresent in any case, but how can it be transcended save through a cerebral effort? I have a feeling that we agree fundamentally, although our definitions of "mind," "invention" and "imagination" probably differ.

March 1, 1983
. . . I went out yesterday for the first time, after a fortnight of grippe and its attendant complications. What a bore! And it takes so long to get back to feeling normal, and not having one's muscles ache. In a few days I hope to feel more or less the way I did last month, before the unidentified bacillae came to visit. . . .

I was still sick in bed when I heard the news last Friday via BBC of Tennessee's death [Tennessee Williams], and in my feverish condition I kept thinking that surely he was only in a coma, and would shortly be back in circulation! I was very much shaken by the news—more than I should have expected to be. Then people reported that Spanish television had mentioned the likelihood of foul play. And I wonder . . .

December 13, 1983
. . . The man in London who had been coming here finally said he wanted to write a biography, and I was forced to tell him that my biography had been written [Paul's own *Without Stopping*] and that I saw no reason why it should be rewritten, at which point he agreed to do a study of the work instead. I wonder if he will actually write the book. I should think that a critical book would be more difficult for the author, but easier for me. There wouldn't be many questions that I should be able to answer, precisely because of what you say: that much of the work comes directly from the unconscious, and thus queries as to why it's the way it is or how it got that way would be unanswerable. I agree with you that such things are important in an attempt to define the writing, but I wonder if it would be possible to find precise motivations for having made it the

way it is. It's hard enough for me to remember the details of my life; the periods of writing are rather like long and short dreams in the midst of living the life, but dreams long since forgotten, and of which the only record is the writing itself . . .

March 24, 1984

. . . Don't you *want* readers to be "disturbed"? For years I wrote *hoping* they'd find the material wayward enough to be upsetting. A strong reaction, either toward or away from, is surely desirable; I don't think the direction is all-important, do you?

October 2, 1984

. . . Brevity. I got back here nine days ago from hospital in Switzerland, imagining that quickly I'd feel well. This idea was proven false. Since my return I've been far sicker than I was at any time in Bern. An infection which in spite of repeated blood tests and masses of sulfa drugs and other supposed enemies, and two intramusculars each day, doesn't seem to have announced its identity or cause. By now I feel so extremely weak and dispirited that I've begun to ask myself if it may not be the moment to think seriously of what should be done in the event I fail to recover . . .

October 18, 1984

. . . Mrabet is cooking for me and feeding me in bed, three meals a day. A godsend, and of course I'm getting better. Whether my weight can be pushed up above 100 pounds remains to be seen. In Switzerland I weighed 103, but then the fever pulled it way down into the 90's, which is really far too little for anybody of my height. Anyway, health is always a depressing (as well as boring) subject. I can now walk fairly well . . .

In September 1986 Paul had an emergency operation in Rabat to bypass an aneurism in the knee. After his return to Tangier, he wrote from his bed at the Itesa, "I'm still alive, if not very happy because of the pain. I imagine that eventually everything will be fine . . ." By November, however, the pain had not relented, and he became less hopeful. "I begin to suspect that it has no intention of going away for good. It makes normal life impossible, inasmuch as I can't even walk to the corner. And I don't want to be confined to bed indefinitely, it goes without saying . . ."

Yet he kept on, as well as he could, with his "normal life." Interviewers and television crews and documentary filmmakers kept coming to his door, and Paul responded at length to their inquiries. Although he had always had a cult following in the underground press, now he frequently mentioned being besieged by biographers, journalists, and moviemakers from the mainstream world. He protested the disruption of his life; yet it was clear that he enjoyed the attention being showered upon him. In May 1987 Bernardo Bertolucci arrived to discuss the filming of *The Sheltering Sky,* and two years later Paul wrote that he had become involved in the filming, as Bertolucci had created a part for him to play—himself—in the movie.

As the years went by and I did not see Paul, a natural distancing took place. The letters between us became less frequent. It seemed likely that with the passage of time he too would recede in my consciousness. But each time a letter arrived from Paul, I would feel once again a strong connection to him, an affection and a sympathy for him in his illness. It was as if through his words, his image had come to the fore, was even for an instant becoming fixed. Then, after a bit, that fixity would dissolve. The image of him in my mind would begin to waver, leaving me not only with uncertainty about him but with an uneasiness about myself—about my own judgment, perhaps.

When I came across profiles of Paul and interviews with him in the various media, I would respond with a curious anger. No, I would think, reading or watching; they're not right. Or am I wrong? Or is there no wrong?

Occasionally I encountered someone who had known Paul in the past, and he or she would talk with me about him. One man said that when he met Paul, he found him cold and distant; a woman told me that she had found him to be caring and thoughtful; another man spoke of Paul's deception, saying he was convinced that Paul never told the truth about anything. Whatever was said, I found myself unable to integrate it into my own fluctuating image of him. It wasn't just that each person had a different image of Paul. Rather, it was that they all seemed to willfully adhere to the image they presented to me, as if they had a crucial stake in that image. Or, to put it another way, it was as if the image had established itself within them as a live and active force.

PART TWO

One day in 1991, ten years after the appearance
of *A Little Original Sin,* a young Italian documentary filmmaker called to say that he was
doing a film on Paul and would like to interview me in
Los Angeles the following week. I declined, giving my
usual excuse, that I did not talk or write about Paul. The
filmmaker persisted. He merely wanted to ask a few questions about Jane, he said.

Soon thereafter I found myself in a very small room in
an old hotel on Hollywood Boulevard. The corridors outside and the lobby downstairs were crowded with delegates
to a convention of science fiction enthusiasts. Some hours
later the filmmaker and his English co-producer appeared,
as well as two technicians lugging lights, many large black
boxes, and innumerable coils of black cable. They shoved
the bed against the wall and piled one chair upon another.
Then the lights were turned on, and the interview began.

After many questions about Jane, which I answered at
considerable length, came a question about Paul. I lapsed
into uncertainty. It was a very warm day, and in the very
small room with the lights focused on me, I began to sweat.
For all my earlier reluctance, I now felt a compulsion to
say something precise and true about Paul. Up to that
moment, not only had I refrained from writing about Paul,
but I had never asked myself my reasons for doing so. Was

it out of gratitude because he had helped me with the book on Jane that I would not subject him to being a "subject," even in my own mind? In response to the interviewer's question, I found myself giving an answer and then, in the next breath, countering what I'd said with an opposite opinion. Then I blurted out another possibility. As I kept wandering further and further afield, I thought about the science fiction convention downstairs, discussing time warps and alien life on other planets.

Two months later I wrote to Paul, telling him of my interest in writing a book about him. I added that I did not know what form the book would take; I only knew that it would not be a traditional biography. When he answered with enthusiasm, I set to work. I listened to the tapes of my original interviews with him. I read or reread all that others had written about him. I consulted his archive at the Humanities Research Center. I read and reread his fiction, noting again the elegance and precision of his language, the brilliance of his narratives. As in my earlier readings, a number of the tales involving violence and cruelty caused me unease.

I tried to imagine going to see Paul after so many years. I could see myself going up in the tiny elevator of the Itesa; I could see myself getting out on the fourth floor and knocking on his door. That was as far as I got. I thought of all the changes that must have or could have taken place in him in the years since I had seen him. I knew from his letters that he had not been well in recent years. Would he be incapacitated in any way, or would he be physically much the same Paul that I had known earlier? And how would he have been affected by fame? When I first went to Tangier, none of his works were in print in the U.S. Now, almost every bookstore I entered had a shelf or half a shelf of his books and books about him.

Two small though nettlesome matters now and again surfaced in my mind. The first had to do with my position as Paul's literary executor. Paul had originally asked me to be his executor in the full sense of the word, which would have involved my going to Tangier upon his death and liquidating and distributing his estate, primarily to Mrabet. I knew that this was not a good situation for me to get into with Mrabet, who had loudly proclaimed in my presence his mistrust of women and Americans and Jews. I had answered Paul by telling him that I was not willing to handle questions about money as money. I would, on the other hand, be glad to be his literary executor, which would involve overseeing the publication of his work. And so it had been arranged in his will.

As I was planning my trip to Tangier, however, I learned—not from Paul, but from Paul's agent—that I was no longer his literary executor. He had written a new will and had appointed someone else in my stead. I was taken aback that he hadn't said anything to me directly, but then why should I have expected directness from Paul? Besides, now that he was internationally famous, now that his published work, his estate, was going to be so much more valuable than before, an executor was needed who knew something about handling money, which I did not.

The other matter concerned what I thought of as Paul's "revisionist" attitude toward my biography of Jane. When he read *A Little Original Sin* in 1980, before its publication, and then again in 1981, after it was issued, he wrote to me of his admiration for the work, for my having been able to make Jane "come alive." But in several articles in recent years, he had mentioned to interviewers that he felt I had placed too much emphasis on Jane's illness in my book. He stated that I had exaggerated the sense of darkness in her life, as she was basically a "happy" person and only changed after her illness. Yet in fact, much of the information confirming the element of darkness in her early life had come directly from him. I was baffled and, as I say, slightly nettled, but I told myself that I could deal with this question directly when I saw him.

I realized that I was about to set out on a risky venture, for though Paul had agreed to my doing a book on him, even expressed eagerness that I do it, I had not forgotten that he was a man who abhorred directness. How, for example, would he deal with my questions that related to the connection between his life and his work? With Jane, I had known intuitively that there was an immediate and direct relationship between her life and her work. Paul, from the beginning, always fervently denied that any such relationship existed for him. Now that I was reading and rereading his work obsessively, however, I could not help noting the crossovers, the obvious links between his life and his work. I could only guess at the strategies and devices that enabled him to keep his sense of the two as entirely separate. Those, too, would be part of what I was searching for.

There was a further risk in this enterprise, a risk that was more difficult for me to define, one that was abstract and yet personal. Now that I was about to do a book on Paul, who had contributed so markedly to my being able to construct the narrative of Jane's life, I was risking something akin to a process of dissolution of that narrative, as if this new book threatened to destroy the substantiality of the earlier narrative within me. This I sensed, though I may not have articulated it so clearly to myself. I only knew that I was going to be continuously on an edge, trying to maintain a delicate balance between different kinds of knowing.

I knew too that whatever my method would be in this new work, it would have to be strikingly unlike the one I had used in the book on Jane. For that book, starting out with no knowledge about her at all, I had traveled to England, to Spain, to Mexico, and to various cities in the U.S., as well as to Morocco. I had interviewed her surviving relatives and many of her friends. I had sought out official records of her birth, of her death, and of her medical condition.

With Paul, I would do none of this. I already knew a great deal of his history. Something else was demanded of me, something ostensibly simpler than what I had done before but in its own way just as difficult, an unraveling where there had already been hidden raveling. I would not interview others about him. I would not seek out official records concerning him. I would simply go to Tangier and see him and speak to him directly. I had come to know him as an essential but supporting character in a confined space. Now I would go back into that same space. Only this time he would be the main character.

13 The Moroccan cab driver shakes his head when I say, "Inmeuble Itesa." "It's near the American Consulate," I manage to convey. As we approach the consulate, I say, "Further on, over there," for I think I recognize the stone grills on the balconies of a concrete building. But when the cab driver stops in front of it, I am unsure. I do not remember the shops on the ground floor or the metal gates covering them. The driver calls out to a gray-haired man in a white djellaba and red fez. "Yes," the man says, "it is the Itesa."

I pay the driver and go around to the front entrance, which is to the side, off the street. Yes, of course, it is Paul's building, though I had not remembered it as shabby. There is the concrete entrance, there is the tiny elevator just inside, making a noise as you step on its floor, as if, suspended in its shaft, it complains of any weight added to its own. (And I recall how Jane had feared elevators, feared them, Paul had told me, not because she felt that they could drop down precipitously but because she feared that they would go up uncontrollably.)

On the fourth floor I ring the bell at number 21. There is no answer. I knock and wait. No answer. I knock a third time, and when there is still no answer, I descend the concrete steps that circle the elevator shaft and go outside. Before me is a rutted driveway, with here and there a scraggly weed pushing its way through the surface. I walk down the driveway to the street. All around are new villas, mixtures of Eastern, Western, and Middle Eastern architecture. Several have roofs like Chinese pagodas. One villa down the street is faced with reflecting glass, like a child's dream of a crystal palace. When I was last here, thirteen years ago, there was nothing on this land save dirt.

Perhaps I had the wrong floor, I tell myself. (No, I am sure it was the fourth floor.) Perhaps Paul is just out. (But Abdelouahaid, who met me at the airport and took me to my hotel, said that Paul would be at home, waiting for me.) Maybe he was asleep.

I go back up again in the elevator with the unsubstantial floor. I get out at the fourth floor, I go to Paul's door—I am sure it is his door—and I repeat my ringing and knocking. Again no answer; again I retreat by the concrete stairway to the front of the building and wait. One must allow for a lot of waiting in this country, I remind myself. A tan dog, of an unrecognizable breed, with several open sores on its side, suns itself in the driveway. The sun is warm but not hot.

Soon a woman with her hair covered by a scarf comes out of the dark interior. I learn, through a combination of gesture and stumbling words, that she is the concierge. When she hears that I am waiting for "Monsieur Paul," she invites me to wait in her flat. She will let me know when he returns, she assures me.

Inside, I am invited to sit on a couch-bed, one of three in the room. Seated on the couch to my right is a handsome young woman wearing a white eyelet blouse and three-quarter-length trousers in a flowered print, gold and brown. She is watching television. The concierge sits in a chair near the open door, mending a child's dress. Now and then she cranes her head to see if Paul is arriving. Against the wall opposite me, the small black-and-white TV is broadcasting a news program in French. Next to the TV is a cabinet containing dishes and glasses, and next to that, an old brown refrigerator.

In my halting French, I say a few words to the young woman. She is a secretary, she tells me, and she speaks Spanish as well as French. She adds that life is hard in Morocco. Everything is expensive, and yet people are paid very little.

The minutes pass while we sit there, the concierge mending, the young woman watching TV, and I watching and not watching the screen, waiting for word that Paul has arrived. The program has changed to children's cartoons and is followed by a preview of a film to be shown on the weekend: *Giant,* with the voices dubbed. There are no commercials. After so many hours without sleep, jet-lagged, I realize that I have leaped a day. (It's May 11, not May 10.) I think of Jane, who sat so often in a Moroccan room with Moroccan women—but that is a memory of a life I have already told.

Two little girls come in, one about six, the other about four, wearing ornately decorated dresses, frilly and at the same time stiff. They are told to stay outside and watch for Monsieur Paul, but most of the time they play inside, giggling as they chase a thin orange cat with a sore on its face. The young woman turns to me and asks if I too am a writer. "Yes," I say. I ask if Monsieur Paul has arrived. The concierge shakes her head. Wait, wait, I am told. Still I am anxious that he might have come in when she wasn't watching. I consider getting up and going upstairs, but I do not want to be impolite.

Another girl enters, about eleven, carrying a school satchel. Her face is sharp, intelligent, and alert. She kisses her mother and the young woman. She then comes over to me, shakes my hand, and kisses me on the cheek. Though the concierge has not been watching out the door for some time, she now stands and announces that Monsieur Paul has returned. I get up and say good-bye to her and to the young woman and the children. As the concierge gets ready to see me out the door, she yells a command to the older girl. The concierge shakes her head and points to her forehead, signifying something about the girl's mischief, even as she smiles with what is obviously pride.

At Paul's door, I ring and then knock. I hear his footsteps coming, and he opens the door. "Oh, there you are," he says, as if he has been waiting a long time. We embrace.

His hair is now completely white, not as full as it used to be, making the shape of his head more visible. (And I recall a description of Mr. Copperfield in *Two Serious Ladies:* "He was very slight and his head was beautifully shaped.") I tell him that I have been waiting in the concierge's flat for him to return.

"I was never out," he says. "I was here all the time."

"So why did she tell me—" I start to ask, then let it go as we pass through the entryway, lined on the left with stacks of old suitcases, long unused, giving off a musty odor. Beyond a heavy woven curtain is his living room, where books and tapes and many compact discs occupy every surface, fill every wall shelf. I have brought with me some small presents for Paul from his friends, along with several sets of towels. He has always told me that one cannot get decent towels in Tangier. When I give him the towels, he thanks me and says how much he likes them, but I think by a fleeting expression on his face that he is slightly disappointed. They are regular-size bath towels, and I recall how much he liked a huge and intricately designed beach towel I brought him years ago.

I give Paul a note from G. "How is G.?" he asks. "Well," I say.

"I hear he made a lot of money."

"Yes, he is retired now and takes a lot of trips."

"He doesn't make money that way," Paul says, and I laugh. Then he adds, "I never made money. I wonder how they do it?"

"They think of it from the beginning," I reply, though actually I have no idea how people make money.

I am struck by how much softer he seems than when I saw him last. Yes, some holding off has gone from him or, rather, some defensiveness. He looks older but not old. I had dreaded deterioration in him, knowing he has had a serious illness. I see none. He is as he was before, with that same luminosity, that same wonderful bony structure of his face, only he is—softer. I do not have a better word.

Claude Thomas, Paul's French translator, arrives. She has just finished translating a section of *The Spider's House,* and she has brought it to him to go over. She mentions how difficult it is to convey in French the development of time in the novel. I remark on the intricate structure of the book.

"You mean the form?" Paul asks, and then he adds, "I don't ordinarily like flashbacks." There is a small quiver in my brain—in my nerves—a reminder that I am here to write a book about Paul, a book that will by necessity involve flashback upon flashback.

At the end of an easy conversation—I remember how conversation with Paul can seem so easy—about mutual acquaintances and about the incidental music he is composing for next month's production of *Hippolytus* at the American School, Paul announces that we are invited to dinner the next evening at the home of a Moroccan acrobat. I arrange to come and see Paul beforehand, in the afternoon, about three.

Claude drives me back to my hotel, the Minzah, and on the way I mention my sense that Paul seems softer than he was. Yes, she sees that in him. "I feel he is happier now than I have ever known him to be," she adds.

At the hotel, fatigued but unable to sleep, I wonder about the concierge. I cannot figure out why she chose that one moment of all possible moments to say that Paul had returned, when he had never been out at all and so obviously had not come in. I tell myself this is just one small unresolved mystery among all the mysteries that lie in wait for me here on this return, this flashback in life.

Walking to Paul's at two-thirty in the afternoon, I find my way easily. Between yesterday and today, I have recovered my sense of direction and place, even though so much has changed in Tangier. Fifteen years ago, when I first came here, traveling on the road from the airport into town, I was stunned by the sight of men dressed in cloak and hood, walking singly by the side of the road, leading a goat or a sheep past untilled land. Yesterday on that same road I saw few cloaks and hoods, no sheep or goats, no untilled land, but rather cars, trucks, bicycles, houses, apartment buildings, a hospital, and many people walking, groups of them, side by side.

Today, as I go up the Rue de la Liberté to the Place de France and follow the Rue de Belgique to the Place de Kuweit, I have that same sense of many people—mostly young people—walking in groups, advancing. There are women in djellabas, more colorful now than they once were (much purple); there are women in the traditional black haik and litham, their bodies completely shrouded, their faces veiled. But there are also many young women in Western dress, even women in jeans. Most of the men wear jeans or athletic suits and running shoes. As I cross over the boulevard near the big mosque and come to the Spanish school, I see how the boys and girls, gathered on the sidewalk outside, speak to each other. In their calling out and their responding, they are indistinguishable from young Americans.

When I arrive at Paul's, another visitor is talking with

him. A young man in his early twenties, he is a waiter at a restaurant where Paul occasionally goes to eat. While we are sitting, we hear a knock on the door. It is an old man— old? perhaps not much older than I, surely younger than Paul—shabbily dressed, with a white stubble of a beard. Paul tells me that he is a beggar who keeps coming to ask for money. When Paul gives him money, the man asks for more to get a shave. "He often asks for money for a shave, but he never gets a shave," Paul says, shaking his head. The man goes away but returns almost at once. He stands at the door holding two huge bunches of flowers that look like calla lilies. Paul goes into one of the other rooms, his bedroom or his study. The Moroccan man goes into the kitchen with his flowers, and I hear him turn on the tap water. Paul comes back into the living room just as the man appears with two huge vases filled with the flowers. "Two?" says Paul. "But I only said one." "It is necessary to have many flowers for the holiday tomorrow," the man insists. Paul pays him for the two bunches, and the man goes away.

Abdelouahaid appears, to drive Paul to the post office and the market. Now the young waiter, who has been sitting quietly, gets up and says that he will return on Sunday. When he leaves, Paul remarks, "I don't know why he comes." But then, Paul often says that about people who come. He does not, however, turn them away.

I get a ride back to the hotel with Paul and Abdelouahaid and say I will see them at eight, when we are to go to dinner. "Do not walk on the streets alone at night," Abdelouahaid warns me. "There are thieves about." "Where are they from?" asks Paul. "Are they from the country?" "From the country," says Abdelouahaid, "or they are young people from the city who watch TV and learn from that about violence." In my room at the hotel, I turn on CNN. They are showing the L.A. riots.

A few minutes before eight, I return to Paul's. Already present are two young American men, aspiring writers, one of them vague from too much kif. Claude Thomas is also there, elegant in black and white. At eight, Abdeslam, the acrobat, arrives. A vibrant man with a beguiling smile, he looks to be in his mid-thirties. He speaks English quite well. Paul and I go in Claude's car with her. The others are in a taxi, which we follow. On the way they stop to pick up Roderigo de la Rosa, the young Guatemalan writer whose work Paul has translated into English, and Roderigo's woman friend.

Abdeslam's house is in one of the new outlying districts of Tangier. We park at the end of an unpaved road and begin to climb a path littered with stones and household garbage. Many of the houses in this sector seem to be showing signs of wear, as if deterioration began at the moment of construction. The sun has set, and it is difficult to see the ruts and the drop-offs on the uneven path. I worry about Paul, laboring up the hill in front of me. I know from the past how when one is with Paul, one feels the urgent desire to protect him. And yet there is always the danger of overstepping a line with him.

We proceed in single file to the two-story house, built of the omnipresent concrete. Inside, to the right of the stairway, is a large unfinished space with a dirt floor. Bicycles and other things are scattered about in the dimness. Nearby two kittens nurse on their emaciated mother. We climb the stairs to the upper floor and enter a space that is the duplicate of the unfinished one below. But this space is partitioned into two rooms—or, rather, partially separated by two concrete dividers three feet high.

The rear space has a dark maroon rug on the floor and is furnished with a couch and two large chairs in the same color, upholstered in a material like flocked velvet. Several straight chairs are brought in so that everyone has a place to sit. In the front room against the stairwell wall, a television set and a videocassette recorder are flanked by vases of artificial flowers. We've brought along the flowers that Paul bought from the man who needed a shave, and now they are placed beside the artificial ones.

Abdeslam goes out and comes back in again with his younger brother; they are carrying a huge stereo. We all sit and watch them set it up—"we" being the two young Americans, Paul, Roderigo and his woman friend (whose name I did not catch), Claude, and myself. Soon mint tea is brought, and kif is passed around to those who smoke. In the past Paul used to start smoking kif at four in the afternoon and continue throughout the evening. But since his operation in the mid-1980s, he has been allowed only one kif cigarette a day.

Now the VCR and the TV are turned on, and a videotape is inserted. Meanwhile the stereo is set to play an accompanying audiotape of modern Arabic music. The video is a preliminary tape of Abdeslam performing, which will be used to produce a final five-minute tape for publicity purposes.

The tape is started, and we watch Abdeslam walk on his hands up a flight of steps to a platform. Next Abdeslam's younger brother places a chair on the platform, and Abdeslam does a set of variations of one-handed stands on the chair. Still on his hands, he jumps down from the chair to the platform and descends the stairs. He returns to the platform—on his hands—where his brother has now placed a low metal table with a tripod base. As Abdeslam supports himself on his right hand on the table, his brother tosses him a brick, which he catches with his left hand. He sets the brick on the table and shifts his weight so that he is balanced on his left hand on the brick. His brother throws him another brick; he sets it in place with his right hand and shifts his weight onto that brick. Then comes another brick and then another, until he has created two towers of bricks. At one point, he sets a brick down off-center, and the stability of the right tower seems suddenly precarious. Bit by bit, standing on his left hand, his feet in the air, he edges the brick back with his right hand until it is aligned solidly upon the others. So he moves, from one hand to the other, from one growing tower to the next, his balance throughout seeming perfect. At the end of the take, he jumps off the towers with a theatrical flourish.

Now comes the second take, an almost exact repetition of the first; following that are seven or eight more takes of the same sequence. Each take is the same, yet not quite the same. Now and then there is a slight variation in the tempo or in the dynamic of the gestures. One cannot see Abdeslam's face, for he is turned away from the camera. There is a curious quality in the upside-down movement, something strangely animalistic and primal. Yet at the same time the whole process seems perfectly fluid and natural to Abdeslam. Perhaps that is what makes it so unnerving.

More kif is smoked, more mint tea is served. Conversation flows in and out of the watching. My attention is on the repetitions on the tape, though now and then I turn to look at Paul and the others. He is at ease, smiling, graceful in his gestures, fluent. The others treat him with a respectful reverence that is also marked by ease.

I hear Paul say something about serial killing, a comment that each detail of the killing has to be done each time exactly the same way, as if it were a ritual reenacted for the community. I think of Jeffrey Dahmer, who killed one victim after another and consumed the remains in secret, beyond the eye of any beholder. "But if no one knows of the act except the killer, how can it be done for the community?" I ask. "Except perhaps," I suddenly volunteer, "there is the community of the selves of the killer. Maybe that's the community it is for, and the ritual action unites the various selves as one."

My comment seems to vanish into the air, unheard, or as if I have said something not to the point. In fact, it was one of those utterances—a sudden thought, or a feeling masquerading as a thought—that seem to voice themselves.

As the tape ends, Paul begins an account of how Abdeslam's younger brother, whom Abdeslam has trained to walk on his hands, went to Holland to perform with a troupe of Moroccan acrobats. Weeks went by, and the manager gave the group only a small pittance, not what he had contracted to pay. Soon they were without money, even without any food to eat. Yet they had to go on giving their performances, growing steadily weaker day by day.

"Is this a Paul Bowles story?" I ask.

"Maybe it will be," Paul says.

14   When I arrive at Paul's at three, as arranged, I seize the moment between visitors to talk to him about this book. He knows from my letter that I do not intend to do a conventional biography, though what precise form it will take has not yet become clear to me. I tell him I have come to the conclusion that I cannot pretend to be objective about him. I have seen how different he is with different people, so that it would be impossible to simply say, He, Paul, is like this. One can only say, He is like this with me.

"Isn't that so with everyone?" he asks. "Probably," I answer, "but with you it is even more so."

The conversation turns to *An Invisible Spectator,* the biography of Paul by Christopher Sawyer-Lauçanno, published in 1989. When Sawyer-Lauçanno first came to him, Paul tells me, he said he was going to write a book on Tangier. Then he came again and said he would write a book about Paul's music. Then he came once more and said he had decided to write a biography of him. Paul says that he told Sawyer-Lauçanno he did not want a biography written, but Sawyer-Lauçanno went ahead anyway. (Of course, it is also true that, even while saying he would not cooperate with Sawyer-Lauçanno, Paul granted him access to all his papers and letters. So while saying no, in a very real sense he had also said yes.)

Paul tells me that he tried to get from Sawyer-Lauçanno's publisher a promise that the biography would be called "unauthorized" but they would not agree. "In the end, Sawyer-Lauçanno rewrote *Without Stopping* and then accused me of not telling the truth," Paul says with a clear show of anger, something I have rarely seen in him. Suddenly he asks, "How can you bear to do this book after that book?"

"Maybe it's just because of that book that I can bear to do this book."

There is a knock on the door, and Abdeslam comes in. He sits with us and assembles the flashlight-pen I have brought as a present for Paul from Carol Ardman. Then he goes into the kitchen and makes tea for us. Presently,

Paul gets up and says he must get ready for another visitor. A teacher from the American School of Tangier is coming to help him with the synthesizer on which he is writing the score for the school's performance of *Hippolytus*. Joe McPhillips, the headmaster of the school, had brought the synthesizer from New York when Paul insisted that there were no musicians in Tangier capable of playing his score. "It is more trouble than it's worth," Paul complains. "I know nothing about computers, so I keep losing whatever I write." But he is being pressed by Joe for the music for Phaedra's long speech right away. "I don't know why he needs music for that," Paul says querulously.

"But Paul," I ask, one of those "why" questions that never take you anywhere, "if you don't want to do it, why do you do it?"

"Joe must have his own way," Paul answers. Then he adds, "I don't care that much about having my own way."

On the way back into town, walking with Abdeslam, I ask where he learned to speak English so well. He tells me he had a job for some years working for an Englishman as a cook. He has had only one year of schooling, in a religious school, but then he had to, or chose to, leave school. Now, however, each evening he goes to Paul's apartment, and Paul teaches him French and Spanish.

I ask about Mohammed Mrabet. When I was last here, Mrabet was often present in Paul's apartment, cutting up his kif on the round wooden table in the living room, talking, threatening, bragging, laughing. But I have not seen him since my arrival. Abdeslam tells me that Mrabet has not been to see Paul for two months. He accuses Mrabet of being "a black-hearted man." Even as I listen to what he is saying, I remind myself how in the circles of those who cluster around Paul rivalry and antagonism are constantly present. "Mrabet took many of Paul's things," Abdeslam insists. Now these things of Paul's are in Mrabet's house. "When Mrabet last came," Abdeslam says heatedly, "he threw the keys at Paul, cursed him, and called him terrible names; he shouted that he was the one who created Paul as a writer. He cursed everyone in the room and called them Jews."

I remember Mrabet's rages as immense, almost mythic in scale, a fury unleashed at anyone he felt had caused him injury, beginning with individuals and expanding to whole classes of beings—Jews, Americans, women. And yet, after such a rage, he might suddenly relent. To Abdeslam I say, "I am a Jew." It is better, I tell myself, to get things straight, as if it were possible to get things straight here in this world of indirection.

In the morning I awake with a sense of discomfort. Once again, here in Tangier, I am having trouble with my digestion, and it threatens to color everything bilious. I am like the butler in Wodehouse's *Leave It to Psmith* (which I am reading at night before going to sleep), who continually complains about his liver. But I do not seem to find the same humor in my own situation.

I recall what Paul said yesterday afternoon: "I don't care that much about having my own way." It has left an odd vibration in my mind, an alternation with its own opposite, for I realize that I do think of Paul as someone who gets his own way.

From my bed, looking out the window, I can see the red brick roof of the hotel and up above it the intense blue sky. My room is on a large inner courtyard; across the way, a series of arches demarcate other rooms, other corridors.

Even the architecture in this place has a sense of implied secrecy, of spaces enclosed against other spaces. I get up and look down upon the courtyard patio, where the hotel guests are having breakfast in the sun or under umbrellas. I notice that one pane is cracked in my window. A gauze-like curtain blows in the light breeze, and there is a muffled noise of hammering, as if offstage.

When I arrive at Paul's at the appointed time, three in the afternoon, the lift is not working, so I climb the stairs to his flat. I knock on his door. There is no answer. Again I ring and knock; again no answer. I pound, much louder this time. Finally I hear his footsteps. He opens the door and apologizes: he had fallen asleep. Earlier he had gone out to take a walk, and when he returned, he found the lift out of order. His leg began to hurt him badly almost immediately after he climbed the four flights. It is a return of the sciatica he has suffered from so severely in the past few years.

"If you want to rest, I'll come back," I say. "No, no," he insists, "you are here for such a short time. We must begin to work." As he settles painfully onto the low couch, he tells me about the blockage of circulation in his leg in 1986. He describes how his leg turned blue; he had no sensation in it at all. The condition developed so rapidly that there was no time for him to get to Switzerland for the most modern medical care. If he waited, he was told, the leg would have to be amputated. Abdelouahaid drove him to a hospital in Rabat, where an operation was performed that day. He uses the term "sympathectomy," indicating that the sympathetic nerve was severed. The surgeon was cold and impersonal, Paul adds, and the food in the hospital was terrible, but, *inch'Allah,* he did recover.

Paul, circa 1915.
Courtesy Elizabeth Kenny.

*At the boathouse on Seneca
Lake, New York, 1921. Left to
right: Ida Bowles, Paul's
grandmother; Anna Fraser,
family friend; Paul; Rena
Bowles, Paul's mother; Claude
Bowles, Paul's father; Veta F.
Robbins, relative by marriage.
Courtesy Elizabeth Kenny.*

*Paul's high school
graduation photo,
1926. Courtesy
Elizabeth Kenny.*

*Paul and Jane, New York,
1944. Photograph by
Graphic House. Courtesy
Harry Ransom Humanities
Research Center, The
University of Texas at
Austin.*

Jane, early to mid-1940s. Courtesy Harry Ransom Humanities Research Center, The University of Texas at Austin.

Paul, Santa Monica, 1969. Photograph by Lawrence Stewart.

Jane, Tangier, 1960.
Photograph by
Lawrence Stewart.

Paul, Tangier, 1977.
Photograph by Jim Kalett.

Paul, Mohammed Mrabet,
and Abdelouahaid Boulaich,
on the roof of Paul's
apartment house, 1977.
Photograph by Jim Kalett.

*The author and Paul in the
medina, Tangier, 1977.
Photograph by Jim Kalett.*

*Paul at work in his study,
1977. Photograph by
Jim Kalett.*

Paul composing, 1992.

Paul in a Tangier restaurant, 1992.

*Paul in the Tangier
market, 1992.*

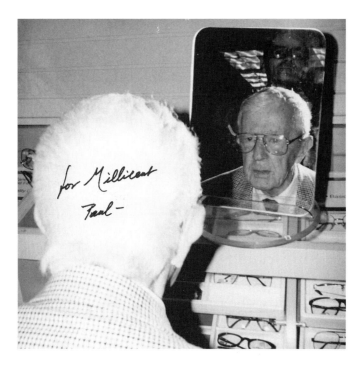

Paul in Atlanta, 1994.
Photograph by Virginia
Spencer Carr.

I turn on the tape recorder, in preparation for bringing up a question about the relationship between Paul's life and his work. I approach it at first in abstract terms. "I want to talk about memory and the imagination," I say.

"Imagination can only work on memory indirectly or directly, but working on it doesn't mean reproducing it," Paul insists.

Of course, I concede, I know that writers do not use their experience just as it is or has been. Yet often, I assert, in the work there are clear traces of memory. "I came across one such trace in *The Sheltering Sky*—the third time I read it."

Paul laughs. "You know it better than I do, certainly."

"When Port is dying, you go into his mind and describe what he is seeing and feeling in his hallucination. It's afternoon, and he's on a street at the bottom of a steep hill. The sidewalks are crowded, and around him people are looking into shop windows, but he knows they are all waiting for something to happen. Suddenly at the top of the hill a car appears. And you use these words: 'It came careening over the crest and down the hill, swerving savagely from one curb to another. . . . He turned and frantically sought a doorway. At the corner there was a pastry shop, its windows full of cakes and meringues. . . . If he could reach the door . . .' But he can't move. He waits for the car to hit him, and at the moment it hits him, he lives through his own dying."

Now I bring up a memory of Paul's, as told in *Without Stopping*. It recounts a terrifying experience of depersonalization he had as a boy, in which he lost the sense of any connection between his body and himself. "You describe going into Roth's soda fountain on a warm summer evening just as the light is beginning to fade. The shop is on the corner, with a swinging door giving on to each street, and as you enter one door you suddenly lose the connection between your body and mind. You or rather your body turns and goes out the second door, and once you're outside, it turns—your body turns—and you go back in the first door, then go back out the second door, then—"

"Then in and then out, and then in and then out—"

"But then as you are coming out, you suddenly see a car come over the hill—"

"Down the hill."

"Down the hill, and you recognize it as your parents' Buick."

"That's right."

"And suddenly you're released. You run to the car and get in, and they drive on. You don't say anything to them about what has happened to you, though you're certain that it was only the appearance of the car that saved you from something terrible. In fact, you never say anything about it to anyone. Years later, however, when you're almost forty and you are writing of Port's death, the memory of that strange and frightening experience when you were a child—"

"I wasn't such a child," he says abruptly.

"How old were you?"

"I was about to graduate from high school. I was sixteen."

"Ah, you were that old. But it was still terrifying, even so."

"Oh, yes, yes."

"I'm not saying that the death scene in the novel and the experience are identical. In the death scene the detail is transformed so that Port doesn't go in and out the door; rather, he is desperately trying to get to the door, but he can't move. In the memory you moved, but you moved without willing it, so it was just as if you, Paul, weren't moving. In Port's mind, the car that comes down the hill hits him and kills him, while in life it's the car that saves you."

"I think it did, yes." After a pause, Paul adds, "I never thought of the two together."

There is a long silence. That is all that is to be said on this subject, he is indicating to me. This far and no further. How does he convey this to me? I cannot say exactly what it is about his face and the tone of his voice. I only know that for him this is the end of the discussion and that to pursue it further will be futile.

Except for the light from a small metal lamp on the corner table between us, the room is in shadow. The window on the outside wall faces onto a balcony, which in turn is fenced in by a concrete grating. The balcony is filled with many huge plants, so that almost no daylight filters through. Paul is slumped on the low couch against the wall to my right. Is he in pain? I wonder.

Someone knocks on the door. It is the teacher from the American School, who has come to see how Paul is getting on with the synthesizer. Paul has several questions to ask him, so they go into the study. As I sit on the couch waiting for him to return, I recall a letter from Jane to Paul in 1947. I cannot remember the exact words, but it was something about doubting her own past experience and how that doubt was stopping her from going on with her work.

Paul reappears, and the teacher leaves; he will return this evening to go over things in greater detail. Paul sits on the low couch. He tells me that inadvertently he has been erasing what was in the machine's memory. Now he knows how to stop that from happening.

I pull from my briefcase the first pocket book edition of *Let It Come Down*. The pages, brittle and yellowed with age, keep slipping from the binding. Paul looks at the cover, which shows a voluptuous young woman flirting with a man at a bar. He laughs and says it looks like a scene from the Bertolucci movie of *The Sheltering Sky*. I mention that I don't like the movie very much. "Sorry to tell you that."

"Why, who does? I don't."

"Oh, you don't like it, either?"

"How could I?"

"I thought he didn't understand the novel at all."

"He thought it would make a good vehicle for him after having received nine Oscars." He laughs, a little.

I leaf through *Let It Come Down* to find a sentence that speaks directly about the imagination. I locate it in the midst of a long description of Dyar's state of mind when he is high on kif, fearful that the Moroccan, Thami, will rob him of his money. " '. . . to assume complete control [of the situation] . . . ,' " I read, " 'he allowed his imagination full play.' "

"That's a very unusual statement," I throw out.

"It is strange. One would wonder in what way would he thus assume complete control?"

"That's what I was going to ask you."

"Well, if he allows his imagination full play, he can then"—and here Paul sighs—"foresee every possibility, whatever he fears. He lets himself imagine everything, so then he can prevent what he's imagining from taking place."

"Then he is able to assert control."

"Yes, but if he hasn't, then it can sneak in."

In the silence that follows there is the implication that nothing further will be said about this subject, that he and the power of his imagination will stop me from going further. Indeed, I am faced by a barrier so complete and palpable—how does he do it?—that it takes my breath away. And yet at the same time I know it is simply Paul that I am facing—Paul, who has agreed so enthusiastically to my doing this book.

Checked as I am, I allude to the past, to Jane. "She didn't think—I don't think—that when she allowed the imagination full play that she would have complete control."

"No, I think she thought the opposite. She felt it would run away with her."

And now (why now?) I bring up his recent "revisionist" statements about the book on Jane, or, rather, I prepare the way to bring them up. "That brings up another thing which I would like to discuss with you. When I came to see you so many years ago, you certainly were at a different point in your life."

He laughs. "I was several years younger."

"I think you've also changed a great deal."

"Really?"

"Yes."

"I don't know."

"You seem"—I pause—"much happier to me."

"Really? That's nice." He laughs again. "I wonder why; I wonder why."

"As if you've come to some kind of peace with yourself about certain things."

"Maybe. But I really don't—I'm not conscious of it."

"You're not?"

"Well, no, I'm not. I don't remember that I was particularly unhappy then."

That he wasn't particularly unhappy then? How can he be saying this? There is more "revisionism" at work here than I anticipated.

"I came to see you at a time when—I think that perhaps all that experience with Jane still weighed heavily upon you."

"Probably, yes."

"It's not that what has been is erased, but—" I stop and prepare myself to speak more directly about Paul's recent statements about *A Little Original Sin*.

"I read this somewhere—" I stop and start again. "You were talking to some interviewer, and you said that in my book about Jane I had presented too bleak a picture of her."

"Ah, I did, yes." And then a pause. "Only because there's so much clinical material at the end. It was based largely on, I think, your meetings with people who hadn't really known her when she was herself, and also with her doctors—"

"But even when she was 'herself,' in her early years, there was a darkness in her vision of her life." It was a vision that he himself had confirmed for me in the telling of numerous episodes about her despair. I remind him of the letters she wrote to him in 1947, how in those letters she described her painful emotional states so clearly and at such great length that she referred to them as "agonizers." He does not respond.

"I also think," I press on, "that in writing the book I was responding to something in you which was still grieving over what had happened with her."

"You were responding to—?"

"To your grief."

"Ah."

"If someone comes to you now and talks about Jane, it is—you are different."

"Yeah."

"Because the years have passed, and there's some kindness in the years passing, if we're lucky," I suggest.

"If you're lucky, yes. You can't remain in the same state of depression. You can—people do—but God forbid."

I have been trying to persuade myself that, as the years have passed, it is perfectly natural for him to want to go forward, to try to remember the happier parts of their life together, and to forget the more painful ones. Yet I am encumbered by the recurrent sense that he has gone forward while I have been left behind.

I refer to a conversation we had fifteen years ago. "There was a point at which you said to me—and I believed you believed it—'I don't exist.' "

" 'I've no ego.' "

"Yes. And then I argued with you, 'That's not so.' "

Paul imitates our conversation from so long ago: "You do exist." "I do not." "You do so."

We both laugh, and I go on. "And then you say, 'Well, if something's not forever, if it's not eternal, it doesn't exist.' "

"A-a-h."

"I think, at least in part, that arose out of the terrible experience you had in the years before Jane's death."

"Yes," Paul says, "it was bad."

"Even when she was in the hospital in those last years, you didn't have the responsibility for her from day to day, but you still had the weight—"

"It was there, of course. Of course. I never escaped from

all that until she died. That was the escape. Then there was no longer the worry."

"Then there was something else; there was the grief."

"But that one can deal with. I think I dealt with it. One becomes philosophical and says to oneself, Everyone one likes or loves dies, or one dies oneself. One or the other. That's part of life, so one has to accept it. That's all. And not make a great *geschrei* about it."

"Actually, in a way"—no, I have not forgotten his pain as he sits before me—"to get older is in some ways very difficult physically."

"Oh, oh, yes." Again he laughs.

"But there are some amazing things that happen in terms of what one can finally accept."

"Yes, how one feels about the phenomenon called living."

"Whatever happens—"

"Everything happens. Bad and good."

"So probably when you look back now, you are much more able to think of Jane as she was in the early years."

"Yes. I don't want to think of her in the later years, naturally. Why? She wasn't herself. Therefore I'm not really thinking of Jane. I'm thinking of an organism which is distorted and ill. Who wants to think of that? I don't. Not if the true thing is so much better. Fortunately, yes."

I struggle once more—it is what I have been after all along—for a simple acknowledgment from him that the core of what Jane was, early or late, was the same. It has to do with her and with him as well: that no matter how one changes, one is still the same.

"With Jane," I say, "even when she was ill, you still saw who she had been."

"One of the last times I saw her when she talked, when

she could say anything—because afterward she couldn't speak—she said, 'My life is a tragedy.' She said it with great feeling. She was lying in bed in the hospital. I didn't know what to say."

"It was true, wasn't it?"

"Yes, of course. But I didn't want to say, 'Yes, that's true.'"

"No. But then you couldn't say, 'No, it isn't.'"

And here he laughs, though it is not quite a laugh. "I couldn't say anything." And after a silence, he adds, "There was nothing to say."

 With Abdeslam I walk back to the center of town. He offers to show me the medina and the house he lived in as a child. We descend to the Socco Chico and enter the old quarter. Winding up through the narrow streets, we come almost to the top, where he points out the house he had lived in. It has one window overlooking the sea. Each day, when he would go down to the water to swim, he would look up at that window and see his mother waving to him, and he would wave back. Next to the house, which is small and narrow, crammed between its neighbors, is a stone stairway. Suddenly Abdeslam flips over and descends it on his hands. It seems natural, everyday habit, yet it is also performance.

We follow a path bordered by a low white wall. Abdeslam is again upright, once again the sociable young man with dark curly hair, who smiles engagingly. Beyond the wall the hillside descends steeply to the sea. The tide is low, and we can see young boys running and playing on the wet sand. Across the water Spain is just visible. I ask him where he learned to be an acrobat. He taught himself when he was a boy, he tells me, practicing every day. He still practices daily, for hours at a time.

As we walk back down through the medina, Abdeslam is stopped several times by young men with whom he exchanges greetings. They grin and wave him on. We make our way through the Grand Socco to the Boulevard de Paris and stop at a café. Abdeslam has orange soda; I have mint tea. At the tables about us, only men are sitting. He tells me he used to perform in Europe in years past but now that it is so difficult to get a visa, he is not able to go there any more. Even here in Morocco, there is little work for him. Once, he and his sister used to perform in the hotels, but now—he shrugs, as if to say, There is no place any more.

Paul has told me that Abdeslam is very interested in dance, so I ask him about dance in Morocco. He shakes his head and dismisses it as what country women do. I had sensed in his performance on the videotape a quality of movement being bound, of an expressive force not given its due. I say something about dance in America, dance as an expressive force, but it is a dead-end conversation. "Nothing can be learned here of that," he responds curtly.

We get up and make our way along the Boulevard de Paris, which is crowded with people, many in groups walking together. The street is clogged with cars, and the scent of gasoline fumes is strong. On the opposite side of the street, several huge concrete structures are under construction. They are the replacement for what was here during the time Tangier was an International Zone, when it was occupied by foreign powers. We walk past the Rembrandt Hotel and turn toward the water. After a few blocks we come upon a small park, a square of concrete and gravel, treeless except for two stunted palms. We sit on a bench and look out upon more large concrete structures—hotels, apartments. Abdeslam does not like the new buildings; he liked the old ones better. When he was young and poor, he goes on, he did not know he was poor. Everyone around him was poor. But since then everything has changed, Tangier has changed; there are many people here with much money.

As he goes on talking, it dawns on me that I am about to be hustled. I recall the smiles and knowing looks of the young men who greeted Abdeslam in the medina as they saw him walking with me, an American, an old woman in their terms, and in their terms rich. Meanwhile, he is telling me that when he performed in Europe he did well and earned money, but now he has to support not only himself but his mother and sisters and brothers as well. His father lives out in the country, where he works as a night watchman. Out there he can be alone and listen to the radio, Abdeslam adds; that is all he wants.

Now that he is the head of the family, Abdeslam does not allow the others to have a television aerial, for then they would watch non-Moroccan television that comes from places like Spain, with violence and pornography. He does not allow his teenage sister, whom he has taught to be an acrobat and who performs with him, to go out of the house unless she is accompanied by their mother. "If she goes out alone," he says, "men would say dirty things to her." Then he adds, "There are some women who like that."

I get up and begin to walk toward the water with Abdeslam at my side. I consider that it would be better to deflect the hustle, if at all possible, to save face for him, as it were. (Does face matter here?) This may well be a preliminary on his part, a testing of the waters, on the edge

of a hustle, not there yet, still avoidable. Almost unconsciously, I fall into a mode of fending off, by turning his
and my attention elsewhere.

In answer to his remark about his sister, I go on to say—
and even as I start to say it, I know it will get his back
up—that in the world I come from, it is important to
women that they have control of their own lives; but I
understand that his is a very different world. "Yes, yes," he
responds impatiently, "I know in America things are different. Here it is the family that matters; it is not just one
person in the family."

As he talks, he grows more vehement, as if he is falling
headlong into his own convictions. Yes, there are more and
more people in Tangier and in Morocco as a whole, he
admits, but no, he insists, it is not necessary to do anything
about it. In the past there has always been enough food to
eat, now there is enough, and in the future there will be
enough too, no matter how many people live here. To use
birth control, he pronounces scornfully, is to avoid the fate
that has been decreed for you.

Shifting the ground of the conversation, I ask him about
himself, if he is married. No, he is not. His family offered
to arrange for a girl for him, but he declined. He speaks
of marriage and its dangers, of what women do to men,
how they destroy men. He tells me how his second
brother's wife destroyed him so that now he is crazy. "What
do you mean, crazy?" I ask. He doesn't want to work, he
sits in the house, he doesn't dress himself, he is dirty, he
flies into rages—he is crazy. His wife did it to him with
magic; she poisoned him with magic. This is what happened to his brother, and now his brain is gone. "Can a
doctor help him?" I ask. No, nothing can be done. Abdeslam knows one woman who did magic to her husband,

and now she brings men into the house even when he is there. The husband sits there; he can do nothing. It is that way with magic.

"Paul believes this," he insists.

Does Paul believe this? I wonder.

At night in the hotel, about to go to sleep, I recall Paul's words at the end of *Without Stopping,* written as Jane was dying in the clinic at Málaga: "I relish the idea that in the night, all around me in my sleep, sorcery is burrowing its invisible tunnels in every direction . . . Spells are being cast, poison is running its course . . ." I remember what Paul said to me about Cherifa, that she performed magic on Jane, that she left strange packets about the house to gain power over her. And I think of Paul's story "The Garden," in which a wife performs magic on her husband with a poison and destroys him. Does Paul believe this?

When I arrive at Paul's in the afternoon, he is at work on the synthesizer, composing the score for *Hippolytus.* He asks me if I would like to listen to what he has done. I follow him into his study, a book-lined room with a table at the center, on which the synthesizer sits. This room, in contrast to the living room, is filled with light. From the window one can see the hills of Tangier, the sky, and the gathering clouds.

I notice in Paul a special openness today. I recall from years ago how at times he seems to allow closeness, as if the distance between himself and any other were at his discretion. He gives me the earphones to put on. When I listen to the tape, I hear a sound immediately recognizable as Paul's musical voice—the beguiling melodic invention, the quick, unexpected rhythms.

Luckily there are no other visitors for the moment, so we can begin to work. We go back into the dark living room. He sits on the low couch in the corner, adjacent to the table with the small, crook-necked lamp, and I sit on the couch at a right angle to him. He winces as he adjusts his position, and I realize he is still in pain, though he says nothing. I tell him about the conversation I had with Abdeslam yesterday, though I say nothing about my sense of the hustle that never became a hustle. He tells me that Abdeslam came last night and told him that he had talked with me—he called me "that woman," Paul mentions— and that he had talked with me in a way that he had not spoken to anyone before. Paul makes no attempt to explain that statement; he simply reports it. I let it pass and ask a question about the idea of fate, as Moroccans see it, particularly in view of what Abdeslam has said about his brother being crazy.

"*Mektoub*—well, literally, it means that which has been written. Everyone's fate is decided before birth. In other words, everybody is passive in the face of *mektoub*. You asked him if someone couldn't do something about his brother; could they take him to a doctor? Ah-h, it's his brother's fate. There's nothing that can be done. It was his fate to be poisoned by his wife."

"Then what about action? Is every act that you do not of your own will? Is it fated that you will do it?"

"It's fated. It's not retribution; it has nothing to do with the Indian concept of having another life and of paying for the bad things you did in your previous life. No, no. They don't believe that. There is no other life. There's just this one, and it's already decided for everyone and will go on being decided forever."

"But Abdeslam still wants to rise in the world," I point out. "He wants a car and other things—"

"Many things."

"And it isn't as though he sits back and says, 'Well, fate will give it to me.' "

"Actually, he doesn't believe that his fate is to be without a car. He believes that all the things he wants are part of his fate, part of his future. So that he can achieve them somehow by reaching his fate, by amalgamating himself with his fate, which is there as an abstraction in front of him, which he has to embrace."

"But how does that work with what he said to me, that when he was performing in Europe, he believed that his fate was going to be for everything to get better and better for him? Now he does not have that sense."

"He doesn't? Well, then, he's grown up a bit," Paul says with a laugh. "He's never discussed all this with me. The moment he began to talk about it last night, he stopped and said, 'I know you don't believe all this.' And I said, 'Yes, I do.' And he said, 'No, no, no, Europeans and Americans, they don't believe in *mektoub*.' "

To me, Abdeslam has said, "Paul believes this." To Paul, at least as Paul reports it, he has said that Paul doesn't believe "this." What happens to belief here? How does it shift and move between someone in the culture and someone outside it? In the short term? Over a long period of time? It is necessary to remember—how could I have forgotten?—that for almost fifty years Paul's daily life has been here, where magic and many other things strange to me are taken for granted. Is it possible for him to believe and disbelieve at the same time, remaining on an edge, not coming down finally on one side or the other?

"Abdeslam is devoted to you," I tell Paul, reporting a statement Abdeslam has made to me a number of times. "Oh, good," Paul answers, his response as unguarded as I have ever heard it. "I hope he is."

"He did tell me that many years before he met you, he saw a picture of you in one of your books, and he said you were so distant from him—you were so far away."

"Well, yes, because I was in a book," Paul laughs.

I pull out my worn copy of *Let It Come Down*. As I leaf through the pages, many of which are falling out of the binding, I say, "This is shredded *Let It Come Down*."

"It has come down," Paul says. "It has come down in life. Ach," he adds, "my mouth is so dry. I'll have a mint. Do you want a mint? They're very strong. That's why I like them; they're the strongest mints I can find. There used to be mints in England that were marvelous. They were called Pontifract's. But you can't get them here, never could. They came in a tin box; the label said 'Pontifract Mints, Curiously Strong.' Isn't that wonderful? These are hard to unwrap. It's coming, here it is." As he hands it to me, he advises me not to chew it. "I never chew them. They last for a half hour."

"Talking about *Let It Come Down*," I say, after the companionable sharing of the mints, "somewhere or other—I guess it's in the introduction to the Black Sparrow edition—you say that all the characters in the book were based on people who had lived in Tangier but had died or gone away."

"M-m-hm."

"And Eunice Goode was based on somebody you knew?"

"Yes, very much. M-m-hm."

"A woman?"

"A woman, of course."

"A woman writer?"

"She wasn't really a writer. She thought she was."

When I laugh, he says, "Mary Oliver."

I am astonished. "The one who used to levitate?" I recall what he told me long ago about Mary Oliver's crucial visit to him and Jane when they were living on Staten Island in 1939. It was after that visit, during which Mary Oliver ordered and consumed vast quantities of liquor and Jane also drank, keeping up with her, that the marriage fell apart sexually.

"Yes. She is Eunice Goode."

"No kidding," I say. "I didn't know she lived in Tangier."

"She came here for a while in the fifties."

"The way you described Mary Oliver to me earlier, I found her very amusing. But Eunice Goode is not amusing."

Paul laughs, and I remember how he reveals information, bit by bit, prompted by some question that releases him, that touches something in him that is ready at that moment to go further. His memory seems to contain many fragments, and from it now this fragment is selected, now that. And yet how smooth his stories are in the writing, seamless, really. No hint of a fragment anywhere.

"So, now," I say, "we're going to skip around a little. This is what is called following a scent."

"Following assent?"

"A scent. S-c-e-n-t. Remember, you told me once that in life that was how you made your decisions, by following a scent. Well, that's what I'm trying to do. Is that somebody knocking at the door?"

"No, I don't think so." Paul gets up. "No, I didn't hear anything. But go on. I just wanted to give this a pat on the back so it might burn." He goes over to the fireplace and picks up the bellows to stoke the fire. I wait for him to come back and sit down before I go ahead.

"All right. The paragraph I'm thinking of is in the last section of *Let It Come Down,* when Dyar is escaping in the small boat, after stealing the money. He's lying down in the boat, thinking of nothing at all, and he remembers a song from his childhood—he's not sure of the words— and then he has a memory, or a series of memories. First he remembers being covered by a patchwork quilt and being tucked in, and his head lying on an eiderdown pillow his grandmother made for him, the softest pillow he ever had. Then the paragraph goes on—"

> And like the sky, his mother was spread above him; not her face, for he did not want to see her eyes at such moments because she was only a person like anyone else, and he kept his eyes shut so that she could become something much more powerful. If he opened his eyes, there were her eyes looking at him and that terrified him. With his eyes closed there was nothing but his bed and her presence. Her voice was above, and she was all around; that way there was no possible danger in the world.

I put down the book. "The sense of a small child having an image of the mother as an omnipotent being—do you remember anything about this at all?"

"Do you mean the actual situation or the writing of it?"

"Either one, either one."

"Well, I remember calling up the sensation of lying there and having her looking at me."

"You could do that?"

"That's why I wrote it."

"You would have been very young when this happened."

"Yes, yes."

"This feeling—the mother as an enormous presence—

is something most people must have when they are very young, but they probably don't remember it consciously. When you read this passage you feel, yes, I know that must have been the way it was. You feel it, more than you remember it. You recognize it as a fundamental experience."

"It's not one experience, it's a repeated one. I do remember not wanting to look at her eyes. She used to look at me, and I would cover my eyes, sitting at the table."

"Would she say something to you?"

"No, she'd just look at me. And it frightened me."

"She wasn't mad at you?"

"Crazy?"

"No, no, angry."

"No, not at all."

"She would just look at you."

"Yes. And I would say, 'Don't,' and put my hands over my eyes."

"And would she say anything?"

Paul laughs. "She would laugh. So then if I took them away, and I saw her looking at me again, I had to cover my eyes." He laughs once more. "That's slightly different from having her leaning over me in bed, though."

Slightly different? Perhaps. Yet the sentence about the mother leaning over him in his bed and becoming "much more" powerful is followed immediately by the sentence saying that if he opens his eyes and sees her eyes looking at him, he will be terrified. The two are linked in sequence, integrated into one passage of thought. First the child wills himself to believe that the mother is all-protective, large, like a sky (like a sheltering sky), not a human being. But then the negation of that belief appears, the realization that if he opens his eyes, she will be nothing but a person and then presumably cannot protect him. So he holds on and wills his belief, even as he knows he is willing it. He shuts his eyes so as not to see her looking at him looking at her, for then all seeing would be the same seeing: he and she would share the same pair of eyes.

And now, looking at him, I go further still, even though I know he will object to what I say. "There's this theory of the Great Mother—you know about that."

"The Great Mother?"

"Yeah, the archetype of the Great Mother."

"Oh," he groans, in mock horror.

"I only bring it up as an idea—that the small child sees in the mother not only the individual mother but the archetypal mother."

"How would the child see that? I wonder."

"Well, the Jungian idea, or at least what I think the Jungian idea is, is that it's built into the human psyche. But I'm not going to pursue that subject."

No, I will not go further on that road. Perhaps it was only another deflection on my part. Great Mother or no Great Mother, it is clear that the image of *her*, what he felt about *her* so early, was to remain so rooted in him that many years later, when he was writing of a man lying in a boat, a man who had stolen money and was fleeing to safety, that image from long ago surfaced as the memory of the man he was creating—as if memory itself were a form of fatality.

16   Paul begins his autobiography with a memory of words and sounds intertwined. He is a child, kneeling on a chair, staring at a clock and a mug on a shelf. He sounds the word "mug" aloud again and again until it seems to lose meaning. He hears the clock strike four. He is four years old. The connection is

crucial and revealing: the clock has struck four, the word "mug" means mug, and, therefore, to himself he can say, "I am I, I am here, it is now." As if it were his true birth. At four.

This revelation took place in the absence of his mother, Rena. She was in the hospital; he was staying in the house of his great-aunt Jen and her husband, Edward, who was the Unitarian minister in Exeter, Massachusetts. It was 1914. Paul's father, Claude, appeared and, taking Paul aside, told him that his mother was very ill. And all because of you, he accused the small boy. Later, when Rena had recovered and they were once again at home in Jamaica, Long Island, Paul asked her why her illness was his fault, as his father had said. She told him that his father didn't "mean" that. It was only that his birth was difficult, that he "had a very hard time coming into the world." He had been a large baby, eight and a half pounds, and his had been a breech birth.

As the years went by, Paul would ask over and over again to be told the story of what had occurred at his birth on December 30, 1910. He was fascinated by the detail. He wanted to hear how he had been delivered with forceps, how he had emerged with a large cut on the side of his head, how his head had been distorted by the pressure of the birth process, how he had been born with jaundice, his skin orange, mottled with yellow.

The story took on an even larger dimension through another event that occurred on that day. The hospital where he was born was run by a Catholic order, and several hours after Paul's birth, fearing for the baby's life, two nuns appeared, to take him to be baptized. His mother refused, holding onto the baby, warning the nuns that if they took him, she would follow them on her hands and knees screaming. Listening to his mother as she told of her struggle against the "dirty creatures" in their black habits with "their old crosses dangling," Paul had the sense that she had protected him from a "mysterious and obscene" fate.

But if there was one story that told of his mother saving him, there was as well a second story to counterbalance it, of his father attempting to do away with him. An incident that may or may not have taken place, it was recounted to Paul when he was a child by his maternal grandmother, Henrietta Winnewisser. According to Henrietta, on the night of a terrible blizzard when Paul was six weeks old, Claude had yanked him from his crib, stripped him naked, and put him in a wicker basket. Then he opened the window wide, put the basket on the windowsill, and went out of the room, leaving Paul with the snow falling on him. If Henrietta had not heard him crying and if she had not run in to rescue him, he would not have survived. Why had Claude done this? Henrietta said she knew why: he was jealous of the attention Rena was paying to the baby.

So there were two stories, told as truth, believed by a child with a deeply embedded talent (a gene? a disposition?) for story-believing, story-making, storytelling from his earliest years. (Speaking before he could crawl, reading by the age of two, Paul was by the age of four writing down story after story in his little notebooks.) Two stories, crucial and encompassing, tending toward the mythic, even the archetypal—well, maybe—two stories in which he was the potential sacrificial being, threatened and then saved.

How does the imaginative child take such stories, such myths, and weave them into ongoing daily life? In each child, in each imagination, the process must be different. For Paul, the story of his father's attempt on his life became a compelling theme, gaining power from what he saw as Claude's continuing enmity toward him as he was growing up. Invoking discipline as the way to shape character, Claude inveighed against any indulgence. Pronouncements were made, edicts were enforced: no playing with other children, no making noise, no leaving toys out, no asking for food or drink . . .

But if this picture of Paul's father is starkly drawn as a narrative with a single theme in *Without Stopping,* Paul's portrait of his mother in his early years never congeals. She remains unfocused, seeming to shift and change with each episode that is told. In one passage, for example, Paul writes that his mother "often spent twenty minutes or a half hour at a time rubbing my nose firmly between her thumb and forefinger." Why did she do this? Young bones and cartilage are malleable, and it is necessary to be very careful what shape they take, she said to him. Making his own private connection for this manipulation, Paul thought of his mother's father, August Winnewisser, whose nose was strangely shaped and discolored because his father had shattered the bones of the bridge of his nose with a hammer when August was young. And August had done the same thing to his two sons. (The source of this bizarre practice, Paul later came to suspect, was an attempt to hide any trace of a Jewish heritage.) As Rena massaged his nose, Paul wondered if such a shattering might be in store for him.

In other passages Rena appears fearful, fearful in particular of Claude's mother, Ida Willa Bowles, whom Rena characterized as a "Strong Woman." (Ida was openly critical of the way Paul was being brought up—he should not be so isolated, he should play with other children.) At times Rena was so intimidated in Ida's presence that she became ill and had to go to bed. "Your grandmother Bowles is the most *suspicious* woman I've ever seen. And your father is just like her," Rena confided to Paul. "Don't ever let yourself get to be like them. It's terrible. It poisons everything."

Yet in another passage Rena is presented as someone who is able to shrug off ordinary caution. When Paul was eight years old and having orthodontic work done twice a week by a dentist in Manhattan, his mother allowed him to go by himself on the subway from Jamaica to the dentist's office. After he left the dentist's office, he had her permission to walk around the city. Rena's sister Ulla reproached her for allowing a child of eight to wander alone in the city. Didn't she worry about him? Wasn't she afraid that something might happen to him? Rena shrugged off her sister's criticism. As for Paul, he was delighted by his mother's trust in him.

In the very next episode Paul recounts about Rena, however, she does not trust him. When he was eight, his father's sister, Adelaide, died, and Paul's mother came to tell him what had happened. She announced that Aunt Adelaide had gone away, that she would not come back. When Paul asked where she had gone and why, his mother walked out of the room. Paul by this time knew about death, and he was so enraged at his mother's evasion of the truth—at what he took to be her failure to trust him—that Adelaide's name became an "obscenity" to him.

There is no single narrative line here, rather a commingling of many lines, of separate strands of narrative. The theme of one is protection; the theme of another, protection subtly corroded by fear; the theme of still another, fear. The fear is hers, it is hers anticipating his, it is both his and hers, it is impossible to tell. In the daily life he shared with his mother, while Claude was in his dental office, Paul was encouraged to enter the inner world of his imagination, where things could be the way he made them be. And when he emerged from that inner world, he shared his stories with Rena, and she listened to them with grave attention.

At night when she put him to bed, she read to him, and they entered another's imaginative world together. She particularly loved to read Edgar Allan Poe's stories. As she spoke Poe's words in her pleasant, low voice, her aspect began to take on the sinister quality of what she was reading. Looking at her, Paul could not wholly recognize her, and this frightened him even more than the stories. During this period he began to call out in his sleep and even to sleepwalk. Claude's way of dealing with the situation was to admonish Paul sternly, "You stay in bed, young man."

Perhaps the most paradoxical story Paul tells about his mother was an incident that took place when he was eight or nine. As his parents were constantly fearful of burglary, the house was always locked, and even Hannah and Anna, the two women who worked as domestics, were not allowed keys. Paul, however, did have a key. One day after school, he let himself in at the front door and suddenly became aware of an intense silence in the house. Usually his mother was at home, but if she was out, Hannah or Anna could be heard moving around in the kitchen. He went into the kitchen; it too was silent and empty. In his mind, one possibility crowded out the rest: a burglar had gotten into the house and was at that very moment in hiding. Terrified, but even more fearful of sitting without doing anything, he went from room to room, starting with his parents' bedroom, pushing aside the clothes in the closet, looking under the bed. Finally he came to the guest room and looked under the huge four-poster bed. "I bent down to look under it and felt my heart explode," he writes. "Someone lay under there, all bunched up. I was unable to stand up and run; I could only stare."

The being under the bed began to make noise and to move. Rena emerged laughing, saying that Anna and Hannah had to go out, and she thought she would see "what would happen if I disappeared too. You wouldn't like it much, would you?" She laughed and brushed it off as a joke. He did not take it as a joke. He was enraged.

Why did she do this? Paul says he does not know. She said it was a joke—a joke about his need for her? about her power over him? about his powerlessness? She seemed surprised that he was angry. But his anger against her (unlike his anger against his father) was not sustained. In a short time he relented. After all, she was the one who had saved him; she was the one who encouraged his imagining. She listened to his stories and, generally, he felt, she and he got along well. It was his father who wanted to do him in; his father was the one he needed to be protected against. He needed his mother on his side so that they would be two against one, two as one against one.

Often he would say to her, "Why don't we go away, the two of us?" And she would answer him, "Where would we go? There is no place for us to go."

However, there did exist a temporary escape into the outer world for Paul—in fact, two escapes. One was to Happy Hollow Farm, the Massachusetts home of Paul's maternal grandparents, August and Henrietta Winnewisser. An extended property of hillsides, trees, and a central meadow, the farm also had a deep brook running through the grasslands. In the story "The Frozen Fields," written in the late 1950s, Paul describes the six-year-old Donald's excitement about the farm he and his parents are about to visit. (In the original manuscript the farm was named "Happy Hollow Farm," but in the published version the name is missing.) "Everything connected with the farm was imbued with magic. The house was the nucleus of an enchanted world more real than the world that other people knew about. During the long green summers he had spent there with his mother and the members of her family he had discovered that world and explored it, and none of them had ever noticed he was living in it."

Happy Hollow Farm was a magic world despite the presence of Paul's grandfather August—he with the shattered nose—a moody man who was subject to sudden rages. To counterbalance this latent violence, there was Henrietta, "strong, calm and sunny." Paul used to look at her and think what a nice mother she would make. "In her presence the world seemed acceptable."

There was also a second place of escape for Paul, in Glenora, New York, with his paternal grandparents, Fred and Ida Bowles. The elder Bowleses lived in Elmira, but they also owned land and several houses in Glenora on Seneca Lake, where the extended Bowles family would gather every summer. Glenora was even more magical than Happy Hollow Farm, with its deep hemlock forests and its high shale cliffs and waterfall at the southern end of the lake.

At night in Glenora Paul could hear the sounds of the katydids and of the waves against the cliffs. "It was good to wake up . . . and hear that music all around me in the air . . ." In the morning, when he explored the woods, he looked for the new growth coming up through the needles: "puffballs, Dutchman's-pipes, fungi like slabs of orange flesh, colonies of spotted toadstools, and best of all the deadly *Amanita* . . ." He would stand "staring down at it in fascination and in terror."

In Glenora he also found a kindred spirit, his grandfather Fred, who loved books, Indian artifacts, languages (he taught himself French and Spanish in his later years), and cats. Most important, he had been a constant traveler in his youth, boasting that he had been in every state of the union. The walls of his study were filled with maps that Paul used to gaze at with wonder, imagining a future life for himself, traveling without stopping, collecting stories and artifacts.

Of course, when he was a child, he might escape for a time into the outer world, but it was always necessary to go back with his mother and his father into that hermetic world where he was an object of constant vigilance. That that vigilance was contradictory as well as constant is suggested by a memory of Paul's from when he was about four. At the time the family was renting an old brownstone house, the first two floors of which served as office and laboratory for Claude, while the family lived on the top floor. For most of the day, Paul was allowed to play by himself inside the house. Then came the one hour when he was told to go and play in the backyard. Once outside, he stood in the yard, enclosed by high walls, and looked up at the house with its nine windows looking down on him with what seemed like nine eyes. His mother tapped on one window and gestured for him to move, calling out, "Don't just stand there." He began to run and move about. Then another window opened on the second floor, and his father called out, "Calm down, don't run around, stop making noise."

Faced with constant yet conflicting orders, sure of only one thing—that his father would prevent him from doing anything he wanted to do—Paul began to practice deceit. He pretended that he liked what he did not like and that he did not like what he did like. But when you do this, he has since said, you only end up fooling yourself.

If one reads *Without Stopping* with assiduous attention to what is not said, to the silences between the paragraphs, one can see Paul's imaginative vision at work, shaping the telling, revealing and withholding secrets at the same time. He reveals to us the rigorous code of behavior enforced in that household, a code that insisted on a surface of politeness, control, and restraint. Not to show what one feels, not to make a display of oneself—this was how one was supposed to act. And if sudden outbursts of anger or fear, naked or surreptitious, occurred, they must be at once buried without acknowledgment. Secrecy was the aim and the rule and the form.

Paul did not learn until he was an adult (Claude did not tell him, but Rena did) that as a young man Claude had wanted to be a concert violinist, but his parents had not allowed it. Subsequently Claude had a nervous breakdown, and only after that did he decide to be a dentist. Nor did Paul know anything about Rena's past, except for a small detail here or there: that she went to the Robinson Female Seminary and that she laughed in scorn when she said it. He did not ask anything further; he says he had no interest in knowing. Paul claims that he didn't even know until he was in his teens that there was any physiological difference between the sexes.

He became an expert at secrecy, keeping things from others and from himself as well. And then one day, when he was sixteen, he went to Roth's soda fountain. He went in one door and out the other and in one door and out the other, over and over, not willing what he was doing. Only the sight of his parents' car coming down the hill saved him, locking him into place again, renewing and strengthening his secrecy.

But there is a power in all that is hidden, in all that is not revealed. It takes hold in the imagination as a parallel narrative, out of which other narratives can grow and evolve and, one day, break through into telling.

 When I arrive at Paul's door at the appointed hour of four in the afternoon, a tall European man is standing there. He too has an appointment at four. No, he is not a journalist or a writer; he tells me he has just come to visit. Paul opens the door and, discovering that he has given an appointment for the same time to the two of us, invites us both in. He waits for the visitor and me to settle the matter. The visitor volunteers to go first, claiming that he will not take long, only twenty minutes or so, and then he will leave. No, no, he does not need privacy, he assures me, as I get up to go outside, so I stay.

The visitor sits on the small couch near the door. It is low for him, and he sits awkwardly. From the first question, his tone is one of confrontation.

"Are you a nihilist?"

Paul says he does not understand the word.

"Don't you believe in the meaning of life?"

"No."

"Don't you believe in hope, in hope for humanity?"

"No," says Paul, politely.

"You have said you don't like Tangier as it is now; why do you stay here, if you don't like it?" Even before the answer is given, still further questions are asked: "Do you smoke kif? What is your life like here? Do you stay isolated in this apartment, seeing no one? Do you go to cafés?"

"I never did like cafés."

"Some people," continues the visitor, not mentioning any names, "say that *The Invisible Spectator* is an accurate picture of you, that you are detached. Why are you famous? Is it because you survived all those guys?"

"What guys?"

"Kerouac, Burroughs, Ginsberg . . . ," the visitor reels off hurriedly (and mistakenly—the latter two are certainly alive at this time). "Why did you come here? You said in an interview you came because you found ecstasy here and freedom."

"I came to Morocco because more than any other country it had been shut off from the modern world," Paul answers.

"Why don't you leave Tangier, if you think it's spoiled?"

"Where would I go? I don't want to go to Europe or Latin America or Asia."

"Of all the guys who came here, who was the craziest?"

"Craziest?" Paul repeats, and after a moment he responds, "Alfred Chester."

"Did you survive because you were detached?"

"I don't know why I survived. Because I was lucky."

Suddenly, without any obvious transition—but what is sequence here?—the visitor mentions that Henry Miller is his favorite writer. Paul does not comment.

"Now that you are eighty-one, are you afraid of dying?"

"No, I'm not. I don't want to suffer."

"What will happen to you when you die?"

"What?"

"What do you think will happen? Do you have a concept of death?"

"It's a completely negative thing," Paul says, "so how can you have a concept of it?"

"Your conception of a world without meaning or religion makes you strange in a country where all the people believe."

"I like to be a stranger."

"When you get up in the morning, do you think how awful it's going to be that day? Are you depressed about what it will be like?"

"It depends upon what I'm going to do, who I'm going to see."

"People feel what a shit this life is," the visitor says.

"I never felt that."

"Do you prepare yourself for death? Because people want to be remembered as nice and good persons, before they die they try to be reconciled to others, to get along with people they've had differences with. Maybe you think of forgiving." (Does he mean being forgiven?)

"Forgiving? There's no one to forgive me. Above all, I'm pragmatic. I take care of things."

"Sometimes," the visitor says—and now the tone of confrontation has turned to one verging on despair—"I think I am bad, that I am at fault."

"No, I don't feel that way. Perhaps I have no conscience. No?"

"I was raised as a Christian, a Catholic. Guilt is persistent."

"The moral of this is, Don't let people be Christian."

"You never have this feeling?"

"I have felt guilty when I was guilty."

"Do you consider yourself to be a great writer?" comes the question, once again in the tone of confrontation.

"Certainly not."

"So then what are you?"

"I'm just a person like anybody else, who left the country where I was born and came here."

"Do you want to be cremated when you die?"

"It's not allowed here."

"What do you plan then?"

"Nothing. You keep imagining I think of death."

"I'm forty-three, and I keep thinking of death all the time," the visitor says haltingly. "You sound like a wise man . . . I'm terribly afraid of death."

"What I'm afraid of is not of dying but of lying helpless, of suffering," says Paul.

"It sounds contradictory."

"If I knew who was going to be near me when I died, I suppose I'd think of making it easier for them."

"Did you have a good life?" The visitor once again appears to be changing course, though to him it may not be changing course at all.

"I took part in life. I was alive."

"Do you feel privileged to have had that life, to have gone to all those places?"

"Yes, I'm delighted, of course, because it gives me a chance to remember, and memory is very important when you're old."

"I think life is unjust," the visitor suddenly announces. "There are people in my country who live drab lives, working all day, doing things they don't want to do. Did you deserve that life? Other people live in misery, and you don't."

Paul answers imperturbably: "There is no such thing as justice. No one deserves anything. Justice is an abstract conception, an aim. It's not real. It would be nice if it was."

But the visitor is not satisfied with that answer. "An American here," he relates, "said to me, 'Life is a whore.' Some people have a chance to paint or to pay a hooker, but others—"

"Hooker?" Paul asks.

"Don't you know that word? Whore." Not waiting for an answer, he goes on: "Did you give Cherifa a lot of money?"

"No, my wife gave her the house; I signed the papers over to my wife."

"What did the death of your wife mean to you?"

"How can I answer that question?" asks Paul, his voice still polite, imperturbable, though he adds that he has time for only one more question.

"Did you feel relief?"

"Yes, an element of relief. She had begun to die sixteen years earlier, and I'd given up hope of seeing her herself, as she had been. Earlier we had given each other our work to read. She was a confidante. Since then, there is not anyone to write for. It was a terrible thing to have happened."

"Thank you very much for talking to me," the visitor says as he gets up to leave.

"I told you the truth," Paul volunteers.

"It's not easy to tell the truth."

"What's difficult is to lie. You get caught in the deception."

When the visitor leaves, I fall back on the couch and groan, "Why are you famous?" Paul shrugs. "They ask whatever they want to ask."

During the visitor's "interview," I have been appalled by the brashness of his questions. At first I said to myself, If it were me, I would have thrown this guy out by now. Why does Paul put up with him? And yet, as the visitor went on, for all his brashness, even rudeness, there was evidence of some terrible need in him that had led him here to ask, even begrudgingly, for advice from a "wise man."

To the visitor Paul has said that he has spoken the truth. When asked if he had had a good life, he answered that he had lived, that he had taken part in life, that he was glad to remember all the places he had been. And what then of what he said to me fifteen years ago, when he described to me his sense of never having really been *in* life? How had he put it? That when Jane died he realized that it was only through her that he had been living. Then, after her death, he felt he was not truly alive.

Is it a matter of multiple truths, one truth no more true than another for him? As if he, Paul, were infinitely adaptable: for each questioner a different response, each one a truth for the moment? Why would that be so surprising? Besides, now that he is eighty-one, what he feels about his life is necessarily different from what he felt at sixty-seven. (Just as now that I am sixty-seven, what I feel is necessarily different from what I felt at fifty-two, when I first came to see him.)

Looking at Paul, I notice how fatigue is graying his face. I know he has had a two-hour interview this morning with a journalist. Then the visitor came with his questions, and now he will be faced with mine.

"Do you not want to talk any more?" I ask.

"No, let us go on."

But I cannot just go on; I am still thinking of what the visitor said about death. He was talking of his own fear of death—of imagining death. In him, fear and horror and rage and guilt seemed entwined with imagining. To Paul, I say that many people think of the imagination as a dark force. They think that when one imagines, one will imagine horror.

"But that's not necessarily true."

"I think it's not uncommon for people to feel that way.

But for you the imagination, from the time you were a child, worked in terms of control and protection."

"Do you have only one earring on?" Paul asks me.

"Do I?"

"Oh, no, I see; there's one on the other ear."

I laugh. "I have two. Anyhow, this is what I've been thinking about," I go on. "In your work, you imagine horror and fear and betrayal in its most minute detail, and yet you control it. Perhaps that has something to do with why he—the visitor—came to see you, why he spoke to you the way he did."

"M-m-m . . . ," says Paul, not agreeing, not disagreeing.

"Take the story 'The Delicate Prey,' " I propose. It is a story of terrible cruelty inflicted by the member of one desert tribe, the Moungari, upon three men and a boy of another tribe, the Filala, and of the subsequent and even more terrible revenge taken upon the Moungari by other Filala. Written in 1948, it was based on a factual account told to Paul about some desert tribesmen.

"I don't think it was a horror story at all," Paul insists. "You could easily have made it one by dwelling on the sadism, by trying to evoke an emotional reaction, which I tried not to do. The whole point is to underplay, to understate. If you're writing about unpleasant things, don't dwell on them. You go quickly through them, and that's it."

To go quickly through unpleasant things? I don't think that's an option for me here. I find myself turning to the episode in Paul's childhood involving Gordon Linville and the Crystal Dog Club. I have been thinking about the imagination and darkness. And here is an incident about imagination and about darkness, though, to put it in perspective, in the scheme of things, it is a child's darkness.

The whole story, in its deliberate planning, its deliberate maneuvering, its deliberate cruelty has remained unsettling to me. I have felt that, even for a child of ten, it was not within the bounds of morality that I subscribed to. You can look at it as arising out of the way Paul himself was treated as a child, I have told myself, as if that were justification. But now, after the interview with the visitor—because of the visitor?—the story about Gordon Linville once again resurfaces.

I tell Paul that when we first spoke of this incident, I had reacted with the feeling that even as a child one should not be "mean," one should try to be "kind." At this Paul laughs.

I bring up an incident from my own childhood. It is an offering of a sort, an effort to show that something in my own past is not so different from his. "There was a boy named Boppo, who lived in my neighborhood in New York City," I begin.

"Oh, what a strange name," Paul says.

I go on to tell Paul that Boppo was about my age, eight or nine, bigger than me but very heavy, an unhappy, complaining kind of kid, perhaps even blubbering, as Paul had described Gordon Linville. I can't recall the detail of what happened between Boppo and me, but I do remember that one day on the street I got into a fistfight with him. That night there was a knock on the door of our apartment, and my father, who was sober for a change, went to the door to answer. Boppo's mother stood there complaining bitterly that I had beaten up Boppo. My father apologized for my action in his most polite manner, but after he closed the door, he laughed like hell. My father thought it was wonderful that I, this little girl, had beaten up Boppo. Of course, my father had always been very small and had had to endure a lot of beatings himself when he was a little kid. He was proud of my being this scrappy kid, and I, who had little enough reason to see him pleased about anything, was pleased that he was pleased with me.

"So," I say to Paul, "when you told me that story about Gordon Linville, I thought, Oh, I would never do anything like that. But then I remembered Boppo, and it gave me pause."

Paul laughs and says, "Yeah, but I didn't beat the boy up."

"No," I say, "you didn't beat the boy up." No, he is not taking my offering. No, I have not been able to move this discussion to another place.

"I didn't touch him," Paul adds. "I helped put a rope around him—"

"Many people," I suddenly say, in another effort to open up possibilities, "go to great lengths to block out what they have done or what they have felt."

"What they have done and feel they shouldn't have done."

"They don't want to feel guilty."

"No."

"But you don't do that, so then—"

"I never felt guilty about that boy. I did when I threw a rock at him and hit him on the head the year before. Oh, yes, augh! I felt guilty because it bled so much. And you do, naturally. And he was"—here Paul wails loudly—"you know, crying. And I thought, That's shameful. Even though he's bleeding badly, he should not cry. Well, maybe he conceived a dislike for me at that point, but I never knew it." It is a metaphorical shrug, if not a physical one.

"In your work," I note, "no matter what actions your

characters take, you make no attempt to put a moral judgment upon them."

"No."

"And because of the absence of judgment, of judging the characters, what's being suggested is that there's a universal internal darkness, that everybody has these dark impulses of one sort or another."

"Well, naturally, I assume they have. My feeling is that if I pass judgment on anyone in the work, I would ruin the material. Why—I mean, what have I got to do with what my characters do? Nothing. They decide what to do, and they do it. If I pass judgment on them, then I would be putting myself into the material."

Abdelouahaid comes in, asks Paul what he wants at the market, serves us tea, and leaves, saying, "Good work," at which we both laugh. But it does not feel like good work to me.

I revert once again to Jane. Is it an escape or another effort at connection? "I've thought a lot about Jane calling you 'Gloompot,'" I say. ("Gloompot" was the name Jane often called Paul in the early years of their marriage because, she said, his view of life depressed her so when she was with him that everything seemed hopeless.)

There is a loud knock on the door.

"Yes, I've wondered about that."

"I think it may have had to do with the darkness in herself that she was trying not to see—but maybe through your darkness she was seeing her own—"

"And so I was to blame?" Paul asks as he gets up.

"No, no, you weren't to blame."

"I mean, she thought I was," Paul says as he goes to open the door to another visitor.

For weeks in the winter of 1937, the lyricist John LaTouche had been telling Paul about this "fantastic girl," Jane Auer. Then one day in late February, LaTouche, the writer Erika Mann, Paul, then twenty-six, and Jane, who had just turned twenty, met outside the Plaza Hotel and went up to Harlem. There, in a dimly lit apartment, they bought joints for fifty cents and sat on the floor and smoked. Paul tried to talk to Jane, but she barely responded. Thirty years later Jane would write of that meeting: "He wrote music and was mysterious and sinister. The first time I saw him, I said to a friend: He's my enemy."

The two met again a few days later at a Sunday afternoon gathering at E. E. Cummings's on Patchin Place in Greenwich Village. Paul was there with Kristians Tonny, a Dutch painter he had met through Gertrude Stein, and Tonny's wife, Marie Claire. Hearing from the Tonnys that the three of them were about to go on an extended trip to Mexico, Jane suddenly announced that she was going with them. Paul was intrigued by this young woman who had invited herself to go to Mexico with a man she had met only once and to whom she'd hardly spoken.

In mid-March Jane and Paul and the Tonnys boarded a Greyhound bus for New Orleans, planning to stop at many towns along the way. From New Orleans they would go west to Houston, where they would cross the border to Mexico. Paul, who was thinking of joining the Communist Party, had, in addition to his extensive luggage, fifteen thousand stickers calling for the death of Trotsky, which he planned to distribute in Mexico. Jane, who had been equipped for the journey by her mother, was carrying a complete new wardrobe, including evening dresses and matching shoes.

On the bus Jane and Paul sat together. They spoke of books they cared for, of people they knew, of their affairs—hers with women, his with women and men. Jane, who for all her wildness was a true daughter of the middle class, made it clear that there would be no sex between them. She was determined to be a virgin until she married.

Jane would later tell Paul that it was on the bus to New Orleans that she fell in love with him. He found her delightful and high-spirited, amusing, unexpected and yet familiar. They shared an aversion to intellectual and literary pretensions. They were alike in their wit and their charm and their brilliance. They shared a deep allegiance to secrecy.

Like Paul, Jane was an only child who lived in great part through her imagination. When she was twelve, her father died, and Jane was left alone with her mother, Claire, a circumstance she later described to Paul as "the worst thing that could have happened" to her. At fourteen she developed tuberculosis of the right knee and was taken for treatment by her mother to a sanatorium in Leysin, Switzerland. Much of the time she was there, from 1932 to 1934, she lay in bed in traction. During her stay at the sanatorium, she was tutored by a Frenchman she greatly admired, though later she would say of him that he was only "well versed in Greek mythology and venereal diseases." In Leysin she also developed a complex set of phobias: a fear of dogs, of sharks, of mountains, of elevators, and of being burned alive. In the spring of 1934 she was released from the sanatorium, her tuberculosis cured, but her leg still caused her great pain. On her return to New York, she was operated on, and her right leg was permanently stiffened so that her knee would not bend.

At the Hotel Meurice, where Jane and her mother went

to live, Claire indulged Jane, bought her expensive clothes, and hoped that she would make a good marriage. But marriage was not on Jane's mind. She became part of a group of young lesbians who frequented the Village. She said she wanted to be a writer, and in fact she did write a novel in French and promptly lost the manuscript.

Through John LaTouche she was introduced to the salon of the art dealer Kirk Askew and his wife, Constance. The painter Maurice Grosser, who met Jane at the Askews, described her as beautifully dressed, prim, and outrageous, limping with one knee stiff, carrying one shoulder higher than the other. In a beautiful, alluring voice, saying whatever seemed to come to her mind, she was the "hit of the occasion," "screamingly funny." Yet she was also puzzling. Virgil Thomson remembered that "people loved her, but what she cared about no one knew."

On the trip to New Orleans and then to Houston, everything went well between Paul and Jane. They talked and laughed; it seemed they were growing closer each day. But once they left Houston and crossed the border into Mexico, everything changed. Suddenly, Paul has recalled, Jane was in terror. She was terrified of the mountains and the precipices. She was terrified of the dogs that ran free in the villages. She cowered on the floor in the back of the bus among the Indian women with their babies and their bundles. She wouldn't even look out the window.

The night they arrived in Mexico City, Jane jumped out of the bus, hired a porter to carry her luggage, and announced she was going to the Ritz, where her mother had insisted she stay. Paul and the Tonnys found a cheap hotel. The next day they went to get her at the Ritz, but she wasn't there. Several days later they found her at the Hotel Guardiola, where she had become ill with dysentery. They tried to cheer her up, assuring her that she would be better by morning, when they would return. But when they went back to get her, she was gone. She had checked out and flown to the U.S. The three agreed that the trip would be easier without her. As for Paul, he did not expect to see her again.

But one day the following August, after Paul's return from Mexico and Guatemala, as he was working on the orchestration for the ballet *Yankee Clipper,* the phone rang. It was a woman whose voice he did not recognize. He responded abruptly, saying he was busy working. The woman said something hesitantly, and suddenly Paul realized that it was Jane Auer. She was calling to ask him to spend the weekend at Deal Beach, New Jersey, where her mother had rented a big house for the summer. Virgil Thomson was also coming that weekend, she told him.

Paul spent the weekend at Deal Beach, and after that, during the fall and early winter, he and Jane saw each other frequently. They began to talk about how amusing it would be to get married and "horrify" everyone, especially their respective families. They fantasized about where they'd go on their honeymoon. (Jane was going to get some money when she married, and they could use it to travel.) But then, somehow, fantasy changed into reality, and the two announced their engagement. Pressed by others to explain why she would even consider marriage, Jane gave one reason after another: her mother wanted her to get married; she wanted to improve her status in the art and music world by marrying a recognized composer; she was lonely. As for Paul, if he had his reasons, he did not express them to others. To himself, he once acknowledged, he simply said, One gets married.

They were married on February 21, 1938, the day before

Jane's twenty-first birthday and immediately set off for Panama on the freighter *Kano Maru*. With them they had two wardrobe trunks, twenty-seven suitcases, a typewriter, and a record player.

All this I have told before in my book on Jane, relying on Paul for my information, constructing a scenario from his memory, as seen through his eyes. But now if I think back to that first trip they took together to Mexico with the Tonnys, I begin to wonder about the swift change that took place in Jane, from high spirits to despair and terror—to darkness—when they crossed that border. Yes, it had made sense when Paul told me of the change. In Leysin she had developed a fear of mountains and precipices and dogs. And here in Mexico were mountains and precipices and dogs.

But now that I am thinking about Paul's life, I am no longer so sure of the scenario I have accepted. When I looked through his eyes, I saw the change in her, the one he told me he saw. Now, however, I am trying to turn, to wrench myself around to look at him in the scene. I have a sense of things wavering and disintegrating, as if my belief in the narrative of Jane's life, arrived at so painstakingly, is eroding.

When I arrive at Paul's at three, he takes some time to come to the door. He apologizes, explaining that he has been lying down. Looking at him, I can see how exhausted he is. Perhaps the pain in his leg is worse, or perhaps he is having a reaction to the medication he is taking for sciatica or for high blood pressure. "Why don't you rest a little longer?" I say to him. At first he demurs, then asks, "But what will you do?" "I can read," I say, pointing to all the books lying about. Finally he agrees, and he goes back into the bedroom to lie down.

Looking at a small masklike sculpture on the mantel across from me, I recall what I said to Paul about Jane and darkness the last time I was here, and I also recall his response, on the edge of irritability. I did not elaborate then on what I meant: that she was someone who lived on the edge of her own darkness and always, from an early age, struggled not to fall into it; but when she was confronted with his darkness, seeing herself reflected in him, she could not escape the darkness in herself that she had been evading.

Once again I go back to that border they crossed in 1937 and to the change in Jane that Paul noticed. I accept that there was a change, but it seems to me that something is missing in the sequence, as if multiple events have been collapsed into a single event. To begin with, Paul has said nothing to me about himself and what he felt at that border, whether there was any change in him consonant with the change in her. I try to project the Paul who is at this moment sleeping in the other room back into that scene. Was he the same as the older Paul, or different? How different?

I think about what he has said and written about his own traveling, about the heightened excitement that being in another country always evoked in him. For him, the stranger the landscape, the more forbidding and mysterious it was, the more he relished being in it. He reveled in all that was unconnected to the life he knew in the U.S., in any sign of another mode of existence, particularly one that was ostensibly more primitive and more mysterious.

In that room in which I once asked question after question about Jane, I recall a passage in Jane's work that I have never discussed with Paul, a fragment from Jane's unfinished novel *Out in the World*. In that fragment Emmy Moore (a surrogate figure for Jane) is writing a letter to her husband, Paul Moore (a surrogate figure for Paul), telling him what she has never been able to reveal to him before. She tells him how lost and estranged she feels when she sees him in a reverie about a world that entrances him but that is alien to her. At such a moment, looking at him, she is aware that he is in the grip of what she calls the "forces of nature," forces which, she insists, have nothing to do with him or with her. But then she tries to describe what she thinks those "forces" are that compel his attention. By the "forces of nature," she says, she means "the forces that work inside us—but seem to be part of—" At that point the fragment breaks off. Emmy Moore—and Jane—could not or would not go any further.

It appears to me now that when Paul and Jane arrived at that geographic border on their first trip together, each came to an edge within: he to the edge of his most intense excitement, she to the edge of terror. He fell with delight into that outer world upon which could be projected "the forces that work inside us." Sensitive as she was to the most subtle changes in others, did she feel his mounting excitement at the very forces she feared? And then, seeing him fall so eagerly into the grip of those forces, was she no longer able to resist her own dark forces, the ones that "worked" within her, the ones she was always struggling to allay? Did she think back to her first meeting with him when she said, "He is my enemy"?

Perhaps too, at that moment in which "and then and then" had collapsed, she foresaw—for she was always anticipating the terrors of the future—a sequence of events in the years to come, when the two of them would continue to cross borders, real and metaphoric, when he would relish the change and the danger, when she would be lost in the estrangement from him and from her daily life.

Sitting in the living room while Paul is asleep in the next room, I find I am strangely dissatisfied with my suppositions. I have a feeling of having simplified, of having rigidified what must of necessity remain undefined and fluid, of having bypassed life in a headlong rush to understand, to analyze. It seems to me that abstraction itself has become a kind of betrayal here. All my former allegiances, to her as a subject, to him as my primary informant, are being tested and altered.

I pick up a book and try to read for a while, but soon I find my eyelids becoming very heavy. I lie down on the couch and immediately fall asleep. Some time later I awaken with a start. There has been a noise . . . a voice crying out, as if for help. Was that Paul, or was it a sound in my own dream? Now what do I do? If I should rush in, only to disturb him . . . Listening intently, I hear no sound but the street noise, muffled. He's all right, I reassure myself as I sit up. You're just confusing dream sounds and real sounds.

Paul walks into the living room, looking much refreshed. Abdelouahaid arrives at just this moment, and Paul, saying he feels better, decides to accompany him to the post office and the market. He invites me to go with them.

At the post office Abdelouahaid goes inside while Paul and I wait in the car. When he returns, he is carrying a large quantity of mail, which he hands to Paul. We drive on to the Fez market. Unlike the central market, which is always noisy, teeming with Moroccans doing their daily shopping, the Fez market is quiet, almost calm. It is smaller; the merchandise is more selective as well as more expensive.

Many of the expatriate Europeans shop here for fresh produce, for meat and poultry, for packaged and canned goods. There are also stalls for baskets, and even one that sells tropical fish.

Today, as he does each day, Abdelouahaid goes to one particular stall to buy a chicken for Paul. (Paul's diet is unvarying. For breakfast: bread and jam, cheese and tea. For lunch: bread and soup. For dinner: boiled chicken, cooked by Abdelouahaid or by the maid.) As Abdelouahaid is making his purchase, Paul and I wander through the market. Here and there he stops to talk. The shopkeepers, all male, greet him in a friendly, respectful way. We stop in front of the shop that sells tropical fish. Just inside the doorway, a dog is chasing a monkey. The owner of the shop picks up the monkey and sets it on his lap. The monkey keeps dodging, trying to keep out of the reach of the jumping dog. The shopkeeper greets Paul, and they exchange a few words. Suddenly another man who has been inside the shop steps forward and brings a lighted match up close to the monkey's face, smiling as he does it. The monkey pulls back in fright. Obviously aware that Paul and I are watching, the man again brings the match close to the monkey's face. He repeats this several times, and each time the monkey cowers. During all of this Paul says nothing.

Even as I am struggling with myself—should I say something? shouldn't I say something?—into my mind comes a memory of a passage in Paul's novel *The Spider's House,* where Lee Veyron, an American woman, is being driven with Stenham in a horse-drawn carriage in Fez. When the Moroccan driver beats the horse with a whip, Lee protests, but Stenham, the expatriate American writer who lives in Fez, asserts that she has no right to come to another country and tell the inhabitants how to behave. No right? Yes, I suppose I have no right. But that still does not stop me from being distressed at seeing the monkey mistreated.

Finally the man who has been tormenting the monkey tires of the joke, and he stops. We move on to another stall, where produce is sold. A black-and-white cat that has been lounging outside the stall gets up and comes over to Paul, and he leans down and pets it. There is a remarkable softness in Paul's posture, in his gentle caressing of the cat. "What was going on in that other shop?" I ask him. "Animals don't like fire," he says. "Except for cockroaches. They flock to the fireplace in my apartment when the fire is lit."

19 It is early evening when we arrive at Claude Thomas's. Her villa, an ornate structure built in 1867, is situated on the summit of the Old Mountain. Claude suggests that we all—Paul; the American photographer Cherie Nutting and her husband, the Moroccan musician Bachir Attar; several young French friends of Claude's; Abdeslam; Roderigo de la Rosa; and myself—join her in watching the sunset from the lower edge of the property. We descend from the main villa down through the gardens, past a small enclosed pavilion overlooking the sea. Below this pavilion, just on the edge of a steep cliff, is a narrow walkway railed off by a low stone wall, aged and weathered to a delicate mauve-gray.

Directly below, we can see a group of dark rocks by the shore, from which fishermen, small figures at this distance, are casting their lines. To the left, in the direction of the setting sun, the cliff ends in a sandy beach that juts out into the water. On the sand is one lone cottage. Before us is a wide expanse of water, the juncture of the western end of the Mediterranean and the eastern shore of the Atlantic as it rounds the North African coast. We watch the sun— orange, huge, distorted by the atmosphere—as it slips below the horizon. In the dying light, the hills of Spain across the straits seem very close. Two small fishing boats move across the water. "During the time of the ancient Greeks," Paul says, "this place was called the end of the world."

With the setting of the sun, the air grows cold. Claude asks Roderigo to go into the house and get a wool cloak for Paul. (Yes, she too has the sense that she must look out for Paul.) Slowly we retrace our steps to the upper garden. Roderigo returns with two djellabas; Paul puts on one and Abdeslam the other. Jumping up on a stone parapet, Abdeslam proceeds to walk on his hands. The wool cloak splays away from his upside-down body, turning him into a fluttering shadow in the dimness. (On his arrival, Abdeslam smiled as he greeted me, saying, "Have you been taking any long walks?")

We enter the main house through a high-ceilinged vestibule and proceed to a large room that is both dining and sitting room. Various beautiful fabrics and rugs are scattered about in an informal manner, and a fire burns in the fireplace. Claude seats Paul in a large chair before the fire. Here, as he was at Abdeslam's house, he is the focus of attention, a revered figure, not just famous but also, it occurs to me, a spiritual presence. I know that Paul would laugh at such an idea.

One of the young French women asks him where he lived in New York; did he ever live in Greenwich Village? "Only in one place in the Village," he responds, "in Oliver Smith's house on Tenth Street."

"But, Paul, you also lived on Patchin Place," I say, the words rushing out before I can stop them.

"There speaks the biographer," says Claude, and everybody laughs, myself included. (I am bemused by the thought of all the facts of Paul's life and Jane's life, marshaled at the forefront of my brain, insisting on their primacy, ready to tumble out and make their connections at the slightest provocation. Even in this social situation, I cannot drop the other aspect of myself, so central to my being here, the biographer or quasi-biographer. When I am with him, my eyes are upon him; they cannot pretend not to be. And he? He knows that I am here, observing, and yet it seems to have no effect on him. At least, that is the sense I have, that he would be the same if I were not here.)

Someone comments admiringly on Abdeslam's skill at walking on his hands on the parapet. Everybody marvels at the inherent danger of what he did. "When I was a boy, I tried to walk on my hands but couldn't," Paul volunteers, "so I gave it up."

"You should have had a teacher," Claude suggests.

"I didn't have a teacher. I taught myself," Abdeslam says.

"In yoga," I note, "the upside-down posture in the headstand or shoulder stand is supposed to produce great health benefits."

"It has to do with the blood going to the brain," says Paul. He recounts an experience he had in India in 1952, when he was confined to a concentration camp, or, more precisely, a "screening camp," for two days because the authorities suspected him of being an "international spy." Paul has written about this camp in his essay "Notes Mailed at Nagercoil," describing its horrors: the overcrowding, the insects, the howling of pariah dogs outside the barbed-wire fence, and, worst of all for him, a loud-speaker continually blaring Indian film music. But now, here in this beautiful room, with others hanging on his every word, he puts a different light on that experience. The camp commandant, he tells us, came to see him the morning of the first day to question him. Suddenly the commandant stood on his head, saying, "I must do this each morning for ten minutes."

Speaking the commandant's words, Paul takes on his voice, his accent, and his facial gestures. It is a brief but compelling portrayal of an official being reasonable, even polite, as he conducts an inquisition standing on his head. Everyone laughs, and I laugh too, but I am puzzled because in his written account of the camp Paul has mentioned only the dark aspects of the experience, the torture by sound and the awful physical conditions. He has omitted the commandant and his headstand.

At dinner Paul is seated at the head of the table, and I am placed at his right. The dinner begins with a pastilla, a Moroccan pie made of a very delicate dough, with nuts and many spices. Presiding at the table, Paul is smiling, at ease. I see no trace in him of his fatigue of earlier in the day. He tells several stories of people he knew in Paris many years ago, one about a large woman everyone called Esther Chester, who gave lavish parties and always interrupted the proceedings with a lecture on history, which was very bor-ing and long-winded. She would introduce the subject: "In the seventeenth century . . ." and then go on interminably. Paul gives a wonderfully amusing imitation of her speech and then takes the part of the party guests muttering,

"She's off again," to each other as they turn away to the liquor and the food.

Though Paul's anecdote about Esther Chester—and about the commandant earlier—has been a performance in a sense, it is not exactly acting. He is in each incident as a participant, but he is at the same time outside it, the controller, the puppeteer, the observer. He is letting (making?) us as listeners see the occasion through his eyes, a fragment of a story, created and performed as a unity. He is our seeing consciousness—and his self suddenly disappears, in a way. Then it is over, dropped, and he returns to the Paul he always is or appears to be.

As we sit over dessert and coffee, Bachir Attar begins to tell a story of Ayse Kandisha, a figure in Moroccan folklore, a woman who preys upon men, seduces them, and leads them to their destruction. A handsome, dark-haired man with an engaging manner, Bachir is the leader of a renowned troupe of musicians from Jajouka, his native village.

There was a man from a village near Jajouka, Bachir begins, who went away to Spain to fight many years ago. When he returned, he announced that he was married to Ayse Kandisha. He said she had entered into him through his breastbone. He always wore an old, dirty djellaba, but he insisted that he had gold, which Ayse Kandisha had given to him. Bachir says he knows the story of this man because the man was the best friend of his father. When Bachir was born, this man came to Jajouka to the family house and, lifting him up, named him Bachir and predicted that he would go far.

One day this man invited Bachir's father to a ceremony in honor of Ayse Kandisha, but his father made an excuse and said he could not go. Other men had told him of being with this man when Ayse Kandisha conferred special powers upon him. Once, they said, a group of men had been walking with him for a long distance out in the country. It was hot, and they were very thirsty. The man asked them, "What do you want?" One man said he wanted clear, pure buttermilk. Then the man who said he was married to Ayse Kandisha went to a nearby stream bed and returned with two earthenware jugs of buttermilk. The others were afraid and would not drink it. But the man said to them, "You asked me for this, and I brought it for you, and you must drink it." And the men drank the buttermilk.

When this man died, Bachir concludes, he was laid out before his burial, and when they undressed him to wash him, they found upon his chest, at the breastbone, grass growing of the greenest hue.

There is a silence after this story. Then Paul tells us that now and then, when Abdelouahaid is driving him, he will point out a man in the street and say that he is married to Ayse Kandisha. Everyone knows this, Abdelouahaid tells Paul, because the man keeps searching for her in places where she is supposed to be found, near running water, near stream beds, near trees. There she is known to possess men and make them mad.

Before I go to see Paul the next time, I resolve to change my ways. Yes, of course, this project is serious, but does it have to be such a grave responsibility? Can't it be lighter? (At this thought, a line from Jane's work occurs to me: "It is not for fun that I do this but because it is necessary to do so.")

When I am with Paul, I ask him how it is that in writing

the story of the camp in India, he left out the funny part, the commandant who stood on his head. He smiles and shrugs noncommittally. I go further and say, "How come, when you're so funny, it doesn't show up in your writing?"

"I don't think I have a sense of humor. A cousin of mine once said to me, 'You have no sense of humor, but you do have a sense of the ridiculous.' And I think it's still true," he adds.

And then, almost immediately he deflects the conversation to Jane and to how funny she was, as if talk of her being so amusing was a safety net. "I think half the time she didn't know that she was funny."

I remind him of her timing, that he and others had told me how perfect it was. "Could she have done that unconsciously?"

"I suppose she had to be aware of that."

"It's a little bit like acting."

"Very much."

"You play a little part, and you believe the part, and then you drop out of the part."

"Of course, she did that all the time in her writing," he notes. "Her writing is very funny."

"Oh, it is very funny." There is a silence. And then I say, "But not the later work, after she was sick—that's not funny." Though I have tried to be "lighter," it seems certain connections cannot be broken, certain thoughts cannot be kept out.

"No. Maybe being aware that she was no longer funny acted as a kind of block—when she wrote, I mean."

Without transition (what is in the space between question and question, between question and answer?) I switch the subject to something Paul wrote about his mother in *Without Stopping*. "Nothing's so much fun as games you play with your own mind," she told him one day when he was a child. After warning him that it is possible to be deceived by thinking that you run your own mind when actually your mind runs you, she suggested a technique to prevent being at the mercy of mind. "You mustn't imagine anything or remember anything or think of anything, not even think, 'I'm not thinking.' . . . You try it. It's hard," she told him, adding that she herself often did this when she rested in the afternoon. "I just go into the blank place and shut the door."

"How do you suppose she came to that?" I ask.

"I have no idea. She didn't say, 'So-and-so taught me.' She just said, 'That's something I used to do, and something I still do. When I lie down, I just forget everything and think of nothing. That's the important thing.'"

"That's very difficult to do."

"I think it is. Thoughts keep coming in. But she said that if a thought occurs to you, just brush it away and concentrate on nothing—that anybody could do it, you just have to try."

"It's a little like that trick of the mind, concentrate on not thinking of an elephant. Right? Only you can't do it."

"No, of course," he laughs. "Or what was it, a rhinoceros, which is even worse."

"But it is puzzling to me, that she came to that herself."

"She always said, 'It's good for you.' I remember that. She said, 'You must do it because it's good for you.' And I thought, Well, if she says so, yeah; but I didn't see why, why it's good for me. It didn't occur to me that I needed anything that was good for me. Except maybe prunes for breakfast."

"It's also interesting that she should have been so fond of Poe."

"Well, I guess she must have liked the idea of being frightened, don't you think? She told me how she used to read Poe at night when she was a girl, sometimes when there was no one else in the house."

"And be frightened?"

"Yes."

"You are your mother's son," I call out, loudly.

Paul laughs. "It's funny, yeah. It didn't occur to me that it was funny. I thought it was quite natural."

20 One morning in the early summer of 1945, years after having given up the thought of himself as a storyteller, Paul awoke from sleep and found himself writing a tale about an old woman. He went on writing, and by the afternoon the story was finished. He called it "The Scorpion."

In the story, an old woman lives alone in a cave hollowed out of a clay cliff by her sons, who have left to live in town. She exists day by day, gathering her own food, killing the scorpions that infest the cave, neither happy nor unhappy, not expecting her sons to return. One day, one of her sons—which one he is, she does not remember—comes to the cave and asks to come in. She says there is no room, but he insists on entering. He tells her that she must go away with him. At first she refuses, but then she agrees to leave with him after she has slept. She sleeps and dreams that she is in a town filled with many people, who may or may not be her sons. She enters a house and is thrust into a room, where she is once again a little girl. She sees a scorpion crawling down the wall and seizes it with her fingers; it clings to her tightly. Realizing that the scorpion is not going to sting her, she feels a great surge of happiness.

She lifts the scorpion to kiss it; it enters her mouth and crawls down her throat and is "hers." Awaking, she tells her son she is ready to go with him. As she leaves the cave forever, she passes by an old man, who often sits outside the cave watching her. The old man calls out, "Good-bye." Her son asks her who the old man is. She says she doesn't know. "You're lying," her son tells her.

In this five-page story, no one has a name. There is an old woman, there is a son, there is an old man. It is an oddly generic story, a mythical story, almost an archetypal story. In the spare narrative are many reverberations of Paul's childhood, including a mother who empties her mind and a son who asks his mother to go away with him—although this son has the power to force his mother out of her hiding place. Throughout there is also the theme of watching and being watched, of "don't look at me," in this case as experienced by the mother.

At the time this story appeared to Paul, he was living on West Tenth Street in the Village. Oliver Smith had arranged to lease the top three stories of the four-story building. Helvetia Perkins, Jane's lover, had taken over the lease for the second floor, Oliver Smith took the third floor; and Paul took the top apartment. Although Jane was living with Helvetia, she saw Paul every day, often preparing a late breakfast for him or having lunch with him alone. Outwardly the living arrangement at West Tenth Street was amicable, but Helvetia's presence was a continual irritant to Paul. He kept warning Jane that being with Helvetia was bad for her, while Helvetia in her turn kept trying to get Jane to break with Paul. Jane resisted both the entreaties and the warnings, and the domestic situation went on in its uneasy balance.

Paul was, characteristically, working intensely, composing incidental music for the theater as well as writing chamber music and songs. In addition, he was writing music criticism daily for the *New York Herald Tribune* and had recently begun a Sunday jazz column. He had just finished translating Sartre's *No Exit.* Unable to travel to Europe or North Africa because of the war, he escaped now and then on short trips to primitive areas of Mexico and Central America. He was not directly involved in the war, having been rejected by the draft board as a "psychoneurotic personality" after an examination by an army psychiatrist.

The precipitating factor for writing "The Scorpion" was an invitation by Charles Henri Ford, the editor of the surrealist magazine *View,* for Paul to be the guest editor of the May 1945 issue, which was to focus on tropical America. In preparation for the issue, Paul read a number of anthropological texts, including the work of Claude Lévi-Strauss, and delved into the myths of several South American native tribes.

As it happened, the anthropological material was not entirely new to Paul. At some point during his second stay in Paris, in 1931 or 1932, he had read in French the work of the philosopher-sociologist Lucien Lévy-Bruhl and had been very impressed by his ideas. Lévy-Bruhl's work dealt primarily with the concepts and thought processes of various "primitive" cultures. Investigating how myths and magic defined their worldview, Lévy-Bruhl developed the idea of *"participation mystique"* (mystical participation). Through *"participation mystique,"* Lévy-Bruhl contended, self and other, subject and object, past and present, animate and inanimate are linked in such a way that there are no clear borders between them. Further, Lévy-Bruhl implied, even in so-called advanced societies, *"participation mystique"* exists, although unacknowledged, in the realm of feeling.

When Paul completed the editorial work on the issue of *View,* he found himself with an impulse to write his own stories once again. As a child, of course, he had written many stories, but in his late adolescence he had concluded that he had insufficient understanding of life in the world to be a fiction writer. Suddenly he began to think of creating stories by adopting the point of view of the "primitive mind." And so it was that one rainy Sunday morning he woke up and found himself writing "The Scorpion," abandoning conscious control by emptying his mind and letting the words flow through his hand to the pen.

Paul had been readied for this telling by many elements in his past experience. His skill in rhetoric and in the integration of sound and meaning through language, his facility for narrative resided in him as old habit, there for the taking. In a more immediate sense, he had been preparing himself for this telling by his daily writing of reviews for the *Herald Tribune,* a process that reinforced his already awesome self-discipline. He had been preparing himself with his music as well. Even as he had submerged himself in his musical studies and written his musical compositions, he had been evolving a precise and impeccable sense of form, one that lay ready to be taken over into the prose. (In fact, "The Scorpion" has built into it a very strong sense of musical structure, with its dialogue almost antiphonal in form, as if one instrument were calling to another.)

But perhaps most important, Paul had been readying himself for this telling from that day in 1942 in Mexico when Jane presented him with her novel. He went over the manuscript word by word and, with her permission, excised sections having to do with a third serious lady, helping her bring it to completion. Reading the manuscript so closely, knowing her as well as he did, he became aware in a new way of the possibilities that fiction offered for the transformation of experience in life.

Once he had written "The Scorpion," one story came quickly after another: "By the Water," "A Distant Episode," "The Echo," "Call at Corazón," and "Under the Sky." All were immediately accepted for publication.

During the mid-forties, even as he was producing stories, Paul continued to function as a composer, a reviewer, and a translator. He wrote ten songs for voice and piano, three pieces for piano solo, his Concerto for Two Pianos, "Tornado Blues" (a four-part chorus of mixed voices with piano accompaniment), the music for a puppet play by Jane, and theater music for many plays, including *Cyrano de Bergerac, Land's End,* and *The Dancer.* In addition he completed translations of works by Jorge Luis Borges and Ramon Sender.

To all outward appearances, he was an admired figure in the artistic milieu of New York. Yet he felt himself caged, shut off from others in a place—a city, a country—that was becoming more and more alien to him. The atomic bombing of Hiroshima and Nagasaki, which ended the war in 1945, remained in his mind as a symbol of the moral corruption that had taken over American society.

One night in May 1947, Paul had a dream of being in a city where he walked through a succession of tunneled streets. When he awoke, he realized that the dream had left him "with a residue of ineffable sweetness and calm." Then it came to him that the city of the dream was a real city, that he had in fact once visited it, that it was Tangier, and that he could return to it if he wanted to now that the war was over.

With the help of his agent, Helen Strauss, he got a contract from Doubleday to write a novel and immediately determined to set sail for Morocco. Along with Gordon Sager, Paul took passage on the SS *Ferncape* to Casablanca. Jane chose to stay in the U.S. at the home of her friend Libby Holman, the jazz singer, to try to work on her new novel. On the day Paul and Gordon were to depart, Paul discovered that his passport was missing. Only after a frantic search was it discovered in Jane's bureau drawer.

In a letter to Paul, after he had arrived in Morocco, Jane wrote, "As for packing your passport away—I thought it was mine—I looked to see whose picture was in it and I dimly remember my own face and not yours. As Libby said when I told her, 'How psychosomatic can you get.'"

Once again, as he had at eighteen, Paul had left the U.S. and his former life behind him. Once again he was about to cross a border, inwardly as well as outwardly.

On board the SS *Ferncape* he began and finished "Pages from Cold Point," a story that propelled him forward into new territory. Told in the first person in the form of diary entries, the narrative begins with a statement about the coming end of civilization through atomic warfare. "Our civilization is doomed to a short life . . . I personally am content to see everything in the process of decay. The bigger the bombs, the quicker it will be done . . . Let it go . . ."

The diary that follows tells of an incestuous affair between the "I" (Norton) and his son. Following his wife's death, flush with the money from her estate, Norton has given up his position as a university professor and has taken his sixteen-year-old son, Racky, to live with him on a tropical island. In an isolated house on an isolated point, he has settled into an idyllic existence with the angelic-looking boy. They swim and they sunbathe; they are waited on by exemplary servants, while Norton, doting on Racky, admires his "extraordinary innocence of vision." He is convinced that even if Racky were to be thoughtless or unkind to him, he would only "love him the more for it."

Soon, however, the idyllic existence is threatened when Norton is warned by the local police that Racky is seducing the native boys in a nearby village and that, if he does not stop, he will be arrested. Norton knows he must tell Racky what the police have said, but he cannot bear the thought of a confrontation and keeps putting it off. It is Racky who resolves the issue by appearing naked and passive in his father's bed. The result is a period of total happiness for Norton.

At the end of one week, Racky abruptly assumes control. He demands that his father turn over most of his money to him, threatening disclosure if he does not agree. Norton submits without any protest, and Racky leaves the island in pursuit of his own pleasure elsewhere. Left alone on the isolated point, Norton clings to the memories of his former happiness, even as he muses upon a world on the brink of destruction.

The stories that Paul had written up to this time were primarily stories of cruelty, often involving a struggle for power, set in exotic locales using as protagonists characters who were distant from Paul. But in "Pages from Cold Point," he was working closer to the bone, confronting fragments of desire, fragments of fear, fragments of feelings of power and powerlessness, and allowing them to be played out against the background of a world on the edge of atomic extinction.

But if it was a leap forward for Paul, it was also a looking back into the past. It was a retelling, though greatly changed, of Paul's first published story, "The Waterfall," written more than twenty years earlier. In "Pages from Cold Point," it was as if he was starting all over again, flexing newfound muscles and talents and knowledge, redoing childhood sentiment.

In the earlier story, the son has thrown himself over a cliff into the waterfall; and the father, though angry at first, is drawn by guilt and remorse into following him, joining his son in death. In "Pages from Cold Point," the union of father and son is not in death but in life. But just as the father surrendered to fate by throwing himself into the chasm in "The Waterfall," so Norton surrenders to his fate when he sees Racky in his bed, asleep on his side and naked. "Destiny," Norton writes, "when one perceives it clearly from very near, has no qualities at all." And of Racky he says that he "lay so still. Warm and firm, but still as death."

In "The Waterfall," the tension between father and son, told through the eyes of the father, is resolved by the father's punishment through death. In this new story, again told through the father's eyes, the tension between father and son is resolved by having the boy allow the father to take him, to become one with him, taking on his innocence and destroying it in the same act. The angry father has become the desiring father. The boy who surrendered and died has become the boy who surrenders and wins.

After his arrival in Morocco, Paul went first to Fez, where he lived in a state of continual excitement. The ancient city was little changed from the Fez he had known before the war. There were no sounds of automobile traffic but only the sounds of bells on horse-drawn carriages. "Outside the walls at Babel Hadid, where my room looked across the valley of the Oued el Zitoun, there were shady paths where the wind rattled the high canebrake."

From Fez he traveled north to Tangier, then on to Spain—to Algeciras, Córdoba, and Ronda—then back to Tangier. He moved from hotel to hotel, finally settling into the El Farhar, where he had a two-room cottage with a fireplace and a wonderful view. He bought an Amazon parrot and wrote to Jane, telling her that Morocco was still what it had been and that she must come as soon as possible. He also arranged to buy the house in the medina, on the Place Amrah, for five hundred dollars, after persuading Oliver Smith to share the cost. However, as the house was not livable, he continued to reside at the El Farhar.

Almost from the moment he arrived in Morocco, he had been working on his novel. Up to this time, his prose work had been in the realm of the short story. But now he was committed to a long prose work, one that would have to be lived with for an extended period of time. He chose as his protagonists a husband and wife, Port and Kit Moresby. Just as Jane had used Paul and herself as models for Mr. and Mrs. Copperfield in *Two Serious Ladies,* now he used himself and Jane as models for Port and Kit. Married for twelve years, they arrive in North Africa, "fleeing the aftermath and memory of the war." They have not had sexual relations for some time. They are nevertheless deeply tied: ". . . a section of [Kit's] consciousness annexed [Port] as a buttress, so that in part she identified herself with him."

Kit has many of the same terrors Jane had. She is fearful of trains, of tunnels, and of trestles. She is fearful of omens of any sort. As for Port, he is described at the beginning as thin, "with a slightly wry, distraught face." He is a man obsessed with the desire to travel, who does not think of himself as a tourist. "He was a traveler."

Shortly after their arrival in Africa, Port goes for a walk alone, but as he progresses into the town an image comes into his mind of Kit, seated at the open window of the hotel room, looking out. For him, she is the spectator and he is the protagonist of the drama he is enacting. But she is not a passive spectator. In fact, the very validity of his existence, Port believes, is predicated upon her watching him. Further, Port feels that Kit and Kit alone knows when he will turn or when he will choose another direction, as if in knowing she has already made the choice for him. In the medina, the choice Port makes is to sleep with a beautiful female prostitute, who tries to rob him.

On their trip to North Africa, the Moresbys have brought along a friend, Tunner. It is as though on this journey of the imagination Paul has acceded to Jane's wishes in life, that they have a third person with them when they travel, to divert her from that "gloom" of his that so weighed upon her. In the novel, of course, the presence of the third person will serve as a crucial dramatic element in the unfolding relationship between Port and Kit.

Living in the world of the novel day by day, Paul began

to incorporate into it aspects of the life he was living. By chance, in Fez and in Tangier, and then in Spain, Paul had met a mother and son whose bizarre behavior piqued his interest. This mother and son became transformed in the novel into Mrs. Lyle and her son, Eric, who play a pivotal part in the destruction of the Moresbys. Port meets the Lyles at the hotel shortly after his arrival and chooses to accept a ride in their car with them, while Kit and Tunner take the train to the desert town where they are to meet. On the train, terrified by the journey, Kit submits to Tunner's advances. When the three meet again, Port becomes suspicious that something has taken place between Kit and Tunner. On the next leg of the journey into the desert, Port arranges to leave Tunner behind. As the two travel further and further into the desert, Port discovers that his passport has been stolen (by Eric), and he falls mortally ill with typhoid.

When Paul came to what was to happen next in the novel, the death of Port, he hesitated. He had never written about death before except in "The Waterfall," and that was only a fantasy of a young boy. But here he would have to stay with Port in his dying, to live out his dying with him. At this point, he says in *Without Stopping,* he decided to hand the job over to his subconscious. He purchased some majoun and, after ingesting it, waited for it to produce its effect. Lying on his bed, he imagined the death of Port and wrote out the scene the next day, using detail from that mind-altering experience.

Whether consciously or not, in telling how he wrote this part of *The Sheltering Sky* many years after the event, Paul omitted a crucial step. As can be seen in a letter he wrote to composer Peggy Glanville-Hicks in December 1947 from the Hotel Palais Jamai in Fez, Paul spent some time waiting for the narrative to resolve itself. He told Glanville-Hicks of his hopes to get permission to travel into the Sahara. Then he mentioned the novel, telling her that it seemed to be "taking a small rest . . . I had meant to kill the 'hero' off halfway through, but I can't seem to let him go. He lingers on in agony instead of dying. But I'll get rid of him yet, I assure you. Once he's gone there'll be only the heroine left to keep things going, and that won't be easy." In fact, while the novel was "taking a small rest," what Paul did was to write another story, apparently totally disconnected from the novel.

"How Many Midnights" is a subtle story of betrayal and abandonment, set in New York on a winter night. It is told through the eyes of June, a young woman who goes to her fiancé's apartment to wait for him to return from work. Van, the fiancé, has given her his keys, an action that she takes as a profound sign of his trust in her. June is very excited, as this is the first time she will spend the night with him and, presumably, the first time they will have sex. As she waits for him, she moves the furniture around to match her vision of the way his apartment should look. She waits and waits for his arrival, but Van never comes. The next morning, discovering that his overnight case is gone, she realizes that he never intended to join her. He did not tell her; he simply allowed her to find out.

Though this story apparently has no relevance to *The Sheltering Sky,* it shares with the novel a preoccupation with betrayal and abandonment. From Port's viewpoint, Kit has betrayed him first with Tunner and then betrayed him a second time by abandoning him while he was dying. In the story, June is abandoned and betrayed by Van, though there is the implication that since she was the kind of woman who would "take over" his apartment, he has some justification in his action.

Once he had written this story of betrayal, it was possible for Paul to "let go" of his hero. He would now be able to write the story of Port's death, with or without majoun. Just as the writing of "Pages from Cold Point" had some-how propelled him forward into the beginning of the novel, so writing "How Many Midnights" served to propel him out of its middle, toward its end. Story resolved story for him.

In December 1947, after several weeks of waiting in Fez, Paul received permission from the authorities to go into the Sahara. He traveled to Oujda, and from there to Colomb-Béchar and then on to Timimoun. In the course of this trip, he found the final resolution to Port's death. This resolution was also a going back for him, a return to the quality of feeling of the episode of depersonalization he had had at sixteen, the severing of his sense of his body from himself. Of that episode in Roth's soda fountain, Paul writes in *Without Stopping* that he never told anyone about it. "I suspected that if I were to put it into words, it would somehow become more threatening and true."

But two decades after the event, as he was getting rid of Port, he finally did put it into words. Altered to fit the situation of Port, the memory was told, and in the telling it became more "true." For all the shuffling of detail, the essential quality of the memory entered with full force into Port's consciousness as he dies, giving it a hallucinatory power.

Once he had managed to kill off his hero, Paul was ready to proceed with the rest of the novel: the fate of Kit as, alone, she escapes into the desert, first into isolation and then into her sexual adventures, specifically into being raped, which becomes so pleasurable to her. At this point in the novel, as Paul has often maintained, a profound change took place in the character of Kit. Whereas earlier she had been modeled on Jane, now, he insists, she emerged as a being totally detached from Jane. (Jane herself was never to believe this discontinuity. In fact, in the later years of her illness, she would keep saying to Paul that he had prophesied her terrible end in Kit's end.)

I have mentioned that in my own reading of this work in 1977, when I came to Kit's adventure in the desert, I concluded that it was in some way connected to Paul's own sexual fantasies. But now, writing this book, another possibility presents itself. What if this narrative of Kit's sexual journey is not a sexual fantasy but is rather an accurate and precise representation of Paul's conception of the way a being—man or woman—would act if he or she were isolated in a universe of guilt, betrayal, grief, and abandonment?

Would this being, this character, in the face of an overwhelming threat to the self, throw himself or herself into a kind of anti-universe of feeling, in which pain is pleasure, humiliation is praise, and violence is tenderness? In such a universe, there would be no distinction between the one who does the betraying and the one who is betrayed, between the one who does the abandoning and the one who is abandoned.

Paul was in Timimoum when a cable arrived from Jane, saying that she was arriving in Gibraltar on January 31 and asking him to meet her. Immediately Paul set out for Algiers and then northern Morocco, a journey that took six days. After Jane's arrival in Morocco with her new lover (whom I called Cory in *A Little Original Sin*), she and Cory traveled through Morocco for a few weeks. Then Cory left, and Jane joined Paul in Fez. There, at the Hotel Belvedere, with Jane writing in an adjoining room, Paul worked on the last part of *The Sheltering Sky*. At the same time, Jane was completing "Camp Cataract," a tragic-comic novella with hallucinatory overtones.

Paul has written about their stay at the Belvedere in a curious paragraph in *Without Stopping:*

> At the break of day we would have breakfast in bed in Jane's room. Then I would go into my own room, leaving the door open so that we could communicate if we wanted. At one point she had a terrible time with a bridge she was trying to build over a gorge. She would call out: "Bupple! What's a cantilever, exactly?" or "Can you say a bridge has buttresses?" I, immersed in the writing of my final chapters, would answer anything that occurred to me, without coming out of my voluntary state of obsession. She would be quiet for a while, and then call out again . . . After three or four mornings I became aware that something was wrong; she was still at the bridge. I got up and went into her room. We talked for a while about the problem, and I confessed my mystification. "Why do you have to *construct* the damn thing?" I demanded. "Why can't you just say it was there and let it go at that?" She shook her head. "If I don't know how it was built, I can't see it."

Yes, I know that there is a bridge in "Camp Cataract." (It is described in the published story in one sentence: "A series of wooden arches, Gothic in conception, succeeded each other all the way across the bridge; bright banners fluttered from their rims . . .") So it is not that I doubt that Jane asked Paul questions about the bridge. But the very selectivity of the paragraph—and of the questions she asked and of his conclusion—suggests how much has been omitted here.

Let me back up a little to go over how it once had been between them. In 1942 she had come to him in Mexico with the manuscript of her novel. At that time, she had been the writer in the family, and he had been the editor-helper-adviser, entering into her fictional world and suggesting the form necessary to give it substance. Now he, as much writer as she, was immersed in his own compelling fictional world. Aided by whatever he could find to help him—the desert, Morocco, majoun, memory—he had been finding his own way in solitude, trying to achieve a mastery in the work that would also help quiet his own internal demons.

She had followed him into his chosen world—Morocco, North Africa. At the Belvedere, they were writing side by side. He was working quickly, with confidence, continuing to maintain his arduous self-discipline, completing the novel for which he had a contract. She had already published her novel, and it had been dismissed or greeted with contempt. She had been trying to write another novel, for which she had no contract, but she had been blocked for months. She turned to him for help, even as she saw him so engrossed in his fictional world. Call it a bridge that preoccupied her. She asked about a bridge, and he answered, with irritation, needing to get back to his own work, to end his narrative of a woman wandering alone and mad in the desert, a woman who had begun as a being modeled after Jane—Jane, who at that very moment, in an adjoining room with connecting doors, is asking him questions about her own imaginative life, intruding into his own.

In coming to Morocco, in the writing of his novel (which

was inseparable from his coming to Morocco), Paul was bringing himself to a break with his past, with what he had been and with what he had been with Jane as well. And if it had been her work, her imagination, that had incited him to return to the exploration of his own, why should it be surprising to think that once launched into his own imaginative work, he should have to protect himself against the power of her imagination? (In that sense, had she become *his* "enemy"?)

Soon after Paul completed the novel, he wrote a story, yet one more story to complete the chain of narratives he had begun when he left the U.S. "The Circular Valley" is a mythical, almost totemic work about a spirit, the Atlájala, residing in a valley. Over the centuries, the spirit has lived by slipping into the body of one human inhabitant of the valley after another. Once inside its host, the Atlájala, who is incapable of experiencing any emotion on its own, experiences the emotions of the host and, at times, can even impel him or her to action before slipping out again to enter yet another host. For all that Paul has maintained that "The Circular Valley" is only a story about the spirit of a place, one cannot help seeing that the story of the Atlájala is an allegory of the fiction writer slipping into a character, then slipping out again.

22 When *The Sheltering Sky* was published in September 1949 in England, it was a great success. In October, upon publication in the U.S., the novel immediately leaped onto the best-seller list. It was regarded as a visionary work. Though set in the exotic locale of North Africa, it was seen by many as an accurate portrayal of the contemporary world, harsh, hostile, and unforgiving.

During the previous ten years, for all that Paul had gained a reputation as a composer of chamber works, songs, operas, and ballets, most of his time had been devoted to writing incidental music for the theater. The purpose of incidental music is to underpin the drama, to heighten the emotional impact of the play; the music itself is to be heard only subliminally. But now Paul had been heard, and heard with approval. He was no longer underlining others' thoughts and others' dramas. Ahead of him was a future in which he would earn his living by his writing. He had brought about a change in his own existence.

In December 1949, finally free to travel as he wished, Paul boarded a freighter from Antwerp en route to Ceylon. Sailing south along the coast of Europe, the freighter, a Polish ship called the *General Walter,* experienced very rough weather, but suddenly off the coast of Portugal the seas became calm. The night the ship sailed through the Strait of Gibraltar, Paul stood on deck, looking south. "I could see faint lights in the fog and I knew that was Tangier," Paul has said. "I wanted very much to stop and see it, but not being able to since the boat went right on past, I created my own Tangier. I started by imagining that I was standing on the cliff looking out at the place where I was on the ship."

He left the deck and went down to his berth, where he began to write the scene that eventually became chapter 8 of a new novel. By the time the freighter reached Suez, he had laid out the plot of the novel and defined the characters, working backward and forward from that initial scene on the cliff. He even drew a series of diagrams to direct him as to where the novel would go. The title would be *Let It Come Down,* the words of the First Murderer as he stabs Banquo in the third act of *Macbeth.* The protagonist would be Nelson Dyar, an American who had spent the previous ten years working as a bank clerk in New York. On impulse, he accepts an offer of a job from an old acquaintance who runs a travel agency in Tangier.

Unlike Port Moresby, Nelson Dyar arrives in Tangier unencumbered by a wife. The character of Dyar, as Paul slips into him, is only vaguely defined or, rather, defined by one feeling—that he has lived a life in which nothing has happened to him. The driving force of the narrative is Dyar's need to bring about a change in his existence.

Soon after his arrival in the city, which is an International Zone, Dyar wanders into the native quarter and has sex with a prostitute. Unlike Port, Dyar has no Kit to oversee and determine his next step. He is a free agent, ready to follow out his impulses wherever they take him. In his further involvement with the prostitute, he finds himself a rival for her attentions with a powerful and unpleasant middle-aged woman. He allows himself to descend further into the seamy life of the city: he is drawn into a fraudulent money exchange scheme through the travel agency; he is recruited by a Russian agent as a spy and paid a small monthly income for his services. Still he continues to have the sense that his life has not changed.

Finally he determines that for once he will make something happen. He steals a large sum of money and arranges with Thami, the shady son of a well-to-do Moroccan family, to hire a boat so that he can escape from Tangier into the Spanish Zone of Morocco. Waiting out the time before his departure, Dyar goes to the house of Daisy Valverde, a European expatriate, who has invited him to dinner while her husband is away. At Daisy's suggestion, he takes majoun and, under its influence, he and Daisy have sex, though the sex is unimportant to him compared to the extraordinary sense of freedom that he derives from the majoun. He leaves Daisy and with Thami sets sail for the Spanish Zone, where he will start life anew.

While traveling in Ceylon and in India, Paul worked on the novel, but it did not progress easily, despite the fact that he had plotted out the entire work beforehand. In late April he returned to England and then went on to Paris, where Jane was living in a hotel with her friend Cory. She was working on her play and also on her novel, the never-to-be-completed *Out in the World*. By July Paul was back in Tangier, concentrating on the novel full time, but it was still offering resistance. To Peggy Glanville-Hicks in November he wrote that he was determined to finish the new book before returning to New York. He had been suffering from digestive difficulties, either from what he called a "liver attack" or from a gall bladder inflammation.

His book of stories had been published in England by Lehmann as *A Little Stone* in August 1950 and in the U.S. by Random House as *The Delicate Prey* in November. James Laughlin, who had published *The Sheltering Sky* at New Directions, was very upset that Paul's agent had gone to the larger publishing firm instead of staying with him, but the money from Random House was much better, so Paul had agreed to make the move. The reviews of the collection in England were very favorable, but some of the American critics took Paul to task for what they felt was an unnecessary emphasis on horror and disintegration and evil, a charge that he vehemently denied.

At the end of February 1951, from Tangier, where he was working on the novel but was still unable to finish it, he wrote in a letter to Peggy Glanville-Hicks a sentence suggesting that although he may have slipped into Dyar, it was Dyar who had taken him over: "As to news of myself—how can one send news of himself if nothing happens to him?"

In July Paul went to Xauen, a hill town in the Spanish Zone, hoping that immersion in the isolated landscape, one that reminded him of the landscapes of Poe, would help him end the novel. And indeed, in Xauen he witnessed a scene that allowed him to bring the work to completion.

Sitting in a café one night, he watched as a man from Jilala went into a trance and performed a bloodletting ritual. Dancing to the beat of drums, the Jilali, under the influence of kif, started to cry out, and the drummers responded with their own cries. Pulling out a knife, the Jilali slashed one arm in time to the beating of the drums, licked his own blood in ecstasy, and then began to slash his other arm and legs and smear the blood on his face.

That ritual performance was to enter *Let It Come Down* as a defining moment in Dyar's life. Dyar witnesses the trance of bloodletting—just as Paul had seen it—and when it is over, he feels freed from fear and from all that has kept him in his cage of nonexistence. He returns to the cottage where he has been hiding with Thami. There, under the influence of kif, suspicious that Thami is plotting to steal the money he himself has stolen, he kills the sleeping Thami by hammering a nail into his ear. (Paul took the method of killing Thami from a description he had read in a psychology book, of a case in France in the late 1800s.) Alone in the Spanish Zone with the money, Dyar has the profound sense that he has finally brought about a change in his existence.

In *The Sheltering Sky,* Port dies in the desert, a victim of his own intransigence, feeling betrayed. Kit too ends up a victim, having dropped out of sight, alone and mad. In *Let It Come Down,* however, the protagonist is no longer the victim. At the end, he is isolated and he may not escape punishment, but he has forced something to happen.

When Paul and I meet again, I bring up the ending of *Let It Come Down.* "It makes me think of Camus's *The Stranger,* when Meursault kills the man. It's as if he is saying to himself, I—Meursault—am doing this. And with Dyar, after the killing, he seems to feel that he has become—"

"He becomes somebody. And before he wasn't." Suddenly Paul laughs. "What you just said reminds me of the old verse of Lizzie Borden. Do you remember? 'She took an axe and gave her father forty whacks, and when she saw what she had done, she gave her mother forty-one.'" He says it lightly and melodically, and we both laugh. "She discovered who she was by giving the whacks to her father."

"You must have been quite conscious of that when you were writing, that he gained his identity by the killing."

"Well, yes, I was conscious of it, sure."

Abdelouahaid comes in from the kitchen and asks if we'd like some bread with cheese. We decline, and he goes out again. He's been having some himself, so he is offering some to us, Paul explains.

I turn to the blood ritual Paul had witnessed in Xauen, which he had incorporated directly into Dyar's experience. "I wanted to ask you about the way a ritual of this kind makes the one who watches feel he is the one who is performing it. At first when Dyar watches the ritual, he's an observer, right? But then during the course of the ritual, he becomes involved, and he begins to feel that he's a participant. He begins to feel that it's happening to him."

"Does he?"

"Well, he says he—"

"I know he feels it's happening *for* him."

"It's done for him but also to him." I pick up the novel and read a sentence describing Dyar's feelings as he watches the Jilali: " 'It was his own blood that spattered onto the drums and made the floor slippery.' "

"He watches this person, and he becomes this person. He is caught up in it. So—"

"Yeah, he feels empathy," Paul says, and I laugh, remembering a conversation we had in which he spoke of hating the use of the word "identification" but allowed that he didn't mind the use of "empathy."

"Had you ever had an experience similar to this before?" I ask.

"Not so intensely, I would think. No."

"This was different from anything that you had ever seen in the sense in which it pulled you in?"

"Of course. Because I was so near. I mean, I could have reached down and touched him. He was right in front of me."

"Had you ever experienced that in the American culture?"

Paul waits before answering. "I look for an example of such a thing back in New York, but I don't think so. One doesn't come up against things like that in American culture, at least not in New York. I've been to churches in Harlem where one feels very strongly, but still one is very conscious that they're doing what they're doing and you're watching."

"The way you describe the scene in *Let It Come Down* makes it seem like an exchange of selves or, rather, a merging of selves between the person watching and the person in the trance."

"Perhaps thanks to kif, thanks to the sound of drums—"

"There's also the power of seeing what this man is doing physically, seeing him slash himself, seeing the blood flow, seeing him smear the blood upon himself."

"Yeah, well . . . ," Paul says doubtfully.

"There's also something in the culture that allows this transformation to happen. Because it not only happens to Dyar, it happens to all the other men who are watching. They too become part of this man."

"I wouldn't say there's a transformation exactly. There's a beginning of one. But it doesn't really happen. You can see that it could, I suppose, if it went on long enough. Dyar might have found himself in a state of trance."

"But he does feel that it's happening to him," I remind Paul. "He feels that it's his blood that is falling on the floor."

"He feels that the purpose of the whole ritual is to bring people together. So it's not just a personal experience, it's a communal experience. And he feels that he is part of the group."

"He also feels that he's been changed through the experience. So then when he leaves the café, he leaves with the sense that he has no fear anymore."

"Does he really?" Paul asks. "I don't remember that."

"Oh, yes. I'll read you the passage," I say. "It's not that

I've got this book memorized, Paul, but . . . ," I laugh as I open to the necessary page.

"I believe you, whatever you say."

"Here is Dyar leaving the café:"

> He walked out into a wide place, dominated by a huge minaret, feeling only acute surprise to find that none of his fear was left. It had all been liberated by the past hour in the café. How he would never understand, nor did he care. But now whatever circumstance presented itself, he would find a way to deal with it.

"He finds a way," Paul laughs, "by murdering Thami."

I mention a book I've read on the connection between ritual and violence and sacrifice. "What you're saying," Paul interrupts me, "reminds me of one of Mrabet's early stories. It was published as 'The Well.' Toward the end of it, he says that he used to watch the sacrificing of sheep, and it made him nauseated. At one point a man looked at him and saw that he was pale, watching the blood drain out, and he put a glass under the vein in the sheep and filled it and gave it to Mrabet and said, 'Now you drink that.' And he did drink the warm blood. And after that he was never afraid. He never felt nauseated watching, which is interesting."

After a pause, I say, "No wonder you stayed in Morocco, Paul. Where else could you have found a communal culture that had that kind of thing built into it?"

Perhaps in other places, he suggests, but in places that would have felt like "other" cultures. "Whereas Moroccans," he says, "one can imagine them being like oneself. They're not, of course, but—"

"But they can be thought of as *not* the other."

"Yes. Oh, yes. I don't think of them as the other."

There is silence in the room. Paul, sitting up,
has slipped into sleep. When I arrived a little
while ago, I noticed how tired he looked. As
we began to talk, he mentioned that he was having difficulty speaking because his mouth was so dry from the medication he had just taken. Soon his eyes began to close,
though he struggled to keep them open. I suggested that
he take a few moments to rest, sitting there.

"No, that would be very rude," he protested. "I just shut
my eyes, but I hear everything you say."

"I'll be quiet," I said.

"No, don't do that."

"Don't do that?"

"No, that would really wake me up if you're quiet." At
this, he and I both laughed, but he went on. "Because I'll
think, Oh, I'm bothering her."

"It wouldn't bother me."

"Well, if you can't talk, it's bothersome."

"I can look at you," I said.

"A lot of good that'll do you," he responded, at which
we both laughed again. So I went on with my questions,
coming to a remark he had recently made that he felt there
was a compulsion in his need to travel without stopping.
But now when his eyes began to close, he did not resist
the closing. His words became slower, and he responded—
though here he was almost asleep—"I didn't know I said
it about me; I thought I said it about Jane."

"That Jane was compulsive?"

"Something she had done. I can't remember." His eyes
closed, and he slept.

I notice that my tape recorder is still running. I do not get
up to stop it; I don't want to make a noise and awaken
him. Seeing him asleep—his head fallen to his left, his

hands clasped in front of him, his mouth closed—I feel a sudden sense of his vulnerability to my gaze and at the same time a deep rush of affection for him. His face is more than ever the face of a boy, as well as of an older being. I turn away. I do not want to intrude upon him. Yet at the same time I feel I do not need to worry about intruding. His sleep does not seem a deep sleep. It seems rather a preparatory sleep. Still I do not stir. I look around the room, at the walls, once ochre, now dark with smoke and time. The ceiling is stained from the rainwater that has seeped down from the roof above.

In the dim light of the overhead lamp, I observe the dark pillows, the dark rugs, the bookcases filled with Paul's works and the works of others, the portable CD–tape player given to him by some of his friends, the huge basket of mail (unanswered), the overflow of letters on the floor. On the wall above the low couch opposite me, next to the fireplace, is a piece of frayed reed matting.

The solidity of things occupying one space, their space and no other . . . the ability of things to stop and be stopped in time, suggesting that in stillness more can be known . . .

I have a sudden sense of the strangeness of the enterprise I am now engaged in. What I am doing has to do with knowing, but not the kind of knowing that comes when you are with someone in daily life. I turn and look at Paul. I am aware of the movement of his breath in and out while he is at rest. How powerful the effect of the breathing of others is upon us.

I have come to a stopping place.

At the sound of a knock on the door, Paul stirs and awakens instantly. There is no sudden surprise in his eyes, the way there is in some sleepers waking. He slips as easily out of sleep as he has slipped in. "I opened my eyes just in time. Probably Abdelouahaid."

"Should I answer it?"

"You want to?" he asks.

"Sure."

"You don't mind getting up."

"No," I say.

"Not as much as I do," he says.

 But, of course, there is really no stopping place with Paul. The next day I find myself back again on an edge, crossing and recrossing a border—a line of the purest defense.

Today Paul leads the way by repeating how incensed he is at what Sawyer-Lauçanno wrote about him. Once again he voices his objection to the allegation that he didn't pay his own way when he was young, that his friend Harry Dunham gave him part of his allowance so that he, Paul, could travel.

"It's not true at all. It's all out of his head," Paul says indignantly.

"But even if it were true," I say, "what would be so wrong with it? Dunham was very wealthy, and you had hardly a cent."

"Nothing, not by my reckoning, of course not. It's true that Harry Dunham gave me enough money so I could get to Berlin, but that's all. Sawyer-Lauçanno couldn't let anything pass. He had to use all that space in the book to denigrate me during the thirties."

It is clear that Sawyer-Lauçanno's allegations continue to rankle, that Paul cannot shake them off. It is like a judgment that has the weight of other accusations riding on it. It is odd to see this in Paul. But then I should know that how anyone feels about money is very mysterious, at the same time as it seems so obvious—that feelings about money can absorb many other feelings and anxieties, can take up old wounds, old losses, and old desires. In more than one sense, money is a medium of exchange.

When I bring up with Paul the question of his feelings about money in his childhood, he recalls an incident from the time he was a boy, when he was staying with his Aunt Mary at her home, Holden Hall. "My parents were there and my cousin Elizabeth. I had an orange for breakfast, and when I had eaten it, I committed the serious error of asking if I might have another. There was a big basket of them on the table. My father said, 'Certainly not; you can't. When you get out in the world, you'll find out that you won't have oranges. They cost money.' So I didn't have the orange. But when I went outside after breakfast with my cousin, she said, 'Don't you pay any attention to him. When you go out in the world, you won't have oranges, you'll have grapefruit.'"

I notice again how when Paul takes on his father's voice, his tone has such intensity and immediacy that it seems the words are being said for the first time, at this very moment, to him.

"So was he saying that you were going to be hungry when you went out into the world?"

"Yeah."

"Was he also saying that because you were someone who lived so much in the imagination, you would never be practical?"

"He didn't say that, but he certainly thought it. Yes. That I would never be able to earn my own living."

"And that you'd be hungry for that reason."

"Yes. Destitute. He was always trying to scare me with this fear of poverty."

"And were you actually fearful of being hungry and being poor?"

"Well, of course, that's what my father told me," Paul says so matter-of-factly that I laugh.

"But though you were so fearful of being hungry and being poor, you still ran away to Europe by yourself at eighteen with almost no money."

I am reminded of a story he once told me about Jane. When asked why she had gone out to walk on the docks in New York late at night, she had said to Paul that that was what she was afraid of, so she had to do it. "Did it work the same way with you?" I ask. "I mean, to go to a strange country with no money. Was that because you were afraid and you had to do what you were afraid of?"

"No, I don't think so. I think I went in spite of being afraid, not because of it. I somehow believed that I would live, that I would survive."

"Even though your father said, 'You're going to be poor, you're going to be destitute.' "

"Well, I thought I probably would be very poor."

"So you always had to save what you had because the next moment might be total destitution."

"Yes, of course. Well, I think it makes sense. I still think it makes sense. Even though the value of money has deteriorated very much."

This all seems simple and straightforward enough when I recall that right after Paul began his journeys out into the world, the Great Depression started, and the economic situation reinforced everything his father had said to him about the difficulty he would face in earning a living. Even as late as the early 1950s, after the success of *The Sheltering*

Sky, when Paul mentioned to Brion Gysin how much he would enjoy having a car, and Gysin told him he could afford a car so he should buy one, Paul was shocked. He had never thought of himself as a car owner, he has written. "Nor had it occurred to me that money was something to be spent. Automatically, I always had hoarded it, spending as little as possible. Brion's suggestion was like the voice of Satan." Heeding Gysin's suggestion, Paul did buy a car, a new Jaguar convertible.

That "sinful" spending, however, remained an exception to his usual behavior. He has continued to believe his father's dire warnings about the poverty that will always lie ahead of him. As he puts it, "it still makes sense," so he errs on the side of caution by not spending. This is so even in the face of the fact that as an expatriate, he has, from the moment of coming here, been regarded as "wealthy" in Moroccan terms. And it is that "wealth" that allows him to define his relationship with Moroccans in a particular way, creating a staging area, an arena where dramas of another sort can be played out.

In *Days: Tangier Journal (1987–1989),* Paul recounts an incident that arose out of a disagreement about money between Mohammed Mrabet and Cherie Nutting, an incident in which he seems to have been only a bystander. It began when Mrabet agreed to build a house for Cherie in Tangier for ten thousand dollars. Cherie gave Mrabet the money, and he started construction but soon ran out of funds. At that point, he refused to give her the partially completed house or to return the money to her.

They were at an impasse when one day Cherie arrived in Paul's flat carrying a huge bunch of roses and lilies for Paul. Seeing a large vase with a small array of white roses in it, she decided to move the older flowers into a smaller vase and replace them with her new bouquet.

Mrabet, who had brought the white roses the day before, went into a rage. (It was during Ramadan, the Muslim month of observance when believers must abstain from food and drink all day long, and Mrabet was even more vulnerable to irritation than usual.) He began to shout, and then he started throwing cushions at Cherie, "and finally," writes Paul, "hauled off and gave her a resounding crack in the face." Mrabet then picked up a log from the fireplace and swung it at her head. Abdelwahab, another Moroccan who was present, intervened and calmed Mrabet down. "But then," Paul goes on, "Mrabet must have felt that he had been bought too easily, and began to bellow that he was in a room full of Jews who should be killed and not allowed to pollute the air breathed by a Muslim."

Although some of those in the room seemed shocked by Mrabet's behavior, Paul himself was not, "having seen other instances of his insensate fury, but I was ashamed that all this should have happened in my flat, and to a guest of mine. In reality," Paul adds, "Mrabet has a bad conscience, and when a Moroccan feels guilty, he attacks."

When I asked Cherie recently if the argument had been settled by now, she said Mrabet had told her that, if she gave him nine thousand dollars more, he would finish the house for her. Since she didn't have the money, she added, Paul gave Mrabet the money. But then Mrabet turned around and sold the house to someone else.

"I don't understand what was going on there," I say to Paul. "What really happened?"

"Well, Cherie asked Mrabet if he could build her a house on this land that she had bought, and he said, 'Oh, yes,' and then she said, 'Well, how much do you think it would cost?' And he said, 'Oh, not much.' And then she said, 'Well, do you think I could get a house for ten thousand dollars?' And he said, 'Oh, you can get a palace,' and so on. So she gave him nine thousand and kept one thousand, after which he built a house. Then he said, 'I've built a house, but it's not for you. You can't have it. It belongs to me.'"

"What was in his mind, do you think?"

"Well, he wanted the house free, no? He saw a chance of having a house and not paying for it. That was all that was in his mind. That's fairly simple. So then he wouldn't give it to her. Then he began feeling guilty—this is my interpretation—so he got very unpleasant to her and nastier and nastier until finally he had this big scene where he socked her in the face in front of everybody. He's crazy."

"But, Paul, when he demanded nine thousand dollars more from her to finish the house and she didn't have it, Cherie says you gave it to him to finish the house for her. Is that true?"

"That's true, but it had nothing to do with her."

"Oh, I thought you did it for her."

"No. By that time, I knew she was not going to get the house. He had spent the nine thousand on it, and it wasn't finished, and I thought better to have a finished house than a half-finished house."

"So you gave him the money."

"So I gave him more, yes. Well, he finished the house. But it's not good at all. He doesn't want to use it."

"But didn't Cherie say he has sold it?" I ask.

"I don't think he has."

"So she doesn't quite understand what's going on."

"No, she doesn't," says Paul. "I don't either."

"Nobody understands it, perhaps not even Mrabet."

"Well, nothing's going on as far as I know," Paul says

and laughs. "He's either sold it or he hasn't sold it. But it doesn't matter; he's not going to give the money to her. He promised if he ever sold it to pay her back. Well, I thought that sounded very empty. He won't, of course. No, of course not."

After this explanation of the incident, I am even more puzzled. The fight took place in Paul's apartment, where, no matter what happens, as I have come to see, Paul is the central figure about whom everything circulates. It was ostensibly a fight about money, but there were certainly other things involved, other jealousies, other resentments, always present in every ongoing drama concerning Paul. In writing the story or in his retelling of it to me, Paul gives no hint of what those other things might be, saying only that he was "ashamed" to have a guest of his treated this way. It seems an odd word for him to have chosen, as if politeness to a guest were the crucial matter at issue, not violence or rage or the possibility that the guest could have been badly hurt.

What puzzles me most is what he said about giving the money to Mrabet because he thought it "better to have a finished house than a half-finished house." It is one of those simple declarative sentences of Paul's, stating a so-called obvious truth and yet suggesting by the tone and the inflection that it is tied by innumerable strands to innumerable levels of hidden meaning.

One day in 1977, I spoke to Paul about the question of privacy and his own personal life. What of his private life belonged in the book about Jane? What did not? He answered that he would talk to me about those situations in his personal life that had a direct bearing upon Jane. Of his own separate, intimate life, of those things that had no connection with Jane, he would not speak.

In all his public statements in the years up to that point, he had been scrupulous in not revealing anything about his own sexual orientation. He made it clear that he thought it was no one's business but his own. I respected his wishes in the matter, and in the book I let those relationships of his that did not involve Jane be understood without defining them in any precise way.

Of course, since 1977 a great change has occurred in how openly people deal with their sexual orientation. Even for someone of Paul's generation, who for so many years was vigilant not to disclose his preference—for legal as well as other reasons—that change has had a profound effect. In the biography of Paul by Robert Briatte, published in France in 1989, for the first time Paul made a clear statement in print of his own sexual preference.

As if yet again having to redefine the terms of our discourse, I bring up the Briatte quote when I next see Paul. "You made a statement to him about sexuality. Do you remember what you said?"

"No," Paul says. "Why would I remember?" He reminds me that he was ill in bed during the entire time Briatte interviewed him. "He had a microphone hung up over my head. And I just talked."

"One of the things that you said to him is that you don't believe in love and you never loved anybody, et cetera, et cetera. But that's Mr. Briatte's book, not my book. In his book, he quotes you as saying that you always preferred men to women and that Jane always preferred women to men."

"I think that's true."

I mumble an assent.

"It is true," Paul reiterates.

"I think that's sufficient. Is that sufficient for you?"

"I don't know what you mean, if it's sufficient."

I'm not quite sure what I mean, either, so I take a step sideways. I speak of there being a "crossover" between sexuality and creativity. (It is as if I am saying, This is not going to be just about sex as sex.)

"There must be. Oh, yeah, there is, I'm sure; yes."

"I don't know whether it's possible to talk about this crossover in abstract terms—"

"Crossover means connection?" Paul asks.

When I nod, he says, "I think that there is a definite connection. Don't you think?"

"I think nobody knows how the connection works. . ."

"It's probably different in everybody; it's probably not a general design."

In Sawyer-Lauçanno's book on Paul, he quotes Virgil Thomson as saying, "Paul had a very low sex drive. It just wasn't important to him." Then he quotes Thomson a second time to substantially the same effect. "Paul was never of an ordinary sexual temperament. How much actual power of ejaculation there was in Paul I never knew but I always guessed it as low."

"That's his idea," Paul answers heatedly when I bring up Virgil's statement. "He didn't know anything about it."

"Why do you think Virgil said that to him?"

"Why would he? I don't know. I don't know whether he was interested in, as they say, putting me down."

"Virgil was—?"

"Yeah, I think he was. All the time I knew him, which was many years, he often showed very definite symptoms of jealousy. He had no reason to. I mean, he was famous, he had everything he wanted. But," Paul corrects himself, "maybe he didn't have everything he wanted. I don't know what more he wanted."

I recall what Virgil wrote in his autobiography about first meeting Paul in Paris in 1931. Paul had come to Virgil's studio with Harry Dunham, and Virgil was dazzled by their blondness and their radiance. Virgil himself, for all his brilliance and wit and charm, was not physically dazzling, while Paul's physical beauty was remarkable in its effect on women as well as men. When I first met Paul, though he was sixty-seven and no longer blond but white-haired, he was still luminous, and I responded to him just the way everybody else did. I tell Paul in a slightly embarrassed way—though luckily one of the benefits of age is that it reduces your susceptibility to embarrassment—about how I had responded to him. "Though," I add, "I didn't mention it. After all, that wasn't why I was there." At this, we both laugh. "So I was surprised when I read what Sawyer-Lauçanno said Virgil had said."

"I was indignant when I read what he wrote because he said more or less, 'He has no sex, it's very, a very low power—very low drive.' I don't know what got into Virgil. He decided, 'Well, I'm going to say that Paul was really asexual.' I guess he got a kick out of that because he always said that creativity and sex went together."

"Oh, he did?"

"Yes. The higher your sex drive, the more creative you were."

"So do you think he was—"

"He was saying I didn't have any talent." Paul laughs. "Very little talent. That was his way of saying it."

I cannot quite believe this, for I remember one of Virgil's comments in a review he wrote in the 1940s in which he asserted that Paul was the best composer of chamber music in the U.S. So what was Virgil's reason for the comment to Sawyer-Lauçanno? I recall that when I went to see Virgil in 1977 about Jane, we talked about her, and Paul was barely mentioned. But in the early 1980s, after my book on Jane was published, Morris Golde, who had known Paul and Jane in the thirties and forties, invited me to dinner with Virgil, and then I saw another side of Virgil besides the composer and writer I so admired. He was witty, cantankerous, even outrageous in his statements about Paul (as well as about others). But it seemed to me that this was Virgil's style, to incite controversy, to see how others would respond, to see whether they would rise to the bait.

To Paul, I say only, "He may have been jealous of you."

"I know damn well he was, but I don't know why. I'm sure he considered his music far better than mine. He certainly was a better critic."

"He was very famous and successful," I admit.

"Yes. I was not. He really had nothing visible, no visible reason for any jealousy."

"Jealousy often doesn't have a visible reason."

"But it has a reason, whether it's visible or invisible." Paul recalls an incident that took place in Paris in 1932, when his mother came to take care of him after he became ill with typhoid. After he had recovered, he says, "I was sitting with her, having a drink somewhere, I don't remember where, and Virgil was there. And he said in the most pitiful way, 'I wish I had a mother that would come and see me.' What the hell. My mother felt very sorry for him. And she said, 'Oh, doesn't he have a mother?' And I said, 'I don't know; I think he has. I think she's alive, living in

Kansas City.' She said, 'Well, why doesn't she come and see him if he feels that way?' "

"Well, for whatever reason," I say, puzzled by the insertion of mothers into this discussion, "he must have been jealous of you for quite a long time to lash out as he did."

"Always, I think. From the time we met. He may have been jealous—why—because Gertrude Stein invited me to her house; I mean, a silly reason like that—it could be."

"Maybe he was jealous because of the life that you led, which was one of freedom and—"

"Well, he had freedom."

"He did?"

"Well, didn't he? It seems to me he had."

"Maybe he didn't think so."

"Why not? It becomes more complicated if he thought he wasn't free and he thought I was. I don't know . . ."

Reading *Without Stopping,* you come to realize that Paul lived a childhood in which almost everything that had to do with sex was dealt with in secrecy. He says that he did not discover that there were anatomical differences between male and female until he studied biology in high school. He maintains that he never saw a male or female unclothed until he took a life drawing class at art school when he was sixteen, and then he felt a sense of disgust at the way the models looked: the women had too much flesh and the men too much hair.

As for any facts about procreation, those too were kept from him. Learning at a young age that mammals were born alive from the mother, he asked his mother a question: if a baby was born from the mother's body, how was it possible that often the baby was said to look like the father? Rena answered by saying that it was a great mystery; no one really understood how it worked. And there the discussion ended.

If by chance something was forced upon his attention having to do with sex in even a peripheral way, he stoically disregarded it. One Sunday morning when he was about seven, he heard laughter coming from the room where his visiting Aunt Emma was staying. He ran in and saw his father in his pajamas in bed with his Aunt Emma, while his mother, at the foot of the bed, was shrieking with laughter. When Claude saw Paul, he got out of the bed and said they must all have breakfast immediately. A little while later his mother warned him that he must not tell anyone that he had seen his father in bed with Aunt Emma.

"I won't; but why?" Paul asked.

"They might think it was terrible," his mother answered.

"What do they care? It's none of their business," Paul said. Nor did he care, or so he remembers feeling. It didn't matter to him what his father and Aunt Emma were doing. What did matter to him—and he held to it with tenacity—was the world he himself could create, a world into which no adult could enter.

In 1919, when he was eight, he started an imaginary diary that he called "Bluey," after the name of his protagonist, a young girl who in turn was based upon a doll he had been given. In this diary, Bluey falls in love with a man called Henry, and Henry falls in love with Bluey. But this love story, if that's what it is, is interspersed with entries on the weather (the temperature and the depth of the snow), on illness, on sudden death, on travel, on Bluey's driving a self-steering car. Henry does say to Bluey in one entry that "they cannot have a child until they get married," but that statement is immediately followed by one about the weather. Bluey and Henry get married, but the marriage is only one brief entry among many others, given no more weight than anything before or after it: "16 degrees. Bluey has a fight with Henry. Bluey yells." "Greatest storm in world's history. 13 degrees. Bluey knocks Henry down . . ."

What sense of continuity there is in the diary derives only from the fact that one day's entry follows another. But the total effect of the work is strangely surrealistic, juxtaposing unrelated facts and events and annihilating elements of cause and effect. By an apparent linkage of events and fact through chronology and then a sudden destruction of that linkage, Paul at eight and nine was able to hold disparate things in suspension in his fictional world. What he knew and what he did not know about sex and the body, what he felt and what he did not feel about love and hate and death, all were kept in place and held apart by the entries that he wrote in solitude in his room.

There was, however, one thing Paul as a child did know about the body, one thing that he was not only allowed to know but was forced to know. This was the vulnerability of the body—all and any bodies—to disease and accident and, above, all, to pain. One of Paul's earliest memories is of his father saying he was responsible for his mother's pain during and after his birth. So the body (his, in this case) was also dangerous: wittingly or unwittingly, it could cause pain to others' bodies.

Even Claude, especially Claude, for all his tyrannical behavior to Paul, was vulnerable to pain. One morning, when Paul was ten or so, his father woke up with the vision in his left eye gone, as a result of a hemorrhage. Claude continued to practice dentistry, never letting his patients know that with only one eye his depth perception was impaired.

His father had always been a hypochondriac, Paul tells us, and after this time, his preoccupation with his own bodily ills increased.

Claude became a believer in Fletcherizing—chewing each mouthful of food forty times, as recommended by a Dr. Horace Fletcher for health—and imposed this practice on Paul. Because Paul was having orthodontic treatment, he was already experiencing pain whenever he ate, which the increased chewing only exacerbated. Every Tuesday and Friday from the time he was seven until he was seventeen, he had to go to the dentist's office so that the screws holding the bands in place could be tightened. "The pain this caused lasted two or three days, generally until just before the next tightening, so that there were very few days in the year when I could eat without wincing."

One day, at about the age of eleven, Paul made a deliberate attempt to explore his own body's response to pain. He had heard some girls at school speak of going to a circumcision ceremony. He asked his mother what a circumcision was, and she told him that when a baby was born, "they take the little penis and cut a piece off the end of it."

"I was thunderstruck," Paul remembers. He asked his mother why it was done. She responded that some people thought it was "cleaner." Paul got hold of a needle and, in the privacy of his room, experimented on himself. He reports that the pain was not so intense as he had expected, "nor was the experience really interesting."

As for sex as sex, its first conscious eruption within him was connected with the imagining of pain. In a letter to his friend Bruce Morrissette, written in January 1930 when Paul had just turned nineteen, he recalled that his first sexual thrills were obtained from reading newspaper accounts of electrocutions.

Only after Paul had run away from the U.S. to Europe at eighteen without telling his parents or the college authorities, only after he had crossed the necessary borders geographically, was he able to have his first sexual experience. In Paris one evening he met two couples, one in their twenties, the other in their thirties. One of the young women, Hermina, invited Paul to join them camping in the countryside. They all spent the night in a tent and in the morning went swimming in the Seine. "After lunch," Paul writes, "Hermina and I took a walk, still in our bathing suits, which made it bad for me when I ran innocently into a patch of high nettles. . . . The nettle stings were not the only initiatory experience for me that Sunday afternoon. There among hundreds of excited ants that rushed over us, while Hermina declaimed such sentiments as: 'I'm the flower, you're the stem,' I had my first sex."

Soon after, a man called Hubert, a friend of Paul's paternal grandparents, arrived in Paris. A couturier who dressed in silk shirts and matching jeweled cuff links, Hubert invited Paul to move into his hotel with him. As Paul recounts it, "And so I moved into the Hotel Daunou . . . and received a further sexual initiation, equally cold-blooded and ridiculous." Hubert had brought a check for two hundred dollars from Paul's father (Paul had finally let his parents know where he was), to be used for clothes for Paul. Instead, Hubert outfitted Paul completely in his own style at his own expense. In his telling of this incident, Paul acknowledges that he took some pleasure in the unfamiliar experience of being made to feel important, even though he found having to make conversation with Hubert boring.

With Hubert paying the way, they traveled in Italy and Austria and ended up in Dauville, where Hubert lost a large sum of money in the casino. Paul was horrified not only because Hubert lost the money but because he shrugged off the loss so easily. It gave Paul "a sick feeling to see money treated so lightly." The next morning he asked Hubert for the check his father had sent for clothes and used the money to purchase a ticket to return home to his family, a step Hubert had been encouraging him to take all along.

Here, as in much of *Without Stopping*, consciously or unconsciously, there is a reliance on the devices Paul had used in writing "Bluey" so many years before. Ostensibly, he is telling a chronological story of a life, his life. But at the same time that he is telling, paragraph by paragraph, he gives equal weight to large things and to small things. He juxtaposes events in such a way that the possibility of linkage to what has gone before is denied.

Yet think of what has gone before. His father has tyrannized him so—or such is his recollection—that the one certainty he has in his young life is that whatever he wants he will not have. His mother has been devoted to him—though even she sometimes makes a quixotic shift from closeness to disavowal of closeness—but she has been powerless to affect his father's judgment that he is never to get what he wants.

Now he has fled from the U.S. to Europe, a youth of eighteen, a beautiful youth at that. (His beauty is never mentioned in *Without Stopping*, as if it would be immodest to do so or as if it had no bearing on anything.) Now several people indicate to him that he is an object of desire. (Perhaps it has happened before; perhaps he has assiduously avoided recognizing what was happening.)

In these two "ridiculous and cold-blooded" sexual initiations, it is simply proved all over again that others (the seducers, the powerful ones) can have desires and their desires can be fulfilled, whereas he (the seduced, the weak one) is not allowed to have desires—so how could they ever be fulfilled?

 I have in mind a letter Jane wrote to Paul in August 1948. She was in Tangier, staying at the Hotel Villa de France. He was in New York, having been called back to compose the incidental music for Tennessee Williams's *Summer and Smoke*. In the letter, Jane wrote that she was making little headway in her pursuit of Cherifa and Tetum, another Arab woman. Then she lamented, "I am in a very poor frame of mind, suffering from what you suffer from in New York—except that it does not seem to interfere with *your* work. I find I can think of nothing else and yet I cannot *bring* myself to leave."

I remind Paul of Jane's letter and of what she said about his "suffering" in New York. "Can you say anything about whether your life was different once you came here? Was it easier than it had been in New York?"

"My life?"

"In terms of the sexual atmosphere," for I assumed the suffering to be sexual, from the context, "was it much more—I would imagine it would have been much more difficult there."

"New York?"

"Yeah."

"Oh, in New York, it was—it precluded any sexual activity. Wasn't any. If I stayed a year—I never stayed that long, but I could stay ten months—there wasn't any. No. How could there be?"

"Because of the mores . . ."

"Yeah."

"And because everybody knew everybody else, and—"

"No," he corrects me, "not because of that. Because of the setup, the disapproval of society, the"—and here Paul sighs—"presence of the police, the possibility of blackmail, all sorts of unpleasant things. So it was best to keep, you know, completely away."

"That made it awful."

"Well—that's not so awful, but it is boring."

"But other people took risks, didn't they?"

"Oh, I think most people did. How they could, I don't know—why they were not terrified."

But once he came to Morocco, I suggest, the situation was such that it allowed him to be freer, not to have to worry.

"Oh, one had different kinds of worry, but they weren't so acute. Remember, it was the International Zone then. They expected Europeans to be crazy, so it didn't matter much what Europeans did."

I ask Paul to say something further about the relationship between a European and a Moroccan in Morocco. Would it be governed by certain rules?

"I think so. Yeah, I think it went without saying. I think it applied to men and women both. What was defined was that the foreigner must supply the Moroccan with money. That's all. The amount isn't important, really. As much as the Moroccan can get."

"But if one enters into a more intimate relationship that still is the primary thing?"

"Of course."

"And so in a way, it limits certain things, or should limit certain things."

"It limits, perhaps, responsibilities."

"But you could still feel affection for the other person—deep affection for the other person," I say.

"You could. M-m-hm."

"But it wouldn't be anything like what is set up in Western mores with romantic love—"

"It wouldn't be like that. No."

"So if one enters into that kind of a relationship, idealization isn't a part of it."

"Oh, I wouldn't think so. No."

"So one looks at the other person and says, 'This person wants money; that's why they're staying with me.' Is it something like that?"

"Well, yes."

"In other words, you don't say, 'Oh, but still they have to or they ought to love me.'"

"If you expect them to, you're crazy. A lot of the Europeans do, and then they weep and wail and wring their hands."

"The way it is in *A Life Full of Holes*," I say, referring to Larbi Layachi's autobiographical novel, published in 1964. It was based on Larbi's narrative as recorded and translated by Paul. In the story, an Englishman becomes so obsessed with love for a young Moroccan man that he neglects the rules that govern the situation. Bit by bit, the young Moroccan takes over and asserts his dominance in the relationship. In this playing out of *tla el fouq*—the struggle to be "top dog"—the Englishman ends up losing all his money to the Moroccan, becoming an object of scorn and derision. Possessed by his own desire, he is unable to extricate himself from the situation.

"That was a true story," I say to Paul, "wasn't it?"

"Yes, I think it was."

In Paul's own fiction, whenever the sexual act appears, it is almost invariably played out as a drama of one person overcoming another, of one person dominating and the other submitting. In the early story "Under the Sky," Jacinto forces a woman tourist to have sex with him, threatening that if she does not submit, he will kill her friends. In "Doña Faustina," the woman protagonist struggles with a man who enters her room at night. After he ties her wrists, she submits to having sex with him and even feels a certain pleasure in the submission. In *The Sheltering Sky*, after Port's death, when Kit is wandering in the desert, she is raped repeatedly by two tribesmen and comes to take great delight in being overcome by the younger one. In *The Spider's House*, there is a single sex scene between Stenham and Lee Veyron. It does not involve rape, but it is a scene that doesn't make sense in the context of the novel. In fact, that scene did not exist in Paul's original manuscript, but he was pressured by his publishers to include a sex scene to make the book more commercially appealing. When you read this scene, you are aware of an almost physical revulsion between the two characters. The true connection in that novel is between Stenham and the Arab boy Amar, a bond that is tender and asexual, a bond Stenham ultimately betrays.

In "Pages from Cold Point," of course, the father, Norton, experiences great happiness in having sex with the son, who has passively placed himself in his bed. But the ultimate outcome of that sexual act is that Norton loses his power and must submit to the boy, a family version of *tla el fouq*.

And then there is "The Delicate Prey," a story of Paul's in which sex and violence are inextricably connected. When I discussed this story earlier with him, he told me he didn't think of it as a "horror" story, insisting that he had "understated the events." "If you're writing about unpleasant things, don't dwell on them. You go quickly through them, and that's it," he had said to me. Now I bring up the scene in the story in which the Moungari, after killing the two older Filali, wounds the young Filali boy and castrates him, then turns him over and rapes him.

"That's an act of absolute humiliation, isn't it?"

"Oh, yes. Sure. This was an insult. The Moungari was really insulting the Filala—all of the people, not just the boy but his relatives, his family, the citizens of his town, and so on."

"But he'd already done such violence to him. He'd already triumphed; he'd already taken everything. So what does the act of humiliation do for the Moungari?"

"Well, for him, it would be pleasant to inflict an ultimate indignity on the boy. That was the ultimate indignity, to use him as a woman. There's no greater indignity for a man, I mean. So he's pleased to do that. When he did that, he could say, 'Well, I've finished; I've done everything.'"

"He's let his imagination take him everywhere."

"Yes. Nasty man," he adds.

Paul wrote this story in 1948, traveling by boat with Tennessee Williams from New York to Morocco. When he finished it, he once told me, he showed it to Tennessee, who said, "You can't publish that."

"That's right," Paul remembers, when I bring up what Tennessee said. Then, imitating Tennessee's voice, he adds, " 'People will think you're a monster!' That's what he said."

"And did you say to Tennessee, 'That's not me?' "

"No. I said," he laughs, " 'Oh, I don't think so.' Well, I could have said, 'But what about 'Desire and the Black Masseur?' "

"I don't know that story of his."

"Well, I think it's much worse than mine."

"What happens in that?"

"A-a-h!" he groans. "A black masseur murders a white man and cuts him up and eats him. I think that's worse. I think that shows that he's more of a monster than I."

"And there's also—if we're speaking in comparatives here—what is the play of his where there's ritual murder and cannibalism?"

"Oh—*Suddenly Last Summer.*"

"Tennessee was one to talk, right? Why did he consider your story so terrible?"

"It affected him strongly, I guess. He read it on ship-board; that made it worse."

"Why, because he was isolated?"

"Yeah. He probably read it and went that way"—a horrified expression comes over Paul's face—"and then reread it and went, 'Auugh!' "

"But when you were writing it, you just followed it through: this man in this circumstance would do this and would do this and would do this. And nowhere in you was there something that said, 'A-augh!' "

"Naturally not." And then he repeats in Tennessee's voice, " 'People will think you're a monster!' "

"Okay, now can we get back to the question of sex—"

"LaTouche wrote a song," and Paul sings it loudly: " 'Sex has reared its ugly head for everyone but me.' "

"What a funny man he must have been."

"He was wonderful. I was very angry with him for dying, for depriving everybody of his person."

With Paul, it is easy to get diverted from one's intention. He slips into anecdote, you're amused, you succumb to amusement. But I have only one day left here on this visit.

I bring up the Moroccan painter Ahmed Yacoubi. Paul first met Yacoubi in Fez in the summer of 1947, when Yacoubi was in his late teens. In the winter of 1948, Yacoubi appeared at the Palais Jamai, where Paul and Jane were staying, with some majoun that his mother had made. In the course of his visit, Yacoubi began to draw pictures on the hotel stationery. Jane was so impressed with his talent that she suggested to Paul that he purchase some drawing materials for him, which Paul did the following day. Paul continued to see Yacoubi during the next few years whenever he went to Fez and was amazed by the progress he was making artistically.

In April 1951, when Jane decided to leave Paris to return to Tangier, Paul drove to the French border in his new Jaguar to pick her up. He invited Yacoubi to accompany him on the trip. It was on the return trip to Tangier that Jane became aware of a change in Ahmed's position with respect to Paul. Seeing the intensity of Paul's interest in him, Jane became very jealous. To a friend, she said of Ahmed that he had "holes for eyes."

Whereas once Paul had helped Jane with *Two Serious Ladies,* devoting himself to her talent as if it were his own, now he was helping Yacoubi with his painting. Paul was not a painter, of course, but he had a very keen eye and was able to make constructive suggestions. Soon Paul was reporting to Peggy Glanville-Hicks that Ahmed was making "magnificent" paintings, much more sophisticated than his earlier work and yet retaining the same directness of vision.

In January 1952, when Jane went to New York, anticipating a production of her play, she took with her a number of Ahmed's paintings and helped arrange an exhibition of his work at the Betty Parsons Gallery. Soon after Jane left, Paul saw a poster in the window of a travel office advertising inexpensive travel to Bombay. He decided to go to India and take Yacoubi with him. "I would drop Ahmed Yacoubi, from the Medina of Fez, into the middle of India and see what happened," he writes in *Without Stopping.* After they returned to Tangier in June 1952, they traveled together to Spain, Italy, and England. According to Paul, Yacoubi "made himself so extremely useful on journeys that I no longer considered going alone and taking care of everything myself."

In March 1953 Paul went to New York, specifically to write the incidental music for Jane's play, which was to be produced first out of town and then on Broadway. During his visit, he stayed with Yacoubi at Treetops, Libby Holman's mansion in Connecticut. By early May 1953, having finished the score, Paul decided to return to Tangier. He had just been offered a commission for a new work, "A Picnic Cantata," by Arthur Gold and Robert Fizdale. Leaving Jane and Ahmed at Libby's, he writes in his autobiography, he "hurried back to Tangier, and rented a piano."

But as I recounted in *A Little Original Sin,* Paul's departure from New York was more complex than he revealed. As he was about to leave, expecting Ahmed to go with him, Libby came to him and said, "I've fallen in love with Ahmed. I feel so guilty, but I can't help myself." Paul returned to Tangier alone; Ahmed had chosen to stay with Libby, who "showered" gold presents upon him.

In early June, however, Jane received a telephone call from Libby, who was very upset and angry because of an incident involving Yacoubi and her six-year-old son. (Yacoubi would later tell Paul that Libby thought he'd tried to drown her son in the swimming pool, but that it was all a misunderstanding.) Libby told Jane she was going to call the police, but Jane persuaded her not to. Instead, Jane arranged to have Yacoubi stay at Libby's townhouse in Manhattan with her, while she arranged passage for him back to Tangier.

After Yacoubi returned to Tangier, he and Paul resumed their former intimacy. In September 1953 they traveled to Turkey, a journey that Paul describes in the essay "A Man Must Not Be Very Moslem." By the time Jane returned to Morocco in the spring of 1954, Paul and Yacoubi were living together.

Paul's relationship with Yacoubi was to change in late 1957 after Jane's stroke, when, during a time of intense political upheaval in Tangier, Yacoubi was arrested. He was accused of seducing a fourteen-year-old German boy. Yacoubi was cleared of all charges and freed in May 1958, but by this time the tie between him and Paul was no longer close. Later, Yacoubi was to marry and emigrate to the U.S.

I met Yacoubi in 1977 in New York, where he was associated with the La Mama Theater. He was perturbed that

I might misunderstand the relationship between himself and Paul, and he insisted that they had not had a sexual relationship. He had married a second time, he told me, and had another child. From other people I was to learn that Yacoubi, even as a very young man, had great "healing powers," inherited from his father and his paternal grandfather. At the La Mama he was respected as a considerable talent: a visual artist, a poet, and a playwright. He died in the 1980s in New York City.

"Once you entered into a creative relationship with Yacoubi, how did that alter the situation that ordinarily exists between a European and a Moroccan?" I ask Paul. "What happens when you introduce, as you introduced, the whole question of encouraging his creativity? Doesn't that put the imagination as an important factor back again into the relationship, so it isn't defined so sharply? Am I making myself clear, Paul?"

"Yes, but you ask what happened when. The very beginning of my association with Ahmed Yacoubi had to do with his drawing."

"So this was not one of those relationships in which there was a defined kind of an exchange. From the beginning, it had to do with—"

"The one we started with, yes. And it always went on, of course. Never stopped."

I bring up the time that Yacoubi decided to stay with Libby. "I guess he couldn't resist it, all that money."

Paul laughs. "I don't know what money he thought she had or would give him. She didn't give him any money, anyway."

"But he must have hoped that there would be some money, eventually."

"Well, she gave him gold, which is as good as money. As good as gold, yes."

"Still, that was a betrayal of you. You had worked with him so carefully, and then he just chose to stay with her."

"M-m-hm. Well, that's what he wanted."

"So you didn't take it personally—as a betrayal—when he did that."

"Well, no, how could I? No. It seemed logical."

"Could I ask you if your feelings were hurt?"

"Feelings were hurt?" Paul repeats and then laughs. "I don't know. I don't know what it feels like to have your feelings hurt."

"Okay," I say, "all right. If that's what you say, I believe you. I'm not going to say that you have to—" After a moment, I add, "I know what it is to have my feelings hurt."

"What does it mean, exactly? Can you define it? Is there no word?"

"Well, one has an expectation of an implied understanding, of how things are and how they will go on. And then the other person withdraws from it and shows you that you were wrong all along in your expectation. And you feel . . . badly. You feel badly that you had hoped certain things and trusted certain things—and that isn't going to be."

At this moment, there is a knock on the door. "That's Abdelouahaid," I say.

"Probably. Well—I was annoyed. I was angry."

"You were angry?"

"Not with Libby. With him."

"You were?" I repeat.

"I was angry, of course. But I knew that was foolish, and I knew also that I could get on perfectly well without him, why not?" And Paul gets up and answers the door.

It was the summer of 1954. After having "taken back" Yacoubi, Paul was living with him in a house outside the Casbah, on the edge of the cliff at Sidi Bouknadel. He was just beginning his third novel, *The Spider's House*. Meanwhile Jane, who by this time found herself almost entirely blocked in her writing, was pursuing Cherifa, inviting her to the house on Place Amrah every day, trying to get Cherifa to move in with her.

Yacoubi had always disliked and distrusted Cherifa. He mocked her because she was a lesbian. He was also afraid of her, refusing to eat any food that she cooked, engaging in ritual washing and praying after seeing her. After Jane discovered some packets of tseuheur (a mixture of antimony, pubic hair, and menstrual blood that Moroccan women used for magical effects) in the house on Amrah, Yacoubi announced that he would no longer go there. He stated that Cherifa was a "witch," that she was trying to "get" Jane, and that next she would try to "get" Paul. He further insisted that Paul not visit Jane in her house and that when Jane wanted to see Paul, she must come to visit him at the house in Sidi Bouknadel.

When Paul agreed to Yacoubi's demands, Jane became very angry; she told Paul that Yacoubi was trying to come between them. But Yacoubi was adamant, and Paul, indicating that he himself was afraid of Cherifa, would not visit Jane in her house. Jane did visit Paul a few times in Sidi Bouknadel during the summer, but when she was there, Ahmed made her feel like a guest. To her close friend David Herbert, she said that she felt "kicked out" by Yacoubi.

Paul, who was planning a trip later that year with Yacoubi to Ceylon, to the island of Taprobane, suggested to

Jane that she accompany them. All through the autumn Jane refused to go. But suddenly, just before his trip in December, when Paul asked her again, she agreed, with the proviso that Temsamany also come along.

Taprobane is a very small island of black basalt, rising sixty feet above sea level off the coast of Ceylon. When the tide is low, it can be reached from Weligama on the mainland by wading across the shallow bay. At other times, the crossing must be made by boat. In 1910 a Count de Mauny-Talvande built a house on the island, taking up a good portion of the available land. The house was octagonal, with a large central octagonal hall called the Hall of the Lotus because of the motifs carved on its pillars and roof. The domed roof, thirty feet high, was supported by eight square pillars and sixteen light columns. Around the Hall of the Lotus was a series of small rooms, open alcoves, which could be shut off from the main hall by curtains. There was no electricity on the island, and the house itself, even in the daytime, was very dark. At night the one bright oil lamp was placed in the center hall. An exotic botanical garden surrounded the house with vines, trees, and flowers that grew rapidly in the hot, dense atmosphere.

In 1949, while visiting David Herbert in England, Paul had seen photos of the island and was immediately entranced by it. On his first trip to Ceylon in 1950, he intended to visit Taprobane, but he never got there. In 1952, when he was traveling in Asia with Ahmed Yacoubi, he went to Weligama and crossed over to the small island. He immediately inquired about the possibility of purchasing it. Later that year, the island became his. Once he had acquired Taprobane, it was necessary to maintain a staff of two servants to keep the house in readiness for his arrival.

But it was not until December 1954 that Paul finally went there—with Yacoubi, Jane, and Temsamany.

Reporting on their arrival at the island in *Without Stopping,* Paul writes that when Jane first saw the house, she said, "It's a Poe story. I can see why you'd like it." Paul notes that she had difficulty with the heat and that she was unnerved by the large number of bats in the trees at night. Yet he also says, "Once we got the right cook, life became pleasant." Each day he followed the same unvarying routine: at six each morning, he had early tea, put on a sarong, walked around the island (a very short walk), watched the sun rise, and then set to work on *The Spider's House.* Yacoubi was also working each day, painting, as Paul had arranged for him to have an exhibit in Colombo. In his account, Paul does not mention whether Jane was working or not. He does say that finally she came to him and told him that she and Temsamany wanted to return to Tangier.

When I told the story of the stay at Taprobane in *A Little Original Sin,* I naturally focused on Jane's experience there: on her trying to write but being unable to, on her suffering from the heat and confinement, and on her difficulty sleeping. Temsamany, who slept in an alcove adjacent to hers, told me that during the night she would call out to him, "Timmie, turn on the light." Temsamany would get up and turn on the oil lamp. Then he'd lie down. A few minutes later, she'd call out, "Timmie, turn off the light." He'd get up, turn off the light, and lie down. Then once again she'd ask him to turn on the light. And so it went all night long.

One day she and Temsamany made a trip to Colombo to get some liquor. To Tennessee Williams she wrote, "The bats hang upside down from the trees at night and in the morning they all fly off at once with a great noise." She signed the letter "The Spider's Wife." Alone on the island with the three men in what was essentially one large room, she began to drink a fifth of gin a day.

Ahmed Yacoubi told me he noticed that Jane was "very upset," but he attributed it to the frequent rains, to the heat, to the lack of electricity and water, to the nighttime noises of the devil dances from the mainland, and to the enormous bats that hung in the trees. Peggy Guggenheim, a visitor who found the island to be a "dream world," recalled that Jane was very depressed and that Paul was preoccupied with his work and with Ahmed. "He was very paternal with Ahmed," she commented.

Now, writing about Paul, I must turn back and look again at Taprobane. Paul has described the island as ". . . an embodiment of the innumerable fantasies and day-dreams that had been flitting through my mind and getting caught there during all the years since childhood." Of course, Morocco was also a place where his fantasies could be fulfilled, but there certain adjustments had to be continually made. To begin with, the government might change at any time, and as an expatriate he might not be welcome. Taprobane, however, belonged to him; he could essentially make of it what he wanted. Further, it was an island, separated from the rest of the world.

On Taprobane, writing *The Spider's House*, Paul was following the course of the friendship between Stenham, the expatriate American, and Amar, the young Moroccan boy, against the background of the movement for independence in Fez. He consciously incorporated into Amar's history a number of elements from Ahmed Yacoubi's history: events from his childhood, his relation to his parents, his religious and political beliefs. He just as consciously incorporated a number of elements from his own history into Stenham's life: Stenham is an American writer who has left the U.S. to live in Morocco; Stenham had formerly been a member of the Communist Party and had then become disillusioned with all politics; Stenham's parents had been unalterably opposed to religion of any sort.

In those chapters of the novel in which events are seen through Amar's eyes, the boy begins to feel a deep devotion to Stenham, a feeling of friendship beyond anything he has ever felt before. For Paul, the writer, this was the first time he had ever allowed tenderness to enter his fictional universe. At the same time, on the island of Taprobane, he was living out his intimate relationship with Ahmed Yacoubi: patron to protégé, generous parental figure to indulged younger man.

And what part was Jane supposed to play here? From their earliest days together, what Paul had most wanted from Jane was that she see as he saw, that she feel as he felt about what he loved. It was obvious to everyone else that on Taprobane Jane was not seeing what he saw nor was she feeling what he felt. Caught up in his interlocking fantasy—the cosmos of his novel and the cosmos of the island—he was able to protect himself from seeing in her what he did not want to see. She also tried to protect him, until the burden became too much for her and she left.

In that early chapter of *The Sheltering Sky* when Port goes out alone to walk into the medina, he thinks of Kit sitting by an open window in the hotel. He feels himself the protagonist of the scene, with Kit as the spectator, the spectator whose gaze gives validity to his very existence, to every choice that he makes. Now, on Taprobane, despite all that had happened between them over the years—her affair with Helvetia, his relationship to Ahmed—despite the presence and influence of Ahmed, Paul apparently still wanted some kind of consent or agreement from Jane to his own existence as well as to his own imagining.

When in the late 1980s Paul spoke to the French writer Robert Briatte about their stay at Taprobane, he said, "Oh, *pauvre* Jane!" and described how much she hated the bats and being isolated and not being able to take a bath or shower. But when he told Briatte about Jane's leaving Taprobane with Temsamany, he added, "*Moi, je suis resté. J'étais assez amer, je ne trouvais pas ça bien de sa part, pas très loyal* [I stayed. I was rather bitter, I didn't find it very good on her part, not very loyal]."

After this visit, Paul never returned to Taprobane to stay. He sold the island in 1957, but because of currency restrictions he was not able to take the money out of the country.

When I return the next day, the last day of my visit, Paul begins by saying to me, "I got a special delivery letter during lunch from Spain, telling me that [Edouard] Roditi has died."

I ask him if Roditi had been ill.

"It's hard to say. He had had cancer at one time, but it was all fine. Maybe a return, I don't know."

"Was he about mid-eighties?"

"No, just my age. A few months older. You knew him, no?"

"I just met him once."

Paul has known Roditi for a very long time (since 1931), and I can see that this news has jolted him. "I'm very sorry," he says, "to think I won't see him again. His friend with whom he had been staying enclosed a letter from Edouard. It was just a one-page letter. His handwriting had changed considerably; it wasn't very good. I could read it because I know his handwriting, but it looked as though he'd written it in the dark or something. In the letter he said that he intended to come to Morocco, but he didn't feel well enough. He apparently died of a heart attack."

I ask about Roditi's work, with which I am not familiar.

"He was an encyclopedia of knowledge and of languages. I don't know how many, eleven or twelve languages that he knew very well and several others that he could read. A real polyglot."

We drift into talking about other things, and I see Paul's eyes begin to close. He shakes himself awake. He says he'll get up and make some tea. "If I just sit here, I'm lulled by your words."

"Lulling words?" I say and mock my own inquiries. " 'Tell me, Paul, about your identification with your characters.' "

"He," Paul says, referring to an interviewer who has been to see him in the morning, "asked me an even worse question. He said, 'What is the meaning of life?' "

"Nobody can ask you that question," I say.

"Well, he did."

"So what'd you say?"

"I said, 'Well, obviously, it has no meaning.' "

"And then that made him feel better."

"He said, 'I lost you there.' "

Abdelouahaid appears and, learning about Roditi's death, tells a story about a man dying and a horse dying. He ends the story with "We all die." Then he leaves. I say to Paul that Abdelouahaid is a philosopher. Paul laughs and quotes the last line of Abdelouahaid's story. " 'We all die.' That's not philosophical. It's just stating a banal truth."

"Of course we know people die. But when it happens—

one moment Roditi is alive, and the next moment Roditi is not alive—there's something so impossible to believe about that."

"Oh, we believe it," Paul says and laughs again.

"What always stuns me when I hear someone I know has died is the instant of change from the person who was alive to the person who is dead. From the being who is to the being who no longer is."

There is a long pause; we both sit silently. Then Paul says, "Well, I suppose that from that feeling comes the desire for immortality, that refusal to believe that life can come to a sudden end forever. People want to—they want very much to feel that they'll go on existing."

"It's part of being human."

"Probably. Maybe animals feel that way, too," he says, and once more he laughs.

"Do you remember," I ask, "when you were a child first learning about death? You must have learned early."

"Why?"

"In *Without Stopping* you say something about going out and looking at poisonous mushrooms when you were a child."

"Oh, yes, *Amanita.*"

"So you knew about death at that point."

"Well, I was taught that as a very small child, four years old. Never touch mushrooms. And don't touch poison ivy."

"With the same intensity?"

"Oh, yes," he laughs. "I felt that if I got poison ivy, I'd probably die too."

"Of course, if you were wandering around your grandparents' property, there must have been a lot of poison ivy to touch."

"No, there wasn't. It didn't grow there. It was a hemlock forest. The ground everywhere was covered with inches and inches of old brown needles. There was no undergrowth. Just trees."

"How beautiful that must have been."

"The smell was wonderful. I loved it. I often dream of it and wish I could see it just once more."

He speaks of the mushrooms, how they pushed up through the needles, "white and yellow and brown."

"And you'd look down at them and think about—" I was about to say "death," but he interrupts me. "Yeah," he says.

"But they were beautiful."

"They weren't beautiful. I didn't think they were. I thought they were frightening."

"But do you remember having, as a child, the sensation that there is such a thing as death and that 'I' am going to die some day?"

"Well, I knew that if you died, that was it. Nothing to do about that. No, I suppose I thought if I don't touch mushrooms, I won't die."

At that moment, for some reason, I am impelled to say something about my own sense of death when I was a child. Perhaps it's because it's the last day of my visit. Perhaps it's a small offering in view of his sadness. Perhaps it is one more way of trying to say that I am not here just as an interviewer.

I tell him that when I was about six my family moved to an apartment in Astoria, Long Island. It was during the Depression, and we moved every few months. "I remember coming out of the front door of the building and looking back, up to the window of our apartment—it was on the third or fourth floor. And at that moment, I knew I was going to die some day."

"You connected the memory of the thought with the image of the window, I suppose."

"Or the looking back—and now I wasn't there any more."

"And being in the window, I suppose, meant life."

"Maybe."

"You went out, you left life, you turned around—"

"And I saw that I wasn't there any more."

"You were only one. You weren't two," says Paul.

PART THREE

| | One day in 1977, about halfway through my
| 29 | first visit with Paul, I had said to him: "There
| | is something about your story 'You Are Not I'
that seems to me to be crucial, central, to your work." "Can
you say what it is?" he had asked me. "No," I answered,
"I can't say." But now in California in 1992, ready to return once again to Tangier, I ask myself, Can you say what
it is?

The story begins with these strange and compelling
words: "You are not I. No one but me could possibly be."
They were words Paul brought over from sleep, unchanged
from a dream in early 1947 (shortly before he had the
dream about being in Tangier that was to alter the course
of his life).

The "I" of the story that follows these two dream sentences is a young woman who has been confined to a mental institution. As she tells the story, there had been a train
wreck the day before on the tracks just below the asylum.
A number of people had been killed, and in the resulting
confusion the main gate to the asylum had been left open
and she simply walked out. Rummaging in the bushes
nearby, she came upon a pile of stones and pocketed some
of them. She then walked to the train and, seeing several
bodies lying on the ground, dropped stones into their
mouths. As she was dropping a stone into the mouth of a

dead woman, she was stopped by a man who yelled at her, "Are you crazy?" She began to cry, saying that the woman was her sister.

Believing that she was in shock, the authorities took her home. The address she had given was, in fact, the address of her sister, who had had her committed to the asylum. Once inside her sister's house, the "I" had the sudden realization that everything in the house had been reversed since she was last there. What was once on the left was now on the right, and vice versa. At the same time, she became aware that her sister, upon seeing her, had phoned the authorities at the asylum to have her returned.

At this point, the "I" determined that she would not be made to do what she did not want to do. She made a "big decision," one she knew would be difficult, but "I had a plan I knew would work if I used all my will power. I have great will power," the "I" tells us. When the attendants from the institution arrived to take her back, the "I" walked slowly across the room, pulled a stone out of her pocket, and put it into her sister's mouth. At that moment, the "I" thought, "This is the turning point." She shut her eyes, and when she opened them, she was her sister and her sister was she. She tasted the blood on her own lips from the stone. Now it was the sister who struggled not to be taken back to the institution, who sat on the bed in the asylum, writing the words of the story on paper. "She never would have thought of doing that up until yesterday," the "I" tells us, "but now she thinks she has become me, and so she does everything I used to do." As for the "I," now she is sitting in the living room of her sister's house, alone and free, listening to the rain fall.

When you have come to the end of the story, there remains an irreconcilable confusion between the "You" and the "I" of the first sentence. And if you start the story again, the confusion becomes even greater. The "You" now seems to refer to the reader as well. No matter how many times you read the story, you cannot quite straighten it out. The question of who is the "I" and who is the "You" is unresolvable.

One hears at the same time the voice of the conquering sister through the conquered one, and the voice of the conquered sister through the conquering one. At the moment of change, of the reversal of the two, there is a silence in which the two are one. Even after the transformation, for all the attempts to distinguish separateness, there remains the underlying confusion in the voice.

I knew from what Paul had told me that in writing "You Are Not I" he called upon images from external sources. He based the image of the house where the sister lived on a photo he had seen by Henri Cartier-Bresson of a street in a village where the houses were on a slope, each house lower than the one beside it but all alike. As to the reversal that the "I" saw within the sister's house, Paul took that from the work of the Viennese psychiatrist Wilhelm Stekel, who wrote of a patient who saw everything reversed. But the essence of the story, the idea of the interpenetration of beings to the point of exchange of identity, the idea of the dissolution of borders between beings had come to him in the night, in the border between sleep and waking. It did not need to rely on external sources.

And is there something about "You Are Not I," I wondered, as my return to Tangier drew closer, that is crucial to Paul's life as well as to his work? Is it possible that this story gives a clue to how he experiences being and the relationship between beings? (And then it would not be simply landscapes where borders could be and indeed must be crossed.)

I remembered a line in a letter Paul wrote to a friend in 1929, after he had visited the writer Carl van Vechten in his Greenwich Village home: "His eyes envelop you. He seems to be gazing at you for long stretches of time, during which you feel yourself passing in and out of him."

I remembered that Paul had written of himself that as a child of twelve he entered into a fantasy "in which the entire unrolling of events as I experienced them was the invention of a vast telekinetic sending station. Whatever I saw or heard was simultaneously being experienced by millions of enthralled viewers. They did not see me or know that I existed, but they saw through my eyes."

I thought of what he had said about his mother, how when she looked at him at the dinner table, he covered his eyes with his hands and said, "Don't look."

I thought of Paul's father, how immense and powerful he had been in his tyranny—how Paul wanted him out of the house, gone. Yet he still lingers on, in Paul's voice, so many decades later.

I thought of Paul's life in Morocco, of how he has chosen to make his life there with people who are—how has he put it?—who are not "the other."

I thought of when Paul left for Tangier in 1948 and Jane put his passport away, thinking, after glancing at the photo, that it was hers, not his.

I thought of Jane's novel: it had been *Three Serious Ladies* until Paul helped with the manuscript and it became two, and then, at the end of the book, the two serious ladies seem to merge into one.

I thought of going to see Paul in 1977, of how there were three figures in the dialogue, and now there were only two.

I became obsessed with something about numbers, with one and two, and also three. But the more I thought about these numbers, the more the figure of Paul retreated from me, taking on a stone obstinacy. I had the sense that I knew less about him now than I ever had. I thought of other stories of Paul's in which one being takes over the other: "The Circular Valley," in which the Atlájala enters into any being at will; "Allal," written in the 1970s, in which a boy enters into the being of a snake; "Kitty," another late story, in which a little girl enters into the being of a cat.

I fell into the kind of anxiety that comes when, in the midst of a story I am writing, I can go no further. At such a time, analysis and rational thought take me only in circles. I can do nothing but wait, submit to uncertainty, wait dumbly for some unexpected impulse to reignite my belief in my fiction.

But this wasn't fiction. It was life.

30 It is late in the evening, December 1, 1992. I am once again in Tangier. Waiting for me at the airport is Abdelouahaid. With him is Pociao (Sylvia de Hollanda), who has translated a number of Paul's works as well as the biography of Jane into German. We have corresponded, but I have not met Pociao before. She is a slim, shy, gentle young woman, obviously very devoted to Paul. She tells me that he stays in bed most of the time now. (Because of the pain in his leg?) At the moment, he has a bad cold.

At the hotel I fall into bed, jet-lagged, longing for sleep. I awake at night from dreams of being cold to find the room cold and damp. Shivering, I get up and turn a knob, which I take to be the one that turns on the heater. I wait; nothing happens. I look for extra blankets, but there are none in the room. I put on my street clothes, including a heavy sweater, and get back into bed.

My journey here has not been auspicious. After the long, sleepless trip from San Francisco to London on a full flight and a long layover at Heathrow, I went to the Royal Air Maroc gate for the flight to Tangier. Sitting on a hard plastic chair, I promptly fell asleep. At the announcement of my flight, I came awake and stumbled aboard with the other passengers. Once in my seat, I settled in with relief. My eyes began to close again, but, alerted by the thought that I must check on my carry-on bag, I looked beneath the seat in front of me to make sure it was there. It wasn't. My essential carry-on bag—with my notes, my tape recorder, my annotated books, specific tapes of Paul's music that I planned to go over with him, and my emergency medications—was definitely not there.

I could not believe my eyes. Up I jumped from my middle seat in the small plane, squeezing past a large man on the aisle. I made my way off the plane and ran back down the ramp to the Royal Air Maroc waiting area. No, my bag was not where I had been sitting. I checked at the gate. "No, no bag has been turned in," the flight attendant said. Perhaps I had left it in the general boarding area in the main terminal. How could that be? I wondered, maniacal as I was about clutching this bag to me wherever I went while in transit. "You have only ten minutes before the plane leaves," the flight attendant called out behind me, as I took off for the main boarding area. I ran through endless corridors and finally got back to the exact spot where I had been sitting for so long. No, my bag was not there either. Faster, faster, I urged myself on, as I ran back through the corridors, ran up the ramp, and got onto the flight just as the door was about to be closed. "Excuse me," I said to the large man in the aisle seat as I prepared to squeeze past him again.

At that moment, a kinesthetic memory returned to me—to my arm, to my shoulder—the memory of the action of lifting my carry-on bag and putting it in the overhead compartment. I checked. Yes, it was there.

I fell into my seat with relief, though now I had another anxiety to contend with, the totality of my forgetting. Just a little lapse of consciousness, I tried to persuade myself, from not sleeping, from jet lag. But I wasn't buying that. The metaphoric meaning of the (almost) lost crucial baggage was too obvious. Still, metaphor is metaphor, and life is life, I told myself. Don't get things any more mixed up than they are. Every return to Tangier must have its prelude.

It is four o'clock on a cold damp afternoon when I enter the Itesa, go up the familiarly creaking elevator to the fourth floor, and knock on Paul's door. Abdelouahaid answers and leads me into the bedroom. Paul is in his bathrobe, sitting up in bed. A butane heater, set near the foot of his bed, puts out a large blast of heat, keeping the room snug on this cold day. Seeing Paul, I feel once again how one picks up with him where one was before, as if you have never been apart. He seems totally at ease, sitting up in his single bed, propped up against the pillows, receiving. A certain reserve, a reluctance to appear before others in anything but impeccable dress has given way in the face of the more pressing demands of ill health.

I have brought with me from the U.S. tapes of a recent concert of his chamber music and songs, as well as some tapes of composer Phillip Ramey's new compositions. I sit on a rickety straight chair. Between myself and his bed is a low round table piled with papers and tapes and letters and medications. I tell him about the concert and about the performance of his "Picnic Cantata" by the New York Festival of Song, which I had attended the previous month and had found exhilarating.

I ask how he is feeling. He says that he has a bad cold; he's had it for over a week and can't seem to shake it.

"But that's not the worst thing," he adds.

He tells me that he is having a great deal of pain because of dental problems. It has something to do with pieces of old roots of teeth in the jawbone now making their way to the surface of the gums and sticking out against his cheek so that he can't eat.

"But that's not the worst thing," he says again.

He leans over and picks up a piece of paper from the round table and silently hands it to me. It is a telegram. It is from biographer Virginia Spencer Carr, saying that she is arriving on December 8 with her friend Mary Robbins, that she has a publisher for her biography of him, and that she looks forward to spending as much time with him as possible.

I am looking at this telegram in my hand, I am reading it, I can hardly believe what I am reading. A second biographer? A second woman biographer? I say bitterly to myself. A second woman biographer here at the same time as you? In an instant I have always believed it.

I swallow. I say that it will be very difficult if both of us—Virginia Carr and myself—want to spend our time with him. There are two of us and only one of him.

He agrees. No, he doesn't want her to come while I am here. But he offers no suggestion as to action. It becomes

246

clear that if I do not do something, nothing will be done. Then there will be the two of us, two biographers vying—fighting for his time, even as he is not feeling well.

I ask if he wants to send her a telegram. He shakes his head no.

I say, "Do you want me to call her?" He says yes and makes a fumbling statement about it being expensive to call the U.S. I say, "I'll do it." Yes, it will be expensive, but I will pay for it, I tell myself; it is for myself that I do this, after all. This is the real world: one salvages what one can salvage. All that stuff about metaphors and anxiety—that engrossing anxiety that has been my constant companion these past days—has suddenly become dim, unimportant. So much for one's internal life in the face of the starkness of competition.

Other visitors come in: Pociao; her husband, Roberto; and another young man, who is a publisher from Holland. We all have tea before I return to the hotel.

First things first, I tell myself. I call the desk and report that my room has no heat. Someone will be up at once, I am told. In five minutes, a man in a white coat comes to my room; he speaks no English but gestures that he has come about the heat. He climbs up on a chair, adjusts an overhead grate, pushes a small lever, climbs down from the chair, and assures me with extravagant gestures that soon I will be as warm as can be. He leaves, and I wait to be warmed. Some minutes go by, and the room is colder than ever. I climb up on a chair and put my hand up to the grate. Cold air is coming out. I get down off the chair and call the desk.

After fifteen minutes or so, a different man in a white coat appears. He does not speak English either, but he does speak a French about as halting as mine. He climbs up on the chair and puts his hand in front of the freezing blast of air. "*Chaud,*" he says. "No," I say, "*froid.*" "Ah," he says, "it is getting warmer. It takes time. It is the *résistance;* it takes time." "The *résistance?*" I say. "The *résistance,*" he repeats. "It takes time? How much time?" "A half hour," he assures me and goes away.

In a half hour, the room has approached the temperature of a deep freeze. I put on my coat and my gloves. I go down to the desk. I lean my elbows on the counter; my head droops.

"I need a room with heat," I say to the man at the desk, who has just come on duty. "What is your room number?" he asks me. "Ah, yes," he says, when I tell him the number. "That room does not have heat. It only has air-conditioning."

I have dinner. I place a call to Virginia Carr. From Tangier, to Tangier, sometimes calls go through, sometimes they don't. Finally, after a long wait, this call does go through. A woman answers; it is not Virginia Carr. She says that Mrs. Carr is out at the moment, but she offers to take a message. I say that I am calling for Paul Bowles, that he is requesting—I do this according to his instructions—that she delay her trip for several weeks. He is not feeling well. And besides, I add, I am here to work with him for two weeks. So, all in all, it will be better if she comes later. I leave the telephone number of the hotel and my room number so that Mrs. Carr can call me back. I wait in my room for the call to be returned. There is no call. But then, there could have been a call that just didn't get through. This is, after all, Tangier.

Sometime that night, awaking from a fitful sleep, I suddenly wonder, Did Paul choose to have another biographer as a way of reducing the pressure he was feeling from me, from my inquiries?

I have already been through uprush of anger, downrush of hurt, chastisement of myself for thinking I have the right to either anger or hurt. After all, I tell myself, he doesn't belong to you; he doesn't belong to anybody. If he wants to have two, five, a hundred biographers, it's up to him. It's his life.

But I am like an animal, licking my wounds, calling up old hurts, old angers to reinforce this new one. Why has he done this? comes the mournful cry. Who knows why? You'll never know why; maybe he doesn't know why. There is a theory that some people hold about Paul that on occasion he sets up difficult and dramatic situations to see what will happen. I don't and didn't subscribe to that theory. I am, rather, among those who feel that when something, someone—one biographer, two—comes along, he doesn't fight it; he accepts it, as he accepts fate. Virginia Carr came along, and that to him was fate. Was that why?

But is it possible that by my presence I have reminded him again of all that happened to Jane, of all that he thought had been settled? And that he has deliberately chosen to diffuse the effect of my presence by encouraging yet another biographer?

Get hold of yourself, I rebuke myself. You have come here to do certain things, to explore certain questions with Paul—questions about his writing and his music. That's what matters. So what if another biographer is coming? When you get right down to it, this isn't even really a biography, is it?

I turn over, and I go to sleep in my warm room. Thank God for physical comfort, at least.

31 I arrive at Paul's flat at eleven-thirty in the morning. It is at his suggestion that I come early in the day, as he has so many visitors each afternoon it will be difficult to have any private time to talk. When I knock, Sana, the young Moroccan maid who gives him breakfast and lunch and who also does his cleaning, opens the door. She regards me with suspicion and has me wait while she goes to ask Paul if I may be admitted.

Once in Paul's room, I sit in the rickety chair, taking out my recorder and notes and books. Paul's cold is about the same, and he is still in pain from his teeth. He has not been able to find a dentist he trusts in Tangier.

"Oh, incidentally," Paul asks, as I am turning on the tape recorder, "did they tell you what the phone call costs?"

"Don't worry about it."

"You should ask," he says. "Make them tell you."

"Don't worry about it," I repeat.

"I'm not worried. I just want to pay it."

"You will not pay it," I insist.

"How do you know I won't?" he asks, in an injured tone.

"I mean, I don't want you to pay it," I say. "Just figure I did it for myself, all right?"

With that settled, I launch into a new inquiry. I am going to do what I planned to do; I will ask what I planned to ask. No matter that there is a second biographer in the wings. I say that I am interested in exploring whether he sees a link between his experience as a composer and his experience as a fiction writer.

"Well, they never could be made into one whole, really, could they?" It's like the difference between cooking and jogging, he adds. "You're doing something different. You're using a different part of your organism. Why would they be all one? They're not. They couldn't be. I always put it that they're in two different rooms. And I go out of one, shut the door, and go into the other. And in there it's different."

One room looks very different from the other?

"Yes," says Paul, "like that room in there—it not only looks different, it's freezing cold."

"What room is freezing cold?" I ask, puzzled.

"The next room," Paul says, referring to his study. I laugh, thinking how different he and I are from each other. I was thinking of some metaphoric room filled with metaphoric furniture, and he is, as usual, holding to the specific.

Now I too turn to the specific, in search of his earliest experience as a composer. I have run across a newspaper article from the 1930s in which Paul spoke of his first instrument being a zither. He described tuning the zither with a skate key, using a system of symbols that he had invented for sharps and flats. I shuffle through my papers, trying to find the article, which described the precise symbols he used. "I can't find it," I say. "I'm so organized, and then sometimes my organization goes to pieces."

Paul laughs and says, "I'm not organized. My disorganization goes to pieces."

He volunteers that his grandfather Winnewisser (the one with the broken nose, who broke the noses of his sons) gave him the zither. I ask if his grandfather was musical. No. And his mother? No. "And what about your father?" (I am stepping into a territory fraught with feeling, musical and otherwise. I remember that Claude had had a nervous breakdown as a young man because his family did not allow him to become a concert violinist.) "Did he ever play the violin at home?"

"Occasionally. Sunday afternoon."

"Did you think of it as very interesting musically when he played?"

"I hated it," Paul says vehemently.

"So that's why you very seldom write for the violin."

"I never stick them in."

"Maybe once, as I recall."

"Oh, I have. Yes."

"But you don't like it."

At his loud "No!" we both laugh. "I at last have accepted the idea of a string orchestra. That's all right. But one violin alone is no fun. I don't like the sound."

"When you began to play the piano," I ask, "would your father ever come in and watch you practicing?"

"Oh, yes. I hated having him come in. He would stand behind me and look at the music that I was reading. And then if I played an A and it was written a B, he would suddenly grab me by the ear and twist it around and say"—Paul slips into his father's voice—" 'What are you doing that for?' " Now Paul groans. "And then he would pound on the A and say, 'Can't you see it's an A?' 'Yes,' " comes the downhearted, bedeviled voice of a child. " 'Then be careful' "—again the father's recriminatory tone—" 'see what you're doing.' " Paul groans again. "Then I couldn't do anything."

"What kind of a system is that, twisting the ears?" I ask.

"Oh, discipline."

Or torture, I suggest.

His father would also get irate because Paul wasn't any good at *solfeggio*. "But I wasn't. I wasn't very quick at figuring out a chord. One note I could, but when it was three or four and then suddenly another three or four, it took time." To be able to do that quickly is a matter of training, Paul informs me, and he hadn't had any training. Maybe some children could pick it up by themselves, but he couldn't. Again Paul reverts to his father's voice: " 'See here, young man, what are you doing? You hear what you're playing? You're playing an A major chord. Look at it again. You see that natural?' " Then in a diminished, sad voice: " 'Yes.' " " 'Well, then' "—with the sternness of the father—" 'observe it.' " Paul groans again, "I was never happier than when he went out of the room."

"He probably said to himself that it was so easy and you were so musical, why weren't you getting it? It could only be deliberate on your part."

"I don't know what he thought I was trying to prove. That I was stupid, I guess."

"More likely that you were deliberately disobeying him."

"Yes, he did think that, but what did he think I was gaining by it? What would have been my purpose? I suppose he didn't have to worry about that. The idea was that his son was not doing what he told him to do. I think that was it. He thought everything was a sign of hostility. What was interesting was that when he was not in the room, I was often able to do it correctly."

"Ach!"

"Of course."

When I say, "How terrible," Paul laughs. "He thought I was a grown-up. Some sort of abnormal creature who really was a grown-up inside. And what are all these little short legs and so on? I never acted like a small child, you see. And he decided that I wasn't, that I was perhaps a version of himself or something . . ." After a moment, he adds, "I remember his mother, my grandmother, used to tell my mother what an awful child he was when he was little. Disobedient and vengeful. She would get him all dressed up, ready to go out to tea or something, and then he would deliberately wet himself. She would come into the room and she would see—'Now I have to change his clothes and all the rest. Why has he done that?' And he would say"—here the voice of a small boy—" 'I just has to.' Of course, it wasn't true at all; he didn't have to."

"But how do we know that, Paul?"

He seems surprised at my question. "His mother said he didn't have to."

I shrug. "That's a very interesting question. I mean, I don't want to take the side of your father—"

"Oh, I don't mind," Paul laughs.

"Look at it this way. Suppose he's the kind of kid that just can't control himself when he's nervous or excited. And then when it happens, his mother says, 'You did it on purpose.' Now maybe it's on purpose, and maybe it's not. Maybe he doesn't know himself. But it's been judged as deliberate disobedience."

"Yeah, well, you may be right."

"And then when he has a child, and the child does something he doesn't approve of, he judges it as deliberate disobedience."

"That all children are like that, I suppose. Well, I'm glad it's all over, anyway," Paul says.

Though I have suggested to Paul that his father's wetting himself as a child may not have been a "willed" action, I know the comment will be sloughed off. Something in Paul cannot and does not want to alter what, I suspect, is central to his vision of his own life: that his father's antagonism was absolutely willful. For Paul, his father had— and still has—the quality of a vengeful god. In his willed tyranny, he remains unchanged and unchangeable, a fixed center.

Yet here is a paradox. In Paul's fiction there is one question that seems to haunt all his characters. That question has to do with the nature of action: are their actions willed, or do they only think they are?

When I return in the afternoon, Paul is alone, but almost immediately there is a knock on the door, so I go to answer. Standing in the hallway are Pociao, Roberto, the young Dutch publisher—and, to my great surprise, Mrabet. Roberto, a tall man with a very sensitive face, is friendly with Mrabet and has apparently encouraged him to visit Paul. I have a brief conversation with Mrabet. Then he goes into the bedroom to see Paul, while the rest of us remain in the living room. I hear Paul say, "Mrabet! I didn't expect you," in his voice a sound of undisguised pleasure.

I am surprised by Mrabet's appearance. Of course, I have not seen him for over thirteen years. In the past when he was here, he filled the room with his complaints, his angers, his laughter, and his boasts about the books that he was writing (which Paul translated and put into fictional form). Now that he no longer works with Paul or has a daily relationship with him, he seems smaller, slighter, as if once he gained energy and power from Paul but now he is diminished, the fire within him banked.

Mrabet comes out of Paul's bedroom and leaves at once. There is another knock on the door. It is the Polish ambassador to Morocco, an avid reader of Paul's work, who has come to pay homage.

After the ambassador departs, I once again go back into Paul's bedroom. No, he does not want to rest; he wants to go on with our conversation. I mention that when I was in New York recently, I talked with composer Ned Rorem about Paul's music. He spoke of his great admiration for

Paul's compositions, and for his songs in particular. "He also said that he thought your prose writing and your music were very different, that the person who wrote the songs wore his heart on his sleeve, but the person who wrote the prose did not."

"Well, I don't know what it means to wear your heart on your sleeve."

"Oh, yes, you do, Paul."

"No, I don't. What does it mean? I've heard the expression, but it doesn't mean anything to me."

"I think what he meant by it was a perfect openness in terms of the representation of feeling, in terms of a direct conveyance of the feeling of the one doing the song to the one listening."

"I would expect that to be the case always."

"In song?"

"Well, yes."

"But not in prose."

"Prose involves the intellect, and music does not. As songs don't involve any intellect at all, you can deal with primal materials so much more easily. But when you come to putting words together, you're treating something completely different, it seems to me. Words—" He stops, then goes on. "Actually, when you write prose, you read it over— I do—as though it were poetry. And if it sounds right, then you've written a good sentence. And you go ahead and you write another sentence. Then you've got to read them both together and see how they go together." And he speaks of the importance of sound for him as he writes, how each line must come out of the line before. "One line and the next line and the line after that."

One line and the next line and the line after that. I am reminded of something that has puzzled me about the third movement of Paul's Sonata for Two Pianos, composed in 1946 for Robert Fizdale and Arthur Gold. The first two movements of the sonata are neoclassical, closely related in style melodically and harmonically. The third movement, however, seems unrelated, with its primitive, even harsh, rhythms, with no true melody, only a succession of tone clusters. "To go for a second to another question, can you say something about the third movement of the sonata? It is very different from the two earlier movements."

"You're right."

"But can you say anything about that sequence?"

"Well, I think it's an error on my part. Stylistically, it doesn't really fit with the other two movements, I don't think. There isn't any logical sequence, I'm afraid. It's all right, musically, if one wants to shift styles between movements. But there really is a great shift."

"You just decided at that moment that was what you wanted to write?"

"No, it's not that simple. I must admit that"—and here he laughs a little—"I needed to finish that piece for Gold and Fizdale. I needed to write a third movement. Instead of writing a third movement, I took an entire movement from *Yankee Clipper* [the ballet he wrote in 1937], 'The Call at West Africa.' "

"Because you needed that final movement?"

"I needed it quickly. It's a bad admission, but there, I'm telling you just how it happened. And that's why there's such a shift in style. I'm sorry I did that. And I've always been ashamed of it. But I decided, the hell with it, I'm not going to write a new third movement after all these years. That's the way it came out."

Of course it's not identical, I note, as the original score was for orchestra.

"Well, of course, I had to arrange it for two pianos."

I go further, still excusing him. (I do not see that he does not need my excuses.) "Almost any composer will go back and use things that he has done before—"

"They do; a lot of them do."

"Even Stravinsky has done this." (I know that Paul considers Stravinsky to be the greatest composer of the twentieth century.)

"Did he? I don't remember, really."

As I get up to leave, once again the conversation reverts to the difference between his prose and his music. "Prose is composed of ideas," he asserts. "Once you're dealing with ideas, there are so many things you want to say."

"Darker, denser things?"

"People accuse me of that. They ask me why my prose was so sinister. I never said it was. I think it has to do with thinking and feeling. What one thinks is likely to be negative, critical, cynical. If I'd been able to express what I thought, in music, I'd have written completely different music, instead of being allegri, happy . . . If I had put it into the music, I might not have written any prose. But I couldn't put it into the music. I wanted to express myself, express what I thought. Something else was coming into it. I scarcely expressed anything in music. I just wrote it."

I mention that I've recently been reading Aaron Copland's *Music and the Imagination,* in which Copland speaks of music as the expression of the total being of the composer.

"Perhaps one needed to have a great deal more technique to have that expression of the total man. I didn't have the technique, nor did I want to have it. I didn't want to express the essence of the total man. I was interested in writing pretty music. I don't see anything wrong with that.

Many people do, however. There are accusations that I never wrote serious"—here an exaggeratedly serious expression comes over Paul's face, and he covers his face with his hands in a gesture of mock suffering—"music, that I did write serious"—he repeats the same gesture—"prose. I was extraordinarily lucky to be able to do both.

"Luck has been so important to me, both good and bad. That's why I accept the Moslem philosophy. One can be religious and at the same time be an atheist," he adds parenthetically. "What happens was determined long before we were born. It's a good thing to believe. It can be calming, can help you through bad moments."

32 One day in 1977, toward the end of my first visit to Tangier, Paul spoke to me of the burden that composing had imposed on him just before he left for Morocco in 1947.

"When you're composing, the mind is in use, but only with musical ideas. Those ideas become obsessive, but you are completely confined to musical terms in solving them. You become hypersensitive then to any sound at all. A rooster crowing a half-mile away will startle you because you're hearing combinations of instruments in your head and the phrase you're writing at the moment. You're listening, and you hear, Yes, there would be a French horn with this, flutes here, et cetera. But you can't hear that, really, unless you have silence. You can't hear it against a real sound. You've got to hear it as though it were being played. And that requires a blank canvas. It's very hard to find that kind of silence in the world.

"If you can't get silence, then you've got to have a keyboard instrument of some sort to work things out on. And that again makes you nervous. I mean, it's a great expenditure of psychic energy to hear the music itself coming out on a keyboard and to try and sing with it and get the notes down in front of you. It's hard as hell."

At the time, he even found that certain music became disturbing because he could not escape it. "When I heard music I did not want to hear, I knew what key it was in and where it was going, and that drove me mad, that I couldn't not listen to it. I had to listen to it, every note."

Some months earlier he had had the experience of his ears betraying him. He heard stray sounds, crickets and church bells and flutes. Certain real sounds began to be distorted in the high register. He consulted a doctor, who told him that this disturbance was caused by an infection in his tonsils. But after a tonsillectomy, the problem with his hearing did not go away.

Writing a column on jazz in the magazine *View,* he inserted a phrase he had brought back from a dream: "Poets have ears, but the world of sound is unkempt, chaotic, and barbarous."

Now, in December 1992, when I remind Paul of what he said in 1977 about the toll composing once took on him, he dismisses what I say, indicating that he never felt such a thing. He implies that I have misunderstood him. But I know what he has said, as I have reviewed the tapes from our earlier discussion. I wonder if he has forgotten what he felt. Or has he merely forgotten what he said? Or is it possible that he never felt that at all, but yet he said it to me? But why would he have done that? It seems to me that it is most likely, as I observe him in the present, that the memory of that darkness, that struggle, has receded with time. Some kinder memory of his relation to sound and to music seems to have replaced that dark memory, now that his writing years have almost come to an end.

I turn to questions about individual works he composed. He responds monosyllabically or not at all. Nonplussed, I try to inquire about his method of composing. I cite Aaron Copland's statement that some composers begin with a rhythm and others with a melody. Paul shrugs it off with "I've never tried to find out how things come."

As often as not, after rebuffing my direct questions about his music, however, Paul does slip into another kind of response, telling an anecdote about a performance of one of his works. For instance, he speaks of the performance of the ballet *Colloque Sentimental,* for which he wrote the score. It had been commissioned by the Marqués de Cuevas in late 1944 for the International Ballet (which later became the Ballet Russe de Monte Carlo). De Cuevas, who had chosen as the text a poem by Verlaine, had selected Salvador Dalí to do the set design and costumes. Knowing Dalí's reputation for outrageousness, Paul was leery of working with him, but he was assured by the Marqués that Dalí would not indulge in any of his usual bizarre jokes. So Paul had proceeded to compose a score in the spirit of the Verlaine poem.

"I remember all that summer I would go up to the Marqués de Cuevas's house and he would say, 'I have a new letter from Dalí.' And then he would read it. It was always about the atmosphere that was supposed to be created by this cold garden and twilight. He said, 'That of course will be in the music.' He was always talking about what the music should be. So I was very sensitive and careful, knowing that Dalí should be pleased—should be pleased in order for the Marqués to be pleased, because he set great store by Dalí's opinions. But it was all such a farce."

When he went to the dress rehearsal, Paul saw that the sets and costumes were quintessential Dalí. The two principal dancers, André Eglevsky and Marie-Jeanne, came on stage wearing long hanks of underarm hair that reached to the ground. Men with yard-long beards rode bicycles, crisscrossing the stage at odd moments during the performance. A large mechanical tortoise, inset with blinking colored lights, continuously zigzagged across the stage.

"You never knew where the tortoise was going. Sometimes it almost went into the pit. It would get right to the edge of the stage and then back up. Everyone was watching that, waiting for something awful to happen. The audience kept whistling, booing, and shouting. The dancers, with their long hanks of underarm hair, were trying to do a *pas de deux.* Well, naturally, the audience was in hysterics at their trying to do a *pas de deux,* stepping on each other's underarm hair—'Get that hair out of my way,'" Paul mimics, gesturing as if he were one of the dancers.

Telling this story so amusingly—his gestures and the alterations in the tone of his voice are masterly—he has once again evaded my questions about his music. The storyteller has used his wiles and devices on me. He has told me something funny; I have laughed; I have been distracted. I am left with the sense that he is a master at holding effect apart from content.

I am also left with a sense of how story operates for him in daily life. There is story as defense, story as distancing, story as transforming device, story as habit (he has undoubtedly recounted this same incident many times before), story as what he falls into automatically, story as stopping place, story as enticement, and, yes, story as revelation, too—in this case, that the sounds he had created so painstakingly were drowned out and lost.

I am left, as well, with the unexplored sound of his music: his chamber works, art songs, pieces for piano, cantatas. I recall the lightness, the wonderful rhythms, the charming melodies, above all the swiftness of the tempo. Even in the slow passages, one has the sense that the music is only waiting to speed up, can barely contain itself before it can rush on without stopping. It is lovely, it is often amusing, it is danceable, it is elusive, it is eminently playful. Even as it incorporates jazz, blues, folk music, and stylistic elements of early twentieth-century French composers such as Maurice Ravel and Erik Satie, it resolutely resists seriousness. It does not seek depth, nor does it allow depth; the movement of feeling is irresistibly forward. (I can think of only a few exceptions to this general statement: his art songs and several short chamber pieces, in particular his Sonata for Oboe and Clarinet.) It is music that offers no access to darker feeling. It does not seize you; it is not aggressive. It offers itself as what it is: extremely clear, almost transparent in form.

And if I think of the prose? No question, it is serious. It descends into deep layers. For all the so-called detachment that some critics have detected in his writing, I see instead something far more assertive, penetrating, even aggressive. Yes, the narrative goes forward; it carries the reader forward. But it is simultaneously driving the reader inward and down into the character's experience, an experience that is, more often than not, a terrible one.

I am left with the writing and the music as two separate rooms. And yet once in the past, Paul acknowledged a linkage between the two. We were discussing his story

"The Scorpion," and I suggested that in that story, as in many other stories of his, the narrative assumed a quality like melody.

"That's so," he agreed. "I think of it as melody. Melody, after all, is a line, and narrative is also a line, a line that just happens as you're writing."

In composing, he went on, "harmony is the emotional underpinning of each moment of the melody. You can take a melody and write it with a certain harmonic sequence and it means one thing. And you take it again without changing a note, giving it a different harmonic sequence, and it has a completely different import." In writing, he said, he thought of the reactions of characters under the narrative line as a kind of harmony.

"Yes," he admitted—this once, and only once—"there is a connection. I do think of a very definite concordance between music and writing, when I'm writing words. When I'm writing music, I don't." And then he added, "Because music seems more fundamental to me than writing."

33 I have been noticing a change in Paul: how much his attention is on the present. It is as if memory (except for a few crucial instances) is no longer an active force demanding attention but an alternative path to be pursued at his leisure.

He is still, of course, suffering from a cold and is afflicted with the pain in his jawbone and mouth as well. He seems to have no solution to the latter pain; he simply endures it. There has been a flurry of activity as several people have tried to find a dentist for him. Pociao has gone to see the German consul and has gotten the name of a dentist from him; I have called Isabelle Gerofi for the name of her dentist. Pociao and I have presented these names to Paul, but he has taken no action. Today I learn that Joe McPhillips has simply taken things in hand and made an appointment for Paul with his own dentist for this afternoon.

If I cannot get to his music directly, I can try another tack, to explore with him how he has written of music in his fiction. I refer to a passage from *The Spider's House,* in which Stenham, the most autobiographical of Paul's characters, listens to the music at an amara, a Moroccan religious ceremony. He and the young Moroccan boy Amar have joined a crowd of worshippers, clustered in a large circle about a woman in white who is singing. " 'The woman's song,' " I read, " '. . . could have been a signal called by one mountain wayfarer to another on a distant hill. In certain long notes which lay outside the passage of time because the rhythm was suspended, there was the immeasurable melancholy of mountain twilight.' "

"Wow!" says Paul. "I was being very poetic."

"Yes, you were, but don't knock it."

I go on:

> Telling himself it was a beautiful song, he decided to stand still and let it work upon him whatever spell it could. With this music it was senseless to say, because the same thing happened over and over within a piece, that once you knew what was coming, you did not need to listen to the end. Unless you listened to it all there was no way of knowing what effect it was going to have on you. It might take ten minutes or it might take an hour, but any judgment you passed on the music before it came to its end was likely to be erroneous.

"That's true," Paul says.

" 'At moments—' "

"What is she doing?" he interrupts, in response to a knocking and banging from the next room, the bathroom.

"She's cleaning the bathroom," I say of Sana, who always works very vigorously.

"She's so noisy. Go on."

" 'At moments the music made it possible for him to look directly into the center of himself and see the black spot there which was the eternal . . .' And then," I go on, "he thinks, '*Cogito, ergo sum* is nonsense. I think *in spite* of being. And I *am* in spite of thinking.' "

"Who says this?"

"This is Stenham."

"It sounds like a European reaction."

There is an even louder noise from the bathroom.

"Oh, now what's she doing?" Paul exclaims.

"She's cleaning."

"She's going to knock that wall down. It's incredible." This is not said in anger, but rather in a voice that knows irritation will bring no change.

"All right, anyhow . . . here, with Moroccan music, you seem to be saying, one has to listen to the very end to find out what the ultimate resolution is going to be. That's what you're saying?"

"That's what I said; yeah."

"And that is not true of Western music?"

"Well, in Western music something continually happens. It goes somewhere, and there's a direction. But in the music that Stenham is talking about, the impression you get is that it's static. And therefore you may not take it seriously and listen since you think you know what's going to happen."

"But that in fact is an incorrect judgment."

"That's right. Yes. You need to listen to it all. Then you can decide what it is."

Now even louder noises come from the bathroom, more banging and something like a crash. "The noisiest place I've been yet," Paul says in mild exasperation. "I can't believe that that girl can make so much noise." I suggest closing the door, but he says the noise will only come through the wall.

I ask about repetition in the music Stenham is hearing, whether the repetition itself, the seemingly static quality, is what makes it possible for him to look into the center of himself to ". . . see the black spot there which was the eternal."

"It's the repetition that brings about the sense of time-lessness?" I inquire.

"Yes."

"And then for Stenham, a man who thinks all the time—"

"Too much."

"—it's the music that allows him to stop thinking and to be."

"I really don't know what he means when he says, 'I am in spite of thinking.' "

I ask him if it would be helpful to go over the entire section in detail to see what Stenham meant.

"Is it—I don't know—relevant?"

"Oh, yeah," I say and laugh. "I think it's very relevant to this evolving thing I'm trying to get at—something to do with music and its effect and words and their effect. Of course, you must have experienced that same timelessness yourself when you heard Moroccan music, and you must also have experienced the way in which it allowed you to have a sense of your own internal 'eternal' sense. Is it fair to say that?"

"Undoubtedly, yes."

Sana enters, wearing a sweatshirt that says "Miami" on it, and has a conversation with Paul. Paul tells me she is saying that some woman is here, that Karim had made an appointment for her to come to see him this morning, but he doesn't know who she is.

At this moment, a young woman enters the bedroom. "Oh, there are two people," I note, for behind the young woman is a young man. Sana goes out, and a conversation begins between the young woman and Paul in French, which I can just manage to follow. The young woman announces that she has read Paul's books and has traveled to the places he has traveled to. She is astonished by how much he and she share. It is like fate that his experience and her experience are so closely allied. Without any ceremony, she sits down on his bed. He asks where she is from. She says she is from Paris, though, as Paul will say to me later, to him she looks more like a girl from the country. She has brought a number of books, and she is very eager for him to sign them. He signs the books. She also wants her husband, a young silent bearded man, to take her picture with Paul. She moves closer to Paul as her husband takes the picture.

During the course of this small drama, I cannot help but see the delight, even relief, with which he welcomes the young woman. It is in sharp contrast with how he has just been with me, with his resistance and evasion in response to my questions. "Is this relevant?" he has asked me. He has never said that to me before, no matter what I asked him about Jane, no matter what I asked him about himself—about sex, or money, whatever. I have an almost physical sensation that he is retreating from me, throwing up obstacle after obstacle as he does so. He is not impolite—no, he would never be that. But he is creating a series of impenetrable walls between himself and me, even making his presence into a wall in this small, overheated room.

Is it something specific about music and words in *The Spider's House* that brought this about? Or does it have something to do with me?

I have not thought enough of how he sees me: that I am associated inevitably with Jane, with Jane's illness, with his depression after her death; that I am for him like a specter returned. In his own space, in that place he has created as his refuge in exile, held captive by his own politeness, I have become an invading figure. I have already invaded once, in pursuit of Jane. But then, in 1977, mired in the cage of his grief, he had been in need of telling. After that his life had changed, in part because of that very telling.

To make matters worse, I am searching for that very thing in him he least wants to acknowledge, that which has remained constant in him over time, irrespective of place, in spite of all the changes he has been through. He must know this, for I said many times to him when I was working on the book about Jane that it was precisely this "unchangingness," this essential quality of her being, no matter how she was altered during her illness, that I was looking for in her. I should have remembered what he said to me one day in 1977, that his "I doesn't exist."

However it is between us, we have started down this road. Shortly, the young French woman will leave, but I will go on, if not today then tomorrow, with my questions. The questions will go on, and the answers will go on and not go on, and *it* (this narrative) will be like the music that Stenham heard at the amara. There will be repetition, there will be small shifts; something will be said and then said again in a slightly different way. I will not know what *it* is until I reach the end.

34 The one window in the room, opposite the door, is covered with a thick black cloth day and night. Paul's single bed is against the wall to the right as one enters, the head of the bed next to the window. The small butane heater stands near the foot of the bed; it is always going, its coils burning red. The only light in the room is from a small lamp on the shelf below the window and from a dim bulb within a fixture hanging from the ceiling. To the right of the door is a low bookcase; on top of it are a Phillips keyboard and some towels and sheets. Behind me, as I sit in the rickety chair opposite Paul, is another low bookcase, stuffed with papers and tapes. Above it, on the wall, is a small painting by Brion Gysin. Looking around this small space, no more than nine feet by nine feet square, I measure the accumulating weight of things.

Paul is just finishing his breakfast, savoring the tea and jam and cheese and toast. He seems very relaxed. He talks easily of Tangier, of a new attempt that is being made to "clean up" the city.

Sana comes in and takes his breakfast tray away. "You finished early today," I say. "You won't have lunch immediately succeeding breakfast."

"Yeah, there'll be a whole hour and a half in between. Freedom."

After several fruitless attempts yesterday to talk with Paul about music and words in *The Spider's House,* I am ready to try something else, a further stripping down to a more fundamental level of sound. I tell him I would like to talk about the kind of sound that annihilates the distinction between inside and outside, sound that is in fact pre-verbal. I remind Paul of an experience he had in Mexico in the early 1940s. He went to see the volcano Paracutín, which had erupted in a field to a height of more than three thousand feet, emitting fire and lava every nine or ten seconds. Paul sat the whole night watching the eruption from a short distance away. He had never heard such a noise, a metallic sound that he felt rather than heard. "It went right up through you," he has said. "I felt I was in the middle of reality."

Does he, I ask, recall other experiences in which there was this intense coalescing between outside and inside through sound?

"Well, there are times when you're in the subway or on the train when a certain kind of vibration is set up that's very deep, set up, I suppose, by the train itself. It's a very low bass sound, which takes over. There was a train that went under the Hudson River that did it very well."

"Because of the change in pressure?"

"Probably the pressure. It made a wonderful sound, and it was a wonderful feeling."

"Of your body vibrating to the sound?"

"I wasn't conscious of vibration exactly, just of that deep sound. It only began at a certain point in the tunnel, and then it ended, of course, long before the train got out of it. It went on for maybe a minute—I don't really remember how long."

"One ordinarily thinks of sound as following a path, from the vibrations of the ear drum through nerve signals to the brain. But perhaps you sense sound in another way?"

"Sounds are sounds," he says.

Yes, sounds are sounds, but what is of interest to me at the moment is sound at a visceral level. "Have you ever had the sense of sound as terrible?"

"Oh, yes," he laughs. "A dentist's drill. It's a sound which is connected with pain, so it's bad." But that's not necessarily part of the sound, he insists, it's the association. "Don't you hate the sound of a dentist's drill?" We are once more in the realm of teeth.

I take yet another tack. I ask Paul if there were certain sounds in his childhood that he particularly remembers.

"I remember on the farm, early in the morning about four o'clock, there used to be a fox. They make a frightening sound. I was terrified of it. It sounds like someone trying to breathe, crying as the breath goes inward." Paul imitates the sound, an uncanny high wail. "I remember being chilled by the sound at that freezing moment of the night when it's colder than any other time."

"Just before the dawn."

"Quite a bit before the dawn. When night can't stand anymore of itself. It gets colder and colder."

"And then the fox cries out."

Paul imitates the fox crying again. "It's not like a dog howling."

"Which you don't like too much, anyhow."

"I don't like the whole canine race," he says, and we both laugh, he a dog hater, I a dog lover.

How old was he when he heard the fox? Older than four, maybe six?

"I don't know. No, I wasn't very old." He pauses. "I'm thinking about other sounds," he sighs. "Sounds that I liked. I liked the sound of the milkman coming in the morning because he came with a horse and wagon, and there were tinkle bells on the horse. Tank-a-tank-a-tank-a.

Oh, that's nice. And then I'd hear him stop. And then I would hear the bottles being set down on the back porch. I found that very comforting. Children have to be comforted by something during the night. And there was no comfort forthcoming from within the house," he adds.

"Even though your mother—I mean, certainly your mother loved you, but there was no comfort?"

"She wasn't allowed to provide comfort."

"For instance, if you would have awakened in the middle of the night and called for her, what would have happened?"

"I'd have been punished the next day. 'What do you mean by calling out in the night, waking your mother up, waking me up?' " he says, taking on his father's voice. "The punishment would have come from my father, of course. And she would probably have said, 'Oh, I didn't mind.' Something like that. Well, I knew better—you don't do that. It's not done. You have to suffer through by yourself. You have to do everything by yourself. You're not going to be helped to do it. I remember once—I don't know how old I was, five or six—my family, they were always going out, leaving me completely alone. They didn't believe in baby-sitters or that sort of thing."

"They'd leave you totally alone in the house?" I ask, astonished.

"Oh, yes, yes, sure. They considered that you had to do that or children wouldn't be self-sufficient. A child has to be completely self-sufficient. That was a belief they had. Once I remember, I don't know why, I woke up and a mosquito was buzzing around—"

"Ugh!"

Paul suddenly begins to imitate the high sound of a mosquito buzzing nearby. "And I fell in love with the mosquito—"

At which I laugh loudly, but Paul assures me, "Yes, because it was there with me. And I remember addressing small prayers to it, saying, 'Dear little mosquito, don't go away; stay with me.'"

"Bite me if you must."

"Oh, I didn't mind that, being bitten. I just wanted somebody there with me."

"And the company of the sound."

"The sound and the fact that it was a living thing, buzzing around my head. I thought of it much later, years later, and I thought what a crazy child I was, offering up prayers to a little insect, only that big, buzzing around, saying, 'Dear little mosquito, don't go away.'"

What he has said has penetrated through to me with great force. It does not matter whether every single element of this incident is totally and factually true—in particular, whether his parents left him alone at age five or six. I recognize the truth as being true for him and, more than that, as essential to him. It is a story that reveals and yet that confines within it an image of a child abandoned, longing, struggling to believe.

For the first time, I consciously put myself in his place. I hear the mosquito. I imagine his terror. I tell him I am amazed at his ingenuity, that at such an early age he found this way—a way out.

"Why, of course," he says.

"But not all children do find a way."

"Well, what do they do if they don't find a way to handle it?"

"I guess they become very disturbed."

"Well, maybe I did. Maybe I'm disturbed," he laughs, and he adds, "still."

No, I do not think of him as disturbed. "I think of you as a survivor," I say.

"Had to. Had to. I don't think I was being particularly clever or inventive. I think I just did what I had to do, just to keep going. You know, get through it, whatever it is."

When I return in the afternoon, Paul's Spanish publisher has arrived. Although Paul is still not feeling well, he has dressed and has come out into the living room to greet his guest. He talks easily, fluidly, smiling, telling anecdotes. (One concerns a conversation between his parents shortly after the newspapers announced that the matinee idol Rudolph Valentino had died. Rena sighed and said, "He was such a handsome man." To which Paul's father responded, "Not any more," and laughed.) The publisher wants Paul to come to Madrid in February or March for a concert of his work as well as for several publicity appearances. Earlier, Paul had said that he would not go to Madrid. Yet now, with the publisher present, he says, after all, he may go.

After the publisher leaves, I can see the exhaustion on Paul's face as a result of the effort he has made. Yet, though he is very tired, he decides that since the sun is still out, he wants to go for a walk on the mountain. So the three of us—Paul, Abdelouahaid, and myself—walk together on the narrow road above the sea, Paul moving slowly, using his cane. At one point he asks—it is the only question about my life I can remember his asking me—how long I have lived in San Francisco.

35 As I leave the hotel the next morning to walk to Paul's, I find a note in my box. It is from Virginia Carr, saying that she and Mary Robbins have just arrived. She has tried to reach me by telephone, first from Atlanta and then from Madrid, but she could not get me. Because she and Mary Robbins teach, they had to come at this time, their Christmas vacation. She looks forward, she writes, to meeting me.

At Paul's flat, there is again the ritual of Sana peering out at me through a partially opened door, then closing the door as she goes to tell Paul there is a visitor, then returning to admit me. When I enter Paul's room, he tells me that Sana announced me as "the woman who came yesterday." Yes, that is what I feel like.

Two things are now told. One is that Virginia Carr has arrived, that she has left me a note. This is my telling. The second is his telling, that he has fallen the evening before. He sat on the chair in his room, the one rickety chair I always sit on, and slipped off. It was around eleven at night, and he was alone. It was a long time before he could manage to get himself up, he says.

He does not seem to have hurt himself. But an image has invaded my mind, of him on the floor, helpless, struggling to get up, and I feel a terrible dismay. I don't know whether to offer help (what practical help can I offer?) or to suggest getting rid of the goddamn chair (would my suggestion be welcome?) or to simply offer sympathy, which I do. I am cautious not to rush in with advice where it may be unwanted. I know that in the U.S. there are electronic signaling devices for older people who are alone to wear in case of an emergency. God knows if such things exist in Morocco.

But since he has fallen, does he want to work? Yes, of course, he wants to go on. I tell him I would like to ask him some questions about "Unwelcome Words," the title story of his last collection, which was published in 1988. The story takes the form of a series of letters from "Paul" to an unnamed recipient, "You." The "Paul" of the story describes his daily life in a series of incidents that are unashamedly autobiographical, as if finally Paul has no need or desire to hide within or behind a character in his fiction, as if he is allowing the gap between imagination and reality to vanish.

I ask Paul if he had a particular person in mind for the "You," and he says, "Well, I couldn't help having Gordon Sager in mind." I tell him that I suspected this to be so, and he wonders why. I remind him of several hints in the story, including a mention of a particular apartment in Tangier that the "You" lived in, which I know was Gordon's. (I had met Gordon in 1977, when I interviewed him for the biography of Jane, and I had come to know him as a friend in the 1980s, when he moved to San Francisco, some years before his death.)

"I began thinking of him as I wrote it," Paul says. "And then I was rather hoping he would never see it."

"He never saw it."

"Good."

I also note that the voice in this story is not far from Paul's own daily voice, his speaking voice, and that too is a departure from his earlier work. "That voice you use when you speak to me or you speak to other people—it's always a little different with each person—but it's not the voice you have used in your writing."

"No."

"But in this one story, you allow that voice to take over. You have it say things that you would say in daily life. For instance, I've heard you talk about the way prices have gone up in Tangier, just as the 'I' does."

"Oh, yeah, yeah," Paul admits.

"And then 'Paul' tells a story about Christopher [Wanklyn] and an old Berber man in the south. That sounds just like a real story that you would tell."

"It is," Paul laughs. "It did happen."

"Next 'Paul' tells a story of sending to New York for a thousand dollars in 1947, and he describes how he couldn't get the money from the Moroccan bank, how they kept denying that it had come in."

"That's true. The whole time they knew right where it was, right there. Another story of a Tangier bank."

I single out two other instances of happenings in Tangier that are probably real: one incident involving an elderly Jewish woman who brought coffee to the men who were constructing the mosque and who was robbed and killed by one of them; the other involving two elderly American expatriates who lived on Social Security, who were attacked by a Moroccan.

"Yes, these are true stories," Paul admits.

And then there is an incident about a woman "Paul" calls "Valeska." I have surmised from the context that Valeska must be an American woman who came to Tangier often in the 1970s to see Paul. I have never met her, but Paul has told me many stories about her.

Yes, Paul tells me, she is Valeska.

In "Unwelcome Words," "Paul" recounts that one day he sent Abdelouahaid with the car to pick up Valeska at her hotel and bring her back to his flat. Seeing that Paul was not in the car, as he usually was, Valeska became very upset. "Where's Paul?" she kept asking.

For some time Abdelouahaid had been nursing a grievance against Valeska; he felt that she was slighting him because he was a chauffeur. So when she asked him about Paul, "Satan must have arrived," the "Paul" of the story writes. Abdelouahaid, with great sadness, told her that Paul was dead. Valeska began to scream and cry. Abdelouahaid helped her into the car, and they set off for Paul's flat, where Abdelouahaid told her Paul was lying on the floor, surrounded by other people looking at him.

"She was literally hysterical when she saw me, safe and sound," "Paul" writes, "and I thought: This is too much, and saw myself taking her to Beni Makada to the psychiatrist. Then she wheeled and shrieked at Abdelouahaid: 'You son of a bitch!' I don't think she's ever forgiven him for his joke, but he's still delighted by the memory of it . . ."

"And Abdelouahaid really did say to Valeska that Paul died?" I ask.

"He did. She was saying"—Paul imitates Valeska's voice—"'Where's Paul? Where's Paul? Where's Paul?'" Over and over. Like a parrot. And he stood very sadly, and he said, 'Oh, he's dead.' Then screech, screech, and squawks, and then, you know, 'Take me there, take me there.' So they started out, and they got as far as the mosque, the big mosque, and then she said, 'Oh, Christ, I left my camera at the hotel.'" He laughs, "She wanted to take pictures of me lying on the floor."

"And then when she came in and saw you, she must have had a fit."

"She did. I was in the elevator on my way down, and she was just coming in with Abdelouahaid, and we met downstairs."

"And she started crying?"

"Yes. And held on to me and was trembling. Oh, awful."

I am intrigued by this story because of what I have heard about Valeska and her obvious obsession with Paul. Not only did she keep coming to Tangier to see him year after year for almost a decade, but when she was home in the U.S., she wrote to him daily, long letters that went on for pages and pages. Many who knew Paul were hard put to understand why he tolerated her eccentric behavior. Yet whenever she came, Paul dutifully saw her; and he did for a number of years answer her letters, though not daily.

"Imagine writing a letter every day, for so many years," I say. "You certainly meant something very important to her."

"I don't know what it was, though. I have no idea what I represented," he says and laughs.

I remind him of an incident he once recounted to me about riding in a train in Mexico in the early 1940s, when an old woman, who was holding a live chicken, came over to him and asked him to hold it for her. As he gingerly took the chicken from her, she said to him, "You are my son." It has happened often in his life—and, I suspect, it is still happening—that even strangers seize on Paul as if he were a figure central to their existence. "It must have been so with Valeska," I say.

"It's embarrassing. But she was so funny; one couldn't help laughing."

"And did she mind your laughing?"

"No, she didn't mind, I think. She noticed it, and she would say, 'Well, I don't know what you're laughing at; it's nothing funny.' Gordon was here one time when she came. He was laughing so much he was rolling back and forth on the floor. She looked at him and said,"—again Paul takes on a high, parrotlike voice—" 'What's the matter with him?' I said, 'Oh, I don't know; he's thinking of something. I don't know.' And the way she screamed at Abdelouahaid was something," he groans.

"But, actually," I remind him, "you did write a piano piece for her. Or, rather, you dedicated it to her."

"Yes, she wanted it because she and some friend of hers were working on two-piano works."

"So she was a musician."

"Oh, yes, she was. But her idea of music was Chopin. And nothing else. Oh, Liszt sometimes. She carried with her a—what would you call it?—a false keyboard. A big long thing, like a piano. With all the notes. It didn't have any sound to it. It was just a keyboard. And she brought it out wherever she was and began doing this—" He runs his hand over an imaginary keyboard. "She'd do this during dinner."

I ask him how he responded when he was with Valeska in public and she acted in an eccentric way.

"I didn't respond at all."

"Ah," I say, and Paul laughs.

I go on with "Unwelcome Words," wanting to linger over it, as if it were a stopping place. Compared to the work written earlier in his life, this story, written in 1982, seems not to be under pressure. The brilliant shaping is there, and the skillful forward drive of the narrative is there, but that pressure that erupts from a writer being driven deep within himself is absent. The writer seems consistently at ease, although one passage does have the quality of an ironic imitation of Norton's wish for atomic extinction in "Pages from Cold Point."

In this passage, "Paul" speaks of his conviction that

> the human world has entered into a terminal period of
> disintegration and destruction ... we can imagine con-
> ditions under which sudden death by fire might be a wel-
> come release from the inferno of life; we might long for a
> universal euthanasia. Can we *hope* for nuclear war—I mean
> ethically—or are we bound out of loyalty to wish for the
> continuation of the human species at no matter what costs
> in suffering? I use the word ethical because it seems to me

that unethical desires are bound to engender false conclusions.

When I read the passage aloud, Paul laughs and says, "It's a strange remark."

"It's just what came into your mind at that moment?"

"Well, yes; I was writing a story."

"So story is inseparable from whatever goes on in your mind and from fact as well?"

"Yes."

"So there's no way that 'story' ever stops. In other words, whatever is going on in your mind, story is always going on in some way or other, even when you think about fact or reality. Would that be a correct thing to say?"

"You mean that whatever is happening at any moment can always be incorporated into a story. You can always see it from that point of view—in the frame. Yes," he adds. "Yes. Sure."

Though much of "Unwelcome Words" has seemed to me to be recognizably from Paul's life, there is one incident "Paul" recounts that I have assumed to be fictional. It is about a dog. I say to Paul, "I know you don't like dogs, but I know also you didn't do this."

"Yes, I did."

"You didn't."

"Of course I did. Why do you say I didn't? I didn't do anything very bad to the dog."

In the passage I am referring to, "Paul" writes to the "You" about his sleep being disturbed all night long for nights on end by a dog barking, and about the steps he has taken to quiet the dog: "It would be better to describe the drastic measures," "Paul" writes, rather than let the

"You" think he "poisoned the beasts. Naturally that was the first thing that occurred to me, but I decided against it because of the suffering it causes." His procedure was time-consuming but effective:

> It involved my staying up half the night for a week in my wait for a completely deserted street. About half past one I would go to the kitchen and prepare the half pound of raw hamburger. One night I would mix Melleril and Largactyl with the meat, the following night I would grind up several tablets of Anafranil . . . There was no more barking after the first night of treatment.

"You put the Melleril and the Largactyl in the meat you gave him?" I ask incredulously.

"That's right. Every day I had to go and buy fresh hamburger."

"Paul, that surprises me. I thought this was imagination."

"I'd mix it in the kitchen, the Melleril and the other medicines that were left over from Jane's illness." (Left over from how many years before—thirteen years—since Jane had last been in Tangier?)

"Oh, no! You would do that?"

"Yes, I was—"

"And then the dog would be sort of like this?" I mime a drugged, confused animal.

"The dog didn't know what hit him. First he would be very excited, running around. And next he would be in a catatonic state." (Finally, the dog's owner decided that it was rabid and had it shot, "Paul" writes.)

"Why didn't you think that was true?" Paul asks.

"I thought you would imagine that. I didn't think you would do that."

"Why?"

"Why?"

"You thought it was cruel. No?"

He is waiting for me to answer. Perhaps I simply do not want to hurt him by saying, Yes, I think you were cruel. Yet I do not even know if it would hurt him or what it would mean to him if I said that. Still, I hesitate. I have not forgotten his fall. Even as I look at him, sitting up in bed, waiting for my answer, I am seeing him fall, seeing him struggle to get up, and he is alone . . .

"Do I think it's cruel? Maybe I do think it's a little cruel. It's just that I didn't think you would do that."

"Well, I think it was much more humane than giving the dog poison because that makes them suffer. This dog didn't suffer at all."

"You just wanted him to stop barking," I reason.

"That's right. I didn't know his master was going to get rid of him, but I didn't care, either. I don't think anyone has a right to have a dog that barks all night outdoors."

"One of the reasons it surprises me, Paul"—I still cannot let this go—"is you're so soft-hearted with cats and birds."

"Not about dogs."

"Did one ever bite you?" I ask.

"Yes," he says, with some indignation.

"When you were a child?"

"No, not at all. When I was an adult. Here."

"No wonder." (Yes, I am wanting to excuse him.)

"I never told you that?"

"No."

"Ach! I was just walking along. Suddenly I felt this sharp pain in my leg and—with a noise." Here Paul barks sharply.

"And of course it had made two holes in my leg. The dog didn't belong to anyone. It was just there."

"You didn't know if it was a rabid dog?"

"No. I rushed to the doctor. He said, 'Well, I can sterilize it, but that won't do any good. You'll have to go and have rabies shots unless you can find that dog, that very dog, and capture it and take it to the gurna—it's a place outside Tangier where they'll put it in a cage and keep it a month. If at the end of the month it's still alive and kicking, then you don't have to have the shots. But, of course, you'll know long before that whether it's infected or not.' So we had to go, Abdelouahaid and I, to the exact place where the dog had been. It had come out of a house that was under construction. It had no reason to be there whatever, but apparently one of the workmen liked it and had given it a place to stay inside, where she had eight puppies. She wasn't rabid at all. But you can't tell. No, she was just, I suppose, asleep and someone walked too near her; and she bit, thinking they might be after her puppies."

"You did get the dog, though."

"Yes, but she bit Abdelouahaid all over. I don't think he took it very seriously. I don't think he was worried about rabies. We took the dog to the gurna, and they put her in a cage with her family. It was winter, and it began to rain. It rained and rained without stopping for weeks. So the cage got filled up with water. She got up on top of a rock and lay there, but the puppies couldn't get up there. So they were around her on the floor, and it was deep water. They all drowned except one. We went every day during that horrible winter rain to see her, and we had to take food with us. The point was, if she ate the food, she was all right. If she refused it, then we knew she had rabies.

She never refused it. She was only too eager to get it. So she was healthy. After a month I had to go and apply for permission to take her out. I had to sit in front of a desk where a man was making out lots of papers all about me and the dog. And he said, 'What is that dog's name?' And I said, 'Well, I don't know the dog; I never saw it in my life. How would I know its name?' 'Oh, no, no, it has to have a name.' Abdelouahaid, being a Moroccan, immediately said, 'Her name is Linda.' So it was put down duly, 'Linda,' and her color and so on. And she had one puppy, one son or daughter, who survived. We took them both back. She was perfectly docile. She didn't bark or bite or anything. We took her back to that house, where nobody wanted her, naturally. But she knew the place. I guess she was happy to be back in a place she knew."

36   When I return to the hotel, I call Virginia Carr, and she invites me to come to her room. A handsome woman with white hair, tall and imposing, answers the door. With her southern accent, she projects an image of cultivated softness; yet the overall effect of her being is largeness, a large personality, a large presence. (Have I mentioned that I am only five feet tall?) I learn that she teaches in the English Department of Georgia State University, that she is in fact the head of her department, that she chairs a number of committees, that she has three daughters and a number of grandchildren, and in addition to all this, she writes biographies. Clearly, she is what Paul's mother would have called a "Strong Woman."

She tells me that she has been writing a biography of Tennessee Williams but has run into some complications about access to papers because of problems with the estate—one of those terrible complexities that can undo some biographers. But it has not undone her. She has simply decided to do a book on Paul first and then later go back to Tennessee Williams. She met Paul in 1990, when she visited Tangier to interview him about Tennessee, and this led to her recent correspondence with him about writing a biography.

We discuss Christopher Sawyer-Lauçanno's biography of Paul. Neither one of us likes it. She tells me she has read my biography of Jane and compliments me on it. I thank her, but a shadow of possessiveness—*my* subject, *my* biography—begins to take hold of me. It's a little like territoriality, although, if you get right down to it, nothing geographic is at issue. Beware of possessiveness, I warn myself; what exactly do you think you possess? It's all nonsense. Nonsense, I say to myself, and nonsense I know. But that's how it is.

I tell her that I am not writing a conventional biography of Paul. I think that if I make this clear, it will help clear the air. That there is no reason for competition, that there is room for many books on Paul—yes, to that we both agree. I say that Paul is not well, that he is very tired, that he is not up to working with the two of us at the same time. (This he said to me as I left his apartment.) Yes, she can see that. But then, after I go, which will be in a few days, he will spend his time with her. (This, too, he has said to me.) Yes, of course, she can understand. "He has no phone, as you know," I say to Virginia, "but he has suggested that you come and visit him tomorrow at three."

I have the sense of being on a tightrope: eager to protect my time with Paul for the few remaining days, not wanting to be unfair, but also not wanting to be a pushover. I can guess, now that I have met Virginia Carr, that if she were of a mind to pressure him, he would surely capitulate. Yes, I know that about him. Yet if that happens, it will happen, I tell myself; and that too will be part of this recounting.

I am being unexpectedly calm. Perhaps it is the effect of Tangier itself, mysterious, unpredictable, but oddly inciting to a kind of fatalism. I recall that in May 1979, when I came to Tangier to go over the manuscript of the biography of Jane with Paul, I carried with me as part of my baggage a replacement piece for Paul's 1966 Ford Mustang—a ball-joint, I think it was. Paul had been unable to find it in Tangier, so I had volunteered to bring it for him from the U.S. It is small and light, he had written to me. In fact, it was heavy steel and took up an entire suitcase. Staggering under its weight, I wondered what it would look like to Moroccan customs officials. Would they suspect it of being a bomb? In the air, as I was crossing the Atlantic, these and similar questions ran through my mind as I visualized myself being interrogated by the authorities. But then, as the plane approached the Moroccan coast and Tangier came into sight, the idea of fate took hold of me. What will be, will be, the thought came as the plane circled before landing. Can an idea, a thought, a belief, be embedded in a geographic entity? So it seemed to me in 1979, and so it seems to be affecting me now, in 1992. (As for the ball-joint, by some fluke my baggage was not checked at all by the customs inspectors. So I was not interrogated, and the ball-joint did get through, and Paul's car was repaired.)

When I return to Paul's at three in the afternoon, Roberto and Pociao and Abdelouahaid are already there. Roberto has planned to take a few photos of Paul and myself and has set up his camera in Paul's study. But when I arrive, Roberto tells me that Paul has fallen asleep. He had dressed and was sitting on the bed waiting, but when Roberto went in to tell him everything was ready, he saw Paul had fallen on the bed, twisted to one side, and was sound asleep. "He was sitting up, and he simply fell back and fell into sleep," Roberto says. "I never saw him that way." He and Pociao are clearly alarmed. Only Abdelouahaid seems to take it as a matter of course. "Paul was sleepy, so he has fallen asleep."

Through the open door of the bedroom, I see Paul, dressed so impeccably, his body half-turned as he lies on the bed. It seems an invasion of privacy to be there, and I turn away. But at the moment of seeing, I imagine him dropping back and to the side, letting go, surrendering control. (I have not forgotten the fall of the night before.) There comes into my mind the thought that he has always had an adversarial relationship to his body. But in old age, the body will have its due, will begin to assert its own control.

Let him sleep, let him rest, Pociao and Roberto urge, and I agree. But Abdelouahaid, who is of a much more practical turn of mind, simply goes in and wakes Paul up and says that Roberto is ready to take the photos.

Late in the afternoon, we go for a walk on the mountain. It is cold, and the wind is sharp, almost biting. The full moon is surprisingly bright as it travels across the darkening sky. Paul walks along, using his cane, stopping occasionally, speaking lightly, being his usual, easy social self. If he is feeling pain, he does not show it. When we return to the flat, he immediately undresses, with Abdelouahaid's help, and gets into bed. Then Abdelouahaid brings him his tea, and he reads the mail. Roberto, Pociao, and I sit in the living room and talk with concern of Paul's fatigue. When Abdelouahaid comes out, I tell him about Paul's fall the night before and wonder if he should be alone at night. Abdelouahaid tells us that he has offered to stay with Paul at night, but Paul has said no. It is up to Paul, we all agree, and let the matter rest.

I go in to bid Paul good night. He says he will see me in the morning. Then, with some irritation, he speaks about Virginia Carr coming the following afternoon. "There will be plenty of time for her to come when you leave," he says. "Do you not want her to come?" I ask. He shrugs, and things are left as they have been arranged. There our conversation ends, but when I get back to the hotel, I call Virginia Carr and say that Paul seems particularly tired. I suggest she come a little later than three tomorrow, in case he wants to take an afternoon rest.

At his flat the next morning, Paul is sitting up in bed having his breakfast, seemingly recovered from the fatigue of the day before. Still I limit my time with him. I go over the material I have selected for the *Viking Portable Paul and Jane Bowles,* which I am editing, and then I leave early.

I spend the early afternoon with Pociao. She laughs when she tells me that when she first came to Tangier, she was uneasy, even fearful of walking alone; but now she feels completely at home. After lunch, we walk to the Anglican church. There, in the courtyard, just as I had seen it in my walk with Paul in 1977, is the small hut of the man who sells chants and potions. Pociao, admitting to neither seriousness nor a joke, arranges to purchase a chant for a friend in Bonn, a young woman who has just had an unhappy love affair.

Walking through the streets of Tangier with Pociao, I begin to realize the lingering effect that my intense involvement with the tragedy of Jane's life has had upon my sense of this place. What was it Jane had said about Tangier in 1968? "It's good for Paul but it's not good for me." Yes, it has been good for Paul—a place attuned to his imaginative life, a place in which he could create a daily life necessary for that imaginative life.

As for Pociao and Roberto, they too lead a daily life in Tangier. They have become so enamored of the city that they have rented a small flat on a permanent basis in a section called the Sharf. When they are here, they work on their translations, they keep house, they go to the market, they buy food, they visit with friends, expatriates and Moroccans. Roberto has also become the European agent for several Moroccan writers, including Mrabet.

But in Tangier I can find no reference or tie to daily life. For me, it remains a setting for drama, a place with an almost mythological impact. If I try to isolate its qualities, I come up with a surface seediness and a rawness of depth, curiously entwined. It is a place where outside and inside seem to have no clear demarcation. I recall the brilliantly shining colors in the paintings that Matisse did here in the early part of the century. I do not get a sense of brilliance here now, but rather of a kind of tarnishing that has taken place at this northern edge of the so-called dark continent, just beyond the southern edge of Europe. Even the light here seems dense, as if in this place it has incorporated something of seedy shadow. And at every corner there is the smell of spices and urine and diesel exhaust, as if every pungency carried with it an alternate substance, a counterbalancing odor.

And the sounds—oh, yes, the sounds—the sounds of the cars in the street, the sounds of the voices—incomprehensible—the sounds of the muezzin at night, secret sounds—sounds like cloaks over words and thoughts.

When Pociao and I arrive at Paul's, well after four, Virginia Carr and Mary Robbins are still with him in the bedroom, so we leave and walk to the nearby American School. In the entry hall is a drawing of Paul by the painter Claudio Bravo. The Paul it depicts is remote and still, made all the more fragile by the loud talk and laughter of the students hurrying out at the end of the school day.

By the time Pociao and I get back to Paul's, it is almost five, and Virginia Carr and Mary Robbins have left. Paul is lying on the bed, exhausted. No, he does not want to go for a walk, he tells Pociao when she goes in to talk to him. He is too tired. Suddenly, querulously (I am sitting in the living room so I can hear him), he says, "It's Millicent's fault. She had them come too late." I try to dismiss it; I say to myself that he is tired and therefore irritable, a human response, after all. But there is a lingering impact in the sound of his words. Judgment from him is hard for me to take, when I have striven so hard to understand his refusal to judge. Come on, quit the mea culpa, I say to myself. Did I not ask Virginia to come a little later in the afternoon, thinking to protect him? Enough of being the den mother in the den of iniquity.

At that moment, the doorbell rings. A Spanish couple, friends of Paul's for many years, have come unexpectedly. They go into his bedroom, carrying with them several presents. Sitting up in bed, Paul smiles, he chats, he is his usual lively, welcoming self. Out in the living room, Abdelouahaid and Pociao and I have tea. Pociao asks Abdelouahaid if there is any way to stop people from staying with Paul too long, from overtiring him when he is already tired. Abdelouahaid says he could not do that: Paul will do what Paul will do.

In my overwrought state, I am struck by the thought of how powerful and unfathomable and capricious need is in Paul. When one is with him, one keeps listening to the hidden sound of his need; one feels impelled by its urgency to action. But then his need may suddenly turn, redefine itself, recede, or make itself small, and one feels one has overreacted. Still later will come the sound of his need again, a siren sound, irresistible, the mirror and reflection of one's own need, perhaps.

One day the Lady of Peace went out walking and she met a cat. "My word," said the Lady of Peace, "what a pretty cat!" The cat looked at her sort of queer and said, "Go home." "The idea! I won't!" said the Lady of Peace. "Hike it home," said the cat. "I won't," said the Lady of Peace, stamping her foot. "If you don't go home, I'll make you," said the cat, throwing some stones. "After all, I don't think you're such a pretty cat," said the Lady of Peace and went home.

"How old were you when you wrote this?" I ask after Paul recites this very early fiction to me.

"About six. You know it's nothing."

I do not think it is "nothing." I ask about the phrase "hike it home."

"I suppose that's what children say." Then he adds, "It sounds more like my father."

I ask Paul if he remembers having imaginary playmates as a child.

"No."

"You didn't?"

"No. Well, yes. I didn't have imaginary playmates, but I imagined a world where the normal size of a person was the size of a kitchen match. About that big." With his thumb and forefinger, he indicates the size. "They weren't my playmates because I didn't exist. I was the head of a cosmos in which they existed. They had names, and they had intrigues, and terrible things happened," he says and laughs.

"But they were so tiny."

"That made the room in which they lived enormous."

"Men and women and children?"

"No children. No, no, no. They were banned forever from my cosmos."

And was there furniture in their rooms?

"In my room?"

"In your cosmos."

"Oh, well, they lived in various pieces of furniture around the room. There were elevators up the sides of the tables and so on so they could get in and go up to their apartments."

"Did your mother know about this?"

"No. You know, children don't tell. It would ruin everything."

"And you weren't inside the cosmos, but it belonged to you."

"Well, I ran it, yeah. But I didn't exist. There was no such person."

"No such person inside the cosmos?"

"Anywhere. As me, no."

"You run it, but you don't exist."

"That's right."

"So you're all-powerful—"

"But they don't know me; they've never heard of me. They do what they do, and that's always because I decided that they should. But they don't know that. It's exactly like having characters in a novel, really."

Sana comes in to show Paul a new mop she has just bought for cleaning. It looks like a window wiper with a very long handle. Paul says, "I bought one of those five years ago or more for cleaning the floor. The woman who worked here before took it and broke it in half purposely, like that." He gestures with his two hands, as if snapping a stick. "She said she didn't want to use it. Don't understand them. They're peculiar."

Now, after talk of Paul's earliest fiction, I turn to his last stories, the volume *Unwelcome Words* (which included the title story). It is as if I am following an arc, from childhood to old age, from the first inventions of "intrigues and terrible things" within a cosmos that he ruled, all-powerful and nonexistent, to a series of tales of "real" events in a "real" world, primarily the city of Tangier. The people in these last stories are "real" men and women, though there are still no children to speak of.

He, Paul, is a character in a number of these stories.

For example, in one of the stories, "Dinner at Sir Nigel's," the narrator is Paul in his own voice, a guest at a dinner party at the house of a British expatriate. During the meal the host, Sir Nigel, expresses such hostility and contempt toward his guests that they all grow silent. The dinner is followed by a "floor show" in which five beautiful young Moroccan women play the drums and Sir Nigel pretends to flay them with a whip. The five women cry out in simulated terror and, at a signal from Sir Nigel, begin to attack each other. When this performance is over, the women are sent to their rooms, and Sir Nigel invites the guests to "spend a little time" with them. Not one of the guests takes him up on his offer. Instead, they say they must leave, and immediately Sir Nigel ushers them out.

"I think you told me once," I say to Paul, "about a man who came here who behaved like this."

"Yes. I was there, at dinner, and saw the whole business," he admits. "With a lot of journalists, English-speaking journalists—Canadian, Australian, British."

"Was he as angry and contemptuous a man as you present him?"

"He was like that. I didn't understand him at all. I don't know what he wanted to prove. He wanted to show off, obviously."

"That he had these women—and then could offer them to his guests."

"Yeah. And he knew damn well no one would accept because he stood there with boots and a big whip in his hand. No, nobody took him up on it. Well, he was crazy. Ach! At the end, I remember, when we left, he saw us out. His house was down away from the road, and we had to go up through pastureland to get to the gate on the road. He was very solicitous and polite, and he opened the gate—there was one woman with us, I've forgotten her name now. Doesn't matter. She was well known at the time as a journalist. He opened the gate for us, and we went through, and then he didn't say what I say he said. I say he said, 'Good night, you bloody swine,' or something. No. He said," and Paul takes on a transparently false, agreeable, gentlemanly tone, " 'Good night, good night, fuck you. Fuck you, good night, fuck you.' "

I laugh. "That's what he said?"

"That's exactly what he said. To the girl and everyone."

"How hilarious. But you didn't want to put that in."

"Well, no, I didn't want to put it in."

"But he said it in just that way?"

"Yes, in a rather mellifluous way."

In another of the stories, "Tangier 1975," the narrator is an unnamed expatriate who, with her husband, has been offered the free use of a beautiful cottage on the estate of a wealthy Swiss woman. The only flaw in the arrangement is that there are twenty peacocks in an aviary close to the cottage whose nightly screams unnerve the narrator. After some months, the rich woman begins to begrudge her generosity and tries to force the couple out by treating them as if they were servants. On the night of a large party, she tells them to stand at a little booth outside the gate and allow only invited guests to enter. After hours in the booth, the narrator and her husband leave their post in disgust. As it turns out, after they leave, a thief gets in and cases the property. Some time later he returns with an entire gang of thieves, who invade the main house. In their search for cash, they torture the rich woman for hours until she dies.

After the murder, the narrator keeps thinking back to the night of the killing, feeling guilty that she and her husband had abandoned their post at the gate, thus allowing the criminal in. The story ends with her statement: "I've tried to think back to that night and sometimes it seems to me that in my sleep maybe I did hear screams but I'd heard those blasted peacocks so many times that I didn't pay attention and now it makes my blood run cold to think that perhaps I did hear her calling for help and thought it was the birds . . ."

This story, too, Paul tells me, came out of an actual happening. A wealthy Swiss woman did in fact "put this very pretty little house way down in the woods at the disposal of this couple and then suddenly began to act in a very high-handed fashion. She must have regretted having offered them the house."

"And so then she behaved that way, making them act as servants, waiting in that little gatehouse at the party—"

"She was using them, yes."

"Trying to force them out."

"Must have been."

"And did she actually end that way?"

"Yes. People thought she had a lot of money in the house. She was a wealthy woman. But she was not the sort to have money around."

I ask him about the peacocks. Yes, there were peacocks in a big aviary, not far from that little house. "They make an awful noise. Ah! You can't believe it."

"I've never heard them."

"It's terrible." Suddenly Paul lets out a wild shriek, imitating a peacock. I laugh at the abruptness and intensity of the sound.

At this moment, there is a loud squeaking noise from the living room where Sana is cleaning. "No, I wasn't talking to you," Paul says. "She sounds as if she were answering."

"She's moving the table with the books to wash under it. That's what that sound is."

"I have to leave her alone."

"People must do what they must do."

"I know."

"I forget that sometimes," I say.

"In this country you're likely to remember it."

There is in Paul an ease in talking about these stories that are not the products of his own invented cosmos. I am reminded of what he said in 1977 in response to a remark I made about Jorge Luis Borges giving up deviousness in his later years. Paul, then sixty-six, had said acerbically, "I liked his deviousness." But now it is as if Paul himself has given up deviousness in his writing, has become content to frame what he has seen in the world around him. Framed, of course, these stories are limited and confined. Their subject matter may deal with bizarre happenings, but the reader is not threatened by them, nor is the writer. They are oddly calm and suggest that some kind of reconciliation has taken place in him with the world as it is. Some peace has come to him, unexpectedly, one might say.

As I get ready to go, I say to Paul that Pociao and Roberto will return to Bonn in two days. "I will be sorry to see them go," I add. Paul says that he too will be sorry. And then he adds, "But not as sad as when you go."

His words, as words sometimes can, come as a stunning blow to me. I am forced back into my own wariness. I stumble over my words, blurting out something about how much it has mattered to me to be here with him. Even as I try to speak directly, I am aware of barriers breaking down within me. For one moment, there is a sense almost like horror of what I have been doing here. And then it comes to me that all of this is a measure of the power of the effect upon me of his being, in this situation, in this room.

That night in a dream, I hold a small child, a boy, looking down at him. At the same time, I am looking up at myself, looking down at this child. My face is marked by the years. It is aged but not worn.

There is a further fragment: I watch two little boys playing football. One seizes the football forcefully from the other, who begins to sob. Then the sobbing one runs out into the street, into the traffic. I cry out, fearful for him, angry at the other.

 Each afternoon, on the way to our walk on the Old Mountain, we drive through a street crowded with houses and shops and then come to a large flat area with neither buildings nor trees nor shrubs. As we begin the ascent of the Old Mountain, we see an old blind Moroccan woman, sitting by the roadside on a rock. She is a very religious woman, like a saint, a poor woman, Abdelouahaid has said. Every day she sits by the road, even in the cold and in the rain. Once, Pociao asked Abdelouahaid to stop the car so that we could give her some money. When my turn came to put the coins into her hand, I was astonished to find that though it was a very cold day, her hand was very warm. She said, "Baraka

. . . ," a Moroccan blessing of which I could only make out the first word.

Of all Paul's works, *The Spider's House* is the one that most clearly confronts questions of belief. Between the two protagonists of the novel, Amar and Stenham, an enormous gulf exists. The young Moroccan boy is a devout believer in the religion of his father and his father before him. The expatriate American writer is just as devoutly an unbeliever in any and all religion. In a crucial passage in the novel, Stenham, the most autobiographical of Paul's characters, recalls that his parents were intensely antagonistic to religion of any kind.

"It was true of your own family, wasn't it?" I ask Paul.

"Yes."

I read Stenham's thought: " 'Above all else, any reference to the doctrine of the immortality of the soul was regarded as the acme of bad taste; he had seen his parents shudder inwardly when a guest innocently touched on it in the course of conversation.' "

"Oh, well, yes. They never, never, never discussed such things."

"But if somebody had the bad taste to talk about the 'soul' in the house?"

"Well, they tried to get the conversation onto another territory. For them, it would be like discussing sexuality. There was something obscene about the idea of the soul and God and all that. They shied away from it, and if they knew that some guest was a Catholic, they were very careful to try and keep all conversation far from such subjects."

"Your parents were very unusual, Paul."

He laughs. "Were they? I don't know."

"You grew up with them, so you can't think of them as unusual."

"No, I just think of them as—"

"Mom and pop?" I suggest.

"He and she," he corrects me.

In another passage in the novel, Stenham recalls that as a young man he had believed in Marxism and had joined the Communist Party. But at the beginning of World War II, he had lost his faith in the party and in Marxism as well. (It was precisely at this time, after the Soviets signed a nonaggression pact with the Nazis, that Paul experienced the same loss of belief.) Stenham reveals that by the time he arrived in Morocco after the war, he was convinced that no belief mattered to him, that nothing was of importance but "the exquisitely isolated cosmos of his own consciousness." Little by little, however, as he stayed on in Fez, even that conviction eroded away. He began to feel that all existence, including his own, was absurd and unreal. In the wake of this, he was beset by a terrible anxiety.

I remind Paul of this passage now. "You write that one day when Stenham is walking in the hills behind Fez, he suddenly comes to the realization that the true source of his anxiety is the fear in himself of eternal damnation."

"Yeah, I never understood that."

"Ach!"

He laughs. "Why I wrote it, even. What was wrong with him that day? When I read it over, I thought, Good Lord, what happened to him? But I have to leave it because that's what happened to him. I suppose," he goes on, "it was something he'd heard of, of course. People talk about being damned, and I suppose his idea of damnation was to have to go on being conscious forever. That would be hell. It would be completely unnatural. Because the whole point of life is that it does cease and that one can cease being conscious. It's frightening to him to imagine there being no end to anything. That would be eternal damnation, of course. It would be like—what? Sartre's idea of Hell in a way. The light was always on [in *No Exit*]; you couldn't turn it off."

After a pause, I ask, "Is this what you're saying to me? You take the situation that existed with your family—all that you were taught early about religion—you take that background, and you give it to Stenham, just as you give him the membership in the party and leaving the party and coming to Morocco. But then when it comes to this anxiety, this fear of eternal damnation, are you saying that here he departs from your experience and goes off on his own?"

"I can't force my ideas upon him, make his actions correspond to my feeling of how they should be."

"He was not like the little match people in your cosmos when you were a child."

"No. They had to do what they had to do. But he didn't. Because he's an invented character that becomes alive for me. Yeah. Therefore he existed."

"And once he exists he has the right to—"

"Anything."

Yet, remembering the little boy who prayed to the mosquito, I am still not convinced that Stenham's experience went one way and Paul's another. An old and discarded thought comes to me: from Jane's earliest years, the question of a belief in God—though not the God of a formal religion, not the God of the Old or New Testament—had been central to what she was. For all that she had thrown herself into the pleasures of daily life, she never escaped this preoccupation. Paul had often told me how in the midst of a conversation with her about daily events, a conversation that had nothing to do with belief, she would bring up questions about sin and salvation. He would say to her that he heard the words she was saying but he had no idea what she meant.

When he spoke of not understanding what she meant, there was in his voice a mixture of exasperation and futility. I remember wondering whether it was possible that, even as she spoke obsessively of what he refused to understand, she was also mirroring something within him? Indeed, he and she, for all their striking differences, often reflected each other, as if, someone once said, they were two parts of the same being.

Is it possible, I wonder now, that even as Paul tells me how in the writing Stenham went one way and he another, those two ways were not as divergent as he insists?

Perhaps what Paul has said to me about Stenham, that he existed and therefore had the right to anything, could just as easily have been put the other way around. Because he had the right to anything, he existed.

Later that afternoon we are walking on the Old Mountain. On either side of the road are the high walls of elegant villas. Here and there a breach in a wall allows you to look down onto the blue Mediterranean. One wall is painted a sharp robin's-egg blue, startling in the sun. It is cool but not cold, and the sky is clear after several days of rain. Paul labors on with his cane, steadily, not showing any pain, though certainly, I think, there must be pain for him in the effort. He tells me that he had a visitor the previous day, a Moroccan now living in New York, who told him that Ahmed Yacoubi had a son, a young man by this time, who had moved to Tangier. So it was not the end of Yacoubi's line, Paul says.

We drive down the winding road past the blind woman sitting on the stone, through the outlying districts, into the center of the city. At the Fez market, Abdelouahaid gets out to do Paul's daily shopping. Paul says he is tired after the walk and will stay in the car. I sit with him, he in the front next to the driver's seat and I in the back. Soon I see his head begin to nod and fall forward; he is asleep. I find myself wanting to reach forward and touch his head, as I wanted to reach forward so many years ago to my children when they were small and sleeping.

It is the last evening in Tangier for Pociao and Roberto, and I go with them to an art opening at a gallery on a side street. The gallery is exhibiting the work of an Iraqi painter who specializes in abstract paintings, characterized by intense primary colors and simple forms. As I stand with Roberto and Pociao, the writer Mohammed Choukri comes up to me. I have not seen him since 1977, when he was working with Paul, who was translating his *Jean Genet in Tangier* into English. (Choukri, born into a poor family, was illiterate until the age of twenty. After he was jailed during the riots for Moroccan independence, he resolved to learn to read and write. Within a few years, he had mastered classical Arabic and had published his first book, the autobiographical *For Bread Alone*.)

Except for his gray hair, Choukri has changed very little since 1977. In his halting English, with Roberto sometimes translating when he lapses into Spanish, he tells me that he is writing a book about Paul "and his circle," a book, he adds, that departs now and then into philosophical speculation. (Yet one more book about Paul . . .) He expounds on the subject of Paul and his contradictions. Paul was someone who would give freely of his time and advice in artistic matters, helping Choukri, encouraging him in his work. But when it came to matters of money, Paul was not so liberal. If it was a question of even fifty dirhams (a little over five dollars) owed him, Paul would be insistent about repayment. Flushed with wine, Choukri grows more voluble. "There exists in me toward Paul the kind of hate that I feel for my father."

"Once, years ago," he says, falling into a storytelling mode, "I went with Paul to Jane's flat. Paul, seeing a cat upon the windowsill—not Jane's cat, but a cat that Jane was caring for—went over to the windowsill and pushed the cat out the window."

"I cannot believe that, Choukri," I say.

Choukri becomes insistent, assuring me that he saw it with his own eyes, that afterward he, Choukri, went downstairs and saw the cat lying dead on the ground.

"But, Choukri," I ask, "what possible reason would Paul have to do such a thing?"

"Paul was very angry at Jane at the time," Choukri responds. "She was out of control; she kept getting up in the middle of the night and going to the refrigerator and throwing food on the floor. Paul was fed up with her," Choukri adds with a flourish and goes off and gets more wine.

That night in my hotel room, I think back to the terrible years of Jane's final illness, to her last stay in Tangier, when Paul had taken her out of the hospital in Málaga at her request. And I think of Choukri's story about Paul and the cat.

No, I do not believe that story. But is it not so that there is something in the air around Paul, around his figure, like a nimbus, a corona . . . something that accretes and absorbs story?

I recall Alfred Chester, an American writer who suffered from paranoia and delusions. He came to Tangier, partly at Paul's invitation—Paul was a great admirer of his writing—in 1963. Chester became obsessed with Paul, revering him one moment as a godlike figure and the next moment believing that Paul was poisoning him. Sometimes when he and Paul were talking, Chester would yell, "Cut out the subconversations!" In the fall of 1965 Chester suffered a psychotic break. Shortly afterward he was expelled from Morocco by the authorities because of his bizarre behavior. In 1971 he committed suicide in the Arab quarter of Jerusalem, where he was living.

While in Morocco, Chester wrote "Safari," a tale of going on a scorpion hunt with Paul (called "Gerald" in the story). Gerald is described as looking fifteen years younger than his age, thin as a boy "but not muscular, full of quick nervous energy, and his hair is still very blond." Gerald is remarkably observant of everything in the natural world, able to remember and classify plants, able to recall smells and colors and shapes. The narrator asks Gerald why he is poisoning him, but Gerald calmly denies that he is doing any such thing. The narrator, who is convinced that Gerald can read his mind, goes on:

> Sometimes I think Gerald is God, at least a local god, or more exactly, a local demon. Africa is not the same as other continents, despite its revolutions, and Gerald has lived here so long that magic and sorcery are more part of his nature than science or the ten commandments. I do actually hear drums at his approach; I can see the bone and

ring through his nose; I can see the hideous paint on his face. He is a witch doctor using the body of a mild English missionary. I believe his mind can create things, can make them up as he goes along, *real* things (so to speak) like this road we were on . . . If the world is illusion, why shouldn't Gerald be the cause of some of these illusions? I know this sounds insane. I probably am insane. Still and all, can't a madman be logical and right?

39 "Think," I say to Paul, looking at the unanswered letters scattered in piles on the floor, "after tomorrow you will be able to answer your letters in the morning."

"Well, how can I with you-know-who?" He is referring to Virginia Carr.

"You don't have to see her in the morning."

"No. Not yet. Incidentally, I have to see her this afternoon."

"You have to see her this afternoon?"

"Last night or yesterday afternoon late, after we got back from the walk, someone came, and Abdelouahaid came in and said, 'The two women in the Minzah sent a messenger to find out when you're going to see them,' as though they were getting very impatient. So I said, all right, I'd see them tomorrow afternoon for an hour at two-thirty."

"They're going to see you today at two-thirty?" I ask again.

"M-m-m. Well, were you planning to come at that hour?"

"No, but—they're going to think I'm a liar."

"Why?"

"Because I have been telling them what you told me to tell them, that they were to come when I left."

"Oh?"

"So now they will think that I have made all this up and that you really wanted to see them."

"Well, I don't know whether they'll think that."

Will they think that? Why have I picked this to say? There is hurt here and anger and once again a sense of betrayal. But I have always known, looking at Virginia, seeing her capacity for action, that if she pushed, Paul would capitulate, no matter what he had said to me about wanting to see only one of us at a given time. I have an overwhelming sense that I have been a fool. (You can see that it was all getting out of hand for me.) I struggle to stop myself from imploding or exploding. It is not your right, I remind myself; if he wants to see her, that's his choice. But that I have allowed myself to be used as an intermediary and then bypassed—it's your own fault, I rage at myself. Besides, it's almost over.

(Of course I was being childish, but simple childishness was not entirely the point. It was the situation, too—yes, still the situation between the questioner and the answerer, between the biographer and the subject . . .)

It happens with others in ordinary daily life, I remind myself, that they become jealous and possessive of Paul. So, too, it has happened to you. I struggle to be reasonable. I think, Here is Virginia, clearly a woman of action; isn't it natural that she should begin to chafe at this inactivity? But I am not here to take her side.

"And so—I mean, you know, it's—you're going to see them for an hour at two-thirty?" I ask yet once more, trying to come to some balance, barely coherent.

"Apparently they're coming, yes. I gave the message to Abdelouahaid, and he relayed it to the messenger outside the door. So I don't know. I assume they will come."

"I was going to come and take a walk with you at four. Are you planning to take a walk today?"

"M-hm-m," he says.

"Okay, I'll come at four."

I tell myself it does not make any difference. I try to say a few words of resolution, of reconciliation. I tell Paul it is not a matter of competition. She, Virginia, will write a book that is totally different from what I will write.

(Do you think I listened to myself? Anger had surfaced and then had gone below the surface, hidden behind inanity. Yet, as I am a poor actress, my face betrayed me; my voice betrayed me. He must have known I was upset and angry. Was he surprised at my anger? Did he even a little enjoy my anger, only half-suppressed? I didn't know. The anger shut me out from seeing him as well as myself. I can't say that I felt very proud of the way I was acting. Still, there it was. It had come out of the situation, out of my history with him, out of what I thought was my history with him, out of my own history.)

"I'm so curious to see how she interviews you, Paul. I wish I could be here hiding in the corner to see." This is not really so, but still I say it. I laugh in a bizarre way, bizarre even to myself.

"Writhing in the corner?" asks Paul.

This time I really laugh. Yes, after all, how transparent I am. "Hiding—and maybe writhing, too. Oh, well, *c'est la vie.* I mean, I don't care if she wants to—if she has decided that I have attempted to—but, look, I mean—" Again, out of incoherence comes the sense that I have to be fair. What can one be in this situation but fair? For I cannot help but see that Virginia is caught as well. That she is more forceful than I does not mean that she is any the less caught.

"Now she will have to be a character in the book," I say. "The appearance of the second biographer . . ."

"Oh, that'll be perfect," Paul laughs.

Yes, I am still in a Paul Bowles story.

"Okay, now." I turn to one final question about Paul's fiction. It is not a crucial question; rather, it is almost a diversion, perhaps a way of defusing what has happened. I bring up "Sylvie Ann, the Boogie Man," which was written in early 1959, after Jane had gone to England the second time to receive treatment for her stroke, after she and Paul had returned to Tangier, and just as the police had launched their investigation of all foreign residents who had close relationships with Moroccans.

"I remember your telling me that Cherifa fled to the hills and that Ahmed Yacoubi was in jail, and you were trying to decide whether to stay in Tangier or not. You did decide to leave, but you wrote this story before you left?"

"Yes."

"What I think is interesting—among all the other things that are interesting about writing—is the moment at which a particular story emerges. Here you are under those tremendously stressed circumstances, and you write a story that comes out of a long distant past." ("Sylvie Ann" is based on Paul's memory of a black woman who worked for his mother as a laundress when he was a child.) "You write it through the eyes of Sylvie Ann, seeing the injustice in her life. Would it be going too far to say that all that was happening to you at the time left you with a sense of injustice? I mean, what was going on with the police and what was going on with the pursuit of the expatriates in Tangier—as well as the situation with Jane."

"I wasn't aware of injustice. It didn't occur to me that there was any injustice around."

"But you felt very uneasy about the situation in Morocco."

"Yeah, we didn't know what was going to happen."

"So it was frightening, right?"

"But that doesn't give one the feeling of injustice, exactly. Just trying to be accurate."

"Could you see anything in the situation of the woman in the story that in any way might have had any resemblance to something in your own emotional state at the time?"

"It's hard to know. It doesn't sound probable, but I don't dare say no."

I remind Paul that he has spoken at times of the therapeutic value for him of writing fiction. "Giving form to an experience somehow sets one free from it. Is that correct?"

"Well, it probably does. That's the therapy of it."

"It isn't chance, then, that one seizes upon a subject and writes a story. It isn't chance that a particular subject comes to you at a particular moment."

"That's a mysterious question. I've never seen any connection, really, between anything I wrote and the external circumstances."

"One can't know the connection, because knowing will impede the fiction. But there is some kind of connection," I assert.

"But one isn't obliged to be conscious of that connection."

"One is almost prevented from being conscious of it."

"At the time of writing—but even now, I mean, twenty or thirty years later—I still don't see it. I mean, I'm not able to tell you."

"Well, it may not be of any interest to you, either, to know if there's a connection."

"To me? Well, it isn't, particularly; no. I would say it was part of analysis, analyzing reasons for things, even analyzing what's in the story."

"Which are things that you don't even want to do. It's just not the way you are."

"No. I'm not very analytical, as you probably know."

"Yes, and, of course, from the beginning you've known that that's part of what I am."

"Being analytical?"

"Yes."

"That's your job," he laughs.

"It's also the way my mind works."

At this moment, there comes to me an idea—no, a feeling that presses upon me with an almost physical force so that even though it is vague, I am impelled to try to put it into words. "Writing a work is not only therapeutic in the sense in which you say it is, but it is like an event in life. An actual event that then has its place in life, as powerful as anything that happens in life—or maybe more powerful."

No, I realize even as I say this, That's not what I mean. Yet that feeling still presses upon me with great force, as if it is pushing me over an edge. I fall into words about life and fiction and fiction and life. "I suppose that what I'm trying to say is that a novel as powerful as *The Sheltering Sky* or *Let It Come Down* comes out of something fundamental within the writer, even as the novel is deeply tied to the world the writer is living in at the moment."

"That is probably true."

"The power of *The Sheltering Sky,* the reason it touches other people, comes out of some deep connection made in your deepest being."

"*Es weiss ich nicht!*" says Paul, as he has before.

"Ach!" I laugh. "I know you don't like to think about it. But it has to be; it has to be."

"I don't know anything about the deep parts of my being. I really don't."

"You know everything about the deep parts of your being, but you just don't want to talk about them or analyze them. Nobody could have written that novel unless there was a very deep connection with subterranean things."

"Well, yes, I agree," he says.

In the silence that follows, I have the sense of a great gap, which Paul promptly fills by recalling that he was writing "Sylvie Ann" during the mornings when he and Jane were packing to leave for Portugal.

"You're packing and you're writing the story?"

"Yeah, it's crazy. And of course I had to take care of Jane."

"How did you do that? How could you take care of her and also write the story?"

"Well, I had to; I felt I had to. I didn't have to, of course, but I made myself think I had to."

"In terms of your sense of responsibility—"

"Of course I had to take care of Jane; that goes without saying. But I didn't have to write that story or any story at that point. I think it pleased me to be writing it at the same time, under such stress. I wanted a story really without any particular stress. On the contrary. It was like a balm." He laughs. "I don't know why."

There is another silence, and now I fill in the gap.

"All right, so—I have something else that I want to talk to you about." I pause and sigh. "Why this is so hard for me to ask you, I don't know. It's only about an idiotic story that Choukri told me. Choukri, who was at the reception, drinking a little wine—he's writing this book about you."

"Well, if you say so. I don't know anything about it."

"He's working out his relationship to his father through you. Sorry," I laugh.

"He's out of his mind, but anyway go on."

"After he told me how much you have helped him, et cetera, et cetera, then he said, 'But there was that story of Paul and the cat.'"

"What?"

"Listen to this story that he believes. I don't believe it, but I have to tell you this because he told it to me. One day—this was when Jane was very ill, so it must have been '68 or '69—he says that you and he go into her apartment. I don't know where Jane is. Maybe she's in the other room. Anyhow, there's a cat sitting on the windowsill, Choukri says. It's not even Jane's cat, it's a cat she's been taking care of. Then, Choukri says, you go over to the windowsill, and you shove the cat out of the window."

"I did what?" Paul asks incredulously. "Threw it out the window?"

"You go like this"—I make a gesture of shoving with my hand and arm—"and you push the cat out the window, and it falls down to the ground and dies."

"And he believes that?"

"He believes it. I said to him, 'Choukri, that's not possible.'"

"That's right."

"But he said"—and here I take on Choukri's voice—"'Yes, that happened.'"

Paul laughs.

"If it was a dog, maybe—" I joke.

"I wouldn't push any animal out the window," Paul says in an aggrieved tone.

"I know you wouldn't. What is it with a guy like Choukri? Is he a mythmaker?"

"I don't know. I don't drink, but—something happens,

obviously." After a moment, Paul adds, "What is strange about the story is that it happened to my gray cat Dubs. I left it with Ann Harbach when I went to America or somewhere. And when Jane and I came back, of course I went right to Ann's apartment and asked about Dubs. And she said, 'Dubs fell out the window onto the sidewalk and was killed.' I was very sad. That's the only thing I can think of that has any resemblance to his story. That's really funny."

"I thought that you should know about this and that he's probably putting—"

"He'll probably put it in his book. I don't understand people's minds," Paul says.

When I arrive at the flat at four that afternoon, Virginia and Mary have already left. They have brought Paul a huge bunch of roses. They have also brought with them a number of his books, which they asked him to sign for them. (I have not asked Paul to sign my copies of his books for me; I don't know why.)

Paul gets ready to go out, and he and I and Abdelouahaid go for a walk on the Old Mountain. It is as it has been each day, the conversation easy and unstressed as we stroll. Paul tells me an anecdote about one of his uncles, his mother's brother, who was terribly "cheap," he says. Once— it was before he and Jane were married—he and some friends had gone up to the country and visited some of his relatives, and as they were walking back to the station, his uncle came by and offered them a ride in his car. When they got out, the uncle asked each of them for fifty cents.

That night I have dinner with Virginia and Mary at the hotel; it has been arranged beforehand. There is a gentility at play here. Virginia tells me of her experiences writing about Carson McCullers. I fall into a known part, becoming the listener. She tells me again how much she admires my book on Jane. She asks me about certain people I interviewed in the book, who had known Jane and Paul well. Do I know their addresses so she can contact them? They're dead, I say, which is indeed the truth. I say it with a perverse satisfaction, which I do not even try to justify to myself.

 And now, at the end, I return to where I began, to the work that led me here fifteen years ago, to *Two Serious Ladies,* the book that Jane brought to Paul in Mexico, the book he changed and shaped, the book that compelled him to return to his own fiction.

I bring up the section describing the arrival of Mr. and Mrs. Copperfield—the fictional Paul and Jane—in Panama, the place to which Paul and Jane sailed on their honeymoon.

"Here they are," I say to Paul, as he sits up in bed having breakfast, "just about to get off the boat in Panama. Mrs. Copperfield is saying good-bye to a woman passenger, and she asks her if she can come and visit her in Colón. But the woman says she wants to spend all of her time with her son, whom she's visiting." I read:

> "That's all right," said Mrs. Copperfield.
> "Of course it's all right. You've got that beautiful husband of yours."

Here Paul laughs.

"That doesn't help," said Mrs. Copperfield [again Paul laughs], but no sooner had she said this than she was horrified at herself.

"And then the woman says, 'Now you've had a tiff,' " Paul inserts.

"Well, now you've had a tussle?" said the woman.
"No."
"Then I think you're a terrible little woman talking that way about your husband," she said, walking away. Mrs. Copperfield hung her head and went back to stand beside Mr. Copperfield.

Paul quotes from memory: "And then he says, 'Why do you talk to such dopes?' "
" 'Why do you talk to such dopes?' " I read.
We both laugh, and Paul says, "I remember that, yeah."
"It comes up several times in the novel, the reference to Mr. Copperfield as beautiful or handsome. I would imagine, if you don't mind my saying so, that Jane felt pleased that you were so handsome."
"She thought I was, maybe. I don't know. She never told me."
"On their arrival in Colón," I go on, "she wants to go to the expensive Hotel Washington, but Mr. Copperfield says to her—"

"I don't believe in spending money on a luxury that can only be mine for a week at the most. I think it's more fun to buy objects which will last me perhaps a lifetime. We can certainly find a hotel in the town that will be comfortable. Then we will be free to spend our money on more exciting things."

"The room in which I sleep is so important to me," Mrs. Copperfield said. She was nearly moaning.

"My dear, a room is really only a place in which to sleep and dress. If it is quiet and the bed is comfortable, nothing more is necessary. Don't you agree with me?"

" 'You know damn well I don't,' or something like that," Paul recalls.

"You know very well I don't agree with you."

"If you're going to be miserable we'll go to the Hotel Washington," said Mr. Copperfield. Suddenly he lost his dignity. His eyes clouded over and he pouted. "But I'll be wretched there, I can assure you. [Paul laughs again.] It's going to be so goddammed dull." He was like a baby and Mrs. Copperfield was obliged to comfort him. He had a trick way of making her feel responsible.

"After all, it's mostly my money," she said to herself. "I am footing the bulk of the expenditure for this trip." Nevertheless she was unable to gain a sense of power by reminding herself of this. She was completely dominated by Mr. Copperfield as she was by almost anyone with whom she came in contact. Still certain people who knew her very well affirmed that she was capable of suddenly making a very radical and independent move without a soul to back her up.

"Without a soul to back her up," Paul repeats—in admiration, in wonder, in amusement.

"She's twenty-three years old, and she's writing this," I say in amazement.

"Let's see, what was she? No, she was twenty-one when she began this. She began it the year we were married, and we were married the day before she became twenty-one." (In the pictures of the two of them taken at the time, she seems even younger. Yet here is her voice, in the passages I read now, ageless—as if there is a third being here, speaking, telling what once was.)

"She is using certain things that did happen on your honeymoon, for example, that you didn't want to go to an expensive hotel—and undoubtedly she did want to."

"I'm sure. Yes."

"Okay. So they find an inexpensive hotel in the heart of the red-light district, and they go to look at some rooms on the fifth floor. The manager tells them that these would be the least noisy so Mrs. Copperfield, who is afraid of lifts—"

"A-a-h," says Paul in recognition of Jane's terror.

"—climbs the stairs, but when she gets to the fifth floor she finds herself in a hall with nothing but a hundred straight-backed dining room chairs. As soon as Mr. Copperfield gets off the elevator, she runs over to him and tells him that it's the ugliest thing she's ever seen. He tells her to wait a second while he counts the luggage; he wants to make sure it's all there." We both laugh, and I add, "You probably did say that."

"Yeah, it's natural."

"Then she says,"

> "As far as I'm concerned, it could be at the bottom of the sea—all of it."
>
> "Where's my typewriter?" asked Mr. Copperfield.
>
> "Talk to me this minute," said his wife, beside herself with anger.
>
> "Do you care whether or not you have a private bath?" asked Mr. Copperfield.
>
> "No, no, I don't care about that. It's not a question of comfort at all, it's something much more than that."

"More than that," Paul repeats, and he smiles.

> Mr. Copperfield chuckled. "You're so crazy," he said to her with indulgence. He was delighted to be in the tropics at last and he was more than pleased with himself that he had managed to dissuade his wife from stopping at a ridiculously expensive hotel, where they would have been surrounded by tourists. He realized that this hotel was sinister but that was what he loved.

"That's Jane's idea, yeah," Paul says, and he laughs again.

"Do you remember," I ask him, "what you felt about Mr. Copperfield when you first read *Two Serious Ladies?*"

"Well, I wasn't sure reading it whether she meant it as a caricature of me or not. So I accepted it. Finally I decided that she did mean it as a caricature. I don't know yet."

"You never asked her."

"No. No. I felt it was none of my business to ask her. Maybe she wouldn't have been able to tell me, anyway. She wouldn't have known."

"After they get to their room," I go on, "Mr. Copperfield leaves to buy a papaya and Mrs. Copperfield lies on the bed thinking."

> "Memory," she whispered. "Memory of the things I have loved since I was a child. My husband is a man without memory." She felt intense pain at the thought of this man whom she liked above all other people, this man for whom each thing he had not yet known was a joy . . .

There is a long silence after I read the words. Here, now, *it* is coming to an end.

"This book," I push on, "like all wonderful books, each time you read it, it's different."

"It's wonderful, yes," Paul says.

"It is wonderful," I repeat. "But it must not have been easy for you to read it at first. I mean, I'm sure you admired it and loved it, but that she was revealing her own feelings about what had happened between the two of you—that couldn't have been easy."

"It didn't bother me. I've read it now, of course, so many times I don't really remember what my initial reaction was. Except I always loved it."

"But you had to be aware that there was a sharpness, a critical edge to it, too."

"Well, of course, I was aware, but then there was that same edge to our relationship and to our conversations. It showed the same kind of—what?—awareness of aspects of my personality that she really objected to or that bothered her."

"But in return would you ever say anything to her if there were any aspects of her personality that bothered you?"

Paul paused. "Well, I don't know. Probably. I don't know."

"Two writers in a family, they cannot help revealing something about the other," I say. "How complicated that is . . ."

"We always showed each other our work," Paul says, "except when she began having her block. Then she wouldn't show anything."

"She never could find the form that would release her."

"Well, at all costs she wanted to avoid repeating herself. She didn't want to write another funny book."

"And yet this book has so many aspects—it's not simply a funny book."

"I'm sure she knew that."

322

Then suddenly he asks me, "Do you think it was a good idea to persuade her to cut out 'Señorita Córdoba' and 'A Guatemalan Idyll' and 'A Day in the Open' from the novel?"

This is the first time that Paul has ever asked me whether it was a "good" idea that he had helped her, that he had made the suggestions that turned *Three Serious Ladies* into *Two Serious Ladies*. I answer him by saying what I believe, that artistically it was the correct choice. But, I add, if one does not speak in artistic terms, if one speaks instead of what imagined beings were within Jane, I cannot guess what the consequences were of his advising her to cut them out.

"They really had no place in the narrative," Paul says.

"They began to act on their own, stepping further and further out of it."

"They just walked offstage," says Paul.

AFTERIMAGES

It was late December 1992. I was on a street in south Los Angeles, approaching the house of "Valeska"—the Valeska of Paul's story "Unwelcome Words." It was a barred house, with locks upon the locks. Across the front door was one locked steel gate; across the front picture window was another. I rang the doorbell and waited. Finally a voice called from within, raspy but not weak: "Who is it?"

I called out my name.

A small slot, thigh high, opened in the front door behind the gate. Through the opening I saw part of a face peering up at me.

I said I was writing a book about Paul, I said I had written a letter asking to see her; but as she had not answered, I had thought the letter might have gone astray. The face disappeared from the opening. I heard locks being unlocked; the door was opened, and the gate was pulled aside.

Before me was a slim woman in her late seventies or early eighties, her long gray hair pulled to the side, held in place with a band. She was wearing a blue bathrobe, zipped up the front, with a red collar. She had been taking a nap, she said. She invited me in. The shades were drawn, and the interior was lit by low-wattage electric bulbs. In the small entry room, large stacks of drawing paper were piled up. Valeska told me that this was her printmaking room.

She led me into the living room, this, too, dark and cluttered, filled with bookcases, cabinets containing glassware and china, a grand piano, and many chairs, including a wheelchair. A teddy bear sat in each chair. On the walls were paintings and drawings, one a portrait of Paul. "Done from a photograph?" I asked. "No," she said, "from life." I was puzzled by her answer. The painting looked just like a photo of Paul that I had seen.

She led me into the kitchen and invited me to sit at the table, around which were two kitchen chairs and another wheelchair. The wheelchairs had been used by her husband, she explained, speaking of him in the past tense. She offered me tea. Sitting across from me, smoking, she said she had not heard from Paul in a long time. Was he well? Without waiting for an answer, she jumped up from the table—her movements were quick and energetic—and went into another room. When she came back, she was carrying a pile of scrapbooks, photo albums, and portfolios. She sat down and placed them on the table before her; she did not open them for me to look at.

I asked her if she had known Paul for a long time. She nodded and told me that she knew him when he was still a composer. "So you knew him in New York?" I asked. Her answer was vague. She waved her hand in a gesture implying that it was such a long time ago she could not quite remember.

(Later I learned that she had first written to Paul in the 1960s, saying that she was interested in creating an archive of his musical work. Paul, never having met her, knowing nothing about her except that she was interested in his music, agreed to send her copies of his compositions. Then, when he came to Los Angeles to teach in 1969, he visited her and her husband in their house. After that, as I have mentioned before, until the early 1980s she traveled to Tangier frequently to see Paul, and when she was not in Tangier, she wrote long letters to him, almost daily.)

I remarked on her many teddy bears—there were a number in the kitchen as well. She got up and went into another room and brought back a huge, brown teddy bear, which she said "The Teddy Bear Man" (Peter Bull, the author of *The Teddy Bear Book*) had given her. He had died several years before, she added. "Only Paul and I are left," she went on. "He says we are too damned mean to die."

She opened an album with photographs from Tangier. As she turned the pages rapidly, I caught glimpses of photos: of Paul, of Paul with Valeska, of Dan Bente, of Mrabet, of Abdelouahaid, of Carol Ardman. She recalled how Mrabet would pick up Paul and whirl him around— Mrabet was strong and Paul was so slight—and how Paul would laugh.

She shut the album. From the scrapbook she brought out a newspaper clipping describing her as a linguist and a musician. The article noted that she had degrees in English and in music, was a member of Phi Beta Kappa, and had taught English as a second language in the public schools. She also taught music to private students. I asked if she would play one of Paul's compositions. She led me back into the living room, sat at the piano, and played a short excerpt from Rachmaninoff. "I can still play," she said, but she did not go on to play anything of Paul's.

We returned to the kitchen and sat at the table once again. She began to speak of a horrifying incident: she had been attacked by a prowler in her house. That was why, she added, there were all the gates and locks. She had been asleep one night and awoke to find a man standing over her, holding a hammer. He had said, "I am going to kill you," and began to hit her with the hammer. After he left—had she fought him off?—she called the police. She could not describe him, she told them, because it had all happened in the dark.

Immediately after the attack, she had a neighbor take pictures of her, using her own Polaroid camera, to show the blood on her face and the blood on her white night-gown. She wrote to Paul about the incident and sent him copies of the photos of herself bleeding. (Yes, I recalled, Paul had told me she had sent him photos of herself bleeding after an attack.) He wrote back, wanting to know more details of the incident. "To use in a story," she said. "He uses everyone in his stories." She did not say it bitterly but rather as a simple statement of fact.

Did I want to see her sculpture studio? She led me out the back door, it too locked and gated, into a neat garden. To the left of the garden was the garage, which she had converted into a studio. Its entrance also was covered by a heavy metal gate. She unlocked the gate and pushed it aside with an effort. "No, I don't need any help," she told me when I offered. "You can tell Paul that I'm still strong enough to do this."

The studio was cluttered with tools and sculptures and yet another wheelchair. She removed a cloth from a sculpture on a work bench and began to chip at the stone with a chisel. Pieces of stone and dust flew about in the air. I could not make out the shape of the work. Like all the other sculptures in the studio, it seemed to be in the process of trying to locate its own form.

We went back into the house, and I prepared to leave. "Before you go—" Valeska said. She jumped up and returned with a copy of *A Little Original Sin* and asked me to sign it for her. I was taken aback. After all, she had known who I was from the beginning.

As we walked to the front door, Valeska said something about a woman in Georgia who was also writing a biography of Paul. Surprised, I asked her how she knew that. She explained that she had a musician friend who taught at Georgia State University, where the biographer also taught. He was the one who had told her of the "contemplated" biography.

I got into the car, and Valeska, who was pulling the gate shut across the front door, called out, "Are you collaborating with her?" She smiled, rather slyly, I thought, for surely she knew we were not collaborating. "No," I said, and I laughed. "We're in competition." But that was not true either.

As I drove away from that brown house, I was left with a sense of gates over doors, of locks over locks, of a being invaded by images demanding form, giving her no rest.

I returned to San Francisco. Slowly and laboriously I began to go over my tapes and my notebooks. Now they had to be converted, digested, assimilated. (Food metaphors kept occurring to me, as if this were a totemic process.) I did not hear from Paul for some weeks, but then in late February I had a letter from him, saying that he had been in the hospital in Meknes for a week and had been operated on for a hernia. He, who rarely spoke of pain, put in a parenthetical remark that the hernia had given him enough pain "for all time." He went on: "I really can't write properly crouched over in bed, but I wanted you to know that I've been thinking of you and hoping you were well." Then he turned to the absence of rain and the problem of drought in Tangier.

I received a letter from Elizabeth Kenny, a cousin of Paul's. (She was actually a first cousin of Paul's father, but she was much younger than Claude, only four years older than Paul.) With the letter she enclosed several photographs of Paul as a child in Glenora, as well as a brief note.

According to Mrs. Kenny, Paul's grandmother, Ida Willa Bowles (Elizabeth Kenny's aunt as well as Claude's mother), the "Strong Woman" who so upset Paul's mother, was "a petite woman who ran the family. She married Fred Bowles, who worked as a traveling salesman for Corticelli's Silk Company. She was my favorite and I often stayed with her for weeks at a time at her home on Water Street, Elmira, New York."

As for Paul's father, Mrs. Kenny said, he was "indeed irascible. He was the only weak spot in Ida Willa Bowles's fine character. He was her youngest child and very attractive physically with titian colored hair. She spoiled him terribly throughout his childhood and business-wise he never made much money although he practiced dentistry in Jamaica, New York, where I often visited. I disliked him intensely. He would sneer at Paul and whenever Paul asked for some small item as a child, his father would [respond] in a nasty way."

The photos of Paul—with Elizabeth and the other cousins, with his mother and father—had that kind of heartbreaking accuracy that seems to accrue to simple snapshots after many decades. They captured a child with others, but it was clear that, even at that age, he was standing apart.

I heard from Paul once more, a brief note that he was better. Then I did not hear from him again. Events in his own life were now taking a new turn. In December 1993 a group of Paul's friends gathered with him in Tangier to celebrate his eighty-third birthday. Although he seemed pleased and happy with the celebration, I later learned, some of those present were concerned about his increasing difficulty with walking, about his staying in bed almost steadily, about his not getting the proper medical care. Then it was that Virginia Carr, who was in Tangier at the time with Mary Robbins for further work on her biography of Paul, made the suggestion that he come for medical treatment to the Emory University Medical Center in Atlanta.

Virginia assured Paul that at Emory he would have the finest medical care and that she would make all the arrangements for him, as well as providing him with a place to stay. Further, as Paul was planning to go to Paris in May for a concert of his work, she told him, he could come directly from Paris to Atlanta with relative ease. The very quality in Virginia that had struck me so strongly in my first meeting with her, her capacity to act directly and effectively in the world, now came into play.

Paul had not been back to the United States since 1969, when he taught for a semester at California State University at Northridge, and he had steadfastly refused to return despite entreaties from many people. But when Virginia made her suggestion, although he put off making the decision for a few months, he eventually agreed to go to Atlanta. And there, because of her active intervention, he would receive the medical care that would save his life.

It was May 1994.

I was walking along the tree-lined streets near Emory University, past new construction, past shining buildings. I turned left and entered the park where, Virginia had told me, Paul was having an excursion with Abdelouahaid. I went over a small rise, and there, up ahead of me, I saw a procession of people, ambling on a curving path. At the center of the procession in a wheelchair was Paul, sitting erect, his white hair gleaming in the sun. Abdelouahaid was pushing the chair. Strolling on each side were fifteen or twenty people, including Carol Ardman, the composer Ben Yarmolinsky, and the writer Gavin Lambert, many of them taking photos and taping videos.

Paul sat in the chair, smiling, talking. There was constant moving and shifting—first one came to talk, then another. Most of the people were young; only a few were older. Some had known him for a number of years, others only briefly. It was a curious group, in which each member had lines of attachment not to each other but to Paul. They moved along the path, through the trees, going in and out of the shade, in and out of the warm Atlanta sun.

That evening Virginia had a reception for Paul. Held in Mary Robbins's condominium, which she had lent to Paul and Abdelouahaid for the time they were to be in Atlanta, it was carefully planned. From five to seven o'clock, only those who had known Paul before, in Tangier, were invited. From seven on, other guests would join the party, colleagues of Virginia and Mary from the university as well as people from the Atlanta arts and literary community.

When the "Tangier" guests started gathering at five, the morning contingent had been augmented by a number of others who had just arrived by plane. How well I knew that in Tangier the very atmosphere in Paul's flat was conducive to small rivalries. But here, on this warm and pleasant evening, with the doors open to the greenness outside, in this ambience of southern hospitality, even the thought of rivalry seemed to have evaporated. Soon champagne was served, and a toast was offered by Francis Poole, an archivist who had met Paul while living in Tangier. First Francis thanked Virginia and Mary for having made Paul's return possible. Then he spoke of Paul's effect on the assembled group. "Each of us has different memories of Paul and Tangier. No matter how long we have known him, it is probably safe to say that as a friend and writer Paul has changed the direction of each of our lives." He went on to say that Paul "has been the greatest teacher I have ever known." Tears came to his eyes as he spoke of loving Paul.

I glanced over at Paul, who sat in a chair, seemingly imperturbable. I wondered if he was pleased. After all, how could he not be pleased? (Though later one woman said to me that at the end of Francis's tribute, she heard Paul say, sotto voce, "I'm not dead yet.")

With the arrival of the second group of guests at seven, there was a shift in the party, a kind of heating up. A new element had been added; a new community of people surrounded Paul. Many came with books for him to sign. There was now a commingling of two groups, of the more "establishment" guests from Atlanta and the more "antiestablishment" (or, in some cases, formerly antiestablishment) friends of Paul's from Tangier. Perhaps it was not exactly a commingling but rather a circling at a distance, polite and circumspect. Under the watchful guidance of Virginia, there were, as far as I could see, none of the "catastrophes" that often marked the meeting of diverse elements in Tangier. As the evening wore on, the gathering took on its own momentum, its own dynamic, its own rise and fall and rise, the mark of a successful party.

By now, Paul was seated in a large chair in the living room. Two by two and one by one, people came up and talked to him. At the same time, he was being videotaped and interviewed by a young Moroccan who was at film school in the U.S. (Yet one more interview . . .)

I thought of the photos Elizabeth Kenny had sent to me, of Paul as a child. I thought of him in his parents' house, going up the stairs to the separate floor, to the room where he made his own world, with matchstick figures, with words. I thought of him as I had last seen him in Tangier, where he had established his own world, how he was—in that world—director, master of ceremonies. And now he had come back to the U.S., that place he had once felt was a prison for him. He was greeting strangers; he was clearly loved, admired, respected. He seemed unflappable, charming, open . . . a smiling, public man.

And Virginia—how could I help observing her too?—seeing how when she came up to Paul, inquiring whether he needed anything, there was an almost filial quality in her relationship to him? Something of the daughter of an aged parent, involving a certain giving over of authority by the parent to the child, an acquiescing to care. But then in the next minute, reassured that he had what he needed, she went off to attend to others, was once again the gracious hostess, at ease, taking care of her guests.

Observer that I was, I too was being dissolved into the occasion. The phrase *"participation mystique"* came to me. I had the sense of having descended with Paul into some alternative space, where fantasies—hopes—needs take up residence, where one is a character, moving—of one's own will—not of one's own will. And now that space was being covered over by the sound of voices, the glasses being filled, the food being served . . .

With a sudden sharpness, as of remembered loss, came the thought, He has escaped me. I recalled the moment I knocked on his door in May 1992, that first moment when I returned to look at him. There was no answer. I thought he was not there; yet he was there.

I thought of something Jane once said, sometime in the early 1960s. Paul and Jane and Christopher Wanklyn were in Jane's flat, talking, and Paul turned on the tape recorder. On the tape Jane says something to Paul. He can be heard going out of the room, saying "What?" and shutting the door behind him. Then Jane said, "There's a disconnection. Even if he's on the same floor, he's in another room."

Hadn't he always been in the process of escaping? Escaping into another room, escaping across borders into another country, escaping into regions within himself, escaping into others, escaping into his characters even as they too are escaping: Port escaping into the desert, Kit escaping deeper into the desert and into sex, Van escaping from June in "How Many Midnights," Dyar escaping from a life in which nothing happens, Stenham escaping the possibility of damnation, the young mad woman of "You Are Not I" escaping into her sister, the Atlájala escaping into and out of others' bodies.

As I looked at Paul sitting in the chair, smiling, basking in the admiration of others, I recalled the words he wrote in 1971 as he was completing *Without Stopping*. He wrote of how he foresaw his own old age: "There I am without teeth, unable to move, wholly dependent upon someone whom I pay to take care of me and who at any moment may go out of the room and never return." He had escaped even his own foreseeing.

Was it any wonder that he had escaped my seeing?

Of course, I too had done my own escaping, escaping into abstraction, escaping from feeling, escaping from my own darkness, escaping from what I should have known. Is it possible, I asked myself, that a small part of me wanted him to escape? And that a small part of him wanted to be known?

It is possible.

It was Tuesday, May 24, my last full day in Atlanta. In the afternoon after Paul had had his nap, the four of us, Virginia, Mary, Abdelouahaid, and I went with Paul to have his eyes examined. After that, we would go to dinner. The next morning I would leave, and the day after that Paul would enter the hospital.

At a large commercial establishment on the edge of a mall, Virginia at once took Paul in for his examination by the optometrist. Mary, Abdelouahaid, and I waited outside. Almost an hour went by. Abdelouahaid said that he wanted to go shopping for a sweatsuit, so I went with him into the mall. When we came back, Paul was still with the optometrist. Finally he emerged, his eyes dilated. He would have to go back in again in fifteen minutes, but meanwhile he would look for frames for three pairs of new glasses. He said he would like to have frames just like the ones he already had; but as they were more than twenty years old, no such frames were available.

A young saleswoman pointed out the hundreds of frames that he could choose from, exhibited in cabinets and on shelves all around the store. Abdelouahaid, holding Paul's scarf and coat—it was a warm day, but Paul was still cold—began to search through a cabinet holding the least expensive frames. Virginia began to look through another display of more elegant frames. I told Paul that I had recently had new glasses made with frames that had a flexible hinge at the eyepiece, something that was very convenient if you were one of those people who kept taking your glasses on and off. The young saleswoman, hearing what I said, went away and brought back three such frames and gave them to me.

Paul sat in front of a mirror. I gave him the first frame. He put it on and looked at himself in the mirror. He took it off and handed it back to me.

I gave him the second frame. He put it on and looked at himself in the mirror. He took it off and handed it back to me.

I gave him the third frame. He put it on and looked at himself in the mirror. He kept on looking. I looked at him, looking at himself.

WORKS CITED

PAUL BOWLES

Novels

The Sheltering Sky. New York: New Directions, 1949; New York: Ecco Press, 1978; New York: Random House (Vintage), 1990.
Let It Come Down. New York: Random House, 1952; Santa Rosa, Calif.: Black Sparrow Press, 1980.
The Spider's House. New York: Random House, 1955; Santa Rosa, Calif.: Black Sparrow Press, 1986.
Up Above the World. New York: Simon and Schuster, 1966; Santa Rosa, Calif.: Black Sparrow Press, 1982.

Short Stories

The Delicate Prey. New York: Random House, 1950; New York: Ecco Press, 1982.
Collected Stories. Santa Rosa, Calif.: Black Sparrow Press, 1979.
Unwelcome Words. Bolinas, Calif.: Tombouctou Books, 1988.

Nonfiction

Their Heads Are Green and Their Hands Are Blue. New York: Random House, 1963.
Without Stopping. New York: G. P. Putnam, 1972; New York: Ecco Press, 1990.
Days: Tangier Journal, 1987–1989. New York: Ecco Press, 1991.

In Touch: The Letters of Paul Bowles, edited by Jeffrey Miller. New York: Farrar, Straus and Giroux, 1994.

JANE BOWLES

Two Serious Ladies. New York: Knopf, 1943.

The Collected Works of Jane Bowles. New York: Farrar, Straus and Giroux, 1966.

Feminine Wiles. Santa Rosa, Calif.: Black Sparrow Press, 1976. (Includes material from the notebooks)

My Sister's Hand in Mine. New York: Ecco Press, 1978.(An extended edition of *The Collected Works* that includes material from the notebooks)

OTHER PUBLICATIONS CITED IN THE TEXT

Robert Briatte. *Paul Bowles: 2117 Tangier Socco.* Paris: Plon, 1989.

Alfred Chester. *Head of a Sad Angel: Stories, 1953–1966,* edited by Edward Field. Santa Rosa, Calif.: Black Sparrow Press, 1990.

Norman Mailer. *Advertisements for Myself.* New York: G. P. Putnam, 1959.

Christopher Sawyer-Lauçanno. *An Invisible Spectator.* New York: Ecco Press, 1990.

DESIGNER
Nola Burger

COMPOSITOR
Impressions Book and Journal Services, Inc.

TEXT
11.5/15 Adobe Garamond

DISPLAY
Adobe Garamond

PRINTER AND BINDER
Edwards Brothers, Inc.